LINKED

IMOGEN HOWSON

Quercus

First published in the US in 2013 by Simon & Schuster
1230 Avenue of the Americas, New York, New York 10020

This edition published in Great Britain in 2013 by

Quercus Editions Ltd
55 Baker Street
7th Floor, South Block
London
W1U 8EW

A CIP catalogue reference for this book is available
from the British Library

ISBN 978 1 78206 185 4

10 9 8 7 6 5 4 3 2 1

Printed and bound in Great Britain by Clays Ltd, St Ives plc

TO PHILIPPA,
who was the very first
cheerleader for this book, all the
way back when it was called
Telepathic Twins in Space—
but who was too intelligent
to let that stay as its title,
so thought up the
current one instead.

ONE

AS ELISSA and her mother entered the waiting room, the sky above Central Canyon City was a chill, predawn gray, the spaceport a colorless blaze on the horizon. Lines and points of light pricked up from the canyon floor far below.

Elissa walked to the window, trying to ignore the tightness in her chest and that her palms were damp enough to leave handprints on the glass ledge of the windowsill. As she stared, struggling not to give in to her creeping anxiety, the sky changed. First from gray to a thin twilight green, hazy where it curved down beyond the spaceport, then—as all at once the sun rose high enough for its light to hit the desert floor—to endless blue, a color deep enough to drown in.

The light made Elissa's eyes water. She blinked and looked away, just as the waiting-room lights went to sleep and a ripple of cold at the back of her neck told her the air-conditioning had come on, preparation against the scorching heat of late springtime in the city.

Elissa shivered. No one ever got the temperature right for her. Four years—a lifetime—ago, Carlie and Marissa used to joke that she was as cold-blooded as the tiny glass-lizards that scrabbled up the sides of the school buildings to lie on the flat, sun-hot roofs.

Pushing the memory away, she turned to pick her sweat-shirt up from the chair behind her.

At the far side of the room, her mother sat, straight-backed and exquisitely thin, a bookscreen in her hands. In the adjacent corner amber lights glowed behind a tiny waterfall that ran over a tumble of pebbles into a small pool. In the background, music—chimes and harp strings—trickled quietly from invisible speakers, and the scent of chamomile and lavender hung in the air. Everything was designed to calm, to relax.

Elissa's hands were still sweaty. She wiped them surreptitiously on the sweatshirt as she pulled it on.

If this guy can't fix me . . .

No one had said it, but Elissa knew very well this was a last resort. How many times now had she sat in doctors' offices, waiting for them to tell her how they were going to fix her, how they were going to make her normal? How many treatments had they tried? The sleep medication, the pain medication, the little electronic device designed to interfere with the signals her brain sent to her body. That last one had seemed to work at first, and her hopes had soared, only to crash when, abruptly, the symptoms returned. Then there was the hypnotherapy and the weird white-noise machine they'd fixed up in her room, which had been supposed to help her sleep but had just filled her room with an infuriating sensation, like a buzz she heard not only with her ears but also with the inside of her head.

The background music segued into a slightly different theme, something with more flute and less harp. The muted lighting behind the waterfall changed from amber to gold. Elissa's mother sighed, flicked a glance up at the clock-shimmer on the cream-colored wall, and brushed her book-screen to turn a page.

Elissa bit at the ragged edge of her thumbnail.

"Lissa, darling, don't bite your nails."

She dropped her hand and turned back to the window, but the tightness in her chest crept now into her stomach, coiling behind her ribs. Every time the doctors had tried a new treatment, from that very first time, when they'd said it was nothing but out-of-balance hormones, they'd promised she'd get better. They'd promised the symptoms wouldn't last. Promised that the treatment—whichever one it was that time—was only temporary. *Give it a week . . . a month . . . four months. . . . You'll be okay for your best friend's birthday sleepover . . . for your date . . . the spring break camping trip. You'll be back to normal, Elissa, I assure you . . .*

They weren't saying that anymore. After this last time—the latest terrifying vision, the pain that had made her scream and scream and scream, the bruises as black as burn marks on her neck—they hadn't promised anything. They'd just made her an emergency early-morning appointment with a new doctor. A specialist. *Specialist in what?*

When the chime came, she almost jumped. She looked around to see the inner door slide open and the doctor—the *specialist*—step into the waiting room. He was a man about her parents' age, with dark brown skin and a mist-gray suit as elegant as the room.

"Mrs. Ivory? Elissa? I'm Dr. Brien."

Elissa's mother was already getting to her feet. Her mouth was a little tight, and her hand bloodless on the bookscreen, but she appeared, as always, entirely in command of the situation. "Call me Laine, please. You're going to help my daughter. I really don't feel I should stand on ceremony with you." This with a slight smile as she took his outstretched hand.

Dr. Brien's smile included Elissa. "What a wonderful attitude. If that's your attitude as well, Elissa, I don't think we need to worry!"

Elissa took his hand in turn. Hope unfurled within her, warm and glowing. *This* one would help. Probably they should have sent her to him years before. Years that she'd spent trying, helpless, to hold on to everything that made up her life, watching as it all slid through her fingers and disappeared.

It doesn't matter. It doesn't matter about all that wasted time, if I can just be normal now. If I can just have enough of my life back to build a new one.

"Please, both of you, come in. Now, I've been caught up to speed with the problems Elissa has been having, but of course you'll fill me in if there's anything else I need to know. It looks as if Elissa's symptoms haven't cleared up the way we thought they would. . . ." His voice continued, an effortless, reassuring flow of familiar words, as they followed him into his office and sat, obedient to his gesture, in armchairs that matched the couch in the other room. Elissa's chair shifted a tiny bit around her as she sat, and then warmth crept through its surface, cocooning comfort around her tense body.

Across the room to her right, a whole wall was a plate-glass window, treated to eliminate reflections, making it look as if there were nothing there but emptiness. The sky stretched into an infinity of blue.

Almost invisible against the brightness, a shining fragment climbed like a rising star. A ship, setting off on its journey across the impossible distances of space. Then two more, tiny sliding glints of reflected sunlight. It seemed incredible that just fifty years ago there'd been no spaceflight industry on Sekoia at all. No Space Flight Initiative. No government-funded training program. *What would Bruce have done, with no space career to aim for? Gone all out for sports instead? Followed Dad into the police force?*

Dr. Brien waved the door shut, then took a seat opposite Elissa and her mother, next to the big corner desk where his screen stood.

"Now, Elissa." He smiled at her again, and she smiled back. "I've been looking at the results of all your tests. Just let me make sure I've got everything straight. There's a note here about some nightmares when you were very young, and a prescription for sleep medication. Do you remember that?"

"Yes. Yes, I do."

Except she'd never called them nightmares. They hadn't been scary, so it wouldn't have made sense. The only scary thing had been her mother's reaction when she'd mentioned them. "Sometimes I think I'm a girl who's not me," Elissa had said, and her mother had stopped dead in the middle of unwinding a clean floor across the playroom, looking up with a face frozen in shock. When Elissa had said the same thing to the doctor—that first doctor her mother had taken her to—"nightmares" had been how *he'd* framed them. It hadn't felt like the right word, but she hadn't known what else to call them, those pictures that came day and night.

She'd gone for "dreams" in the end, even though that hadn't felt quite like the right word either.

"And the medication, did it work?" asked Dr. Brien.

"Yes."

It *had* worked, way back then, but she hadn't liked how it had made her feel. Slow, almost . . . muffled, as if they'd given her invisible earplugs. So when at the end of the month the medicine ran out and her mother checked—*Are you having any more of those funny dreams? You need to tell me, Lissa, if you do*—she'd said no. And when the dreams had come back, she just hadn't said anything else about them.

She taught herself to ignore them instead. She learned to shut the pictures out of her daytime, learned to forget the dreams as soon as morning erased the darkness from the bedroom. As she got older they came less and less often, until it took hardly any effort to forget they'd ever been there at all.

She'd thought, earlier, how that had seemed a lifetime ago. That time before the symptoms.

If I'd known. If I'd only known I was living on borrowed time, I wouldn't have bothered freaking out about all the tiny things that used to upset me. When I got to high school and Bruce—and freaking Cadan—still kept treating me like a little kid. Not being able to get matching shoes and swimsuit for Marissa's sweet teen pool party. Not asking for help when I didn't understand simultaneous equations and being pulled up in front of the whole class. When I was sure Simon was going to ask me to the Newbies Prom and he never did.

She'd had friends—two best friends, and a whole heap of others. She'd been asked to most of the parties that mattered. She hadn't yet had an official boyfriend, but she'd known, from giggling *oh-my-God-don't-tell-him-I-told-you-what-he-said* conversations with Carlie and Marissa, that there were at least three boys working up the courage to ask her out. Her grades were good enough. She'd been promised driving lessons, and her own beetle-car if she passed her test the first time.

She'd had everything, and she hadn't even realized.

Until . . .

"Until . . . ," said Dr. Brien, and she nearly jumped, suddenly terrified he was reading her thoughts. But he was looking back at his screen. "Until about a year after you started menstruation, yes?"

Agh. She ought to be used to that sort of question by now, but all the same, heat flooded her face. "Yes."

He picked up a universal pen and sketched a rough square on his desk. The lines glowed briefly green, then the wood finish cleared to show a note-taking surface, smooth and translucent.

"Why don't you tell me about the symptoms, the way they began?"

Again. Going through it all over again, with doctor after doctor . . .

But *this* doctor was going to fix her. She straightened a little in her chair, determined not to leave out anything that might help him figure out what he needed to do. *If it works . . . oh God, if it works this time, I might be okay for graduation. I've been a freak for half my time at school, but if this works, if they can all see me looking normal when we graduate . . .*

"Okay." She swallowed. "The pictures—they came back."

For years they'd been nothing but flickers in her mind, fleeting and indistinct, easy to ignore. But when they returned, they were bright, vivid with detail, appearing as if lit by lightning flashes in her brain. And this time they *were* like nightmares. White-masked people, needles and syringes, huge humming machines she dreamed she was clamped into—and she woke biting down screams.

They brought pain, too. Pain that struck like lightning, white-hot, out of nowhere. She would have been able to hide just the pictures. But even if the pain hadn't been bad enough to make her cry out or faint or—worst of all—throw up, she wouldn't have been able to hide it. Because just as with the pictures came pain, with the pain came bruises.

Dark splotches creeping out from the nape of her neck up onto her jawline, or sometimes unexpectedly around her temples, or in thumbprintlike marks on the sides of her neck. Every morning when she looked in her mirror, she'd flinch from the sight of new marks.

Dr. Brien was nodding as she talked, making the occasional note in scrawly writing that shone a dark, wet green, as if he were using real ink.

Elissa told him everything she could think of that he might need to know. She told him how her grades had slid down to almost failing. How she'd kept blacking out at school. How sometimes the pain wrecked her sense of balance and she fell, adding explainable bruises to the mysterious ones.

She didn't tell him absolutely everything, though. He didn't need to know about the times she hadn't been able to get her makeup to cover the bruises, about the times at school when people had whispered about her—not always far enough behind her back. He didn't need to know that, after one too many no-shows at parties, canceled shopping trips, and sleepovers ruined by screaming fits and late-night emergency calls to her parents to pick her up, even Carlie and Marissa had stopped inviting her anywhere. Or that, after all, each of those three boys had asked other girls out instead.

Nor did she tell him how, to start with, her parents had put their own social lives on hold, but when a year had passed and there was still no sign she was going to get any better, they'd started going out again, leaving her at home with medication, their number to call, and a pillow to scream into. *I'm sorry,* her mother had said. *Really, I am, Lissa. I don't want you to feel abandoned, and we're just on the end of the phone. But it's not like we can even do anything if we stay in with you, and your father's work contacts . . .*

Dr. Brien flipped his pen over, touched the nonwriting end to the surface of his notes, and transferred them to the upright screen, leaving the square blank. "So, hallucinations—'pictures,' as you say. And phantom pain and bruising. They all come together?"

"Yes."

"Every time? You don't get, say, bruising without the pain first? Or the pictures without any pain at all, like you did when you were very young?" He watched her face, waiting.

Not anymore. "No." Then a thought struck her.

"Elissa?"

"I . . . I didn't think before, it was so vague . . ."

He waited, pen blinking its ready signal, a tiny emerald spark at its tip.

"The pain—yes, it normally comes with the pictures. But sometimes, I have just a—well, I guess it's a hallucination, but I never really thought . . ."

"Why is that?"

"It—they—sometimes they come at night, so it feels more like a dream. If there's no pain I don't remember them much.

I didn't think . . ." She looked at him guiltily. If she'd thought of this before, if she'd told someone, would it have helped earlier?

He smiled briefly at her. "Don't worry, Elissa. So, you have hallucinations *without* pain that might just be dreams. Such as . . . ?"

Such as waking up crying in the night, shaking with sobs that didn't seem like hers, bursting with misery and rage . . . feelings that didn't seem like hers either, and that faded almost immediately, leaving nothing but bewilderment behind, and a fatigue that dragged her back down into the depths of sleep.

She'd been looking down at her hands, twisted in her lap—it was easier to talk if she didn't have to watch him listen—but now she glanced up. Dr. Brien had laid his pen down, and was tapping out his notes on the upright screen instead. He'd tilted it away from where Elissa and her mother sat, so she couldn't see what he was writing.

"These particular hallucinations, Elissa. Are they *just* feelings—emotions? Is that all?"

She blinked. "I . . . Like I said, they don't have any pain with them . . ."

"I mean, do you see anything? Are you aware of your surroundings? When you have your 'pictures,' they're associated with images of people in white masks—scientists, presumably. In these night pictures, in these dreams, is it the same thing?"

"No. I don't think I really see anything. I guess . . . I'm just in bed."

"Your own bed?"

She stared at him, confused. They were freaking *hallucinations*. What did the furniture matter? "I don't know. A bed. It's dark."

"All right." He smiled at her. "Don't worry, Elissa. You're doing great. I'm just collecting as much information as I can. Anything that happens in your brain draws on all sorts of other data—movies you've seen, music you've listened to, conversations you didn't even know you'd heard. And sometimes the type of data it's drawing on helps us make a more accurate diagnosis. Now, if that's all you can remember, let's move on to your latest recurrence of the symptoms." He pulled down the corners of his mouth. "It sounds like a nasty one, from what I've been sent. Suppose you tell me about it."

As she obeyed, her stomach cramped. Ever since it had happened, late yesterday afternoon, she'd been sick with fear that it was going to come again. The pain had been . . . *oh God, just awful.* She'd been at home, thank goodness, and it had come so suddenly, so violently it had taken her feet from under her. She'd fallen, halfway up the stairs to her bedroom, dropping the orange juice she'd been holding, doubling over, retching bile onto the pale carpet.

"And the pictures?"

"White masks. A machine. A huge machine, much bigger than the others. And wires. They were putting wires into my head. Something . . . my hair, I think it got burned. There was an awful smell."

The smell had still been in her nostrils when she'd come around, making her feel sicker, making her think for an insane moment that her hair had really burned, although when she'd put her hand up to it, it had been soft and undamaged.

"So with this one, the pain was worse than before?"

"Yes," she said, not wanting to think about it.

"All right." He tapped in the last bit of information, nodding a little at the screen as if he'd been doing sums that all added up the way he'd expected. "This was yesterday. And you've had nothing—neither pain nor pictures—since?"

She started to agree, then stopped. She hadn't thought before—after that awful pain nothing could have had anything like the same impact, and she'd been thinking of them as dreams, anyway . . .

"I did have another picture. Last night."

Dr. Brien looked up at her, a sudden movement. "Last night?"

"Yes. I— Do you want to know about it? I don't know if—"

"Yes." An infinitesimal pause, then: "Please, Elissa, if you would."

Something about it—the swiftness of his response, the quick jerk of his head as he'd looked at her—trickled discomfort through her. Suddenly she didn't want to tell him about anything else. Especially not about the dream.

Which was dumb. She'd already agreed with herself to tell him everything that might be useful, *anything* that might help him fix her.

"I . . . Okay."

It had started with something that was neither pain nor picture. A feeling of heat, of electricity in her hands, of brightness exploding like fireworks in her head. A half-familiar feeling, which she might have dreamed before. But this time it had been like a *focused* firework explosion, a feeling that she'd summoned it, that it was hers to control. Then a sensation of directing it outward. Of restraints breaking off her wrists. Of triumph.

And then the fire.

"A fire?" His voice was unexpectedly sharp. "Where?"

"In a building. A big building—like a hospital. Or a school, I guess." Like she had earlier, she thought, *Why does it matter? It's a hallucination.*

"All right. And you were?"

"I was running away from it."

His fingers tapped briefly over the keyboard. "So, a building on fire, and you were . . . escaping it?"

"Yes."

"And this dream, it was vivid, like the other ones you've described? It wasn't what one might call a normal dream?"

"It was vivid."

And it had been. If she shut her eyes she could still see the flames licking up halfway to the pitch-dark sky. She could still conjure up the memory of people fleeing, screaming, of herself running barefoot over rain-wet grass, fighting fatigue like darkness that swelled inside her head. Locking her hands into the wire loops of the fence, pulling herself up and up, knowing the electricity was off and yet having to force herself to keep hold of the metal. Dragging off her hoodie to put over the barbs at the top, still catching her arm on a wicked spike, the adrenaline racing through her veins meaning she scarcely felt the pain. Thinking that after all this time, she'd managed it, she was out, she was free.

When she'd jerked out of the dream, out of sleep and up into full wakefulness, she'd been exhausted, the aftermath of a headache lingering like poison fumes in her head, the smell of smoke still in her nose. As if this dream too had left bruises, but bruises inside her head rather than on her body.

She couldn't bear to say all this to Dr. Brien, though. She described the dream baldly, leaving out the details, the smoke that had smelled of chemicals and hot metal, the feel of the cold grass under her feet. The feeling, wonderful and terrifying, of triumph. Of freedom.

He obviously felt she was telling him plenty, though. He listened intently, his eyes on her face, fingers racing over the keyboard.

Next to Elissa, her mother sat very still, hands locked in her lap.

"Is that all?" asked Dr. Brien. "The dream ended there? When you'd climbed the fence?"

"Yes." The links had cut into her hands, she remembered. And halfway down the other side, her foot had slipped and she'd fallen, landing with a skull-shaking thump on the ground outside the fence. But that was where the dream had cut off short. She remembered nothing else.

"Nothing else? Nothing later?"

"No."

"Not even which way you turned?"

Which way? The unease rose now within her, like cold water creeping up through every vein. He *couldn't* need to know that. Okay, he'd explained the significance of his questions, but he couldn't *possibly* need to know which imaginary way she'd turned after she'd escaped an imaginary building and climbed an imaginary fence.

"I don't know," she said. "I don't remember anything else."

"All right, Elissa." He smiled at her, his face friendly, relaxed. "You've done extremely well. I know it must seem extraordinary to have to tell me all these details. But trust me, the more data I have, the more helpful the diagnosis I can make."

She smiled back. In her lap her fingers uncurled. Until this moment she hadn't realized she'd been sitting with her nails digging into her palms.

Dr. Brien tapped the keyboard once more, then glanced back up to Elissa. "Oh, one last thing. If you don't know, it's no problem. But if you do, then, again, it's just very helpful data that we can use."

"Okay."

"In the hallucinations, do you register what you're wearing?"

"*Wearing?*"

He smiled again, exactly the same warm, reassuring smile. "What our dream selves dress themselves in says a lot about our state of mind. You might put yourself in something you were wearing in real life, or something that doesn't quite fit. Sometimes outfits end up incomplete, or unusual— embarrassing." He chuckled a little. "Trust me, even if you were wearing nothing at all, you wouldn't be the only person who's dreamed that."

"Oh. Okay. I . . . no, nothing weird. Pants, I think. Like . . . yoga pants? Pale—I don't know if they're white or just a light color. And a T-shirt, the same color . . . I think."

"Right. So you were wearing that again in your last hallucination?"

The memory came back, a flash opening up the details in her brain. She'd been running in the dark, keeping to the shadows, knowing her clothes would help conceal her. Knowing too that she'd never have made it this far if she hadn't gotten hold of them, thankful all over again for that careless staff member who'd let her off-duty clothes snag on the edge of her locker, who hadn't checked to make sure the door was properly shut. . . .

She hadn't been wearing the light-colored clothes. She'd

been wearing black. Black pants, and a long, hooded top she'd pulled up over her head.

Elissa looked up to tell him and saw him watching her, waiting for her answer. He was still smiling, but the smile was slightly rigid, as if he were deliberately holding on to it. And there was that sharpness in his face again, a look as if she were giving him numbers and he were adding them up—some to make the sums he'd expected, and some he hadn't.

She didn't lie. Never, really. Not to her parents, not to doctors. But now, all of a sudden . . . Obeying an impulse that came too fast to think it through, she kept her gaze steady and held her hands still in her lap, making sure not to make any guilty, betraying movements. "Yes. That's what I was wearing."

"Thank you, Elissa." He made a couple more key taps, then flicked his hand up, opening another page. "Right. Having looked at all your test results and the reports your own doctor sent me, and hearing how your symptoms have escalated, I think it's very clear we've gone beyond the stage of being able to treat this with medication. Do you understand that?"

"Yes."

He leaned forward a little, put his hand on the desk, palm down, as if he were reaching out to comfort her. "Now, didn't I tell you not to worry? We're going to take a more permanent approach, Elissa."

He twisted the screen around, tapped a key, and an image sprang up.

"Look. There's an abnormality *here*." He glanced at her, smiling. "Don't worry, it's not cancer or anything like that. This is an area that, in the vast majority of people's brains, is mostly inactive. On this map you'd see it as a gray area.

Here, though, see these fine lines? That's a sign that, in your brain, this area has become very *over*active. Probably because of the stimulus of a hormone surge, as your other doctors have mentioned. I won't confuse you with too much science"—he smiled again—"but basically this area links to memory, imagination, dreams. It's grabbing a whole lot of external data—TV, movies, bits of current news, things you might not even notice you're taking in—and turning them into a kind of ultravivid loop playing in your head. And the more it plays, the more it forces a physical response from your body. Hence the pain. It's like the pain you think you feel in dreams, but it's so vivid it's actually having an effect on you physically. Does that make sense?"

He gave her an expectant look, eyebrows slightly raised.

It did make sense, but . . . *My clothes. Why did he want to know about my clothes?*

"Elissa?"

She jerked back from the questions repeating silently over and over in her ears. He was explaining how he was going to make her better, for God's sake. She needed to *listen*. She nodded. "I'm sorry. Yes, it does."

"It's pretty confusing, I know! I've given you the most basic explanation, but obviously there's more to it than that. Now, what we're going to have to do is perform a relatively minor operation. It *is* brain surgery, so in a sense it can't be minor, but I can assure you that with my team you'll be in the best possible hands. Of course, there is risk involved, but we keep it to an absolute minimum. What we're going to do is use a very accurate laser to kill off some of the brain cells in this area, toning down its potential for activity, as it were. If you'll look at this image . . ."

He explained it well, with carefully chosen, unalarming graphics illustrating his words, but it all came down to the same thing: He was going to open her head and burn something out of it. And now that she'd had a minute to gather her thoughts, it *didn't* make sense. She *didn't* understand. She understood the procedure. But the pictures in her head . . . surely if they'd come from random data she'd picked up all the time, they'd vary? Why, in the dreams, was she always someone else—the *same* someone else? *And why did he want to know about the someone else?*

"All right, Elissa. Do you have any questions?"

Oh, but *hell*. It *had to* make sense. He was the *doctor*, for goodness' sake. What did she know about the brain and how it worked?

She shook her head, then, collecting herself, answered politely. "I don't think so, thanks."

"Okay, then." He smiled at her, flicked the display away, and tapped the toolbar to bring up another display, this one scrolling pages of text. "This is the agreement, Elissa. Your parents have already given consent, of course, via your normal doctor, but at your age we need your consent too. I suggest you have a quick read of it, make sure you're comfortable with everything."

All at once Elissa was freezing cold, stiff in the chair. As if she'd just heard the words for the first time, she heard them repeating in her head. *Surgery. Brain surgery.* And: *There is risk involved. Relatively minor . . .*

Only relatively. "If—if I sign it—"

"If you sign it today, we can get you admitted in just four days, on Monday—"

She interrupted him before she even knew she was

going to open her mouth. "Four? *Four days?*"

"Yes. We've got an opening, so I've provisionally booked you in. Tomorrow's the last day before spring break, isn't it? You'll be out of school for a week? So you won't even need time off. And the sooner we can get it over with—" He stopped, watching her face. "Elissa, you realize your condition is deteriorating? I don't want to alarm you, but I can assure you we don't want to leave this even as long as another week."

His eyes remained on hers, his expression open, his eyebrows drawn together in a concerned frown. Part of her wanted to make him tell her more. *What's the risk? How much risk?* But part of her seemed to cower, hands over her ears, not wanting to know. After all, what choice did she have?

"I— Okay. I'm sorry. I just . . . It's so soon."

Mrs. Ivory reached out and put a hand over Elissa's. Elissa turned her hand over, held on with a desperate, tight grip she couldn't manage to relax.

"I know," said Dr. Brien. "But like I said, the sooner we can get this over with the better, right?" He pulled a slim tablet from a slot on the desk and handed it to her. On its screen the same text showed. She scrolled down to the bottom of the document. Her name was already inserted under a dotted line, waiting for her signature.

"You read that through now, all right? Can I offer either of you a drink?"

Elissa shook her head, politeness forgotten, scrolling back through the document. It was all a jumble, medical and legal stuff she hadn't a hope of understanding. She knew all the stuff about never signing something you didn't understand. But her parents had already signed—there were their digi-sigs, next to the space for hers—so it couldn't be anything bad, and she'd never understand some of the language, even if she tried all day, and she was keeping the doctor waiting. . . .

Why did he want to know about my clothes? Why does it matter?

Oh, for God's sake, Lissa. After all this time, someone was saying he could make her better. Not *maybe*, not *probably*, not with the stupid drugs and treatments and sleep machines that hadn't ended up doing anything, but with something real. Surgery. Like the way they cured cancer and appendicitis and the injury from that time Bruce hurt his leg playing antigrav-ball. A real treatment, a treatment that was going to work—that was going to make her normal.

She scrolled to the bottom of the document and signed it.

Elissa Laine Ivory.

"Excellent." Dr. Brien was smiling at her again, calm and pleasant, and her anxiety fizzled away. It was just paranoia, based on nothing but nerves and lack of sleep—and the fact that she'd collected even *more* bruises since she'd been at school yesterday, and she had no hope that no one would notice.

"So, Monday morning, yes?" He was talking mostly to her mother now. "I'd like you both here—and Mr. Ivory, if he's able, of course—at eight. Now, before you go, how about those drinks?"

They had the drinks—a water for Elissa, a no-cal latte for her mother—and Dr. Brien and Mrs. Ivory talked about the current weather programs, the measures the city authorities had taken to contain the latest incidence of Elloran superflu, and a recent news story about how a couple had managed not only to have an illegal third child but also to somehow escape detection for an astonishing six years.

Some twenty minutes later she and her mother thanked

him, said their good-byes, and went out to wait for the elevator to take them down to reception.

As the elevator descended, her mother put a hand out to
touch Elissa's arm. "Try not to dwell on it," she said. "It'll be
over soon."

At the touch, Elissa wanted to lean her head on her mother's
shoulder and sob. But it was bad enough she was going to be
late for first period—and showing bruises that hadn't been there
yesterday. No way could she walk into class with red eyes.

She nodded instead, drawing herself tight as a protection
against the tears that wanted to come.

They went out through the reception area and onto the
wide, tree-lined shelf where the office stood. Chlorophyll-
stained sunlight dappled the ground, and the pavement was
sticky with the drops of lime that had fallen from the leaves.
This was the rich side of the canyon, with nothing but residential shelves above and below. There weren't even any of
the slidewalks that in the last five years had extended nearly
everywhere within the canyon. People came and went by
beetle-car, or by the private elevators that traveled in shafts
inside the cliff, or not at all.

This doctor, he must earn a lot more than ordinary doctors. Well,
he was a specialist, she knew that. But all the same, this whole
setup, it was way out of their normal league.

Her heart was beating faster than normal. She felt it in the
pit of her stomach.

"Mother?"

Mrs. Ivory had reached the wider area at the end of the
shelf where the little beetle-car gleamed scarlet in the sunlight.
Tiny drips of sticky lime speckled its domed roof. She pointed
her key at it, and the sides sprang up to let them in. "Yes?"

"That doctor . . . Dr. Brien . . . Why did he want to know so much about my dreams?"

Her mother slid into the driver's seat, then glanced up at her, eyebrows raised. "Sweetie, he explained. Every bit of data—"

"No, I know. But stuff about the clothes I was wearing? Which way I went? It's just . . . I don't get why he was asking all about that."

"Lissa, really, it's no good asking me how it all works. If I'd thought I was up to graduating at Dr. Brien's level, I'd have stayed in medicine after you were born. I don't have a clue about brain disorders—I don't know why they need the information they do. But honestly, sweetie—get in, you're already late—you can be sure if he was asking for information, it's because he needed it." She smiled at Elissa, reaching across to pat her knee before she started the car. "He wasn't asking for his own amusement, you know!"

"Yeah. I know."

The beetle-car lifted off the ground, the buzz of its propeller sending a vibration like a shiver through the seat and into Elissa's back, then dropped away from the edge of the shelf into clear airspace.

"Mother . . ." The question hovered: *What if I don't have the operation?*

"What is it, Lissa?"

She couldn't say it. The doctor's voice echoed in her head. *Your condition is deteriorating. We don't want to leave this even as long as another week.*

"I'm just . . . It's scary."

Without taking her gaze off the glinting spiderweb of the intersection approaching beneath them, her mother reached over and put a hand on Elissa's arm. "I know, sweetie. If any of the other treatments had worked . . . But this is it. We have to take this one. You can't live the rest of your life this way."

The beetle-car connected with the intersection, locking on to the monorail. From the corner of her eye, Elissa saw the shadow of the propeller disappear as it folded itself into the upper dome of the car. Then they were down in the steel spaghetti of the upper levels of the city, other beetle-cars and skycycles clattering past them, pedestrian slidewalks sliding by underneath.

"I'll drop you off on the roof, okay? I thought we'd miss rush hour, but looking at this traffic . . . I'm not spending half an hour on ground level."

"Okay." Elissa pulled her bag up from the passenger-side footwell. If she hugged it to her, she could—sort of—calm the churning in her stomach. Just a bit earlier, when she'd first met the doctor, the surgery had seemed like the answer to everything. But now . . . *My condition's deteriorating. I'm having brain surgery in four days.*

The yellow reflective lines marking the landing spaces seemed to rise up toward them.

And now—oh God—school.

TWO

ELISSA PRESSED her thumb to the thumb pad next to the students' entrance, and the doors slid open on a rush of chilled air that, despite all the purifiers, still managed to smell of sweaty shoes and bubble gum. She pulled the cuffs of her sweatshirt down over her hands.

The doors slid shut behind her, cutting out all the dusty blaze of the spring day, closing her in with refrigerated air and the anemic, heatless sunlight that filtered through the antiglare windows.

She had only forty seconds after entering before the truancy system would kick in to send auto-messages to her parents. Otherwise she'd have gone to the bathroom, tried killing a little time there until she was too late to do anything more than sit in on the next lesson. Instead, she pulled her bag up over her shoulder, fingers tight on the strap, and made her way along the network of corridors to the girls' changing room. Second period. Phys ed.

The changing room was already a buzz of voices as she opened the door—a buzz that, just for a moment, dropped as she entered. Under the makeup she'd applied along her jawline, up behind her ears, the bruises she couldn't quite hide throbbed, responding to the sudden attention of twenty pairs of eyes, as if the combined gazes had an actual weight to them.

Elissa reached up to open her locker and pulled out a T-shirt and shorts, not looking up, not letting her face register anything. Behind her, after the space of a few heartbeats, the buzz started up again.

She tried to change quickly, but her fingers were clumsy—even after three years, she'd never gotten used to those breaths of silence when she came into a room, never gotten used to being the subject of so many stares—and she was almost the last to be ready, left fastening her shoes as the changing room cleared.

"Hey. Lissa?"

She looked up, aware of her face tightening as she did so, unable to keep it completely expressionless. Marissa stood in front of her, sleek and tawny blond, her long legs bare between her close-fitting black shorts and her black gym shoes, tanned a perfectly even shade of brown.

"Are you okay?"

Elissa stared at her. "What?"

Marissa shifted, tucking her thumbs into her back waistband. "I just . . ." Her eyes met Elissa's for a moment, then she looked away, a sudden irritated movement. "Jeez, whatever. It's not like you're hiding those bruises from anyone, you know?"

Elissa stood. A million years ago there'd been the three

of them, Carlie and Rissa and Lissa—and yes, it had sounded dumb when you said their names like that, but they hadn't cared. Best friends forever. They'd all said it, before they came up to high school. They would make new friends, sure, but they wouldn't forget each other. They'd stand up for each other against anyone who tried to bully them. They'd meet up every weekend, just like they had since they were eight years old.

A million years ago.

"Is that what you want to know about?" The memories made her voice cold. "Who are you finding out for this time?"

Marissa rolled her eyes. It had been two years, but she knew very well what Elissa was talking about. Back then, Elissa had thought they were still friends. She'd made the mistake of telling Marissa the reason for her latest absence. And the next day she'd come into school to be met with not just the familiar whispers but outright laughter—and echoed phrases that she knew could only have reached them via Marissa.

That was when she'd gone past a group in the corridor, felt them turn to watch her, and heard, for the first time, the murmured comments. *Attention-seeking. Sad.*

"I'm *asking*, that's all," Marissa said now. "This is, like, the tenth time you've been absent since the semester started—"

She'd counted? For a moment Elissa almost opened her mouth to say . . . she didn't know what, exactly. But oh *God*, if she only had someone else to talk to . . .

She caught herself just in time. She and Marissa hadn't been friends for years, but their parents still saw each other—at the Skyline Club, at parent-teacher evenings.

"That's what your mother told you, didn't she? Did she tell you to talk to me too?"

The guilty color rushed into Marissa's face again. "Look—"

"No thanks." Elissa pushed her locker door shut. "I'm really not that interested in being the topic of the day at your lunch table. I'm late. I had a doctor's appointment. That's all."

"God, Marissa, didn't I tell you not to bother?" The voice at the door was as cold as Elissa's. She looked over to see Carlie, dark and curvy, with silver-spiked hair, the standard black gym outfit making her look like a cartoon assassin. "It's Elissa's choice. She'll get help when she's ready to."

Get help? Fury fizzed up into Elissa's face. Her vision blurred. What did Carlie think all the freaking *doctors'* appointments were for? She clenched her hands, opened her mouth—

"*Girls.* What are you doing in here?" Ms. Frey came up behind Carlie, looking irritated. "Carline, I told you to check to see who was left, not stand here chatting." Then her gaze went beyond the doorway, into the room. "Oh, Elissa! I didn't realize you were back. Now—girls, come *on*, out of here—Elissa, are you up to joining in this morning? No headaches? No dizziness?"

Obedient to her impatient gesturing, they were out of the changing room now and in the gym, so the teacher's question was asked in front of the whole class. Again, Elissa felt the weight of twenty stares, heard the merest whisper of laughter. She'd thrown up in this class before—not just once but three times.

"I'm okay," she said.

"Well, if you feel unwell, make sure you tell me, all right? Anything—dizzy, blurry vision . . ."

". . . like you're going to throw *up* . . ." The whisper—then the giggles—came from behind Elissa. Ms. Frey didn't react.

The teachers never whispered or laughed, obviously. Ever

since her symptoms started, the whole school staff had been scrupulously considerate about letting her out of class, sending her to lie down, signing permission slips without even asking what they were for. If they, too, thought she was attention-seeking, they didn't say so.

Sometimes Elissa thought it might have been better if they'd been less tolerant, if they'd sometimes shown impatience about late homework or made her stay in at break time.

As the two team leaders chose their teams—every girl being picked in turn, the waiting group dwindling around Elissa, the single constant—she clenched herself against the tears she wouldn't let prickle her eyes.

Four days. This time, although the thought still came with an icy fist closing on her stomach, she didn't find herself wanting to shut it out. She found herself repeating it like a charm. *Four days, and someone will tell them I'm absent not because of some weird mental thing that no one can understand and that I might have made up and that I could be doing to myself, but because I'm having surgery. Real, genuine, get-well-soon-Elissa surgery. And when I come back, there'll be no more blackouts, no more bruises I can't cover up. It's way too late to ever be popular again, but I don't have to be the class freak anymore. I can be just ordinary.*

Four days, and they'll make everything better.

After school Elissa walked out of the ground-floor students' entrance into sunlight crisscrossed into wedges and stripes by the network of rails and slidewalks rising all around the school building, and into heat that enveloped her, as tangible as a freshly dried towel.

In the mass of other students pouring out of the school—thinking of not much beyond logging on to get the messages they weren't allowed to check at school, or making their way to the recreation sections of the city, or getting home and turning on their favorite of a billion TV shows—she was all at once anonymous, completely uninteresting.

She let her bag drop down from her shoulder long enough to pull off her sweatshirt, feeling the sunlight pour over her bare arms like hot water from a shower, the knot of tension at the back of her neck dissolving.

A whole day and no hallucinations, no pain. *After four days, when I've had the op, that's what every day is going to be like.* The thought of the process, the actual surgery, tried to edge into her mind, like an itch starting to develop. She pushed it away. She wasn't going to think about what the doctors were going to do to her. She was just going to think about the result.

She pulled her bag back up onto her shoulder, joined one of the lines of students filing their way off the platform outside the school, and stepped onto the slidewalk that would take her home. As she stepped onto its rubberized central strip, safety fields quivered against her body, raising the hairs on the crown of her head, on the exposed skin of her arms. When she'd been little, she'd always been scared the fields would suddenly switch off, leaving her wobbling, miles up in the air, and even now, if she looked down for too long, the sickening swoop of vertigo would begin in her stomach.

She'd always preferred the old-style stationary walkways, built during the colonization of the canyon, where you were protected by permanent railings that curved over your head; sometimes there were even solid roofs in order to protect pedestrians from any falling debris. There were fewer of those walkways now, though, as the ubiquitous solar-powered slide-walks gradually took over.

The slidewalk Elissa stood on rose in a deceptively slow helix, curling around and around through the crowded lower levels to join the first intersection. Elissa changed to the higher-speed slidewalk signed SPACEPORT, feeling the vibration of the separate safety fields briefly merging as she hopped from one slidewalk to the other, then she was swoop-ing fast toward the west side of the city.

As the wall of the canyon side loomed before her, the slidewalk divided, the high-speed section zigzagging farther up to the very top of the canyon where the spaceport spread out all along the plateau. Elissa sidestepped onto the slow-walk. It spiraled up, then leveled out to take her along the side of the shelf where her house stood.

A semitransparent wall ran along the edge of the shelf. As Elissa glided past it, sensors picked up her ID, and concealed gates slid open. She stepped through the sixth gate onto the cool grass of the narrow communal garden that separated the row of houses and the edge of the shelf.

A tiny stream, protected from evaporating into the hot, dry air by an invisible shell of a force field, wriggled in between the circular paving stones that led from house to house. Above the flat roofs of the homes, dusty green leaves on the cliffside plants rattled against each other like tiny paper quills, each curled in on itself to conserve moisture.

Elissa's house stood at the end of the shelf, a narrow shrub-filled gap between it and the far wall. The middle panel of its front wall was glass, and at this time of day her mother hadn't switched on the privacy setting, so Elissa looked straight through into the tiled entrance hall at the central staircase that rose through all four floors.

The front door recognized her and withdrew into the walls, glass disappearing into glass so seamlessly, it looked the way ice looks when it dissolves under warm water. Cool, cedar-scented air drifted out around her.

"Lissa?" Her mother's voice came from the kitchen at the back of the house.

"It's me." She went in, dropping her bag next to the door as it slid back into place behind her. She pulled on her sweat-shirt as goose bumps sprang up on her arms.

Mrs. Ivory was standing by the countertop at the far end of the kitchen, dropping mixed lettuce leaves, cucumber, and red onion into the separate chutes of the salad maker. In the wall oven next to her, a chicken turned, roasting, its smell sealed away with all the heat and spitting golden fat. A box of lemon-meringue pie mix stood next to the multimixer.

"How was your day?" As always, the question was edged with anxiety, an anxiety that was never there when she asked the same question of Elissa's father, or when Bruce called home.

"It was fine."

"No . . . ?"

"No hallucinations. No anything." Elissa touched the but-ton of the drinks dispenser and watched as sparkling herb tea poured, fizzing, into the waiting frosted glass. When the pains had begun, her doctor had recommended she cut out caffeine, and although it hadn't seemed to do much—*any-thing*—she'd gotten into the habit of avoiding it and had somehow never gone back.

Mrs. Ivory shut the salad maker. The water sprays switched

on, hissing against the inside of the transparent lid. "We're eating early this evening. Did you remember Bruce is coming home for dinner?"

Elissa took a gulp of ice-cold tea and shook her head. "What time is he coming?"

"Six. If he can get away in time. He said they had flight maneuvers all day . . ." She sounded a little distracted, stepping back from the oven so she could see in through its door, but her tone still changed when she said the words.

Bruce had been in the Space Flight Initiative training program for four years now, and whenever his mother referred to him, especially when she used one of the terms he'd only started using once he'd joined—"flight maneuvers," "sim exercises," "firepower"—pride colored her voice.

Generations back, when the first settlers had come to Sekoia, the planet had seemed to be pure potential. Mineral-rich, it had promised a lucrative export industry. The terraforming process to transform the deserts at the center of each continent into habitable environments was already taking place. With the prospect of fast progression to first-grade-planet status in mind, the government at the time had thrown the process into high gear. And the population—as the populations of recently settled planets always did—had expanded quickly, willing to put up with a few years' overcrowding in return for their eventual Eden.

Except the terraforming process had gone wrong. The high-speed techniques—which, shortly afterward, were banned—had backfired. The deserts had become not just uninhabitable but toxic, even to the native species. Animals and plants had died, leaving Sekoia hovering on the brink of complete environmental crisis.

The government—a new, hastily voted-in government—had had no choice other than to direct every available resource into stabilizing the planet. They'd instituted food and energy rationing and strict population-control laws, and had gone deep into debt to the consortium of first-grade planets with whom they'd hoped to trade on an equal basis.

They'd managed to halt, although not reverse, the faulty terraforming. They'd gotten the population under control before it had reached starvation levels. They'd saved Sekoia.

But when it was done, they were left a long way from Eden: heavily in debt to the consortium, and with an outdated spaceflight industry the rest of the star system had left behind years before. With no way to match the high speeds of the new generation of spacecraft, Sekoia's hoped-for export industry had been left dependent on hired transport. Which meant that any profit they made from exporting their native—and valuable—minerals was more or less swallowed up by the costs of exporting them in the first place.

Amid controversy and the resignation of several senior ministers, which Elissa had learned all about in history classes, the government had taken the dangerous step of borrowing *again*—and at a terrifying rate of interest—from the consortium. They'd gathered further funds from the emergency "Recovery Tax" they'd imposed on a furious and panicking population.

And the government had poured every scrap of that money into setting up the Space Flight Initiative, recruiting people willing to work in it, and developing their own spaceflight technology.

Thirty years ago SFI-sponsored scientists had broken through, perfecting the top secret superfuel that powered their ships into hyperspeed. Now Sekoia was out of debt, and finally competing on an interplanetary scale, running their thriving export industry and providing high-speed transport for goods and people across the star system. Working for SFI in any capacity—cleaner, food tech, anything—was pretty prestigious. But the most prestigious career path on the whole planet was to be an SFI pilot—or to be in training as one.

Like Bruce.

I don't care. It doesn't matter that I can't be high-flying, test-acing Bruce. I don't want to be, not anymore. If I can just be ordinary . . .

As Elissa's mother picked up the box of pie mix, shaking it to settle the contents away from the top, her voice changed again, to something more conscious. "Did you see Marissa at school today?"

Elissa stopped in the act of lifting her glass for a second gulp of tea. The memory of that half minute in the changing room was a sore place in her mind, something she wasn't ready to look at again.

She shrugged. "I saw her."

"Did she talk to you?"

"A bit."

Mrs. Ivory's lips tightened. "Lissa, please. Don't make me keep asking. What did she say?"

Elissa put the glass down on the countertop and crossed her arms over her abdomen, her shoulders hunching. "She asked me if I was okay."

"And?"

"I didn't want to *talk* to her. Mother, we're not friends anymore."

Mrs. Ivory tore open the box with a sharp movement. "The way that girl's treated you is a disgrace. I said to her mother, as if this hasn't been hard enough for you—"

"Oh God, *Mother.*"

"She should *know*, Lissa! When I think of how long you were friends, all the times we had her at the house, took her out with us . . ."

"Mother, it's no good. We're just not friends anymore. We haven't been friends for ages."

"And is that *your* fault? All this time her mother hasn't paid any attention to the whole situation—it's just simply not good enough. Now you're going to be better again—"

Elissa stared at her mother, feeling sick. "Mother, we're not going to be friends when I'm better. We're not going to be friends. Ever. *Ever.*"

"Look, Lissa . . ." Mrs. Ivory's brief flash of irritation seemed to have died. She poured the pie mix into the multi-mixer, added three cups of water, and shut the lid. "Yes, she's treated you badly. I'm never going to *like* the girl. But you've got another year at school—you're going to need to pick up a social life again. Once you're better, things can go back to normal."

It was exactly what Elissa had been thinking earlier. *Normal. Ordinary.* But she hadn't even begun to get as far as thinking about picking up the threads of her old life again. And now, visualizing trying to do that, letting down any of the barriers she'd built over the last three years . . .

She crossed her arms more tightly over her body. "No. I'm never being friends with her. Not with any of them. Even if the surgery works—"

"When. *When* the surgery works."

"*When* it works. I'm still not being friends with them."

The salad maker beeped and its lid flipped open. Mrs. Ivory

took a quick look at the crisp, frilly edges of the lettuce, the cucumber and onion that had been turned into green-edged ribbons and purple-edged rings, paper thin and translucent, then pushed the lid shut and touched the chill button. "Lissa, there are some things you have to be proactive about. You don't have to love the girl. Her or Carline. But you need a route back into a social life. You can't afford to be stubborn about it. If they already feel bad about the way they behaved . . ." She lifted a shoulder before going across to the oven and hitting the switch to unseal its door.

The hot, greasy smell of the roast chicken swept out into the room. When Elissa had come in, she'd been hungry. She wasn't anymore.

"Is that why you talked to her mother? Told her"—she stumbled on the words, could only make herself say them by making them a quote—"'as if this hasn't been hard enough' on me? To get her to feel guilty?"

Her mother gave her a tight smile. "Just paving the way a little." She set the chicken on the countertop. Its skin was crisp and shiny with oil. "People will do what you want, Lissa. You just have to find the right way to get them to."

"But I don't *want* . . ." *But I don't want them to know I care. Don't want to let them in. Not now. Not anymore.*

It was no good saying so. Her mother had never had to go from being the girl who was picked, if not first, at least second, to being the one who—every time, every single time— knew she was going to be picked last. She didn't know what it was like to sit alone at lunchtime, holding a book, not looking at anyone, pretending she didn't care, when once she'd been on the inside of a whole group of friends. She didn't know what it was like to avoid going to the washroom in case she ended up trapped in a stall listening to the people outside talk about her, not wanting to come out till they'd gone, not wanting them to see her face and know she'd heard what they'd said. Not wanting them to know she cared.

Mrs. Ivory dropped the empty pie-mix box into the recycler next to the sink. "Lissa, are you listening to me? You need to remember that, all right?"

Elissa let out a quick breath. "Yes. Okay."

The look her mother gave her was intent. "I'm right, you know. You'll find out."

Elissa picked her glass back up, raising it to her lips to avoid meeting her mother's eyes. "Yes." The bubbles fizzed against the roof of her mouth, and the prickles rose into the back of her nose. Sharp and ice cold, a feeling like needles. Or like tears.

Bruce arrived just after six.

From her bedroom Elissa heard the door chime as it let him in, then her mother's voice coming through the wall speaker. "Lissa, come on down. Bruce is here."

And of course Bruce mustn't be made to wait.

"Coming." Elissa stood and told her computer to go to sleep. Her homework faded out and her own face appeared, staring at her from the suddenly mirrored screen above where she'd been sitting. The keyboard folded itself away into the cream surface of her desk, leaving it marked by no more than the faintest hairline crack.

Sometimes she wondered if her parents wished they'd stopped with one child, wished they'd never applied for the license to have another. Or maybe—the thought came, stinging—that they hadn't used up that precious second license on *her*. If they'd had another Bruce—all-star, high-flying Bruce . . .

As she came down the central staircase, set to stationary to encourage healthy exercise, he was still standing in the entrance hall, tall and clean in his dark blue SFI uniform, dark hair clipped close to his head, talking to their father. Who had obviously managed to get home early too, although normally he worked late.

"Hey, Lis, how you doing there?" Bruce's voice was cheerful, his smile wide, lingering a little longer than usual.

So, he knew about the operation. Her mother must have spoken to him earlier. Was that why he'd come?

She shouldn't resent it. It wasn't Bruce's fault that his last four years had been a glittering trajectory of high-scoring exams and flawless test flights, that he'd jumped from standard SFI training to the fast-track pilot program and would be flying his own ship before the end of the year. Nor was it his fault that for her the last few years had been such a very different story.

She shouldn't resent it. But . . .

"I'm fine," she said, and slid past him to ask her mother if she needed help in the kitchen.

They ate in the dining room, amber afternoon sun falling in blobs of light and shade across the table, leaf-dappled both from the potted vines near the windows inside and from the cliff plants outside.

Elissa's mother served the chicken shredded into salad and mixed with garlic dressing and wafers of shaved parmesan. There was a basket of rolls, fresh from the breadmaker, and butter that melted into golden oil on the warm bread.

Neither Elissa's father nor Bruce asked how her early morning appointment had gone. Her mother must have spoken to both of them—and Elissa supposed there wasn't any point talking about it now, any more than there'd been any point talking about the attacks of pain that had sent her rushing from other dinnertimes. There'd never been anything any of them could do; there wasn't anything they could do now. She just had to go through with the operation like she'd gone through the pain. Either it would work or it wouldn't.

Please, God, let it work . . .

"So Cadan and I are in the simulator . . ."

Elissa's attention came back to what Bruce was saying. His face was alight with interest, a mouthful of chicken and salad waiting, forgotten, on his fork. "And it went perfectly, the whole thing. Evade, escape—we've done it hundreds of times, we ought to be able to do it in our sleep by now. So they sent us out to do it for real, told us we'd be graded on this one."

He gestured with the fork. "They've been using the robo-wings with us now—tiny, unmanned ships, just built to fly attack patterns. They're armed with blanks, obviously, and so are we. If we get in one good hit, it's supposed to flip them into retreat mode. We win, job done."

"Eat your salad," said Mrs. Ivory, smiling at him.

Bruce grinned, then popped the forkful into his mouth. "So we're out there in empty airspace," he said around the chicken. "I'm riding shotgun, Cadan's flying. And they send six of the things after us. *Six.* We thought they must have decided they'd been babying us so far, or someone in Control was having some fun with us." He finished his mouthful and took a long swallow of water. "We took five of them out—no problem, just like the sim, and it's not like we haven't done it in the air before. But the sixth—I hit it, and it kept coming. Cadan started laughing, he said even the robo-wing knew I was shooting like a girl. But then he took a shot square on its flank; if we'd had real firepower, it would have split it in two. And it still kept coming. We were blasting it, and it wasn't registering any of the hits—it just kept on in its attack pattern. We were pretty sure it must just be malfunctioning, and it wasn't like it could do any real damage, but every time it blasted us, it would rock us, you know? And we were getting pretty pissed—" He checked himself, glancing at his mother. "Sorry, Ma. Pretty annoyed." He took another mouthful of salad, chewed, and swallowed. "Cadan said he was damned if we were going to lose grades because of some piece of faulty AI. He told me to hang tight. Hey"—he shrugged—"I'm in a five-point harness, you know? No one's hanging tighter than me."

"And then what did he do?" asked Mrs. Ivory.

Bruce laughed. "He just drove the ship toward the ground. Full speed. The robo-wing comes after us, still blasting. Cadan takes us right down to the ground. I swear, I could smell the dust. He judges it to a hairsbreadth, then yanks the nose right up and takes us into a climb. We're going up, almost vertical. Our bodies are used to most of what we put them through now, God knows, but my nose started bleeding, and Cadan's face went green—I thought he'd throw up, which is no pretty sight when you're flying that pattern! Then there's this god-awful crash from behind us, and a fireball—I could see the flash reflected in all the mirrors. He'd led the robo-wing straight into the ground."

His mother put a hand to her mouth. "He *destroyed* it?"

"Oh, yeah. Wiped it out. It's scrap."

"But, my goodness, aren't they terribly valuable?"

Bruce laughed again, nodding, tearing a piece off a roll to mop up the last of his salad dressing.

"Is he in trouble?" asked Elissa, interested in spite of herself. Cadan Greythorn was an arrogant pain—she didn't care about his high-flying career, but she wouldn't mind hearing how someone had finally cut him down to size, maybe told him that, after all, he wasn't God's gift.

"I thought we'd both be, for sure. We were had up before the chief, and I thought—well, I didn't know what they were going to do. I was pretty damn nervous, and Cadan was nearly as green as he'd been in the air. He said later, once he'd crashed out of the adrenaline rush, all he could think about was how much it was going to add to his debt if they made him pay for it—and whether they were going to dock his grades, too."

He grinned at Elissa. "They made us sweat for a good five minutes before they put us out of our misery. Turns out the robo-wing *wasn't* faulty. It was part of the test, and we'd aced it."

"By *destroying* the robo-wing?" Elissa's voice went high with indignation.

"Exactly that. That's what they were testing us on, thinking outside the box. In a real combat situation it could have saved our lives." He leaned forward. "Imagine it was a pirate ship, Lissa, huh? They're not going to give up till they've torn your ship to pieces. If you can outmaneuver them like Cay did—"

Elissa managed not to roll her eyes. Bruce and Cadan had been friends since their early adolescence, when they'd met at the SFI-sponsored pre–flight training academy. Cadan, the only one on an all-inclusive scholarship, had thought he was all that back then, and unfortunately, Bruce had always taken him at his own evaluation. And when they'd both started expecting *her* to do the same, as if she had nothing better to do than be cheerleader to a pair of boys with toys . . .

"If he had to drive the other ship into the ground, I guess it was just as well you weren't practicing in space." She tried to keep her voice neutral so no one would accuse her of being pettily critical. Which she *wasn't*; it was just freaking *Cadan* who, even more than Bruce, never put a foot wrong. He destroyed SFI property, and it turned out even *that* was the right thing to do. Of all the people on the whole planet, he was the only one who could annoy her when he wasn't even there.

She hadn't kept her voice neutral enough. Bruce leaned back, raising his eyebrows at her. "Trust me, Cadan would have worked out a way in space, too. And if you think pirates don't pursue ships into planets' airspace, then you haven't been paying attention to the news. There's a whole lot of planets that don't have orbital police, you know, let alone flying patrols within the atmosphere."

"*Yes*, I know. Jeez, I'm not stupid—"

"All right," said Edward Ivory, cutting across the conversation that was not quite—yet—an argument. "So, your grades?"

"Still all-but-perfect. In fact"—Bruce grinned, his face alight all over again—"we're looking at our first sole-charge flight in the next couple of days. There's an opening in one of the trade routes—a pilot and copilot both out of commission. It's not a complicated job—just as far as Mandolin. Two days there, two days back—but no one in the regular corps can be spared, so we've been told that they're likely to jump a couple of cadets up to full service, just for the duration."

"Really?" Mr. Ivory's eyebrows went up a little. He often seemed somewhat removed from everyday life, detached, as if half his awareness were moving in a place elsewhere. But right now he was fully present and interested.

Elissa reached for the water, not saying anything, *not* being petty. The movement made the bruise at the base of her neck twinge, a tiny stab of pain that sent a needle of nausea up into her head. "Why do you think you and Cadan will get it?"

Bruce gave her a look again. "Oh, only because we're the highest-scoring flight pair in the whole of the training school? Take it from me, little sister, we're going places you can't even imagine."

Elissa flushed.

"Bruce." Mrs. Ivory's voice was sharp.

"Jeez, Ma, I didn't mean because she was sick. I meant because she's not SFI."

Which, to be fair, was probably the truth. He was sometimes completely irritating—mostly because of the whole let's-worship-Cadan thing—but Bruce had never been spiteful. Elissa bit her lip. She shouldn't have said anything.

"Okay." Mrs. Ivory stood up. "Has everyone had enough? Bruce, would you bring in the leftover salad, please? Lissa, you take the bread. I made lemon-meringue pie, Bruce."

"Amazing." He followed her into the kitchen, holding the salad bowl. "You know, Ma, I kind of think the food at school is improving, but it's still got nothing on home cooking."

"Oh, Bruce." She laughed. "Well, you know I like to cook . . ."

The lemon-meringue pie had come out perfectly, the meringue even and crunchy all the way through, melting to sweetness on Elissa's tongue, the lemon layer silky, sweet, and sharp on its crisp base. Bruce left—*at last*—the subject of Cadan and told a couple of other funny stories about life at the training school. Mrs. Ivory talked about a woman she'd seen at the Skyline Club who'd had six different procedures on her face and who now looked so completely different that the first time she came back, the club ID system didn't recognize her and wouldn't let her in.

After dessert, as they slid the plates and dishes into the center of the table and Elissa's mother touched the clean switch, Bruce turned to Mr. Ivory. "Any souvenirs today, Dad? Or have I missed out on this month's collection?"

Edward Ivory gave his faint smile. "You haven't missed out. I do have some in my bag."

The center of the table sank, whirring softly out of sight, and a fresh surface slid across to fill the gap before the whole table lowered its position and the hidden cleaning program came on. Their chair seats softened, armrests hummed up from the sides to settle into position, and the chair backs reclined slightly. Behind where Mrs. Ivory sat, the coffee machine switched itself on.

"Once we have our drinks," she said, her voice firm. "I refuse to look at illegal gadgets without coffee."

Edward Ivory was a police officer, high up in the tech-crime unit. When Bruce and Elissa were younger, they'd been endlessly fascinated by his stories of the criminal ingenuity some of the tech-criminals used, and with the impossibly clever confiscated gadgets he occasionally brought home for a more leisurely analysis than he could manage at work.

This time, he had a window-melter that would soundlessly rearrange the molecules in a sheet of glass, dissolving a window. He produced another gadget that would send a signal to jam slidewalks or elevators, forcing them to a halt, and one that would deactivate safety fields.

When he took that out—a harmless-looking thing like a slim black pen—Mrs. Ivory gave an exclamation of concern. "Edward, you shouldn't have that, surely? It's terribly dangerous—"

He smiled a little across the table at her. "It's neutralized—this and the window-melter. We wouldn't let them out of custody while they're still active, trust me. And I'll be locking them in my study tonight."

He put the pen thing on the table, where it rolled slightly back and forth before coming to a halt. He reached for another object.

"This one, though, this still works. And it's a clever one. See, Lissa?"

It was a credit card, one of the sleek, translucent ones you had to reach a certain income bracket to even be considered for. The numbers across it, though, were all zeroes, and the tiny identipic in its corner showed nothing but an emoticon—a little smiley face.

Bruce was grinning. "Okay, so what? Tell us, Dad."

"It's the latest scam—well, two scams, put together. It's a morph-card. We confiscated what must have been a sample batch—hopefully in time to stop them from flooding out into general circulation. Look." He held it up to his face and spoke very clearly. "Changeling. Chameleon. Camouflage. Edward Ivory. *E-D-W-A-R-D* space *I-V-O-R-Y*. One, two, three, four."

A ripple of color ran across the card, a haze like vapor on water. All the zeroes changed to a line of different numbers, and the identipic . . . Elissa leaned closer. The emoticon had changed to her father's picture, and the name stamped across the middle of the card was his.

"No *way*."

Bruce leaned forward too. "That has to be the coolest thing. Total fake ID?"

"Fake money, too."

"Seriously? But how? The minute you scan it—"

"The minute I scan it, the payment goes through. That last number I said, that becomes my private ID number, so I can put it in on the keypad."

"It actually looks like it goes through?"

"No, it actually *does* go through." Mr. Ivory grinned, pleased with having caught out his son. "I can go shopping with it, and money will change hands—well, change accounts. But at any point I want to, I can erase my ID from the card, and at that point the money will simply evaporate from the shop's account."

Bruce rocked back in his chair. "Evil *genius*. Can I have a try?"

Their father shook his head. "It can't go out of my possession. I'm sorry. It's—in its way—as dangerous as the field-jammer. It's no good for access to anything high-security, obviously—they haven't worked out a way to fake thumb-prints, thank the Lord—but as far as we can work out, it has no spending limit. And of course it will get you access to plenty of lower-security places."

Bruce shrugged, capitulating. "Okay. How does it work, then?"

"Ah, now that's the *really* interesting thing." And he was off into a long explanation involving security loopholes and hidden pathologies, leaving Elissa—and, she thought, probably

Bruce, too, despite all that nodding and "mm"-ing he was doing—way behind him.

The front door chimed as Elissa's parents and brother finished their second cups of coffee, and Bruce got to his feet. "It'll be Cadan. He said he'd be coming by and that he'd give me a lift back to the base."

"Oh, ask him in for coffee," said Mrs. Ivory.

Oh please, do we have to?

"I'm sorry, Ma, he won't have the time to stop. Curfew's early tonight—we've got some intense exercises tomorrow. I have to get going; no one *likes* to miss curfew, but Cadan is what you might call hung up on it!"

Mrs. Ivory smiled. "Well, you can understand that, given the circumstances."

"Being the scholarship whiz kid? Well, yeah, sure." He disappeared out into the entrance hall, and in a moment Elissa heard him greeting Cadan, and Cadan's voice answering.

"Come through a minute while I say bye to the family . . ."

Elissa looked up as they came in, composing her face to politeness. Cadan Greythorn was not quite as tall as Bruce, and a little broader across the shoulders. His dark-blue SFI jacket was fastened up to the neck, and his fair hair, even as short as it was, stuck up at the back where he'd pulled his helmet over it.

"Good evening, Mrs. Ivory, Mr. Ivory. No, please, don't get up—I'm literally here just to kidnap your son. Hey, Lissa."

Elissa gave him the merest possible smile.

"You're on your skycycle tonight?" Mrs. Ivory asked.

Cadan nodded. "It's a nice night for it. I was coming back from the east side as well, and it saves me a bit of time."

"Visiting your parents?"

"My sister. She and her husband finally moved into family accommodation—I was visiting their new place."

"Oh, that must be a relief for them," Mrs. Ivory said.

"Absolutely! They'll be starting their family any day now." He glanced at Elissa. "Hey, Lissa, what do you think about Bruce and me getting our first sole-charge flight soon?"

Bruce had moved to kiss his mother good-bye and shake hands with his father. Her parents' attention was on him, and for a moment Elissa felt free of the obligation to be as polite as they'd expect. When she was little, she'd hung on every detail of Bruce and Cadan's flight training, but a lot had changed since then.

She gave Cadan an indifferent look. "Bruce said that might happen."

"Only 'might'?" Cadan laughed, all superior and confident. "It's pretty certain now. Watch for a ship taking off at twenty-two-hundred tomorrow night, okay? 'Cause it'll probably be us."

It was too much, seeing him standing there on the brink of his glittering career, hair all coolly messy from his skybike helmet, thinking she had nothing more important to think about than watching the sky for a ship he and Bruce just might be piloting. *Like I have headspace to spare for thinking about him when he's not right here forcing me to!*

She lifted a shoulder. "Sorry. I'm planning on washing my hair."

For a moment something like lightning flashed in Cadan's gaze as it met hers. Then the brief spark of what could have been anger was gone, swallowed up in the untouchable self-belief that was his default mode.

He looked down at her, eyebrows slightly raised. "Okay. You keep those priorities straight, princess. After all, we wouldn't want you slipping up and, you know, *excelling* in any of your classes, would we?"

Heat flooded Elissa's face. She stared at him, caught between hitting back with the nastiest thing she could think of—if she could think of it—or defending herself. *I'm not lazy! I'm close to failing my classes because I can't work, not because I won't.*

But it was too late. Bruce had said his good-byes, and her parents were turning for a last word with Cadan.

Elissa slid out of her chair and crossed to the window, her insides in knots of anger, waiting for them to finish with the good-byes, waiting for Cadan to get gone.

"Okay," said Bruce. "We're off. Bye, Lis! Take care."

She looked around as briefly as she could, avoiding Cadan's eyes, and lifted a hand in a wave.

Their boots trod across the entrance hall. Cadan said something, and Bruce, indistinct, replied. Then the door shut out the sound of their voices.

Elissa realized she'd closed her fingers so tightly around her glass of herbal tea that she was in danger of shattering it. As if the anger had let it in, there was a sudden hollow, falling sensation in her stomach. *Four days. Four days and I'm going in for brain surgery.*

"Elissa? Are you all right?"

Elissa looked around to meet her mother's eyes. She could say how scared she was, but she didn't dare. If she said it, if she spoke the words, she might lose all her nerve. And there was no other option. *I have to have it. I have to.*

"I'm just completely tired," she said, momentarily taken aback by how normal her voice sounded. "I guess I'll go upstairs and shower."

She felt, rather than saw, the fractional relaxing of her mother's posture. "All right, dear. You go up. Come down when you've changed if you need another drink. And, Edward, for goodness' *sake*, lock those things up before something goes wrong."

Elissa left the room to the sound of her father's quiet answer, and climbed the staircase to the top floor, where her room was. Her stomach was still swooping, and her hands were cold. She was never going to be able to sleep, not yet, but it was easier to be alone than having to keep up a brave face in front of her parents.

I have to have it. I have to.

Even a hot shower didn't seem to warm her up; although once she was wrapped in her fleecy red bathrobe, the air-conditioning off and her window open to let in the warm night, she started to feel a bit better. She still wasn't going to be able to sleep, though.

She curled up on her bed and told her computer to come on. The mirror-screen woke immediately, angling itself toward where she sat. *Welcome, Elissa*, scrolled across the screen.

There were a million distractions she could request: movies, funny videos, games. Even chat rooms she could hang out in—if she'd ever be able to forget that every one of the people in those chat rooms would react to her symptoms exactly the way her real-life friends had. She wasn't in the mood for any of them.

Bruce's words scrolled across her mind. *You haven't been paying attention to the news.*

Freaking Bruce, with his perfect life and his golden-boy copilot. If his world was a nightmare of pain—hallucinatory pain, that her stupid brain was doing to *itself*—he wouldn't have the attention to spare for the news channels either.

"Breaking News," she said, hearing her voice ring out defiantly in the quiet room.

Images flowed out across the triple-leafed mirror-screen. Tickers sprang up at the top and bottom, and a little embedded talking face appeared at the side.

They were broadcasting updates on the stuff Dr. Brien and her mother had been talking about earlier. The quarantining of an entire residential shelf in response to the Elloran superflu outbreak. The sentencing of the parents who'd had the illegal child. After that, a failed ecoterrorist attack at a major spaceport on the other side of the planet. Then the eighteen-year-old nicknamed Lizard Boy who'd had body modifications that gave his whole body scales. That made the woman at her mother's club seem pretty much normal, thought Elissa, then, *Why Lizard Boy? Lizards don't even* have *scales.*

Local news scrolled along the top, flickering as the ticker jumped from one section of the screen to another.

"Electrical fault blamed for last night's catastrophic fire at the manufacturing plant . . . ," came the news announcer's voice.

And all at once images filled the screen.

Flames licking up halfway to the pitch-dark sky. People running, screaming. Behind the flames, glimpses of a big building—like a hospital, or a school.

Images she'd seen before. In her dream, last night.

THREE

HTTH   EERHT

"WHAT?" Elissa spoke out loud without meaning to, her mind blank, her body frozen in shock.

The computer flickered, confused, then flashed up a command box.

"Dismiss," said Elissa automatically. She found she'd risen to her knees, hands clasped in front of her, tight under her breastbone. The fire, the fire on the screen, on the news—she'd dreamed about it last night. Not *afterward*, not because her brain had seized on external data and turned it into a loop in her brain. She'd dreamed it *while it was happening*.

But I can't have. They're hallucinations. They're all hallucinations, the doctor said so.

Her heart was banging. This couldn't be right. It made no sense. You couldn't have a hallucination that turned out to be *real*.

And as if to prove that *nothing* made sense, that she was in control of nothing in the whole world or the whole universe or her whole life, with no warning the room blinked out.

She was *elsewhere*. In someone else's body, looking through someone else's eyes.

There was the cold, gritty feel of dried mud and grass beneath her curled-up legs, the taste of dust and metal in her mouth. All around, the night pressed against her, thick, hot, and full of noise. Something thundered over the bridge above her head, then faded into the distance; not the quiet rattle of a beetle-car but the rumble belonging to a heavy-goods vehicle.

She was shivering, in bursts that hurt all over her skin. Her arm ached, the place where she'd torn her skin on the barbed fence throbbing in a pulse that kept rhythm with the pulse of her blood. The cut must have gotten infected. She'd been weak and sweaty since noon today, and now, around the hot red line on her skin, the flesh was hard and swollen, too painful to touch.

I don't dare go back into the city; I can't get into one of those medical centers without ID.

She'd thought she'd do better than this. Thought she'd been so clever. She was out, but she wasn't any nearer to freedom than she'd been before she'd escaped.

She pulled the ragged hoodie closer around her, shivering into it. But it didn't help. The effort of moving sent another wave of cold through her body, and in her bones an ache began. She put her head down on her knees. *If I sleep, maybe I'll feel better when I wake up.*

Then a last thought, as the hazy darkness of fever-induced slumber took her. *And if I don't wake up, that will be a kind of freedom too . . .*

Elissa came back to herself with a jump, her whole body jerking so that the bed bounced beneath her. On the screen across the room, the images played the voices talked, far too bright, too loud. She put her hand up to mute the computer and found she couldn't make the signal because her hand was shaking.

"Mute," she said, and her voice was shaking too.

All the pictures, ever since she was tiny, had felt real, but that one . . .

The picture of the fire was real. It happened. And if that had been real . . .

What if they were all real? What if the pictures, all along, had been what they felt like, glimpses into someone else's life? The images of elsewhere, of the rooms and corridors she hadn't recognized, the—

Oh God.

The machines. The injections, the clamps, and the shrieking, awful pain. The bruises—every few days the new bruises, marks of what had been done to her helpless body. What if they weren't something weird and self-destructive in her mind? What if they were echoes of what had been really happening, to another girl somewhere in the world? A girl who'd finally escaped, running through smoke and fire, tearing her arm on the barbed wire of a fence. A girl who was now lying on wet, filthy grass, fighting an infection that could kill her.

But who? And *how?* She didn't live on some awful third-world planet in the backwater of the outer edge of the star system. This was Sekoia, technologically advanced, civilized, with the lowest crime rate in its entire sector and a whole fleet of laws on human rights. This couldn't be happening, not here.

Elissa put both hands to her face, shutting out the world as if she could shut out the thoughts—or at least slow them *down*, turn them into something that made sense. Okay, the picture had *felt* real, but it couldn't be. She must be having some kind of . . . *Oh, I don't know, psychotic break? Something? The doctor said, he said my condition was deteriorating. If this is what he meant, then it does make sense. It does make sense, and all I have to do is go for the surgery like we already planned. . . .*

But the fire. Even if she could dismiss the picture of the girl dying under the bridge, she'd dreamed the fire, too, and the fire had happened.

Elissa took her hands down. The bridge, the dirty grass, the sense all around her of a place that belonged only to emptiness—she was pretty sure she knew where it was. It was the plateau above their shelf, at the top of the canyon, where the spaceport stood. Heavy-goods vehicles and long-distance trains ran across it, lifted off the ground on steel tracks. And all over it the grass was dirty with fuel residue, both from the wheeled vehicles and from the spaceship launchpads, farther away across the plateau.

The spaceport itself was tight with security, but not the wilderness between it and the edge of the canyon. Pedestrians didn't go up there—why would they?—but there was nothing to stop them if they wanted to.

I could go and look.

It was dumb, of course. It *must* be nothing but the worsening of symptoms the doctor had warned her about. But being there, feeling the girl's fear, the pain in her arm as the infection took hold . . . Elissa couldn't leave it like that. If for some unknown, beyond-bizarre reason she was picking up thoughts from a real person, it had to be because of her illness—the abnormality, whatever it was, in her brain. Come Monday, when they fixed it . . .

Once I have the surgery, I won't get the visions anymore. If this girl is real, if she does need help, this is my only chance to find her.

Elissa slid off the bed and grabbed her school bag from the floor, then went into the shower room to rattle through the medicine cabinet for painkillers, fever-relief tablets, and anti-infection spray. She had a bunch of stuff in there left over from preparations for a camping trip the year before. *Will they be strong enough?* The painkillers would be, God knew—they'd been prescribed for Elissa just this last month. *But what if her fever is as bad as it felt? Will I be able to get stronger stuff at a pharmacy, without authorization?*

It doesn't matter. I'll work it out later. And if I get there and there's no one, at least I'll know it's just me being crazy. Then I'll have the surgery and it will all go away. It'll be over, finally, forever, and I won't need to think about it anymore.

She zipped the bag shut, turned to the door—and stopped, her brain catching up with what she was doing. How stupid was she? She didn't even know which bridge the girl was under. And how was she going to get out of the house without her parents knowing?

She paused a moment, forehead furrowed so hard that it began to hurt, fingers tight on the strap of her bag.

She could at least go and look. There were slidewalks all over the nearer edge of the plateau, put there for emergency use and for the maintenance crews. It wouldn't take her too long to check the closest roads. And if she didn't actually go through the house holding her bag, and if they didn't catch her going out through the front door, if she did run into her parents on the way out, they wouldn't know she was planning to leave the house.

The thought came, unexpected. *That picture was completely vivid—is it because she's nearer than she's ever been before?* And then, more disturbing: *Is she coming closer to me on purpose? Does she know I can feel her?*

Oh God, this was all too weird. Elissa straightened, pushing the thoughts away, then went to the open window at the far side of her bed. Her bedroom looked out over the end of the shelf. She leaned out and dropped her bag to land neatly between two flowering bushes. It thumped as it hit the ground, and she jumped to attention, listening for her parents' voices, but it must have sounded louder to her than to anyone else, because the rest of the house stayed quiet and unalarmed.

Okay.

Behind her, her bedroom door gave a gentle buzz as it slid open. She spun around, her skin prickling with guilt.

Mr. Ivory stood in the doorway. The overhead light bleached the color from his face, showing every line. "Lissa, are you all right? I . . . wanted to check on you."

She stared at him, blank, hardly understanding what he'd said.

"Lissa?" He came into the room. "What's wrong? Is it the operation?"

For a moment she almost opened her mouth to tell him, then rationality swept in. What she was planning to do—it was crazy. If she said anything, if she said she thought she had some kind of link to a real person—they'd freak out, both of her parents, think she'd gone completely insane.

She bit back all the words she wanted to say. "I guess. It's kind of scary."

"Yes." For a moment he looked as if he were about to say something else. The lines in his face drew themselves deeper. She'd never thought of her dad as old—he wasn't yet fifty, nowhere near middle-aged, even—but suddenly, staring across the room at him, she saw how he would look when he was.

The words didn't need biting back anymore. They fizzled away, dissolving as if they'd never been.

It wasn't just that her parents would stop her from going. It was something else as well. For three years, as the drugs and the sleep meds and the hypnosis were prescribed and didn't work, as the doctors stopped giving time frames for when she'd get better, she'd seen the worry grow in their faces.

Everyone—everyone in her family, that was—accepted that it had been three years of hell for her. Now, as Elissa looked at those new lines on her father's face, she remembered, despite time after time of resenting that he and her mother could at least get out of the house and away from it, that it hadn't been much easier for them.

And now, on the brink of the cure they'd been hoping for all this time, if she said anything that would make them think her condition was getting so suddenly *worse*, that she could no longer even distinguish between hallucination and reality . . . *She* was scared enough. She couldn't do that to them as well.

"But I'm okay," she said, meeting his eyes, deliberately lying to him for the first time she could remember. "I'm nervous, but I'll be glad when it's over."

For an instant her father's face stayed still, the lines harsh in the unforgiving light, and Elissa's thoughts wavered, momentarily confused. *I thought he'd look relieved. Why does he look like that? As if he's . . . he's . . .* She couldn't think of the right word, and then her father smiled at her, his face relaxing into a normal expression. It was all right. She'd convinced him, and he wasn't worrying about her anymore.

"Good girl," he said, the words he'd been using all her life, from when she was tiny and she'd remembered to close the storybook he'd been reading her, to when she got top grades in her logic class her first semester of high school.

If she hugged him—especially right now, with awful secrets in her head and a bag hidden in the bushes outside—she'd start crying. So she didn't. She smiled at him instead, as if, as far as she was concerned, they'd finished talking and she was just waiting for him to go. After a moment he stepped back outside the room.

"Good night, then, Lissa."

"Good night, Daddy."

It was only after the door had slid shut behind him that the word she hadn't been able to think of came to her. The expression that had shown for that fleeting moment on his face . . . it had been grief.

She waited, sitting cross-legged on her bed, while his footsteps went away across the landing, while her mother's voice came from the staircase as she went upstairs, as water ran in her parents' bathroom. Her heart rushed blood through her eardrums, and she had to deliberately relax her hands to stop her nails from digging grooves into her palms.

Outside her window the sky slowly darkened to full night, lit from below by the haze of city lights, the languid streaks of spaceships rising against the darkness.

The house settled into silence.

Elissa drew in a breath that shuddered between her teeth, and slid off her bed. The pants she was wearing, loose and comfortable, were okay to go out in, but she took off her bathrobe and replaced it with a dark hooded top. She slipped on a pair of shoes, then went softly out onto the landing.

Her parents' door was shut, and no sound of voices came from behind it.

Elissa went down the stairs, stepping as lightly as she could, one hand on the rail, as if that would help her tread less heavily.

In the entrance hall she opened the control panel and deactivated the door-chime before she went out.

The night was even warmer than it had felt in her bedroom. Low down, only a little way above the plateau, clouds had begun to gather, milky gray in the lights they reflected from the city far below, seeming to concentrate the heat and sweat of the night as if under a blanket.

Her bag was around the side of the house, behind a tumble of flowering creeper that she had to more or less wade through, fighting the tendrils that wound like wire around her legs. The scent of the petals was sweet and heavy in the darkness. She hooked the bag's strap over her shoulder and checked that her ID card was in her hoodie pocket. Out this late, if she met law officers, they'd be *completely* likely to ask her for ID, and although they could scan her and match her up with their database, she'd get by a lot quicker if she could just wave her card at them.

Back at the front of the row of houses, she touched the dip in the wall that indicated the concealed sensor, and a section of the wall slid open to let her out onto the slow-moving slidewalk as it slid past alongside the shelf, over emptiness.

It took her past the end of the shelf to where she could step onto the fast section that spiraled her up toward the spaceport plateau.

As the slidewalk reached the edge of the plateau, it leveled out, sliding into the groove set for it in the ground. The safety fields switched off.

Elissa stepped off the slidewalk and was left standing in an odd landscape, a leftover mixture of undeveloped grassland and the shiny, high-tech slithers of other slidewalks. Ahead of her she could see the dart of fire where another ship took off into the dim gray sky.

Away over to her left a chain of lights briefly glittered then blinked out, showing where a high-speed train had just torn up from the city and disappeared over the horizon. Its thunder rumbled through Elissa's imagination. *The sound of trains going over a bridge. The hot shiver and ache of fever. The feeling of giving up, of failure . . .*

She'd thought, somehow, stupidly, that all she needed to do was come up here and look. She'd forgotten how big the plateau was. The spaceport itself was a far-off bulk against the sky. The grassland dwindled gray into the distance. And now that she was thinking properly, she knew there were far more than a handful of the huge metal roads that sped the long-distance trains away to other cities across the whole of the continent.

For a moment she stood still, her stomach tightening, her skin hot and sweaty. *This is no use. I'll never find her. I'll wander and wander around here, risking getting picked up by security . . .*

No. Think. She dragged her hoodie around her, for comfort rather than for the warmth she no longer needed.

She had wondered, a disturbing idea, if the visions were getting clearer because the girl was coming closer. She'd go with that, try the nearest road first.

If I never find her, I'll never know. I'll wonder always if it was real, if I could have done something.

She stepped onto another slidewalk and let it take her through the patchwork of light and dimness, past areas of grass that grew waist high, combed through by the scouring breath of the hot wind, past the dark slices of the drainage ditches that crisscrossed the plateau, insurance against the sudden drenching rains that would come in the autumn. She slid from shadow into the glare of tall lights, so bright that they bleached all color from their surroundings, turning her into a grayish girl traveling over grayish grass. Then she slid back into the shadow that made her almost invisible.

The slidewalk curved, and almost before she knew it, she was sliding alongside the buttresslike supports of one of the roads. She jumped off, stumbling slightly on the tangles of grass. *It's not the right place. She was farther down, out of sight. She can't be here.*

The road towered up above her, a dull gleam in the dark where she stood, flashing bright higher up where the light from one of the tall lamps fell on it. Its supports stood solid in the grass in front of her, but others dwindled into the dark . . .

Into the dark of the drainage ditch just feet away from her.

If Elissa hadn't known the girl was there, she'd have thought the huddled shape, darkness against darkness, was nothing but a pile of garbage collected into a corner by the wind. As it was, she could see it was a person, worryingly still, curled in the crook between the grass and the side of the road support.

The side of the ditch fell away, precipitously steep, the grass on it long and dried glass-smooth by the sun and wind. Elissa's descent was a slide, scarcely controlled at all, made faster by the weight of the bag on her back, the grass slithering through her fingers rather than providing handholds to slow her down. She reached the bottom to find blood streaking her palms where the grass had made tiny shallow wounds like paper cuts.

The girl hadn't moved. Refusing to listen to the alarm

suddenly thrumming in her head—*she's dead, it's too late*—Elissa got to her feet and made her way along to where the figure lay.

The girl was still breathing, a tremor that showed in her huddled shoulders. She had her head buried in her arm so that hardly anything showed except a dark head, the hair damp and straggling all over it. She was wearing a black, baggy hooded top covered in frayed holes. Just the back of one hand showed, pale and grubby, on the grass.

Elissa knelt and spoke gently. "I'm here."

Is she even conscious? If she's in a coma or something, what am I going to do?

The girl shifted and put her hand out, bracing it against the grass. With an effort that made her arm shake, she lifted her head.

Elissa's breath stopped.

She knew the girl's face. She'd seen it before, more times than she could count. In mirrors, shop windows, drowned and wavering in swimming pools, indistinct in the night-darkened windows of her house. She'd felt its contours under her fingers every time she'd applied moisturizer or sunblock, every time she'd gotten washed, every time she'd put her hands up to try to ride through a violent headache.

This girl, this strange girl under the road, who'd been tortured and had escaped, the girl so sick she might not recover—she had Elissa's face.

FOUR

IT WASN'T just a similarity, not just a likeness of dark hair, dark eyes, pointed chin, and high forehead. The girl had the tiny crooked bump at the bridge of Elissa's nose; the exact shape of her mouth, the bottom lip fuller than the top so that, unless she tried not to, she would always look slightly sulky; the splotches of freckles over her cheeks; the few stray hairs at the end of each eyebrow that Elissa, for the last five years, had made sure to pluck out as soon as they grew. The girl's hair was cut shorter than Elissa's, and her face was thinner, the cheekbones sharper, but all the same . . .

She's me. She looks just like me.

After a long moment where Elissa couldn't gather any thoughts beyond that sentence repeating over and over, she realized the girl wasn't staring back at her. Her head was still up, but she clearly wasn't fully conscious. Her eyes were shiny with the glaze of fever, her hair sticking to the sides of her face. She put her hands out, a fumbling, clumsy movement.

Elissa's own hands flew back, an instinct-driven reaction she made before she knew she was moving.

Jumping from blankness into hyperactivity, her mind had suddenly thrown up a million weird terrifying ideas from horror movies. Cosmetic surgery. Identity theft. Clones—not just the partial clones routinely used for life-saving procedures, but full-body clones—somehow spontaneously developing self-awareness. The girl looked exactly like her. Was her thumbprint the same as well? Her DNA? If she, Elissa, disappeared now, in this minimum-security wilderness, her parents not even knowing she was out of the house, could this girl take her identity, take over her life, and no one would ever know?

Elissa set her teeth, biting down the thoughts before they flooded her whole body with panic, before the instinct to run took over completely. All the time she'd been growing up, she'd had glimpses into this girl's mind. Whoever she was, whatever she wanted, Elissa had never caught a hint of anything that indicated the other girl was dangerous.

Elissa put her hands out deliberately, keeping them steady, fighting back the panic, and clasped the other girl's hands.

They were the same as hers. Which shouldn't have been a shock—the girl had the same *nose* as her, for goodness' sake—but was, nevertheless. She suppressed a wave of something more akin to revulsion than fear—this was wrong, it just felt *wrong*—and as she got it under control, she registered the second thing, that the girl's skin was damp, and radiating heat like a glow that seeped out into the air around her.

The girl's fingers curled around hers, clung. She blinked, focusing on Elissa's face, and the girl's face stilled suddenly. Something swept into it, a wave of something more than relief, more than recognition, something Elissa couldn't name. The girl opened her mouth. Her voice was ragged, scratchy and sore-sounding. "Lissa?"

She knows me. She knows my name. Elissa's stomach turned upside down. For the first time she realized what she should have thought of before, that the window she'd had into this girl's brain hadn't been just one-way. It was one thing to get glimpses of someone else's life; it was something else entirely to think someone else had had glimpses of *yours*.

The girl's hands tightened. "Please—don't be scared. I swear . . . I'm not here to hurt you."

"You know my name." Elissa's own voice sounded unsteady, not just frightened but completely off-balance.

The girl wasn't listening. "I just wanted to see you. Just . . ." Her head dipped, but she brought it up with a jerk, her face tight with effort. "I haven't come to ruin your life. I know you have parents. I know I can't—I know I'm not legal. I just wanted . . ." Her voice faltered, her head sagging again. Her hands were all at once even hotter where they clutched Elissa's, and a flush burned in her cheeks.

She's really sick. She needs a doctor. But I can't just call one. I don't know who she is, or who the people are she escaped from. I can't do anything that might let them know where she is.

Elissa bit her lip. She'd thought she'd felt helpless and out of control before, but that was nothing compared to how she felt now.

Okay. This is why I brought medicine. I can at least sort out the infection, get the fever down.

She slid her hands from the other girl's, slipped her bag off her shoulder, and dug through it for the meds and the half bottle of water left over from her day at school. She shook two of the antifever tablets into her palm. "Here, take these."

The girl's eyes opened again, focused on the tablets—and she jerked back, so violently that the tablets flew out of Elissa's hand and disappeared in the grass. The water slopped out over Elissa's hand.

"What are you doing—" She broke off. The girl's pupils had contracted to pinpoints; her whole body was stiff, her mouth clamped shut. With a sudden shock of cold, Elissa noticed the bruises that extended along her jawline, down onto her neck. Bruises that were an exact match to Elissa's.

Elissa took a long breath, then spoke gently. "It's all right. They're just for the fever."

"Sorry." It was a whisper.

"It's okay." She shook out two more pills. "Can I give these ones to you? I brought some water to help you swallow them."

The girl nodded. She took the tablets and gulped most of the drink down in one huge, gasping swallow after another.

Elissa watched her. She hadn't brought enough water. And the meds she had brought—were they even strong enough? She didn't know who the girl was, was completely freaked at her eruption into her life, but if she *died* because Elissa should have called an ambulance and didn't . . .

"I'm just going to spray some medicine on your arm too, okay? It'll feel cold, that's all."

The girl flinched when the spray hit her swollen arm, but she didn't make a sound. She was obviously trying to drink the last bit of water slowly, but she looked as if she were having to make an effort not to gulp it down as she had the rest. Elissa found herself chewing the side of her thumbnail sore, trying not to look worried, watching for the signs the meds were working. They were supposed to work within minutes, but the girl seemed so sick . . .

And what am I going to do with her? Even if these meds do work, if she gets completely better, what do I do with her then? I don't know who did this to her, or how to keep her safe. I don't even know where to begin—

When the thought came, it was like a light switching on in her brain. How stupid was she? She hadn't wanted to tell her parents about going out to find the girl because she hadn't wanted them to think she was even sicker than they'd realized. But now . . . *She's here, she's real. It's* not *me going mad. All along the doctors got it wrong. The abnormality in my brain, the thing they want to operate on to remove—it's not what they said. It's a link. A telepathic link with a real person.*

All at once she was floating with relief. Whatever awful organization had been keeping this girl, however crazy it seemed that *anything* like this could happen nowadays on a high-security, low-crime planet, it didn't matter now. Her parents could fix it. Her dad would know who to call to keep the girl safe, to get the organization raided and shut down. Her mother hadn't worked in a hospital since Elissa was born, but she'd still know better than Elissa what the girl needed. They might not even have to take her to a hospital—her mother could make her better at home, where she was safe and private.

Elissa looked down again at the girl. She'd finished the water, and the bottle had rolled out of her limp hand. She was lying with her eyes shut, flushed and damp, her breathing heavy. Her clothes—the torn hooded top and a pair of dark pants—were covered with darker stains from oil and grass, and her hair was filthy, hanging over her face.

She'd never make it as far as Elissa's house. And she looked like a vagrant—if they passed any police officers, they'd ask for ID for sure.

Elissa would have to leave her here. Once she told her parents, they could come out here in one of their beetle-cars and take her back home.

She cleared her throat. "Listen . . ."

The girl's eyes opened. They were a little more lucid.

"Listen," Elissa said again. "I have to go get you some more water. And more meds—I don't think what I brought you is going to work fast enough."

"You're leaving? Now?" The girl's whole face tightened, as if to meet a blow. The shadows under her eyes showed all at once even darker, as dark as if they, like the marks on her neck and under her jawline, were not just shadows but bruises.

"I have to," said Elissa.

"Don't tell anyone." The words were so urgent, they came out like a shout even though the girl was still speaking in not much above a whisper.

"I—" Elissa stopped. The girl was half-delirious with fever; anything that Elissa could say about how her parents would help her wouldn't register, would just freak her out even more. "Okay. I just need to get you more water and meds, all right? I'll leave these meds with you now, though, and I'll be back in, like, less than an hour."

The girl's eyes stayed fixed on her, huge and dark, her face still tight, her cheekbones seeming to stand out even more than they had before. "You're coming back?"

"Yes. I promise. You don't need to worry."

Finally the girl nodded. "I . . . I couldn't find you. I thought it would be easy, I thought . . . Can you tell me where you live? So this time, if you don't come back—"

"I'm going to come back." For an instant the horror-movie thoughts poured back in. Elissa had already *said* she'd come back. Why did the girl need her address? What was she planning? *I don't know her. I feel as if I've grown up with her, but I didn't. She's a stranger—a weird, secret-experiment stranger who looks just like me.*

Then their eyes met, and after a split second Elissa recognized what lay in the other girl's eyes. She was afraid. Whatever had driven her to try to find Elissa, it was stronger than Elissa's own motives for looking for her. And now she was terrified she'd lose Elissa again.

It didn't seem right, or normal, but then, nothing about this whole situation was normal.

"You don't need to worry," she said again. "But of course I'll tell you how to find me." She gave instructions, as detailed as she could make them, directing the other girl back across the area around the spaceport and to the right slidewalk junctions.

"Our shelf is Acacia Sixteen. The slidewalks have the codes marked on them—A16. Once you get onto the shelf, we're apartment twelve, right at the end, on your right. If you go around the side, you'll be under my window."

The girl's lower lip was bloodless where she was biting it. "Okay," she said.

Elissa hooked the bag back up over her shoulder.

"I won't be longer than an hour, all right? You won't need to come and find me."

"Okay."

Elissa gave her a half smile, uncertain, wavering, then turned to walk into the shadows of the ditch, looking for the steps that would take her back out.

It was twenty minutes of walking before she found them, but once she was up on the plateau, her journey back across the outskirts of the spaceport was easy.

Her house stood dark and silent, the blankness of a house whose inhabitants were all asleep. Elissa slid noiselessly in, the only sound her own heart beating high up in her ears.

Her parents would have been asleep for ages. And she wouldn't be just waking them up; she'd be waking them up to tell them this beyond-crazy story. They'd probably think she was having nightmares, brought on by the stress of being pre-op or something. Elissa caught back a half-hysterical giggle and, aware she was putting off the moment when she'd have to wake them, went into the kitchen to refill a few drinking bottles with water and grab a handful of energy bars. Maybe the girl would need something to eat, too, before they even got her home.

She dropped the bottles and bars into her bag and came back out of the kitchen as she began to zip it up. Okay. She'd promised the girl—*and I can't keep thinking of her as "the girl"; she must have some kind of name, mustn't she?*—she'd be back within an hour. She couldn't put off waking her parents any longer.

As she came out into the entrance hall, the zipper of the bag got stuck. She paused in the shadows of the hall, standing between the bottom of the staircase and the front door, fiddling to free the zipper from the loose thread it had snagged. It came free and she pulled it shut, hitching the bag strap farther up her shoulder.

"*Lissa?*"

Elissa jumped so violently she bit her tongue. For a moment she couldn't even think where her mother's voice was coming from. Then the landing lights snapped on, and

Elissa looked up and saw her, standing at the head of the stairs.

"Lissa, what's going on? What are you doing?"

For a moment Elissa couldn't make sense of the shock and anger on her mother's face. Then she realized how she must look, standing here in the middle of the night, bag on her back, face frozen in fright.

And to add to the guilty picture she made, her brain had frozen too. She couldn't find the right words to even begin to explain. Instead she stared up at her mother, pinned still, caught motionless like a criminal in freeze-beams.

"Edward! Edward, come here now!" It was a shriek, angry and frightened, the sort of shriek she'd give if Elissa *were* a caught-in-the-act criminal.

The note in her voice unfroze Elissa. "Mother, don't. I'm not—it's completely not what it looks like—"

Her mother didn't seem to hear. *"Edward!"* She came fast down the staircase, hand hardly touching the rail, mouth set hard. "How dare you, Elissa. How *dare* you, when it's all arranged. Where the hell do you think you're going to go?"

"Mother, I'm *not*. I'm not going anywhere. I'm not running *away*." It was too crazy to even have to say it. Her mother couldn't think she'd just take off. Since when had she ever done *anything* like that?

Mrs. Ivory grabbed her arm. "Don't you *dare* think of moving. How can you *do* this, Elissa?"

Elissa's father had come down onto the landing, looking half-dazed in the light. He walked down the stairs, tying the belt of his bathrobe tighter. "Laine? What's going on?"

"Look! Look what she's doing!" Mrs. Ivory's hand tightened on Elissa's arm. "She's out here with a bag. With her operation in four days' time!"

"No. *Listen* to me. I'm *not running away*."

Her mother shook her arm. "You little liar, you've got a bag with you!"

A flush heated Elissa's face. She didn't lie to her parents. She *didn't*. And her mother wasn't even giving her a chance to explain.

"I'm not running away. I went out secretly because I didn't want you to worry. I found something—"

"Found something? What on earth are you talking about? And what do you mean, went out? You've been out *already*? It's past midnight!"

"You're not listening to me!" Elissa raised her voice, the heat from her face flooding into it. "I'm not sick. It's not hallucinations. There's a girl—our brains are linked somehow—she looks just like me—"

Her mother's fingers froze on her arm, biting through her sleeve into her flesh. *"What?"*

"That dream I had—the dream I told the doctor about. It was real. The fire was real. Mother, *listen*, they've been doing awful things to her. She escaped, she came to find me. You have to help her." She stopped. Her mother's face had gone utterly still, her lips pressed so tightly together that the blood had gone from where they touched.

"Mother, please. She's sick. She needs help."

Her mother's pale lips opened. "Edward. Call Dr. Brien."

"Laine, is that really necessary? It's two o'clock in the morning."

Mrs. Ivory turned her head to catch her husband's gaze. A muscle jumped in her jaw. *"Call him.* He said her condition was already deteriorating, but this is even worse. She's having a hallucination and she thinks it's real. He's going to have to move the operation forward."

Elissa had thought she was prepared to convince her parents it wasn't just another vivid dream. She'd known she'd have to explain it—several times, maybe. But she hadn't been prepared for this, hadn't been prepared for her mother to completely refuse to believe her, to not even *begin* to listen, to go straight from accusing her of running away to declaring that she wasn't in control of what she was seeing.

"*No*. I'm not hallucinating."

Mrs. Ivory's eyes came back to Elissa. They were wide with panic, but it was not only panic that showed on her face. She had the look of someone trying to work something out. The look, Elissa realized suddenly, of someone preparing to lie.

"Elissa." Her voice was one of forced calm. "You *are* hallucinating. You're sick, you have an abnormality. Dr. Brien said—"

Dr. Brien said. Suddenly a puzzle piece fell into alarming place.

"*Dr. Brien* asked me a load of questions about her! He *knew* she was real—he was trying to find out where she was going, her clothes—"

"Elissa." Despite the calm voice, her mother's hand was still painfully tight on her arm. "He was asking for data about your hallucinations."

"He was *not*." She dragged at her arm. "Let *go* of me."

"When you're in this hysterical state? Absolutely not. Edward, will you call Dr. Brien?"

"Laine, come on now." Elissa's father moved forward. "I really don't think calling Dr. Brien at this time of night is going to help anything. We can call him in the morning."

"And what are we going to do if she's gone by morning? Edward, you *know* what's at stake here. You *know* what we signed. If she's not here for the operation—"

Anger flashed through Elissa, swift and hot. "I'm not even *having* the operation anymore! I only ever got all that pain because of what they were doing to her. She's escaped, I'm fine—"

Her mother's eyes blazed into hers. "You're *not having it?* How dare you say that to me! Do you want to be a freak your whole life? I won't have it, Lissa. Fine, Edward. If you won't let us call the doctor, come here and help me get her under control."

Under control? Like I'm a badly behaved animal?

"Let *go* of me!"

Elissa jerked her arm down, hard enough to break her mother's grip, and flung herself away toward the door. She hadn't planned on doing anything so drastic as walking out, but her mother was talking as if they were going to force her to have the operation whether she agreed or not. She'd accused her of running away—well, she damn well would, then. She'd call them tomorrow when they were ready to listen to her—

But then, unbelievably, her father was there, holding her instead, his fingers enclosing her upper arm. She pulled away from him, but while she'd broken out of her mother's grip, she might as well have tried to escape a handcuff as her father's hand. For the first time not just anger but fear rose within her. This was her *father*, he had never hurt her, he wouldn't—

"Let go," she said, shrill disbelief sounding in her voice. "Dad, let *go*."

He didn't. When she looked up at him, his face was closed, more distant than it had ever been. No trace of the man who'd come to her room earlier, who'd asked her if she was all right.

She pulled harder, beginning to panic, feeling his

fingers motionless and unyielding around her arm. *"Dad."* Instinctively, she tried the tactic that—surely—couldn't help but work. "Dad, stop, you're hurting me."

It didn't work. "Elissa, no. Stop struggling."

"Let go! Let *go!*" Her voice went into a shriek. This couldn't be happening. Her mother, maybe, but not her dad, not her *dad*. He hadn't called the doctor when her mother had told him to. *He* hadn't said he didn't believe her. He was on her side. Wasn't he? *Wasn't* he?

"Elissa, come with me."

She struggled, but she didn't have a hope. He half-marched, half-dragged her away from the door, up the stairs, and to her bedroom, her mother hurrying behind.

He walked her in front of him into the room, then let her go. She flung away, over to the other side of her bed, clutching her bag to her chest. Her face was wet with tears she hadn't noticed till this minute.

Her mother followed them in. She shot Elissa a look that could have cut steel. "How dare you cry about this? It's me who should be crying."

Elissa stared at her. "*What?* Because I don't want an operation I don't need?"

"You do need it."

"I don't! I'm not having it!" She backed away farther, over to the wall next to the window. "I don't consent! I'm not having it!"

"You are," said her mother. "And you're having it tomorrow."

When Elissa tried to speak, the words would hardly come out, so choked were they with tears and helpless fury. "You can't have them operate on me against my will!"

"Lissa," said her father, and she looked at him, still thinking he *couldn't* be joining in with this, he *couldn't* be. But his face showed nothing but grim agreement with her mother. "There are things you don't understand. This operation— there are several reasons it's necessary."

Elissa's tears dried up as suddenly as if they'd frozen. She stared at him, icy cold, seeing the familiar face but feeling as if she looked at a stranger. "You *can't*," she said, but her lips had frozen too, and her voice came out not sounding like hers at all. "You can't make me have an operation I don't want."

"We don't have the choice," said the stranger standing in her father's place, not meeting her eyes.

"No." It came out as a whisper, the sort of horrified whisper that was all she'd been able to manage when she was tiny and had woken in terror from bad dreams. "No, you can't. You can't."

But they weren't listening anyway. "We're going to have to lock her in," said her mother, and her father nodded, a single grim movement.

"But— What? *What?* You can't lock me in my *room!*"

They didn't even answer. Instead her father went out of the room, and her mother made to follow him.

"No, *no*." Elissa scrambled over the bed, went toward them, trying to look past her mother to catch her father's eyes. She didn't understand anything of what was going on, but she knew, beyond doubt, that her mother had lied to her. Her father, though . . . "You can't lock me in all night!"

Her mother put her hand up to the override switch on the wall outside. "For God's sake, Elissa. This is for your own good. If we don't secure you now, I'll have to call the enforcement agents to take you in. You don't want that, do you?"

The door slid shut in Elissa's face, and she heard the click of the internal bolts driving home. They'd done it. They'd seriously locked her in.

Driven by shock and fury, she opened her mouth to shriek through the door, then stopped as if an invisible hand had been laid across her lips.

Her mother had lied to her. And Dr. Brien had lied too. Her instinct that morning, not to tell him what the other girl was wearing, had been right.

Which meant . . . What did it mean? That they knew her pictures were real? That they'd known all along? That they . . .

Nausea turned her stomach upside down. "Oh God. Oh no." They'd known what was happening to the other girl? They'd known about the . . . Her mind shied away from the word she needed, but it echoed in her head all the same. *Torture*. Someone had been torturing that girl, doing some kind of horrific . . . *experiments?* . . . on her. And people, official people—doctors and ex-medical professionals like her mother and police officers like her father—other people knew about it. And did nothing.

The cold spread all over Elissa's body. This wasn't just as simple as some kind of illegal organization that only needed someone to find out about it to get shut down.

The images of the fire came back into her mind. That building—the newscaster had called it a manufacturing plant. People knew about its existence; people knew it was there. So unless its real purpose was *unbelievably* well-disguised, it must be officially sanctioned . . . by someone.

How far does this go? Is it not illegal at all?

Her stomach turned again, and goose bumps raced all over

her body, not just from cold but from a spasm of nausea she had to fight to control.

The other girl, whom Elissa had left still sick and weak, doctored with nothing but some basic pain meds and an antibiotic spray, was in danger. She'd escaped less than twenty-four hours ago, and she didn't have a hope of staying free much longer. They were going to find her, take her back. And Elissa, who'd promised to return, who'd promised to help her, was trapped till the morning in her freaking *bedroom*.

She went to the still-open window, and her fingers gripped the ledge. She leaned out, searching the smooth white-plastered wall for nonexistent hand- and footholds. There was nothing. If she tried it, she'd kill herself.

She was trapped, trapped until the morning, when they'd come for her and take her off to have her head cut into, to burn out the thing linking her to that other girl.

They won't do it, surely? Surgeons, nurses—if I say I've withdrawn my consent, they won't force it on me. They can't. Surely, surely.

Who was she kidding? Look what they'd done to her double. Did she really think they'd hesitate to do a little brain surgery on her, to stop her from revealing their secrets?

And her mother had said *enforcement agents*. A step up from ordinary police, enforcement agents were Special Forces, with extra powers of arrest and detention, who got their orders directly from one of the other government departments.

It's that important, then. This thing. This link.

What else would they do while they were in her head? Erase her memories, too? Leave her blank and happy, not remembering any of this, not knowing she'd been lied to, never finding out who the other girl even was, or why and how she looked identical to Elissa?

They could, she was sure of it. They could take away her link *and* her memory, and then that would be it.

She sagged against the wall, trying to think, her hands pressing her eyes shut. Her thoughts ran like paint in water. When her head jerked up, she realized she hadn't been thinking, but dreaming. She was shivering, cold even in the warm air drifting through the window.

She dragged the cover from her bed, wrapping it around herself before she went back to kneel at the window. She *couldn't* fall asleep. She had to think how she was going to get out. In the morning, when they let her out to take her to the surgery, she had to be able to get away then. If she just *ran*?

Twice more she pulled herself awake, heart banging, dizzy with fatigue. She had to stay awake. She had to make some kind of plan. She couldn't just fall asleep without . . .

Her thoughts dissolved again.

Elissa jumped awake, chest hammering, from a dream of someone calling her.

The lights in her room had dimmed themselves and gone out. Outside, a little gray light crept through the darkness. It was nearly morning. She'd slept half the night.

"Lissa!"

She shot upright to lean out into the semidarkness, from where the voice had come.

Down among the shrubs between the house and the edge of the shelf, a pale blur of a face showed, and a figure, a shadow among shadows. The other girl had remembered the directions. She'd come to find her.

Elissa leaned out as far as she could. She didn't dare shout too loudly, but she cupped one hand to her mouth to try to direct the sound only where she wanted it, and called down, "They locked me in."

Indistinct in the dimness, the girl made an incomprehensible gesture. Elissa shook her head, spread her hands to try to signify, "I don't understand." Jeez, they were in this state because of a telepathic link, but their connection wasn't good enough to let them communicate over a few feet of empty air? Not that the other girl could help even if they *could* communicate.

At least I can help her, give her the chance to get away.

She reached for the bag she'd put the food and water in, took her ID and a handful of money out of her pocket, and dropped them in on top of the snack bars. She had no way of knowing if the ID would work for her double as it worked for Elissa, but on the chance that the girl's thumbprint was as identical to Elissa's as her face was . . . *What I need is one of those morph-cards Dad showed me and Bruce.*

What I need *is for my parents to take my side.*

She made "look out" gestures, swung the bag over the sill, and let it go. "There's my ID in it," she called, as loudly as she dared. "And money. The ID might work for you. You need to get out of the city—"

The other girl spread her hands this time. *What?*

Elissa let out a breath of frustration. "Wait," she called, cringing at how loud her voice seemed, even though she'd hardly raised it above a whisper, then pulled back into the room to grab something to write on. Her book tablet would break if she dropped it from here—damn it, did she not have *any* old-fashioned paper around?

She found some eventually, in the shape of a tiny satin-covered notebook, a gift from some social event her parents had risked taking her to, and she fumbled with the equally tiny sequined pencil to write down what she'd been trying to tell the other girl. Then she had to find something solid enough to attach it to so that when she dropped it from the window, it wouldn't flutter or bounce away over the wall. She shoved it next to her pillow in its pillowcase, leaned out to drop it down, and stopped midmovement.

The bag had gone. And so had the girl.

Elissa strained her eyes into the shadows for a moment—*she was just there, where would she go?*—but the shelf was empty. She straightened, one hand still clutching the pillow, confusion and frustration coiling inside her.

"Hey," she called, trying to hiss the word. There was no answer. Panic made her hand slide on the smooth wooden sill. Where had she gone? Was she coming back? "Hey. *Hey!"*

An enormous crack split the air. It seemed to come from all around, filling the world. Outside, the gray flared red, a split-second lightning flash the color of blood, exploding the night into flame.

The wood was suddenly warm beneath Elissa's hand. She snatched it away. Smoke trickled from under the sill, the plaster beneath crazing from the heat building under it.

She backed away, dropping the pillow, her breath stopping in her chest.

Fire. I said don't lock me in, and they did, they locked me in. They locked me in.

She ran for the shower room, grabbed a towel, and flung it under the faucet. Old safety lessons sprang into her mind. *Keep the smoke out. The smoke will kill you before the flames. I have to keep down low. I have to—*

From over by the door something went *clunk*, a

mechanical sound like metal bolts springing back.

Oh. She straightened, the panic dying instantly, leaving her feeling stupid. All her life she'd known about the safety programs that went into effect in the event of fire, bomb threat, or earthquake.

There was no point standing here wondering how a fire could have started just when she needed one. She fled across the room and hit the doorpad.

On the landing, smoke clouded up under the ceiling lights, and a tremble of flames seeped through the wallpaper. Her father loomed suddenly out of the smoke to grab her arm. "Lissa! The house is on fire. Come with me, come with me now. We have to get out."

I have to get out before you freaking lock me up again. But she wasn't going to argue now, with the sound of fire roaring up from below, and all the doors miraculously unlocked, and the girl she had to help waiting somewhere out there on the edge of the shelf.

Elissa hardly felt the treads of the stairs beneath her feet, didn't need her father to hurry her down them. On the ground floor fire roared from the kitchen at the back of the house. A window cracked with a sharp sound; something else went up in flame, hissing and sizzling. In the breakfast room vines curled, blackening, and flakes of burned leaves blew with the hot breath of the fire into Elissa's face.

They tumbled out through the front door. Billows of spitting-spark-speckled smoke obscured the whole shelf, but through them Elissa could see other front doors opening, people coming out wrapped in bathrobes.

"Laine! Laine!" There was a frantic note in her father's voice. "Can you see your mother?"

"No." The fear in her father's words clutched at her. She cast a look around.

"She was calling the fire services, she was supposed to be out here already." Her father looked around again, searching the crowd. His hand had dropped from Elissa's arm.

Across the grass, in a muddle of people, the exit to the slide-walk stood open. But she couldn't go. Not like this, not without knowing if her mother was still in the burning building . . .

Fear tied a knot inside her chest. *I have to go find the girl. I have to help her. But my mother—*

"*Laine.* Thank God." The crowd had parted to show Elissa's mother, standing near the slidewalk exit, her phone in her hand. As Elissa registered that she was there, that she was safe, she saw her turn, shielding her eyes from the flames to look up at the sky.

Emergency vehicles hovered overhead, flashing blue lights, sleeker and faster than beetle-cars, some spraying foam in huge arcs to smother the flames, some with the trident-caduceus sign of the med-services, some displaying the trident and scales of justice of the police.

And one with a different sign: a trident with a lightning-bolt handle. Not firefighters, medics, or police. Government enforcement agents.

A house fire didn't require enforcement agents. Her mother hadn't been just calling people to come and put out the fire, she'd been calling people to come for Elissa.

Elissa didn't even consider the possibility they might be there for something other than her. They weren't, she knew it. They were here to make sure she didn't get away, here to make sure she made it into the operating room, here to make sure she didn't tell all their secrets.

"Run," said her father very quietly, and pushed something into her hand.

She threw a frantic, confused look down at what it was. It was two of the morph-cards from the stack he'd shown her earlier, their translucent surfaces reflecting the flames.

Frozen speechless, she jerked her head up to meet her father's eyes. The fire threw his face into harsh lines of light and shadow. "Run," he said again.

The first of the emergency vehicles landed on the shelf. Elissa flung a glance at it in time to see two men getting out. Dark clothes, bulletproof vests, guns visible at their waists.

"*Now,*" said Edward Ivory, and he pushed her. "Go find her. Go *now*."

The men were looking around, getting their bearings. Elissa couldn't afford to wait any longer. She took off, racing across the shelf, making for the exit to the slidewalk.

She had to dive right by her mother, and Mrs. Ivory grabbed at her, caught the flapping edge of her hoodie. "Lissa! Stop right now!"

Elissa pulled away. The zipper caught, then broke, and the hoodie slid off her arms. She was free again, running for the exit, her mother left holding nothing but an empty garment.

She swerved, crashed into someone, pushed free but found the exit blocked by a press of bodies.

"Stop!" An unfamiliar voice, the voice of one of the agents. "Elissa Ivory, you're ordered to stop!"

She didn't stop. She flung herself sideways, skidded on the grass, recovered, and took off running along the shelf.

Behind her came shouts, her mother's raised voice, then pounding feet. The agents. Both bigger than she was, fitter, faster. And armed.

All at once she was running flat-out, faster than she'd ever thought she could. If she could get to the next exit, out onto the slidewalk, she could reach the intersection and disappear into its constantly moving tangle.

She threw herself at the next exit, banged her hand down on the sensor. The gate didn't move. They'd jammed it. The agents—somehow they'd jammed it to block her way down to the main slidewalk system, to block her escape.

She ran again, mind racing ahead of her flying feet, trying to picture what lay ahead of her. Grass, the bland blocks of houses, all the way to the end of the shelf. Nowhere to hide. If she could only get down to the intersection . . . but if they'd blocked one entrance, they could block others.

She lost a precious half second trying the next gate, and she was right, it was blocked as well. She heard their feet behind her and took off again, heart pounding in her ears. If she could reach the last gate before they could jam it, she could still get through and away.

The end of the shelf was coming up fast in front of her. If the gate wouldn't open, she was trapped. She'd left herself nowhere to go. She kept running, chest hurting, knees weak, hoping against hope that something, some miracle, would intervene before they reached her.

The corner of the last house loomed up at the edge of her vision. She flung herself toward the last exit sensor as if she were flinging herself at the miracle that hadn't come, that wasn't coming. It was no use, she was caught—

The gate slid open.

Elissa fell through it, landed on her hands and knees on the slidewalk outside the shelf, the safety fields switching on so suddenly, it felt as if she'd been given an electric shock.

She scrambled up and threw herself onto the track that led away from the shelf, running the way you were never supposed to run on the slidewalks, because if you ran too fast, the safety fields couldn't hold you—

As she thought it, she felt the tremor on her bare arms, the here-and-gone-again flicker of the safety field failing. Terror flashed through her. She started to slow, then a little way behind her the slidewalk gave another tremble as someone else—two someone elses—jumped down onto it.

A different terror took her. A memory that wasn't her own, a memory like a spike and flare of lightning all through her brain, a memory of nothing but pain she couldn't describe, pain so huge it blanked out words.

This time she hardly noticed the tremor of the safety field disappearing. She took off, running the way she hadn't run since she was little, feet pounding on the slidewalk. She reached the next junction, sidestepped onto the fastest slidewalk, and tore along that one too, down and down and down in a spiral that took her farther and farther from the men chasing her, farther and farther from her shelf, her house, as if she were running from everything screwed up and awful about her whole life.

Two more intersections. She jumped onto the southbound slidewalk, then the northbound one farther down, zigzagging, no longer hearing their feet above her but not sure she'd lost them, not daring to slow down or even look back.

Her heart was thundering in her ears now, each breath tearing at her chest. She had to find somewhere safe so she could stop. She had to think.

She jumped another intersection, her knees wobbly under her, choosing a route that ran directly under another one, so no one coming from above her could see where she'd gone. She threw a quick look around herself, getting her bearings, trying to picture the nearest place to hide. Once she got down onto the city floor, there'd be cameras everywhere, something that had always made her feel safe before, something she'd always thought only criminals needed to fear.

Am I a criminal now?

She pushed the thought aside, imagining the section of the city she'd end up in if she kept going down. She was still nearest the west side of the canyon. Where could she go? A place without cameras, a place you didn't need ID to get into . . .

The old playground. Relief zinged through her, momentarily eclipsing the fatigue. She hopped slidewalks again. The old playground lay at the base of the west side of the canyon. It had been practically camera central years ago, when Elissa was little, but then the antigrav soft-play complex opened farther along the city side, and the playground fell into disuse. Teenagers used it now, traveling there in couples and hiding out in the playhouse and the triangles of shadow cast by slides and climbing frames. The city council had kept the cameras going for a while, but then there'd been some scandal about alleged inappropriate behavior from one of the police officers who'd had the job of scanning them, and then a whole human-rights-and-privacy argument, and in the end the city had taken the cameras away and instead put up signs that the playground was no longer a secure place for children to play.

Chest heaving, knees shaky, Elissa stepped sideways off the slidewalk onto the platform two stories above the bottom of the canyon and descended the static stairs that ran down the cliff to the city floor.

This early the playground was deserted. Pools of light showed here and there from the lights strung above the whole of the city, glinting off the shiny plastic of the abandoned play equipment. No cameras. She was—for the moment—safe from pursuit.

As the last of the adrenaline drained from her body, Elissa's legs folded under her. She went to her knees on the cold, slightly bouncy playground surface.

When she put her hands out to stop herself from collapsing entirely, the morph-cards fell in front of her. She'd been holding them in her right hand all this time; their edges had left red grooves in her palm.

Her father. He'd told her to run and shoved them into her hand as if he knew, no matter how far she ran, that she wouldn't get far without them. If she remembered how to use them, that was.

There was a combination of words, she remembered that. But right now . . .

She put her head down, breathing gulps of the sweaty predawn city air.

She'd run away from home, from her parents—from law enforcement agents, for goodness' sake. She was in possession of a confiscated, illegal method for getting fake ID and credit. But right now nothing mattered except that she'd stopped running, she could breathe again, and she was alone.

"Lissa?"

FIVE

EVEN FROM the position she was in, Elissa jumped, a stupid sort of bunny hop that made her feel like an instant idiot. She snatched up the morph-cards and swept them into her pants pocket. She looked up at the slight, dark figure making its way across the playground, avoiding, as Elissa had done, every patch of light.

"You scared me." Her heart was banging again, and adrenaline rose back through her body, making her hands twitch and every exhausted muscle tense. The girl hadn't been able to find her before—Elissa had had to give her the address. But now, when Elissa had managed to throw *law enforcement agents* off her trail, two minutes later, all the same, here she was?

"I'm sorry." The girl stopped a few feet from Elissa, her stance hesitant. The bag Elissa had dropped down to her was slung across her back.

"How did you find me?" Once the words were out, she

realized they sounded like an accusation. But then, they kind of *were* an accusation. She didn't owe the girl anything, after all. Sudden sickness swept over her. *I've run away from everything that matters to me for someone who's pretty much a stranger, for someone I don't know enough . . . really . . . to be able to trust.*

"I'm . . . not sure." The girl rubbed the side of her hand on her cheek, bit the edge of her thumbnail. "I . . . Meeting you, maybe, for real? The link between us? I just knew where you were this time. I couldn't do it before."

Okay. That made sense. The sickness settled into a knot of unease in Elissa's belly. It hadn't gone, but she was no longer taut all over, poised on the edge of fight-or-flight.

The girl unhooked the bag and dropped it to the ground, then knelt beside it. Her chest was heaving even more than Elissa's had been, and in the faintly growing light her face showed colorless, smudged with marks like shadows where dirt had mixed with sweat. But she was kneeling upright, her shoulders straight, her eyes clear.

"You're not so sick now," Elissa said.

"That medicine was amazing. I slept for a while. Then I read the package and took some more—two doses—before I came to find you. The swelling on my arm has gone down." She looked straight across at Elissa. "I know you don't trust me. I . . . That's okay. I get how you wouldn't."

"I—yeah." It made it better, somehow, that the girl had said it. "I just . . . A few hours ago I still thought you were a hallucination."

The corners of the girl's mouth turned up a tiny bit. "It's easier for me. I always knew you were real."

Elissa had her breath back now, and she knew she had to use this place of respite, of safety, to think. They had to go somewhere even safer, where they'd be even less likely to be pursued. But vital though that was, she *had* to ask the girl another question first.

"What is all this? Who's doing it? And what for? And who *are* you?" Okay, so that was another four questions. But she couldn't stand this not *knowing* any longer—if she didn't get some information, she'd go absolutely freaking crazy.

The girl took another breath, settling her shoulders back in a way Elissa recognized as bracing herself for something unpleasant. She'd done it herself, before a doctor's appointment, before walking into school . . .

"I'm a Spare," the girl said.

"A what?"

"You don't know about us? Not at all?"

"*No.* I don't have a *clue.*" She swallowed down the frustration spilling into her voice. "What's a spare?"

"A nonhuman human-sourced entity? You haven't heard of that?"

The answer was even more *no* than it had been before, but Elissa didn't say it. *"Nonhuman?"* Her voice went shrill, hovering on the edge of control. "You're *nonhuman?*"

Over thousands of years of colonizing the known universe, no one had ever found *Alien sapiens,* life-forms with anything closer to human intelligence than Old Earth's apes. Was that what this girl was saying she was, an alien life-form who looked like a human?

"Human-sourced nonhuman. I'm, um . . ." The girl bit her lip again, pulling it into her mouth, an anxious movement. "I'm *your* Spare. I'm genetically identical to you. I . . . come from you."

The idea had crossed Elissa's mind before, part of the

horror-movie stuff she'd tried not to think about. But she hadn't really expected the girl to say it. She had to force the word out. "Cloning?"

"Not exactly . . ." The girl's voice trailed off. Her eyes fixed, wide and anxious, on Elissa's face, but Elissa was out of patience.

"Just freaking *tell* me. I'm trying to help you here, and you're making me play guessing games!"

The girl flinched. Everything she'd gone through, and a raised voice could make her look as if she'd been hit? Elissa stared at her for an irritated, bewildered moment before the thought—unexpected and unwelcome—struck her. *Not just a raised voice*. My *raised voice*.

"I'm your double," the girl said. "There's this rare abnormality, sometimes, in pregnancies. The egg, it splits into two embryos, develops into two identical fetuses."

"*What?* No *way*—that's impossible. Sometimes people have two babies, but they're not from one egg, they're not *identical*."

The girl shook her head. "No, really. It was a lot more common thousands of years ago. They had a whole name for them. They called them 'twins'—it means doubles. It died out for—oh, just *forever*—until there was some kind of spontaneous mutation thirty or forty years ago. But the second fetus, it's not human. It's"—her eyelids flickered—"*I'm . . .* just a replica."

Elissa's head was swimming. "But you—what's *different* about you? You look the same, you feel pain. How do they decide?"

The girl lifted a shoulder. Her face was very set, Elissa noticed suddenly, held still as if it were clamped down over pain or grief. "Our brains are different. The link, between you and me? That's one of the differences. For you, it should have died way back, when you were still small. After the birth, once they separate the twins, it doesn't normally last beyond the first few years—"

"Wait. *Wait.*" There was too much to take in. Elissa was only managing to grasp a tiny bit at a time, as if the normal connections in her brain were on a go-slow of information overload. But one thing suddenly got through to her in all its meaning.

"You were *born* with me? You're my parents' child? My . . ." Her whole brain locked up for an instant, as if it were threatening to send her a stack of error messages. "You're my *sister*?"

The girl looked at her, her lip looking almost bruised where she'd bitten it, and a slow flush rose into her face. "I'm your Spare. I'm—I'm not legally defined as anything else. I . . ." She swallowed, the flush rising all around her eyes. "I've always *felt* you were my sister. Back when I was really young, I used to see into your life lots of the time. I knew what was happening to you, what you were feeling, who you were. But you—you didn't even know I was real. You don't feel the same way, and I'm not asking you to. I'm—really, I'm not asking you for anything."

Elissa couldn't speak. Something had caught in her throat.

The girl swallowed again. There were no tears in her eyes, but her mouth trembled when she tried to speak, and when she'd gathered herself and begun again, her voice quivered. "I just . . . I just wanted to see you, to see your world, and then . . ." She trailed off. She looked very tired suddenly, and years younger.

I'm supposed to believe she's not human? Elissa's hands had clenched themselves in her lap. *She's gotten all the way over here, and she's frightened, and still recovering, and she wants me to know she's not asking for anything from me?*

There were a million things Elissa still didn't understand, some of which the girl might be able to explain, some of which she probably wouldn't. Right now none of them mattered.

There were security cameras all over the city. And even where there weren't, the girl—the twin—looked exactly like Elissa. Anyone, anywhere, would notice there was something odd about them. Something wrong. They had to fix that first of all, before they could even use the morph-cards.

Where can we go? Just for an hour or so, long enough to change how we look so we're not so easy to track?

Once more Elissa dragged her thoughts together, summoned memories of the section of the city around them.

Of course. They were almost on the edge of the business district; it was two intersections away. Business travelers came through it every hour of the twenty-four, staying for a few hours or days in the pod-motels, one- or two-person self-service rooms. If you stayed longer than a night, there'd be ID checks, and alarms if you didn't complete them. But for just a couple of hours . . .

She pulled the bag over and rummaged inside it for the money she'd dropped in earlier that morning. There wasn't much, but what there was would stretch to a two-person room for a night. After that . . .

The morph-cards seemed to tingle in her pocket, and her father's voice came to her. *Changeling. Chameleon. Camouflage.* She did remember how to use them. And she damn well would.

"Come on," she said. "You've seen a *lousy* bit of my world so far. This isn't going to be a whole lot better, but it'll have food and a hot shower. And then we'll think what to do."

The girl blinked at her. "You're—not going back home?"

For a moment it was like a mini earthquake rocking the ground beneath Elissa's feet. *Not going home. Is that what I'm doing? Not just tonight, but ever?*

She looked the other girl in the eyes. "I don't know," she said. "I—right now I can't think beyond getting somewhere where we can get ourselves to look different. But after that I'm not going anywhere till I've worked out how to keep you safe."

"You don't have to. I didn't—" The girl swallowed again. "I didn't plan this. Your life—it's so perfect, and I . . . I don't want to wreck it for you."

"Perfect?" Elissa could almost have laughed. "Not even close."

"But that's my fault, isn't it? It's the link, sending you echoes of . . ." The girl trailed off again, shrugged. "You know. But they're going to do that operation, and you won't feel it anymore. You can just go back to being normal."

"*What?*" Elissa's voice went up, incredulous and horrified. "You think I'm still going to go through with it? *Now?* When I know what it's for, when I know what they're burning out of me? No *way* am I letting them do that!"

"But you . . ." The girl stopped, swallowed. "Look, I get your thoughts, okay? Not all of them, but flashes. Enough for me to know you want to be normal. Having me turning up like this, I know it's . . . I don't *want* to ruin things for you."

Elissa got to her feet and picked up the bag. "My life is *nowhere near* perfect. My parents—they've lied and lied and let me think there was something wrong with me, when all the time . . ." Her teeth gritted against one another. Her parents *must* have known at some point what was really going on. If the link was supposed to die off like some sort of weird psychic umbilical cord, then presumably that was what they'd been hoping for. Presumably, too, at least some of those stupid, ineffectual treatments had been meant to help kill it off. *That white-noise machine—was it some kind of psychic damper? The drugs, too?* But for three years, *three years*, they'd let her struggle with misery and loneliness and attacks of pain like lightning strikes, losing her friends, losing any kind of normal life . . . and they'd let her think it was her fault, that something was wrong with *her*.

"You're not ruining anything. All you've done is show me how fake my whole life has been." Her hands had closed into fists again. She forced them to relax, drew in a breath. "It wasn't perfect even when I thought it was. You haven't wrecked anything, and I'm not leaving you till I've got you somewhere safe."

And either the words, or her voice, or something in her face got the message across, because her double said nothing else.

The pod-motels were built around the sides of a building shaped like a giant, upright cylinder, the streetlights catching their curved windows with a smooth plastic gleam. Elissa fed money into the interface by the sealed-shut entrance, keyed in two persons for five hours—the minimum time you could stay—and waited when the display told her to, her heart suddenly thumping, hand hovering over the little tray where their room keys would be dispensed.

She was using physical money, not credit, but all the same, nightmare ideas of being traced came into her mind. You couldn't avoid all the cameras around here. She'd told the other girl to keep her head down, and they were both wearing their hair trailing around their faces, but if an alert had gone out, if a camera picked them up and an operative was on the ball . . .

The keys, narrow slips of plastic coded to the room number on the display, slid into the tray. The pod-motel entrance sprang open.

Elissa scooped the keys up. "Come on."

A staircase spiraled from the center of the ground-floor lobby all the way up the height of the tower, but it was only for emergency use. Elissa slid her key into the slot next to one of the elevators that stood around the outer edge of the room. "We're floor twenty-six," she said to the other girl, keeping her voice low. She'd never *heard* that there were security microphones in the pod-motels, but security had been getting tighter and tighter over the whole city—the whole planet—in the last few years.

Sekoia had almost none of the terrorism you heard about on other planets, but what it did have were completely strict immigration controls. Like everyone kept saying, an already-overcrowded planet couldn't afford to let even a few illegals slip through.

The elevator door slid open. Elissa led her double in, dipping her head, checking that the other girl copied her, so the security camera in the ceiling corner wouldn't get a clear scan of their faces. Would the pod-motels be a good place for illegals to stay for the one night they could get away with before they had to give ID? Or did they go somewhere else, somewhere completely low-security, way off the radar?

The elevator shot them upward with a stomach-dropping rush. Elissa ran the keys through her fingers, staring at the numbers on the wall display as they changed—zero to sixseveneightnineten in as many seconds. She wasn't only thinking about illegal immigrants. She wasn't, really, thinking about immigrants at all. *Is there anywhere totally safe from cameras and mics? If there is, dare I go there? Dare I take us both into some kind of . . . criminal underworld?* She grimaced. Jeez, she didn't even know what to call it. She was so not cut out for this.

The pod-motel was everything it was supposed to be: surgically clean, equipped with beds, nutri-machine, shower cubicle, and toilet, and so tiny there was only just room for them both to stand on the floor at the same time.

Elissa dropped the bag on the floor, scrubbed her hands across her face, and dialed two coffees from the machine. The night before, it had seemed like the worst thing in the world to go to sleep instead of staying awake to think of a way out. But now . . . *Thank God I did. If they've tracked us, if they know we're here, they'll be here in half an hour. Even if we needed to, we wouldn't dare sleep now.*

Another thought came, clamping a steel grip around her throat. *If they do come, I've trapped us. In this little room with one exit and one way down.*

Elissa took another gulp of coffee, feeling the unfamiliar caffeine buzz through her brain. She hadn't had a choice. They had to get changed before they could use the morph-cards, and they had to have privacy to do it.

The other girl was perched on the edge of the lower bunk. Against the fat white quilt and pillow, she looked even grubbier, shabbier, than she had before. And in the close quarters of the podroom, she smelled. Unwashed and sweaty, sharp with a scent Elissa identified with illness and anxiety—the smell of sickrooms and exam rooms and her own bed when she woke from a nightmare. *Oh, wait.* As Elissa moved, she caught a gust of scent from her own body. *It's me who smells.*

She flushed, hoping that however the link between them worked, it hadn't picked up *those* thoughts. But then, she'd never picked up that type of inconsequential thought from the girl, only flashes of emotions that came through stronger: pain, terror, rage. "You probably need some food, don't you?"

"I found some in the bag when you dropped it out?" The girl's voice went up as if the sentence were a question, as if she were asking permission to have eaten a couple of snack bars. Once again something caught in Elissa's throat. She *didn't* feel like the girl was her sister. Despite the link with her she'd had all her life, Elissa still didn't feel she knew her, didn't feel the connection with her she'd once felt with Carlie and Marissa. But all the same . . .

"No, I mean real food."

"I . . . yes. But didn't you use all your money to pay for the room?"

"Not quite, no. And anyway, food is covered in the price. Do you know what you want—" She broke off. "No, it's okay, ignore me. I'll get you a standard meal." She dialed the nutri-balanced option. The girl looked beyond thinking about what she wanted. Let the machine do the thinking for her—at least she'd get the right balance to help her recover.

A familiar covered tray slid out of the bottom of the machine. Elissa peeled the lid back and handed the tray to the girl, looking over her head out the window, alert for flashing blue lights. They'd been in the room five minutes.

Twenty-five more and I'll believe we're okay. For now at least.

She dialed another coffee and a pot of cereal for herself. She wasn't hungry, but like she'd said, food was included in the price of the room. And if they did have to run again, she could at least get some extra calories to keep her going.

The girl was eating hungrily, scooping up the basic curly grain salad and protein dressing as if Elissa had discovered some kind of secret gourmet function on the machine. Elissa squeezed herself down to sit cross-legged on the floor, eating her cereal, watching the girl for a minute.

For an instant, sitting there, she was rocked by the weirdness of it. Here in this tiny room she was on the run from her own planet's police, with a girl who was her mirror image, her literal double, her—what had she called it?—*twin*, whom she hadn't even known existed before today.

Then the girl—*twin*—looked up and caught Elissa's eyes, and the weirdness vanished under the weight of a million things she had to think about.

She fished the morph-cards out of her pocket and handed one over. "We have to program these, okay? They'll give us ID, and we won't get anywhere without ID. And more money, too."

The twin turned the card over in her hand. It gleamed a little in the glow of the room, the dot-eyes of its emoticon catching the light unevenly so that it looked as if it were winking. "It's fake, right?"

"Completely fake." A little ripple of triumph crept through Elissa's fatigue. "It's the one bit of good luck we've had, don't you think?"

The twin's eyes came back up to hers. "Where did you get it?"

Memory crashed over Elissa. Her father, his face in the light of the fire that had driven them from their house. The urgency in his voice, in his hand as he pushed the morph-cards into hers.

"My dad," she said. Then, "He knew. He knew about you. He told me to run."

The twin's face was blank with incomprehension. "He *knew* about me? But the hosts—they don't know. They're not told."

"He knew. He said 'Go find her.' And my mother—both of them, they *both* knew. Once I told them I'd seen you for real—"

"You *told* them?" The twin's voice jumped.

Too late Elissa remembered she'd said she wouldn't tell anyone. "Look, I'm sorry. It was completely the wrong thing to do. But I—honestly, I thought they'd help you—us."

"So they—" The twin swallowed. There was a pulse beating in the side of her throat. Her eyes seemed all pupil. "The—the people chasing you—they know I'm with you?"

"I guess. I mean, they won't know for sure, will they? They didn't see us together. They didn't know you'd come after me and find me." The twin's eyes were on her, the pupils still huge, blackly dilated. "But . . . yes, they're after both of us."

"We won't be able to stay here." The words sounded spiky with panic.

"I know. I *know*. It's just for now, while we change how we look and I work out what to do. With the morph-cards we can figure out our fake IDs, find somewhere else to stay for tonight."

She looked at her watch. Another fifteen minutes to go. The sky outside their window was full of lights, from beetle-cars, flyers, and distant spaceships taking off. But no emergency blue flashes, no sound of sirens. She rose to her knees so she could see the nutri-machine's display and began scrolling through the menu. "We need hair dye, makeup. Colored contacts. Sometimes these machines have a toiletries option for the stuff you might run out of or need suddenly." She kept scrolling. "Okay. Hm. No colored contacts, but there's hair dye and false eyelashes and a whole pile of makeup. That'll do till I can go out and—"

The twin had leaned sideways so she could see the list of products. "But all those—they're not included in the room, are they?"

"No. I'll have to pay for them separately. It's okay, we've got enough money for that."

Two minutes later Elissa had a double handful of almost everything she'd been able to think of—and the sky was still empty of blue lights. She pulled open the door of the tiny shower cubicle at the end of the room and climbed onto the top bunk so she could see her reflection.

She'd found Freckle-Fade, which lightened her already-pale skin to the color of milk, wiping out her freckles as if they'd never existed. And a sachet of copper-colored Curlio. She'd never used it before; it was banned at school, and she hadn't exactly felt like using makeup or hair color for fun, rather than camouflage, for the last few years. But now it couldn't have been more welcome.

She unrolled the protective gloves, slid her hands into them, and then squeezed the Curlio out of its tube and rubbed it into her hair. It slid over her soft dark locks like liquid metal, giving them a shine that seemed to reflect every scrap of light in the room, tightening them into copper ringlets. Amid the blaze of hair, her face seemed even paler and narrower than before, although her eyes still stared out from it, familiarly dark, betraying her. She needed colored contacts. After they were both disguised, she'd take them to the nearest mall and get contacts for each of them, as well as different clothes.

She unscrewed the tube of lip-plump lipstick and applied it carefully over her lips, watching their shape and color change and become more pouty, redder. They tingled momentarily, then stung. Once she was done, Elissa stared into the mirror. Well, her *parents* would probably still recognize her, but she looked a long way from her normal ID picture. And with a new name and a matching ID card . . .

Now that she was no longer kneeling, gasping for breath in a shadowy playground, remembering what her father had showed her before was completely easy. Elissa held the card up to her face, thinking of the first random names that came to mind. "Changeling. Chameleon. Camouflage. Rissa White. *R-I-S-S-A* space *W-H-I-T-E*. One, two, three, four."

The surface of the card rippled, the zeroes changing to a line of random numbers. The identipic became a tiny face with wild red curls, white skin, and a pouty, bee-stung mouth, and the name across the center of the card read RISSA WHITE.

She tipped the card so the twin could look at it, watching her eyes widen. "Okay, now I'll use my card to buy the stuff you need. We'll have to get to a mall to get colored contacts, but we can change your hair and skin at least."

Outside, a siren gave a sudden wail, wrenching open the quiet, coming nearer. Every cell in Elissa's body jumped. She froze, eyes fixed on the window, waiting for blue lights to flash across the glass, for flyers to descend . . .

The siren noise crescendoed until it was almost on top of them, then wailed itself away into the distance. All of Elissa's breath left her body so fast, she went dizzy. *Not us. They weren't after us. It's an emergency call, that's all. It could have just been an ambulance, not even the police.*

She leaned down from the bunk and turned on the screen set in the wall just above the nutri-machine, her heart stuttering, ready to race. The siren had awoken a new fear. She'd run from her home, been chased by law enforcement agents. They could accuse her of a crime and put out a public alert for her.

But there was nothing. Elissa skimmed through the news channels, ending up on Breaking News, and neither her nor the twin's face appeared on the screen.

From the bunk below, the twin was watching her, her face pale and tight. Elissa sent her a smile that she hoped was reassuring. "They're not making any public announcements. As long as we fix the identicalness, people won't be paying us any attention."

The twin nodded. "I didn't think they'd say anything about me. I'm not supposed to exist. But you . . ."

"Well, there's nothing—even if it's only nothing *yet*. I guess if they can't acknowledge you even exist, they can't exactly accuse me of committing a crime."

"They'll be looking for us, though."

"Oh, I believe you," Elissa said. She didn't need to make any effort to remember the emergency flyers, government emblems on their sides, gliding down onto her residential shelf. The armed men who'd arrived in them. They hadn't even hesitated. Just taken straight off after her. *And it was my mother who called them.*

She couldn't think about that yet. Earlier that morning it had been all a blur of fear, panic, and needing to get away. But now, thinking back, knowing her mother had called the police on her . . .

The twin was still looking up at her. "Your parents," she said.

Elissa reached out to adjust the volume control next to the screen. For a moment she couldn't answer, couldn't look down to meet the twin's eyes. *Don't ask me about them. Don't talk about them. Don't reach into my mind and see what I'm feeling.*

"You said they knew?"

Elissa nodded, head turned away.

"Do you . . ." The twin's voice was hesitant, as if she knew Elissa didn't want to answer. "Do you know *how* they knew? At the facility they told us we had no connection with them, they didn't even know we existed. I . . . Maybe they were lying, but I don't see why they would."

Elissa shrugged. "They must have been, though. My parents"—again the memory returned—"they *definitely* knew."

"They're not government officials or something?"

"My dad's in the police. But they wouldn't be an exception, not to something like this." She swung her legs over the edge of the bed and dropped onto the floor, paying excessive attention to her movements so it would seem natural not to meet the other girl's eyes. "My mother used to be a medical lab technician. But you said you weren't supposed to *exist*. They can't go around telling everyone who's police or medical about all this if they want it to stay that way."

"How long ago?"

Although Elissa didn't look at the twin, she felt the gaze of the other girl on her back. "How long ago was she a technician, you mean?"

"Yes."

"She stopped when she was pregnant with—" Elissa hesitated. "With us."

"When she was pregnant? Not after you were born? I

thought people normally worked most of their pregnancies?"

"I guess they do. She said she had complications. She'd had Bruce, my br—*our* brother—with no problems, but when she was pregnant again, they wouldn't let her go into labor naturally. . . . *Oh.*" Now Elissa did look at the twin, her eyes wide. "I guess that was because of you. Is that what they do? Take women in for surgery so they can drug them and take their baby without them ever knowing?"

"I think so."

"But how do they ever cover that up? And how often are they *doing* it? They must have to falsify records and everything, and all it would take is one person to find out."

"That's why I wondered if maybe, being a medical worker, your mother *did* find out."

Cold settled like a weight in Elissa's stomach. The knowledge hit her afresh. Her mother had known a lot more than Elissa. How much *had* she known? Had she *not* been drugged into unconsenting unawareness of what they were doing to her? Had she known all along? *And then, when I started to suffer the consequences . . .*

She couldn't think about that now. She didn't have time. "I don't know," she said, her voice low. "It doesn't matter now. Let's just get you disguised, okay?"

Using the morph-card for the first time made the muscles all down each side of her spine tighten, made her skin prickle, her whole body going on alert for the sound of alarms shrilling. She told the twin to open the door and stand in the doorway in case some kind of auto-security setting jumped to red alert and locked them in.

But it was fine. She scrolled through and made her selections, seeing the total cost growing on the screen. She tapped

in the new number—*1, 2, 3, 4*—and watched the items shower
into the dispenser.

Elissa scooped them up and dumped them onto the lower
bunk. "It's okay. You can let the door shut now."

The twin moved away from the door, and it sprang softly
closed behind her. "It worked?"

Elissa tilted the card, watching glints of reflected light
swim across and through it. "Yes."

Run, her dad had said, pushing the card into her hand.
Giving her the means to escape—and to save her twin. But
earlier that night he'd helped her mother shut her in her
room, told her she had no choice about the operation.

He'd known, like her mother had. But whereas her mother
had been intent on complying with whatever the doctors
demanded of them, her father had . . . what? Only conformed
when he had to, when he couldn't get away with anything else?

*If I could ask him, if I could get in touch with him when my mother's
not there.* With everything that had gone on, would he go to
work today, like normal? If she called him when he was there,
with no one else around, would he tell her what was happening? Would he make sense of it all for her?

She picked up the hair dye. "Are you okay with going
blond?"

"Yes."

Elissa flicked a glance at the other girl. She'd known she
would say that. Elissa certainly didn't want to bleach her
own hair. The copper color was only temporary, but bleach
wouldn't wash out. Since yesterday her life had turned into
something she didn't recognize, and if she had to lose her
real hair as well—

She caught up with herself then, and shame washed over

her, a hot, stinging wave. Like bleaching your hair was the worst thing that could happen?

"You don't have to," she said, and was ashamed all over again when it was an effort to say the words. "If you want to keep your hair, it's no big deal—we can do mine and use more of the copper stuff on you instead."

The twin's eyes met hers. Silence hung between them for a split second. "Honestly. I don't care. And those curls"—she grinned, a sudden flash of amusement that made her look, for the first time, like any normal girl who'd led a normal life, with school and friends and parents—"they're pretty. Let's not get rid of them yet."

Elissa grinned back at her, suddenly warm with a flicker of something familiar, something she'd always taken for granted until she'd had to do without it. "Okay. I'll sort myself out while you shower, then we'll dye your hair and get your face done too. If we fake-tan your skin and leave me pale, and straighten your hair as well as bleaching it, that'll make us look really different. I *think*, anyway—"

The girl turned to the shower cubicle, then paused in the middle of unzipping her hooded top. "I can put the dye on myself, can't I?"

Elissa blinked at the sudden tight sound to the words. "Yeah, of course. It'll be easy enough."

"Okay." The girl didn't glance back, just resumed undressing, but the tension had gone from her voice.

Elissa turned away to dial another drink from the machine, then sat on the edge of the lower bunk. She'd changed in the same room as other girls before, but *this* girl's body would be identical to her own, familiar and strange all at once, and she didn't want to look. Once she heard the water come on behind her, she turned back. The other girl obviously hadn't had any trouble working out the control panel. *Well, I guess they must have had showers at the . . . whatever it was where they kept her. In the pictures it always seemed completely clean.*

The scent of orange blossom drifted out on steam into the room, momentarily fogging the air, before fans whirred softly into life. Then the drying program came on with a soft roar of air. In the cubicle the twin shook her head, water spraying from her hair and evaporating before it hit the walls.

Tension was coiling inside Elissa again. *We need to get this done. We have to move on.*

She didn't even know *where* yet. Over to the other side of the city? Or should they catch one of the high-speed trains that cut across the desert to other cities? *And if I call my dad, will he help us? Or . . .*

The cubicle opened to let the twin step out, and Elissa looked quickly away from what felt suddenly, disorientingly, as if she were seeing a come-to-life reflection of herself.

In the periphery of her vision, she saw the twin pull her clothes back on, then hesitate, watching Elissa.

Elissa looked up, then patted the edge of the upper bunk. "If you sit up there, you'll be able to see yourself in the mirror. Once you've got it all applied, the instructions say it only takes ten minutes." She smiled. Unlike before, it felt like an effort, and the thought came, sliding through her like poison. *What have I done? Tied myself to looking after this girl who I don't know, who's not even a friend, let alone a sister. Is this what I'm going to be doing forever, sharing rooms with her, finding new places to hide, new people to be?*

The hair dye did only take ten minutes. When the other girl washed it off in the shower, her hair showed blond through the foam, then under the heat of the dryers it turned pale, a soft curly drift the color of cream.

As she stepped back out of the shower cubicle and pulled her clothes on once more, Elissa handed her the straightening serum. "Here. If you use this, you can go straight as well. You don't need much, just a couple of blobs." She watched for a minute as the girl squeezed some of the faintly shimmering serum into her palm and reached up to rub it through her hair. "No, smooth it through right to the ends. Look, if you turn the ends around the hairbrush, you can hold it straight while it sets." She stepped up to the other girl, reached out to take control of the brush.

The twin flinched, jerked away, then froze, fingers clamped over the back of her head, not speaking, not looking up.

And now Elissa knew why. The other girl had moved fast, but not fast enough. In that moment when Elissa had touched the hairbrush, she'd also touched the back of her double's head. And she'd felt something through the hair. Something that wasn't identical to Elissa's head. Something that shouldn't be there.

It was a hole. A neat, smooth-edged hole, hidden under the hair that fell over it, just at the base of the girl's skull. The flesh all over the back of Elissa's neck tightened with an instant of agonizing memory. That's where the pain had come from, rocketing out from the base of her skull, spreading bruises all around her jawline and up the back of her head. Not just from a clamp they'd put on her skull, but something they'd inserted *into* it.

WHEN ELISSA could control her voice, she said, "Is that what they did to you?"

The twin nodded, an infinitesimal quiver.

"You don't want me to see?"

Another quiver of her head, this one a sideways shake.

"It's . . ." Elissa bit her lip, trying to think of anything *close* to the right words. "You know it's not your fault, right? You don't need to be . . . ashamed. They did that *to* you. They just randomly decided to take you—"

"It's not random." The twin's voice was hardly audible. "It's my brain, it's different."

"Yeah, but *both* our brains are different. It's not like the link goes just one way. And even if it is different . . . This whole not-human thing—I don't believe it. I felt what you were feeling. You look just like me. You feel the same kind of things. Being able to do something different—it doesn't make you not *human*."

The twin didn't say anything for a long moment. Then her voice came, muffled. "I always *felt* human. When they told us we weren't . . . I was around thirteen. It was when we reached puberty. Before then they brought us up like normal children. They have to do that—it has to do with our brains developing properly. But when they told us, it felt *wrong*. It felt like a lie."

She shifted where she stood, leaning against the side of the bed, her fingers still white on the back of her head, her face still turned away. "Maybe it was the link with you that made me think that too. Even though it didn't stay as strong as when we were small, I think it still lasted way longer than it was supposed to. And like you said, I felt what you were feeling. And they said *you* were human—real, declared-legal human—so it kind of felt to me that if you were, I was too."

Elissa hesitated, then put her hand out to lay it on the twin's back. She didn't have anything to say, couldn't think of anything to help.

Under her hand the twin's body relaxed a tiny bit. She eased her hands off her head, let them fall by her sides. "Some of us—in there, some of the other Spares . . . they burned out. The procedures were too much, and their brains couldn't handle it."

Elissa's stomach clenched. If the twin was going to talk about what had happened to her, if she was going to give details . . . *If she had to go through it, I should be able to hear about it. And I can't tell her not to tell me. But I don't know if I can listen. I don't know if I can bear to hear.*

"And other Spares. They just . . . went."

Elissa swallowed. "Died?"

"No. Went. Became . . . not there. Like they were still alive, but they weren't." Her hands moved to twist together in front of her. "*None* of us were people, we were told that, but when that happened to those Spares . . . before, they'd at least *seemed* like people. Afterward there was nothing there at all."

Elissa tried to keep her hand open, comforting, on the twin's back, but she couldn't help the not-quite-suppressed shudder that went through her from shoulders to fingertips. "I . . . God, I'm sorry."

"I was scared it would happen to me. I was scared. When the procedures started. But I . . . If I reached out, you were there, and I . . ." Her head dipped, her shoulders hunching. "I didn't think about it hurting you as well. I don't know if my reaching out is what hurt you—I don't know if the pain would have gotten through anyway." She was speaking fast now, as if trying to get all the words out in one big rush. "And when I did think about that, I tried to stop, but the link was too strong, I couldn't do it. I think my reaching out to you like that—I think I made the link stronger again. I know, after the first couple of times, I started getting flashes of your memories the way I hadn't for years. I'm sorry, and I didn't mean to wreck your life, but I think, if it hadn't been for that, I'd have burned out—or gone—too."

"It's okay." Elissa spoke automatically, but as she did, she realized it was true. The twin might have sent the pain through to Elissa, might have reestablished a connection that was on its way to dying off completely, but suddenly it didn't seem to matter whether she had or not. What mattered was that she'd reached out to Elissa, and it had helped. *I never mattered like that to anyone before. I never helped anyone—not like that, not so much that it might have been me who saved her life.*

She put her other arm around the twin, feeling how stiff the other girl was, how tightly her hands were clenched around each other. For the first time it wasn't an effort, touching the strange-familiar body, close enough that she caught the clean scent of the other girl's hair, felt the tension in the thin shoulders. "It's okay," she said again. "It was *them*, not you. And we're going to fix it so you don't ever go back."

In her embrace the twin's body relaxed a little. "You don't need to hear about it. I'm sorry."

"Hey." Elissa shook her a little. "You don't need to keep saying sorry. Jeez, the whole freaking *world* should be apologizing to you!"

The twin gave a breath of laughter. "Okay."

"Okay." Elissa let her go, stepped away. It didn't exactly seem like the right time to ask, but none of the other times had seemed like the right ones either. She realized she was chewing her lower lip and deliberately released it. "Do you have a name?"

The twin shook her head. "We had numbers."

After everything else Elissa knew about what her double had gone through, that shouldn't have been a shock. But it was, all the same. *Numbers*.

"Well, you have to have a name now." Her voice came out with an edge to it, an edge she instantly tried to soften. "At least you get to choose your own!"

"I . . ." The twin wound another piece of hair around the brush, pulled it out straight. "I already did . . ."

"Oh?"

"I can't use it. I know I can't. I . . . In there, once they told us what we were, I only managed to believe I was a real person because I knew *you* were a real person. I took your name."

"You—oh." Elissa didn't know what to do with that. Her instinct was to say, *No. You're not doing that. I'm already sharing my face with you—I'm not sharing my name.* But she had no right. Their whole lives, she'd had everything and the other girl had had nothing. "Um . . . so you want to be called Elissa?"

"No. No, that's not what I meant. I thought of you as Lissa—that's the name everyone calls you, that's the name you have in my head. And I"—she hesitated, head dipping lower, not looking at Elissa—"I thought of myself as Lissa's twin."

After a moment Elissa put her hand out, touched the girl's arm. "That's okay."

"I know I shouldn't have. But I never thought I'd actually see you, and I—"

"I said it's okay." Elissa paused a moment, hand staying reassuringly on the girl's—*my twin's*—arm. "But it's no good for the morph-cards. We need to think of something. Something that still means the same thing, but that sounds like a real name for the cards." She chewed on her thumbnail, thinking out loud. "Lissa's twin. Lissatwin. Letwin. Etwin. Satwin. Satin? Satin's a real name. It's kind of dumb, but it's real."

"Okay." But the muscles around her twin's eyes had tightened. It wasn't okay. She'd been told she was nothing but a number, a human-sourced nonhuman, and she'd fought back by choosing her own name. It wasn't just a name—it was the thing that had kept her human. Kept her alive.

"Oh! How about Lin? That could be short for Lissa's twin, and it starts with the same letter. And *also*, for if we need to keep changing our IDs, we could change it just a tiny bit, to Lynette or Linda. Or, um, Linnet, or Lindsey . . ." She trailed off, watching her twin's face.

"Lin. Lynette." The other girl said the words slowly, as if feeling the shape they made. "Lin."

"I mean, you don't have to have that. We can think of something else."

Her twin smiled, a sudden bright flash of . . . Elissa couldn't think of the right word. It was more than happiness, more than pleasure. *It's—oh*. It was a flash of what looked, for the first time, like joy.

"Yes. I'll be Lin."

Elissa found herself grinning back at her twin, her own smile so wide, it hurt. *We're doing it. We're getting her away from those people and what they did to her. We're declaring that she's as human as I am. Her own person.*

"All right," she said. "Now let's finish up so we can do the morph-cards."

Twenty minutes later the cards showed Rissa White and Lynette May, one a milk-pale curly haired redhead, one a blonde whose sleek hair brushed cheeks that glowed with a faint golden tan.

Thank God they were done. Now they could grab some colored contacts and different clothes, check into another pod-motel, and think about where to go next.

Elissa shoveled all the debris of their disguises—empty tubes and sachets, disposable hairbrushes—into the disposal and recycling chutes, checked around for anything they might have left or that might be useful, then zipped shut the bag she had brought from home.

As she did so, a phrase from the screen, only half-heard, caught her attention. ". . . say the residential fire was caused by an electrical fault . . ."

She looked up, and the shelf where her house stood was

showing on the screen. The grass outside it had been trampled into the ground, squashed and muddy, and the glass fronts of the houses nearby were opaque, not because of privacy settings but because of the blackened scorch marks streaked all over them.

She leaned over and turned the volume up.

"Despite the extensive damage caused, fortunately no lives were lost in the fire that last night raged through eleven houses of a residential shelf in Sector Seven-West." The news presenter, as news presenters did, was repeating more or less the same information over and over, a soundtrack to the images flashing on the screen. "The firefighters who were on the scene within minutes have suggested that the blaze may have been caused by an electrical circuit overheating in the house where the fire began, number twelve. Extensive damage has been caused, and all residents were forced to evacuate. . . ."

Elissa glanced over at Lin, who was sitting on the edge of the lower bunk. "That fire—look, they're saying it started in my house. It was completely the weirdest thing. You must have seen it. It started so *fast*. And it was the only thing that could have gotten me out of the house. I'd almost forgotten about it, but jeez, talk about miracles!"

The corners of Lin's mouth curled up a tiny bit. "It wasn't a miracle. It was me."

"What? What do you mean? How could it be you?"

"You don't know? You couldn't tell—through the link?"

"Tell *what*?"

"It's one of the things about my brain that's different. I'm electrokinetic."

"Electrokinetic?"

"I can control electrical currents."

"*You* started that fire?"

Lin's face froze, as if Elissa's tone had shocked her. "Yes."

"And that—oh my God, is *that* how you escaped? The fire the other night—you did that, too?"

"Yes."

"And they didn't know? They didn't know you could do that kind of thing? They didn't have safety precautions?"

Lin shrugged a shoulder. "They knew several of us had a level of psychokinesis from when we were quite young. They kept track of how it matured. But mine, it kept developing, even after the procedures started, and by that time—" Lin's face went hard, acquired a shut-in look. "I knew not to let them know how strong it was. I kept practicing, and I got good enough, finally, to push up the current supplying the whole complex. I got it to leap the fuses, and it set the place on fire." She grinned, a flash of triumph. "So then, when you said you were locked in your room—all these doors, they have the same safety thing built into them."

There was an awful feeling in Elissa's stomach. "You started a fire. In a housing complex."

Lin frowned. "Yes."

"But"—Elissa took a breath—"it was people's houses. They were *sleeping* in them—it was the middle of the night. And you— It was a *massive* fire, it went up like an explosion."

"I know. Like the one in the facility."

Elissa swallowed. "You could have killed someone."

Her twin stared at her. "I knew the sensors would pick it up before it got anywhere near you."

"I don't mean me! *Other* people! There are other people in that building. There's safety measures and all that stuff, but people die in house fires all the time. You could have killed them!"

Her heart was thumping as she looked at Lin, waiting for her to register what she'd done, waiting for her to look as stricken with guilt as Elissa felt. She'd put all those people in danger—people who had nothing to do with what was happening to them, people who hadn't even known Elissa was locked up.

Lin did look distressed now, biting her lip, her eyes fixed on Elissa's. But her words weren't anything like the ones Elissa wanted her to say.

"Why should I care about that?" she said. "Why are you upset? No one's dead. The fire services were on their way when you escaped."

"Because *you could have*—" Elissa broke off. "I can't explain. If you can't see why there's a problem, I can't make you understand."

"Lissa . . ."

"Stop it! I can't— If you don't see how awful it is to put all those people in danger and not even think about it, not even care, I can't talk to you. I don't know what to do with you."

"Don't. Lissa, don't, don't." Even under the fake tan Lin's face showed white. "Don't not talk to me. Tell me. I don't understand. I was saving *you*. I don't know any of those people. I only know you. Why are you saying I should care about them?"

Despite Elissa's horror, Lin's distress caught at her. Elissa frowned, staring at her, feeling as if they were speaking two different languages. "You . . . ," she spoke slowly, feeling her way. "You weren't *trying*—you didn't actually *want* to kill them?"

"I didn't *want* to, no."

"Okay. Maybe it's me who's not understanding. You didn't *want* to kill them, but you didn't care if you did?"

Lin opened her hands in front of her and stared down at the palms. "I guess. I mean, I wouldn't have *enjoyed* killing them, but . . . them dying or not, it's got nothing to do with me. I don't know any of them. You're my twin, but they're just . . . nobody."

"But *why*? I don't get why that makes a difference. They're other *people*."

Lin flicked a glance upward, her hands still open on her lap. She looked suddenly exposed. "Not to me."

"Not— Oh." *Right.* Lin had been raised like a lab animal in a facility, intended to be used for the benefit of legally declared humans, creatures different from her. Maybe Elissa couldn't expect her to have Elissa's own automatic connection with the species that was biologically hers. To the rest of the world, Lin was nothing more than property. So, to Lin, what were *they*? What were other people to her? Not the ones who'd held her prisoner, but others, outside the facility, neutral and uninvolved?

After a hesitant moment Elissa asked the question out loud. She'd expected Lin to fumble for an answer, but she didn't. "They're not anything."

"None of them?"

Lin tugged at an end of her hair. "Well, not you."

"But . . . ?"

"All the rest. Yes. I saw some of them, when I was coming through the city to find you. I saw people who were looking after their children, and people who thought I was one of them, and they smiled at me." She looked at the screen, where the news presenter had moved on to an earthquake over at the other side of the continent. "But every single one of them, if they knew what I was . . ."

"They'd want you sent back?"

"Yes."

"You don't *know* that . . ." But Lin looked at her, her face blank, and Elissa's words trailed away.

She's not a psychopath. She's not. She cares about what I think. Psychopaths—sociopaths?—they don't care about other people's feelings.

But Elissa's stomach was churning, her chest as tight as if there were a weight on it. Inside her head, flames roared, the impossible, out-of-control flames that had torn through her family's house just a few hours ago. *Lin could have killed so many people. She was doing it to save me, I know why she did it, but to not even care what might have happened . . .*

As Elissa turned off the screen, and then as they went out of the room and down in the elevator, the arguments beat at her. Lin had sounded beyond callous, but it wasn't her fault. There was no *reason* she should care about any of the people in the whole city, on the whole planet. *Look what we—our government— did to her. She's entitled not to care about any of us.*

But what if that's it? What if what they did, what if it's broken something inside her? What if I've run away with—what if I'm protecting—someone who really is a sociopath—a dangerous, electrokinetic sociopath?

What if there's a very good reason they kept her locked up?

They stepped out of the motel into a glare of sunlight. It was early still, the city lying half-drowsing in the pre–rush hour calm, but the sun was already hot, promising a boiling day to come.

"Where are we going first?" said Lin.

The sunlight showed her clothes to be even shabbier, even dirtier, than they'd looked under artificial lights, her bare feet peeking out under the hems of her pants. The sleek blond hair, the flawless sheen to her face, made her look quite unlike the girl of yesterday. But she didn't look as if she belonged in Elissa's world either. Elissa's clothes weren't exactly shiny and clean, and they smelled of sweat, but they still looked a lot more expensive and cared for than Lin's. She hitched the bag farther up onto her shoulder.

"Clothes and shoes first," she said.

She led the way onto a slidewalk, heading toward the nearest twenty-four-hour mall. Lin followed her obediently, the unquestioning trust in her face making her look like a little girl. *She's not a sociopath. She's damaged, that's all.*

Elissa shook her hair back, hitched the bag up again. *And anyway, I can't think about that now. Right now we just have to think about disguise.*

The mall was made up of glass-fronted galleries built one on top of another within the cliff. As Elissa paid for their new clothes with her reprogrammed morph-card, tension pulled all her muscles tight, made her clumsy so that she fumbled with the card as she slid it through the scanner, and had to press cancel and do it a second time.

Phantom alarms rang in her ears, and when for a split second she met the shop assistant's eyes, she had to force herself not to jerk her gaze guiltily away.

Lin stood quietly next to her, blond wings of hair hiding her face. The same tension held her too—an invisible aura that seemed to vibrate across the space between them.

The assistant shook the pants and tops into practiced folds, slid them into a carrier, and dropped the shoes in on top of them. "Take your card, please. D'you want a hard-copy receipt?"

"No, thanks."

The assistant's gaze met Elissa's for a further moment, then moved incuriously away. "Thank you. Have a nice day."

Elissa left the counter, new clothes safe in the carrier in her hand, Lin close behind her. The assistant had hardly seen them, hardly registered them as individuals. They'd been customers, that was all, yet more customers in a day full of them. *She won't even remember us. If people ask, if they track us here and go around asking for sightings . . .*

They were back out in the main area of the mall, bathed in the muted sunlight coming through the glass. People wandered past them, adjusting their direction without properly looking up from phones, myGadgets, or from conversations with their companions. There were other teenage girls here and there, girls walking in twos or threes, often wearing clothes not dissimilar to Elissa's and Lin's, some laughing, some talking quietly, heads together.

Like me and Lin. In this whole place we're just two more teenagers. Until it's schooltime, no one's going to pay us any attention, notice us any more than they're noticing all the other girls like us.

She looked up and caught Lin's eye. "It's okay," she said, not loudly but not particularly quietly either. "No one's noticing us. We're just blending in."

Lin gave a quick breath, and the almost-tangible shiver of tension in the air faded, died away. "Let's change into the new clothes now, though."

Elissa sent her a little grin. "Oh, completely. I feel like I've been living in this outfit my whole life." She caught herself too late, and a flush burned up into her face. *Could I sound more overprivileged? Saying that? To her?*

But Lin's lips just curled in a smile. "Yes. And think how I feel."

"Gah. I'm *sorry*."

Lin shrugged, dismissing it. "Let's get changed."

Elissa had bought clothes that were cute and fashionable enough to transform both girls into yet another pair of teenagers on a quick mall fix before school. Three-quarter-length jeans and a long floaty white top for her, loose exercise pants and a close-fitting sleeveless tee for Lin. And new sweatshirts with deep hoods.

She rolled up their old clothes in the carrier and stuffed it into one of the trash cans in the washroom they'd ducked into to get changed. As she straightened, she caught sight of one of the mirrors and almost jumped, thinking for an instant that a stranger was watching her. But it wasn't a stranger. It was her own reflection.

It was obviously her, once she looked closer. But for that one instant she'd seen herself and thought it was someone else. And the girl standing close by, with sleek blond hair and the graceful, clinging lines of dark pants and T-shirt—she looked nothing like the desperate, dirty runaway of less than a day ago.

Once, when Elissa was six, she'd been playing hide-and-seek at a friend's party. Running in a panic while another girl counted, she'd found a hiding place behind the one-way glass of the shower cubicle in the friend's parents' bathroom. She'd stood silently, hardly noticing the moisture seeping through the soles of her socks. She'd been dizzy with the triumphant knowledge that she was invisible and the others weren't. Even if they looked straight at where she stood, she would see them and they would never see her.

The seeker had given up in the end, and the friend's mother had gently reminded them all that the grown-ups' bathroom was out-of-bounds, and the game had continued with Elissa feeling chastened. But now, seeing her and Lin's eyes looking out of unfamiliar faces, under unfamiliar hair, she remembered what it had been like, seeing but not being seen, as safe from scrutiny, discovery, as if she'd turned truly invisible.

Her shoulders relaxed as a knot she hadn't even realized was there untied itself and slipped away.

"Where do we go now?" said Lin from behind her.

Elissa turned. "We can pick up colored contacts from a machine—we'll do that first. Then we'll go to one of the parks, where there aren't many cameras, and plan our next step. I was thinking it would be a good idea to leave the city."

But even as she spoke, other thoughts flowed up into her mind, washing through what she was saying. The first thoughts, it seemed, since she'd run from her home in the early hours of the morning, that weren't frantic, charged with panic. Thoughts she wouldn't have been able to have until she'd reached this new calmness.

We can leave the city. There are high-speed trains leaving all the time, and the morph-cards will pay for any tickets we like. But I don't need to do anything that drastic just yet. Not just yet. Dad helped me escape. He went along with Mother, but it must have been just to calm her down. He can't have meant to force me into an operation I don't need anymore.

And Mother—she was just overreacting. She was freaked out

because she thought I was running away. I've been gone for hours now. If I'm gone for another night, she'll start to realize how crazy she was. I can call them. We can talk sensibly.

Then, a thought came that shot relief through her so fast, it nearly made her dizzy: *I can talk to* him *now.*

Earlier she'd wondered what her father would do if she called him. But now it seemed dumb to have even wondered. He'd helped her escape, hadn't he? Of course he'd help her now. Tell her where she should go, how long she needed to wait till her mother had calmed down. Think of other ways of helping Lin.

"Lissa?" Lin's voice was a little sharp, anxious.

Elissa looked at her. "I'm going to call my dad."

Lin's face froze, her eyes suddenly huge. "What?"

"I'm going to call him. He gave me the cards, remember? He's on our side."

But Lin was shaking her head. "No, no, don't. They'll find us. Lissa, you *can't.*"

"He'll *help* us."

"You thought they'd *both* help us, and they locked you up—"

"That was because of my mother! My dad *helped.*"

"No. *No.* It doesn't mean he'll help us now. He did what your mother said, he locked you in. He only gave you the cards when you were already going to escape. He's not going to do anything else, Lissa."

A wave of heat rose behind Elissa's eyes. She remembered to keep her voice low, but all the same the words snapped like a crack of electricity. "Don't you tell me what my dad's like!"

Lin's face went still. She opened her mouth once, then shut it again. Her shoulders hunched. "Okay."

"Look. I don't know what to do at this point. My dad will help us figure it out. It's not like we have a lot of options."

There was a little frozen moment, then Elissa picked up her bag and went out of the washroom. Silently Lin came behind her.

If you don't like what I'm doing, you don't have to come. Go sort things out for yourself; go do something else.

Except even in her anger—*who the hell does she think she is, telling me about my dad?*—she knew it wasn't true. Lin did have to come. She was dependent on Elissa to help her. *And she has nowhere else to go. She came to find me. That was all.*

It was awful to matter so much to someone.

She led the way to the nearest phone booths. They were soundproofed, which was just as well, because they stood next to a courtyard filled with chairs and coffee tables and dominated by a large newsscreen.

Elissa looked up at the screen as she went past, her stomach tightening a little, but the stories were all more or less the same as earlier that morning, and although the shelf fire was referred to again—the earlier facility fire seemed to have passed its current-news date and wasn't mentioned at all—there were no additional details.

The tightness stayed with her, though, as she fed two of her last few coins into the slot next to the phone screen, looking at the stylized vines of the WELCOME display. She could use the morph-card for this, too, but it made her edgy, and after all, she didn't need to while she still had some cash.

She tapped in her father's name, scrolled through the short list of other Ivorys that replaced the vines display, and clicked on the familiar name.

The connecting icon, a single vine stalk, drew itself across the screen, curling out in long spirals and little tendril twists—first just dark green, then other colors as the leaves and drooping, graceful flowers began to color themselves in, outer edges first, bleeding color toward their centers.

The edge of the screen was smooth, and hard enough to push dents up into Elissa's fingertips where they pressed against it.

Her father *had* gone along with her mother, but only to start with. Just like he'd agreed to the painful braces Elissa had worn when she was thirteen, braces that the orthodontist had said were scarcely necessary but that her mother had insisted she wear. Like he'd agreed to the summer school her mother had sent her to when she was ten, where she'd been homesick for two weeks before they'd come to take her home. He hadn't interfered; he'd agreed that both were for Elissa's own good.

But when the braces had given her a toothache that had woken her in the middle of the night, he'd brought her painkillers and taken her back to the orthodontist to check that the braces had been fitted correctly. And when she'd called home from the summer school, sobbing, for the third time in two days, he'd persuaded her mother she should come home early.

I know him. Not Lin. I know he'll help me.

The connection chime sounded, the vine blew away off the screen as if a silent wind had turned it to dust, and her father's face appeared. He was in his office—*thank God, I thought he would be*—and he only looked up as the phone connected. His eyes met Elissa's, and his whole face seemed to jerk in shock.

After a split second, when his face was so still it might have been no more than his photograph, his lips moved, silently, very slightly. *No.*

Suddenly Elissa was near tears. She'd been coping okay: She'd gotten them fed and washed and disguised, was on the edge of making plans for what to do next. But she wasn't *supposed* to be doing all this. This was something that *adults* were supposed to do.

"Daddy, I need help." Her voice wavered.

"No." This time he said it out loud. "Cut the call. Get out."

"Daddy . . ." Tears stung the inside of her nose. Her chin shook. "I really need help. I don't know what I'm doing."

Her father's eyes met hers in a long, agonizing stare. She waited for him to say something, waited for him to save her, help her, tell her what to do.

Lis. He didn't speak out loud, just formed her name with his lips. Then he mouthed something else she couldn't quite pick up. . . . *help you . . . out of the city.* And then one final word, a word he'd said to her in the gray dawn of that morning, standing outside the blaze of their burning house, pushing an illegal form of ID into her sweaty palm. *Run.*

Then his face blinked out and the WELCOME screen returned.

For a moment she couldn't believe he'd cut her off, couldn't believe that was it. Her hand went to the screen as if she could summon him back, but all that happened was that the familiar menu of choices appeared. *Would you like to make another call? Would you like information on current special offers? Would you like to end this session now?*

Numbly she touched yes to end the session, and her left-over coins chinked into the tray below. She scooped them up, feeling their smooth coolness between her fingers, the way they slid together with a tiny scraping sound.

"Elissa."

Elissa swallowed. "He told us to run. I said I needed help and he wouldn't. He didn't help me."

Lin stepped close to her, taking her arm in a grip that was nearly painful. "He helped as much as he could." She shook Elissa's arm. "We have to go. We have to do what he said. They must be scanning the phones, and your dad knew."

Elissa's hand froze around the coins. "He—what? They're doing what?"

Lin shook her again. "Lissa! Snap out of it! You thought he'd swoop in and save you because he's your father? Like you thought your parents would help me—an illegally escaped nonhuman—just because you asked them to? Listen to me. They can't help with this. Even if they *wanted* to—and for all I know, your dad does want to—they couldn't. They don't have the power to. Either we help ourselves or—" She stopped, her eyes fixed above Elissa's head. "Lissa, we have to get out now. *Now*. What's the best way out of this place?"

"What is it? What are you—" But the next second she didn't need to ask. Above her, her own name blared out from the speakers next to the newsscreen. She turned, cold all over, her gaze moving to the screen as if pulled against her will. Her own image, dark-haired, dark-eyed, hugely magnified, stared out at her.

"Residents of Central Canyon City are asked to be aware of a teenage runaway who may be at acute risk. Elissa Laine Ivory, seventeen years old, disappeared from her home last night. She is believed to be in the company of another girl of her own age, who may be holding Elissa against her will."

No. Oh, no. She'd thought they wouldn't be able to put out an alert for Lin—Lin, who was supposed not to exist. But of course they could do this, mention an unnamed girl, say that Elissa was at risk from her. They must have prepared the whole statement beforehand, had it ready for as soon as they located her. A statement full of cleverly judged phrases that would make a city full of law-abiding citizens feel personally responsible for looking out for her, for the vulnerable teen-age runaway she was supposed to be.

And then, as if that weren't bad enough, as if to drive home that calling her dad had been the *worst possible* thing she could have done: "The last confirmed sighting of Elissa was five minutes ago, at the Sand Springs Mall. Citizens at the mall are asked to be particularly alert, and to call authorities should they believe they've spotted the runaway."

SEVEN

ELISSA was frozen no longer. Heat and adrenaline raced through every vein in her body. In a quick, reflexive movement she jerked her hood up over her hair, pushing the wild spirals of copper curls forward to shadow and conceal her face. At the same time she was mapping out routes in her head, not just the quickest ways out of the mall but also the routes where they'd meet the fewest people. The fewest kind, concerned, all-too-watchful people.

Next to her, Lin was shivering. She'd pulled her hood up too, and in its shadow her face was gray. She held her morph-card in fingers that had gone so pale, they looked bloodless. "It's okay," Lin said, although she spoke so low and her voice was shaking so much that Elissa could hardly pick up the words. "You don't have to—you've already done so much. I—" She swallowed. "Thank you for helping me. Thank you for the card."

Elissa's hand shot out to grab her arm as she moved away. "What? What are you doing?"

Lin's lips were as bloodless as her fingers. "If I go now, you can just go back. To—to your normal life. They're after us, and if you keep running, you'll end up being a criminal too. And I never meant that. I never *meant* this for you, Lissa."

"You're going to *go*?"

Lin nodded, pale lips pressed together, face set. She was going to do just that. After finding the sister she'd known about all her life, the sister whose link had kept her alive through fear and torture, she was going to leave so that same sister could go back to her nice, normal life. So she could have the link burned out of her brain, so she could forget.

Elissa's hand tightened on her twin's arm. "You're not. We're staying together. I know I was a complete bitch to you, but that doesn't mean it's okay for you to leave."

"I— Lissa, it's not because of *that*."

"I know." She moved her hand, twitched out the creases she'd left in Lin's sleeve. "Okay, listen, we're going to the top floor. There's a whole kind of roof garden—it gets completely crowded later on, but right now it'll be okay. Then there's like a back route out down to the slidewalks—it's all old-style stuff, just bridges and walkways, so it hardly gets used." She continued talking, not particularly quietly, as she led the way to the elevators at the end of the gallery, sparing a scrap of attention to be amazed at how relaxed her voice sounded.

Inside she was all coiled and burning tension, hyperaware of the tone of voice of anyone who passed her and Lin, of every gaze that touched them and then moved away. They were just the same as before, a pair of teenage girls, familiar, unremarkable. But now Elissa was aware that everyone they passed gave them a second, sometimes a third, glance, paid them just a little more attention than before.

They'd *had* to come here, they'd *had* to get clothes, but—oh, *hell*, it was the worst place possible to have an alert put out for them, a place full of lazily browsing, slow-moving people with time and attention to spare for news broadcasts, for noticing the unusual. And here Elissa was, hiding beneath the merest skin of a disguise, going around with a girl who, despite all their efforts, was still the same height, had the same face shape, the same hands, moved in the *same freaking way* as her.

Run, said her father in her head.

Oh, Daddy, it's too late for that. Their only chance was to get out of the mall as smoothly as she could manage it and then disappear in the anonymity of the city outside.

Except now that the alert was out, was there anywhere they could go where they'd be anonymous? Two teenage girls, traveling together without parents or grown-ups anywhere nearby, in a city made famously low-crime by an intricate network of security, cameras, alarms, and ID checks, a city that was ultrasafe for anyone who stayed within the law—and terrifying for anyone outside it.

There were two people waiting for the elevator, and the door opened as Elissa and Lin joined them.

They slipped inside, moving instinctively, without discussion, to stand by the far wall, their backs to the other occupants.

The elevator was built at the far end of the mall gallery, against the glass wall of the building. As the elevator slid upward, the glass of the mall and, farther down, the rock wall of the canyon fell away beneath them.

We'll get up to the roof, out to the walkways. Get back down into the city.

If only they could get out without being spotted.

"What class have we got first?" Elissa said, grabbing at random for something that would sound normal, would make her and Lin seem like two ordinary girls leaving the mall on their way to school.

Lin hesitated too long before replying. "I—languages?"

Elissa bit back a flare of irritation. *I'm having to think of everything, having to do everything, and you can't even sound as if you know what you're talking about?*

But if I hadn't insisted on calling my dad . . .

She spoke through the wave of cold, drenching guilt. "Oh no, it's okay, I remember. It's health and hygiene. Listen, you know that party this weekend, I'm going to wear my red dress, okay? As long as you don't want to wear your blue one, 'cause they're way too much alike and everyone will be all . . ." She talked on, an endless rattling of words that didn't mean anything, as if she were running some resurrected program from a life she hadn't had for years. It sounded horribly fake to her own ears, and although she kept talking, kept churning out meaningless phrases, the skin at the back of her neck began to prickle with an awareness of being watched. Those other people who'd gotten into the elevator, were they looking at her? Were they already taking out their phones to call the police, the mall security guards?

She couldn't bear it. She threw a look around just as the man opposite her glanced up from the myGadget in his hand.

Their eyes locked. Elissa couldn't move, couldn't look away. He'd been reporting them. The stupid disguises they'd wasted so much time on hadn't done any good.

He'd recognized her. He was reporting them.

The man gave Elissa a quick, uncomfortable smile, then looked back down at his myGadget. As he tilted it, its screen reflected briefly in the glass wall of the elevator. Game scores. He'd been checking game scores, that was all. Maybe he hadn't even heard the news alert yet. If he'd only just entered the mall, if he hadn't been near the newsscreens . . .

Elissa leaned against the handrail, floppy with relief, forgetting to look away, forgetting to carry on talking. In the glass across from her, the reflected display on the man's myGadget changed. A news ticker scrolled backward across it.

No. Oh, no. Elissa's stomach dropped as if the elevator had plummeted. *Click away. Look at something else. Something else—*

Too late. From the little colored, moving reflection, Elissa's own face looked out at her. She couldn't see the mirror-text scrolling across it, but she knew what it said. *Elissa Laine Ivory, seventeen years old . . .*

The man was suddenly very still, the myGadget motionless in his hand. He lifted his head and looked straight at Elissa.

At the same time, the elevator came to a halt. At the seventh floor, not the top, but it didn't matter.

Elissa was at the opening door in two strides. "Lin. This floor."

"Wait a moment," said the man. "Are you that girl? The runaway?"

Elissa shook her head, backing out of the elevator, Lin by her side. "No. No, I'm not."

"*Wait* a minute now!" The man took a long step toward them, but they were out of the elevator, hurrying away along the gallery floor.

"Hey, someone!" The man's voice rose behind them.

"Those girls—they were on the news alert! I'm calling the police!"

"Lissa—"

"I know. Run."

Up on this floor, there weren't many people around. But all the same, as she and Lin took off down the long gallery, Elissa heard a scatter of concerned voices beginning as other people caught the man's alarm.

Another man put out a half-unwilling, ineffectual arm to bar their way, and a woman stepped in front of them, but they dodged, not breaking stride, running as if running itself could get them away, keep them safe.

One set of elevators was behind them, and the others were way at the far end of the building. But halfway through the mall moving staircases connected the floors, zigzagging up and down the cliff face. Elissa jerked Lin toward them, avoiding a couple of slow-moving mothers with toddlers and an older couple walking arm in arm.

Then they were on the staircase, racing up past the people who stood on it, who were turning surprised faces to stare. They reached the top of the stairs, the next floor. Elissa flung a glance up as she and Lin swung around the corner and jumped onto the next staircase. Two more floors till the roof, that was all, they could make it—

For an instant she thought the ringing was only in her head, then she realized it was the sound she'd been dreading since the motel—the sound of alarms ringing all over the building. Then the screech and scrape of security grilles cutting off the ground-level exits. Then more raised voices, these ones confident, authoritative. She spared a quick look back. Security guards, two of them, taking the stairs three at a time, gaining on them.

"They're coming," Lin said, panting.

Elissa had no breath to agree. They hurtled up the rest of the staircase, pushing past the few people who didn't move quickly enough out of the way. The girls jumped for a moment onto the static floor of the next landing, and rounded the corner onto the last extra-long staircase. Only a handful of people stood on this one, letting it carry them slowly up to the top floor: a businessman talking on the phone, a young woman with a baby in a sling, an older man with his walking support leaning on the stair above him. If the girls could just get up to the top of this last staircase, just keep running till they made it, just get out—

Oh God. They'll have locked those doors too. Not every door had one of the expensive high-security grilles, but they could all be shut and locked. And by now they would be. *We'll get up there and it'll be a dead end, we'll be trapped.*

But she couldn't do anything but keep running, hoping that somehow they'd be able to get out anyway, hoping that something would happen to save them. They were halfway up the staircase when the guards appeared at the bottom and began to make their fast climb up. One of them shouted something.

Déjà vu caught Elissa, a moment of dizziness like vertigo. She'd been here before, running from men in charge, men commanding her to stop. Running with no hope of escape. Last time an eleventh-hour miracle had saved her, a last-minute stroke of luck that had left a gate unlocked. A miracle like the fire that had gotten her out of her house—*Wait.*

As if Elissa were running so fast that she'd left her brain behind, her thoughts suddenly caught up. The fire *hadn't* been a miracle. It had been Lin. And the gate—the sealed gate, too?

"Can you open the doors?" Elissa gasped, breathless. "The doors at the top, if they've locked them?"

Lin cast a wild look at her. "What?"

"The way you did the fire? Electrokinesis? *Lin*, can you do it?"

Lin stopped dead in the middle of the staircase, so suddenly that Elissa had leapt five more steps before she realized and turned to look down at Lin. A long length below them the guards had overtaken the young mother, were racing up toward where the businessman stood staring, phone call forgotten. The older man moved sideways, ready to get out of their way.

"*Lin*, don't stop—"

"*Yes.*" Lin's face was flushed and sweaty, but now it took on an extra glow—one of triumph. "Yes, I can do that." She grinned, a wide flash of teeth. "And more. Hold on tight."

"What—" But even as Elissa spoke, the staircase shuddered beneath her feet. She grabbed with both hands for the handrail.

The staircase shuddered again, a vibration that went all through it, then stopped dead. The guards, climbing two steps at a time, hands only loosely on the rail, were jerked off their feet. One stumbled, snatching for the rail; the other fell on one knee, hands flung out to break his fall. The businessman's phone flew from his grasp, and it, too, fell, bouncing from step to step.

"Lin, be careful. Don't . . ."

Lin wasn't listening. Her grin spread wider. "Hold on tighter."

The staircase began to shake.

It went in a wave, down from where Lin stood, each step

lifting a little, sending the movement into the one below it. Then again, faster, the steps lifting higher, one wave after another, like ripples running down a length of ribbon.

The guard who'd fallen had been getting back to his feet, but the wave of motion threw his hands off the rail, flung his feet from under him. He gave a cry of pain as he went down, his knee hitting a step. The older man's hands, sharp-knuckled on the handrail, lost their grip. He fell heavily on his side, grabbing uselessly for his walking support, his face a mask of surprise and panic.

The wave came again, this time strong enough that even Elissa, standing above where it began, felt it shake the steps. And again. On the handrail Lin's hands were clenched as tightly as the old man's had been, her feet braced apart, her teeth bared in what might be effort, or what might still be that grin of triumph. And again came a wave, stronger. This time the steps didn't fall back into place. They crashed and grated, forced out of shape, a heaving avalanche of broken metal.

With each wave the old man was bounced down another section of treacherous broken slabs of sharp-edged metal, his walking support rattling after him, knocking against his hands as he scrabbled for a hold, tumbling helplessly down toward the businessman.

The guard had given up trying to stand. He'd locked his hands around the rail, his head shielded behind them. Where his knee had hit the step, the metal edge shone wet and red.

Elissa couldn't look away. Far below a woman screamed, and a baby gave a sudden terrified wail.

"Lin," she said again, her voice thin with horror. "Lin, please, stop."

Lin looked up at her. She spoke through clenched teeth, in a voice Elissa hardly recognized. "They're after us. We have to get away."

But you're hurting them! They're just ordinary people, and you're hurting them! If she said those words aloud, said them to Lin, would they even register? Would they do anything at all?

"We *can* get away," Elissa said instead. "If you can open the top doors, we can get away now. Lin, *listen* to me, you don't need to do any more."

Lin glanced down the still-shaking staircase. The businessman was gripping the heaving rail, one leg braced against it, the other leg braced against the old man to keep him from falling any farther. Below him the guards clung to the rail, the movement vibrating through their arms, through their whole bodies. The pants fabric of the one who'd fallen was bunched up above his knee, clinging to his leg, dark and wet. Farther below, the mother was the only one not holding on to the handrail. She lay, body curled around her baby, each wave jerking her violently up then down, crashing her into the steps, jolting her down onto the next few stairs. She didn't move, didn't put out a hand to save herself, her whole body nothing but protection for the baby she held.

On the rail Lin's hands slowly relaxed. And as they did, the rippling, crashing staircase began to judder, an earthquake coming to an end.

Lin looked back and began to climb up toward Elissa. "Okay," she said. "Let's go."

A hundred different thoughts battered in Elissa's head; a hundred different sentences burned her throat. Lin had looked down, had seen what Elissa had seen, and— *Oh God,*

*it's not registering at all. It's like she doesn't even see it. And I asked
her to—I asked her to use electrokinesis. Knowing what she did last
time, knowing how she doesn't react like normal people—I panicked
and let her do it again.*

"Elissa?" Lin's look of bright triumph faded. Her eyes were
dark with worry, her face drawn with sudden fatigue. "Are
you okay? I didn't hurt you?"

*She's not a sociopath. She doesn't just care about herself. Look.
Look—she cares about me, she can't have anything really wrong
with her. And if she hadn't done something, we wouldn't have gotten away.*

"I'm okay," Elissa said. She didn't look back down at the
ruined staircase, at the people struggling to their feet. The
air still rang with a cacophony of alarm bells, and there were
plenty of other security guards in the building, and any minute now law enforcement agents would arrive. Elissa drew in
a long shuddering breath through her teeth, turned, and ran,
hearing Lin's feet pounding after her.

The doors to the roof were locked, their translucent sili-
con edges clamped tight. Elissa and Lin came up to them,
panting, and for a moment all Elissa's other anxieties were
drowned in a flood of panic. If they couldn't get out, if they
were trapped here while the enforcement agents caught up
with them . . .

"Can you do it? Can you open them?"

Lin put her hand flat against the seal, her forehead crin-
kling in a frown. "Wait a minute. They're heavy, and sealed
so tight. I could move them, but it's easier if I find the electrics of the switch . . ." Her voice trailed off. She screwed
up her eyes, and her fingertips went white where they rested
against the door.

Something seemed to explode in Elissa's head, a noiseless firework flash, an impossible constellation of sparks. A tickle in the palm of her hand, like a nerve gone suddenly, itchily insane.

The doors sprang open. Heat hit her; hot air and the dazzle of unfiltered sunlight washed over and through her. The weird sensations died before she could try to define them, and they blurred into a memory.

In the sunlight Lin's face was pale, a sheen of sweat along her hairline, shadows like bruises all around her eyes. Elissa remembered suddenly that less than twelve hours ago Lin had been lying feverish in a ditch. That less than forty-eight hours ago she'd been held prisoner in a government-sanctioned facility. That she had a *hole*, for God's sake, in the back of her head.

"Come on." She took her twin's arm and pulled her gently out into the blaze of sunlight and heat, out across the wide sweep of the rooftop, paved in frosted glass, between the pots of palm trees and trellis screens of carefully trained scented flowers. At the far end of the roof, the sun glinted on safety rails arching over a walkway at the head of a flight of static stairs. "We just have to get out of here, back down to the slidewalks, and we can disappear again."

Lin nodded. She looked more than tired. She looked hollowed out, as if she'd used every scrap of energy, of willpower, to get this far. As though, if she had to do anything else, she might not make it.

If we can just get down from here before they send anyone else, Elissa thought. *If we can just get a chance to hide for a bit, to rest.*

She hoped, but in vain. They'd only just reached the walkway when she heard the flyers coming.

They came surging up from below, appearing over the edge of the mall building, sleek and narrow-bodied, shining silver in the sunlight. They were designed to maneuver in the smallest spaces; they'd have no problem landing on the roof. And once there—

We've been running and running. Lin's already exhausted from what she did back there. We can't, *we can't do any more.*

But as the sound of the flyers' propellers changed, as they backed in the air, preparing to settle into place on the roof, fresh adrenaline kicked up through Elissa, and new heat ran through her veins.

The girls took off down the walkway, feet echoing on its metal surface. There was a staircase at the end, a spiral of steps that would take them down to the next walkway, then another to take them down to the next, down and down the cliff face to a final wide platform on the level where the slide-walks began.

We can't make it. Not all the way down. They'll catch up.

But there was nowhere else to go, no other escape route. Elissa ran, Lin's feet an echo beside her, Lin's breathing in her ear, the whine of slowing propellers behind them. She ran into a maze of shining steel stairs and safety rails, of eye-watering bright blue sky, of sunlight bouncing in dazzling bursts of silver fire from steps and bars, and, beginning three stories below them, the snakelike spiral of a staircase that was entirely covered.

They reached the end of the walkway, clattered down the spiral staircase at the end, then along another walkway, then descended another short flight of stairs. Elissa's hand, wet with sweat, slid on the rail as she swung around onto the next floor. She lurched, nearly falling, then wrenched herself back up as the long curve of the covered staircase came back into view. For a moment her vision blurred with fear and fatigue and the endless dazzle of the sky and sun and steel. The smooth coiling shape of the roof drew her eyes down and down, dizzying, blurring, pulling her gaze to follow its shape all the way down until it spread out in a wide fan, into a roof covering the mechanism at the start of one of the slidewalks. The fan curved up at its farthest edge, a graceful curved lip like the curve at the top of a wave, or the curve at the end of a playground slide.

"*Lissa!* They've landed, they're coming!"

Elissa cast a split-second look around them. Another flight down would take them to the walkway that joined the covered staircase. But if they just made it to the end of the walkway they were on now, they'd be directly over it.

She spun around. "Lin. Listen. Can you—"

"No." Lin was shaking her head, her face pale and clammy, her eyes like black holes. "I'm finished. If I hadn't—the moving stairs—I used so much energy."

Above them men's feet pounded along the first walkway. Elissa's chest was heaving; every breath seemed to tear its way through her lungs. "You don't have *anything* left?"

"Not enough to do it again." Her gaze clung to Elissa's. "I'm sorry. I'm sorry. If it was just opening another door—but I can't stop them, not anymore—"

All at once Elissa understood what Lin thought she was asking her to do. "It is! That's all it is. Quick, quick, this way."

She pulled Lin along the walkway, hearing the clatter that meant the law enforcement agents were on the spiral staircase above them. If she was wrong, if Lin couldn't do this or if it didn't work, all she'd done was trap them like rats in a disposal chute.

They came to a halt at the end of the walkway, directly above the roofed staircase, safety railings all around them. Elissa put her hand up to the railings. "Lin, can you bend them? Enough to get us through?"

"Through?" Lin looked down. Her eyes caught the long spiral of the roof and snapped wide as she understood what Elissa was planning. *"That?"*

"How else can we get away? Lin, quick, we don't have time—"

She wouldn't have thought it was possible for her twin to go even paler, but as Lin closed her hands around the railings and shut her eyes in concentration, every scrap of blood seemed to drain out of her face. Her lips turned blue, and the shadows under her eyes showed so dark, it was as if someone had pressed their thumbs hard into the sockets, leaving bruises behind.

A shudder went through Lin, from her tensed shoulders to her fingers, bone white on the metal. Her teeth clenched, and her face went tight, every feature standing out sharper than before.

Above them, the thump of feet.

Oh God, Lin, you have to do it. If we've gotten this far and can't—

The bars shuddered as Lin had shuddered. Wavered as if Elissa were seeing them through a heat wave, then bent slowly, fluidly apart. There was just enough space for a teenage girl to slip through, then to get her balance for a moment and drop onto the wide silver stripe of roofing below and begin to slide.

They'd be miles away from the law enforcement agents

within seconds. They'd buy themselves time to hide and rest and plan. It would be easy—fantastically, ridiculously easy.

And, looking at the roof for the first time without the safety railings in the way, Elissa knew she couldn't do it. The twisting staircase seemed to swirl and swoop below her, sending spirals of nausea up behind her eyes, into her stomach. She must have been crazy to ever consider it. They were so high up, so *high*, and there were no safety fields, no bars, no glass walls to catch them if they slipped too far, slid helplessly off the roof to fall and fall and fall . . .

"We have to," said Lin, white-faced, hand on one of the warped rails.

"I can't. I can't do it." Cold sweat broke out all over Elissa's back. "I'm sorry. I should never— We'll just have to keep running."

"Lissa, we don't have *time*."

Elissa looked again at the narrow ledge they'd need to climb onto, the drop, the roof spiraling down and down and down. The nausea twisted, tight and cold inside her, making her start to shake. "I *can't*. I just can't."

Lin dropped her hand. "Okay. Then I'll have to fix it myself."

"What?"

"I'm not going back there. They're not getting me. I can start fires, remember? Interfere with electric currents?" Lin glanced up through the crisscrossing metal above them, up to where the flyers had landed. Her face was not just set but merciless, her eyes like ice. "I can reach their fuel tanks," she said. "I can send them up like fireballs."

She raised her hands, palms open.

"Oh God, *no*." Elissa grabbed her twin's hands and dragged them down. "They'll have pilots in them!"

Lin jerked away. "Then what am I supposed to do? Stand here and wait for them to take me?"

"No. *No*. Oh God. Oh God, you just can't. You *can't*."

"What choice have I got? What choice are you giving me?" Lin wrenched her hands free, turned that blank, merciless face upward.

In a split second of horror so intense it was like precognition, like a vision unfolding in the air in front of her, Elissa saw what would happen, saw what Lin could do. She saw the flames burst from the flyers' engines, saw their propellers go crazy, spinning out of control. She saw the machines flare up, death traps spewing flames, coffins for the still-living men inside them.

Elissa's heart was pounding so hard, every inch of skin seemed to feel it. Her mouth was so dry, she couldn't swallow, and her hands were cold and clumsy. But she had no choice. She grabbed the railing and swung herself up onto the ledge. "Stop," she said. "I'm going. We're going to get away. I'm going now."

And she dropped from the ledge.

An instant of falling, of terror exploding all over her body, of her vision blinking out. No time for thoughts, just wordless, white-hot fear.

She landed. On her side, with a jolt that knocked the breath out of her, and before she could even gasp, before she could even register that she'd landed on the roof, that she was okay, she hadn't missed it and gone plummeting through miles of empty air—before she could even register the clang that meant Lin must have landed as well—she was sliding. Down and down over cold smooth metal, no handholds, no friction, completely out of control, down and down and around and around, the sky and the sun and the silver flashes of steel spiraling with her, faster and faster, around and around and down and down. Every moment she expected to go flying off the edge, flung out into the empty air.

Head whirling, vision completely screwed, for an instant she left the ground and found herself suspended in midair, stabbed through with terror like ice and fire. Then she hit something and was flung back, to fetch up against another hard, smooth surface, this time with a jolt that seemed to grab and shake her as if she were nothing but a spindly bundle of bones.

She tried to gasp for breath, but her lungs wouldn't work, and all she could do was make a thin crowing sound.

Then Lin crashed into her, and any tiny bit of breath left in her body was punched out of it all over again.

Somewhere law enforcement agents were still after them, with weapons and flyers and tracking devices. Somewhere were her parents, who couldn't help her. Somewhere there were doctors and police she couldn't trust.

None of it mattered. The only thing that mattered was that she was no longer running, sliding, falling. She was lying still, in a world of pulsing black spots and stabbing spears of light. And, gasping and wheezing, dragging the air in as if it were fighting against her, she was starting to breathe again.

The black spots cleared. The world returned. The stabs of light resolved themselves into sunlight on steel. She and Lin were lying on the fan-shaped slab of roof at the bottom of the structure they'd slid down. They'd slid so fast, they'd actually left the surface of the roof for a moment—the thing she'd hit, the thing that had flung her back, was the lip at its edge. Hundreds of feet above them the law enforcement agents were tiny dark figures. The flyers hadn't taken off yet, but any second now they would.

Elissa pushed herself to her hands and knees, then to her feet. "We have to get moving," she said to Lin, and as she said the words, horror heaved within her, turning her stomach upside down. What Lin had been going to do to the flyer pilots . . . that was worse than the shelf fire, worse than the moving staircase.

It's not her fault. What they've put her through . . .

But this time the thought, the counterargument she seemed to have been dragging up all day, had no force to it.

As they climbed down off the roof, then hurried across the platform onto the fast-moving slidewalk, the horror lay like a cold weight in the pit of her stomach. Lin's fault or not, if she was willing to do that, *anything* like that . . .

It's inhuman. As soon as she thought the word, she tried to unthink it, delete it from her mind. But it was too late. *Oh God.* What if they were right, the authorities who'd declared Lin not human? What if she really was lacking some vital part of her brain—what if she really had neither conscience nor empathy?

Then she's dangerous. Really dangerous. And that alert—was it telling the truth? Am I at risk? Or if I'm not, if I get immunity because I'm her twin, what about everyone else?

They changed slidewalks, taking one down toward the northern edge of the city where a park had been built along the banks of an artificial lake. There was no longer safety in numbers, in losing themselves, two anonymous teens in a larger crowd. *And I don't dare take her among people. Not now that we're in danger of being caught, of being chased again. If she—if next time she—*

Neck prickling, Elissa glanced back to check if they were being followed, and as she did so, she realized Lin was watching her, had been watching her since they'd climbed off the roof.

Lin's face was still the color of dirty paper, set in tense lines that spoke of fatigue and, as Elissa's eyes met hers, of something that looked like fear.

"You know I was lying, right?" she said.

"I—about what?"

"About setting the flyers on fire?"

Elissa found she'd crossed her arms over her chest, a comfort . . . or a barrier. "No. I don't know. You sounded pretty sure to me."

"No. No. I was lying. I had to get you to jump and I . . ." Her voice trailed off; her eyes fixed anxiously on Elissa's face. "It was all I could think of."

The slidewalk doubled back on itself before starting the slow looping descent to the canyon floor. Elissa's fingers curled around her arms, into the gap between her upper arms and rib cage, holding herself even tighter, holding herself together. She wanted to believe what Lin was saying, she *wanted* to, but . . . *If I believe her, if I believe she's not some kind of psycho, and I trust her, and something happens . . .*

"Lissa, you believe me, don't you?"

"I . . ." Elissa's eyes met Lin's again. She couldn't bring herself to lie, but if she said no . . . "I— Look, the staircase, back at the mall—"

"They'd have caught us if I hadn't done something!"

"Yeah. I *know*." Elissa dug her nails into her arms. It was true, what Lin said. And if she could just believe that necessity was all it was, if she hadn't seen Lin's face as she watched the people . . . *If she hadn't been smiling . . .*

Elissa couldn't talk about that. Not yet. Not now. She swallowed. "Look, you did start a fire. At my shelf."

"And you didn't like it. You said you didn't like it, so I'm not going to do it again." Lin's face was anxious, intent. "Lissa, up there—I couldn't have, even if I wanted to. You saw me—I could only just do the bars."

"Oh." Elissa hadn't thought about that. Hadn't, she realized now, been thinking clearly at all. Lin was right. "So . . . you really weren't going to . . ."

"Really."

The slidewalk dipped down among the first branches of the tallest trees in the park. Leaf shadows rose up around them like a shoal of flickering ethereal fish. Elissa pushed her fingers up into her hair, scraping her nails over her scalp, trying to force herself to think clearly. "Okay. I get it. I believe you." She hesitated, not wanting to say anything else, wanting to leave it there, but at the same time feeling the edge of worry—of fear—at the back of her mind, like the flicker and blur of vision before the start of a migraine.

"What?"

Elissa looked up at her twin. "If you *had* been able to, and if they'd caught up with us . . ."

Lin was watching her, the leaf shadows flickering over her face, her eyes steady, a surprisingly adult look in them. "You want to know if I'll kill people to save us?"

"I . . ." She hadn't expected Lin to put it as bluntly as that. "Yeah, I guess."

"I don't know."

"Okay." Elissa swallowed. "I . . . okay." *Okay. She doesn't know. That's reasonable. She didn't say yes, and she's running for her life—it's not fair to judge her by normal standards.*

"Can I ask you something now?" Lin said.

Elissa looked at her, waiting.

"If I had . . . if I do kill someone—"

Elissa's careful reasoning fell apart. "God, Lin, *please*. Don't *talk* about it like that—"

"I didn't say I was *going* to!" Lin's face was aggrieved. "I said *if*!"

Oh, jeez, it's like speaking a different language. Elissa took a long breath. "Okay. All right. Go on."

"Will you hate me?" her twin asked.

"Will I hate you? You mean, if you . . ."

"Yes."

Elissa took another breath. The slidewalk made one last slow curve, lower, lower until it sank a bare half inch below the close-clipped grass. They'd left the tops of the trees far above, and now they drowned in a green twilight. A long way off, from the direction of the spaceport, distant thunder rumbled: a ship taking off.

Elissa stepped off the sluggishly moving slidewalk, onto grass so soft it seemed to bounce beneath her feet. Lin followed her.

"Lissa . . ."

Elissa stopped, turned to face her twin. "Honestly?"

Lin nodded, face tight.

"Okay, then, honestly—I don't know." She hesitated, watching Lin's face. "I'm sorry, okay? You don't see it like I do, and I can—kind of—understand why you don't. The fire, the staircase—no one got . . . *really* . . . hurt. But if you—if you actually kill someone . . . I don't know if I can . . ."

She stopped. Lin's face was set so stiff that it had gone expressionless, and her whole body had tightened as if she were bracing herself against pain.

Something caught at Elissa, something that tightened her own chest, made it momentarily hard for her to swallow. There was nothing else she could say, nothing that would make it better.

"Lin, look."

Lin lifted her chin, met Elissa's eyes as if with an effort before she spoke. "I'd promise not to if I could. I— I don't want to make you hate me." She swallowed, and Elissa saw her throat move as if she, too, found the movement hard to make. As if Lin's throat too were suddenly tight and dry. "I can't promise. If they come after me, if I can't get away and it looks like they're going to take me back . . ."

She stopped talking, gave a little helpless shrug.

Elissa opened her mouth, then shut it. *That's how it leaves us, then. They're going to keep coming after us—after her. Wherever we go, out of the city, across the far side of the continent—even if we get on a flight over to the other side of the planet—they can send alerts everywhere. Wherever we go, they'll catch up. And if she's desperate, if she's trapped . . .*

Despair swept over her. *It's no use. Whatever I do, wherever we go, there's nowhere for her to be safe long enough to learn to be fully human. Nowhere on the planet that's going to be far enough out of reach.*

The words echoed inside her head. Like another echo, a long way off rolled the distant thunder of the spaceship. *Nowhere on the planet.*

There were other planets. Strewn all the way across the star system. Ones that shared laws with Sekoia, had trade agreements, extradition treaties . . . and ones that didn't.

"That's where we'll go," she said. "We're not going to stay here. We're going to go off-planet."

EIGHT

WHEN ELISSA had said it, it had felt like the obvious answer, the obvious escape. But early that evening at the edge of the spaceport, as she approached the Space Flight Initiative student accommodation tower block, the certainty came to her that it was not an escape—it was nothing but another dead end.

She tipped the peak of her cap farther down over her face as she left the fading golden sunlight for the cool shadows of the main lobby, with its banks of lockers around every side and its staircase rising above her. She and Bruce hadn't been particularly close growing up, and since she'd gotten sick and he'd gone off to SFI, what closeness there was between them had dwindled further. And if her *dad* hadn't been able to help her—

She cut the thought off, crossing the lobby floor to reach the foot of the stairs. Her dad hadn't been able to help her because she'd phoned him, and his phone had had a trace on it. They could have done the same to Bruce's phone too, which was why she hadn't tried calling him first. Of course, coming in person to where he lived wasn't the safest thing to do either, but she was pretty sure they wouldn't have bugged his *bedroom*. There were cameras, obviously, but . . . Climbing up the flight of stairs to the first landing, Elissa caught sight of herself in the shiny doors of the lockers on the far side of the lobby, and despite everything, she had to bite back a grin. Her own *parents* would have a hard time recognizing her right now. If the low-security student accommodation cameras picked up her true identity, then they were a hell of a lot better than everyone said they were.

Her copper curls were gone. Her hair, stripped back to its normal dark brown, was bundled up into her cap. She'd wiped all her makeup off, apart from the camouflage cream that concealed the fading bruises on her jawline and neck, and in the shadow of the cap—GO TEAM something-or-other, it said—her face looked thin and pale. She was wearing boys' pants, baggy enough to conceal the treacherous girl-curves of her bottom and thighs, and a too-big jacket hanging open over an equally baggy T-shirt. She wasn't sure she looked exactly like a boy, but she was pretty sure that *whatever* she looked like, at least she wasn't easily recognizable as Bruce's little sister.

She didn't have a cover story to tell him. She'd thought and thought about it, but she hadn't come up with anything more compelling than the real story—that their sister had been taken away at birth, imprisoned for seventeen years and tortured for three, and that Bruce was her only hope of escape.

The only thing Elissa wasn't planning on sharing with

Bruce was that she had to get Lin away not just for Lin's sake but for the sake of everyone she might come into contact with—the agents tracking her, and the innocent bystanders with whom she might collide. Again and again, as if set on a closed loop in her brain, Elissa felt the mall staircase shake beneath her feet, saw the blood seeping from the security guard's knee, heard the terrified wail of the baby clutched too tightly in its mother's arms. And then she saw what had never happened—the flyers going up in balls of flame, their propellers exploding, flinging shards of hot metal all around them. Lin hadn't done that—*couldn't* have done it, not then. But in the future, if they were trapped again . . .

I have to get her off the planet. I have to get her somewhere she won't be tracked, won't be chased, won't be in danger.

And Bruce, with his pilot's license and spaceship . . . *If he won't help me, I don't know what I'll do.*

Elissa cut off that thought too. She'd climbed to the third landing and was scanning the doors, looking for Bruce's room number. She'd only visited him twice before, early on in his training, and although she knew the number—seventy-three—it took her a moment to remember which way to turn. *He has to help me. He has to. He said they were piloting a goods transport flight soon—it won't even take him any effort, it won't be any risk. He can drop us on Mandolin. It doesn't even matter where, as long as there's a spaceport so we can catch another ship, lose ourselves somewhere on another planet . . .*

She found the door and reached up to press the buzzer next to it. Her finger slipped a little, and she realized that despite all her determined calming thoughts, her hands were damp and her heart was beating, uneven and fluttery, in her throat.

The echo of the buzzer reached her faintly through the door, but no other noise followed it. No footsteps of Bruce coming across his room, no sound of the door being unlocked.

Elissa checked her watch again. He *must* be there. She'd chosen the time specially—training would have finished for the day, but it wasn't quite the time when he and the other trainees would go across to the main building for dinner. If he was going home for dinner then he might have left by now, but he'd been home just the night before—no way would they give him evening leave again so soon.

She pressed the buzzer again, harder, as if the action alone would force a response.

Still nothing.

Again. Nothing. This time the echo seemed to sound in Elissa's head, buzzing up inside her skull, making the edges of her thoughts go fuzzy. He had to be here. He was—*oh God, he's my last resort. I thought of him—and his spaceship—and was so relieved that I didn't think about a backup plan.*

Ten minutes away, in the small, sterile-clean room of another pod-motel, Lin was waiting. She'd been scared—white-faced, trembly-lipped scared—of Elissa leaving her. Elissa had had to pretty much bully her into staying where she was. *I'm so much less obvious by myself,* she'd said, over-riding Lin's protest. *If you come with me, all you'll do is put us both at risk. And if Bruce sees you before I've explained, you'll just completely freak him out. You have to stay here. You have to.*

So Lin had stayed, sitting cross-legged on one of the narrow beds, her back against the wall, fingers wound tightly in her lap. And Elissa had come without her, promising that it was the only way to get her to safety, promising that when she returned, it would be with—well, not a spaceship, but at least the promise of one.

And here she was in disguise, in horrible baggy pants and a cap with some dumb slogan on it, and Bruce couldn't even be in his *own freaking bedroom*—

With a soft hush of displaced air, the door next to her slid open. "Can I help you?" said a familiar voice.

Elissa snapped her head up. In the doorway of the next-door room stood a tall, fair young man in the dark blue SFI uniform. He stepped out onto the landing as if he owned the whole building, and Elissa's heart sank. Of all the people to run into, it had to be him. Cadan Greythorn.

"Can I help you?" he said again, and Elissa realized she'd been staring, dumb, as if someone had hit her pause button. She'd only thought of getting to Bruce; she hadn't thought of what she'd do if she met one of his friends whom she knew, anyone who might recognize her.

She cleared her throat. "I'm, um, looking for Bruce Ivory?"

"Bruce? I'm sorry, he's still in quarantine. He should be okay for visitors in a couple of days, but—"

"Quarantine?"

Cadan's attention sharpened. "Damn, you didn't know? He's not sick, don't worry; it's pretty much a precaution, that's all."

"Precaution against *what*? What's *wrong* with him?"

"Contact with Elloran superflu." He leaned against the side of the door. "Turns out the girlfriend of one of the cadets lives on the quarantined shelf. He went to see her and left before the quarantine order. They tracked him down, but by then he'd been in contact with a whole class of cadets, including Bruce. They've had antiviral shots, and now they'll be in quarantine for three days minimum. I can take a message if you want—" He stopped. His eyes narrowed suddenly. "Wait a moment. *Elissa?*"

"Shut up." The words leapt from her mouth. "Don't say that out loud."

"But what the *hell*— What are you doing?"

She didn't pause to think. Panic overrode her concern for Bruce, her desire to know what had happened to him. She barged past Cadan into his room, grabbing his sleeve and pulling him with her, slamming her hand up on the control panel so the door sprang shut. Then she swung around, fingers still clutching the smooth fabric of his jacket. "Don't tell anyone. *Please.*"

"What on earth are you talking about?" He frowned down at her. "What are you doing? Do your parents know you're here?"

Elissa's heart was beating in her throat. She should never have risked coming here. On Cadan's wrist the smooth surface of his minicommunicator gleamed blandly up at her. He could have building security here within minutes, and then the police, law enforcement agents, surgeons and staff from the facility where they'd kept Lin . . .

"It's not like they're saying," she said, frantic. "Listen to me. I'm *not* at risk—"

Cadan's eyebrows went up. "Who's saying you're at risk?"

She halted. "What?"

"No one's saying *you're* at risk. Jeez, princess, easy on the drama, huh? *You* weren't in contact with the flu. It only happened this morning."

His gaze swept down her body, then back up. He was suddenly frowning. "What's this about, anyway? You heard what

I said, right? Bruce doesn't have a *cold*. He's in quarantine for *Elloran superflu*. That's serious stuff—you can't play dress-up and think you can sneak in to see him. Do you have any idea of the health risk if it spreads?"

She stared at him, momentarily speechless, trying to make sense of his attitude. Easy on the drama? Sneaking in to see Bruce? After that citywide announcement that she was missing, that her companion could be a danger to her? After the security alert, the police chase?

Half a second later, understanding clicked into place. Cadan's face was tight, not just with irritation but with fatigue. His uniform wasn't quite as pressed-looking as she'd seen it before; the buttons on his cuffs were undone, and the sleeves were creased from where he'd rolled them up. And where the long evening light fell through the window and onto his face, it glinted off a roughness that was fair end-of-the-day stubble.

He'd only just gotten in from training. He'd been out all day. He hadn't seen the alert.

If he hasn't seen the alert, if he doesn't know . . .

But before her brain could start picking over all the possibilities, he spoke again. And now it was mostly irritation in his face—and a touch of disapproval.

"Well? Did you think they'd make an exception for you or something?" He leaned back against the door, arms folded. "Look, I know current affairs aren't your strongest point, but even you must know about the risks Elloran superflu poses to the population."

"What?"

The disapproval in his face deepened. "Seriously? Jeez, Elissa, I know you're used to getting what you want, but there are some things even your parents can't protect you from."

Heat rushed up into Elissa's face. Used to *getting what she wanted?* He'd hardly even seen her for the last four years, and now he thought he was somehow qualified to offer assessments on her character?

She opened her mouth to tell him that, given everything that had happened to her over the last twenty-four hours, Elloran superflu—*or* current affairs—was the least of her worries. Then she stopped.

Bruce, with his access to a spaceship and his license to fly, wasn't here. But Cadan was. And Cadan didn't know anything about what had been happening.

She swallowed the explanations she'd been about to throw at him and took a long breath, willing the angry color to die out of her face.

Cadan was watching her, looking suddenly wary. "What?"

She met his eyes. "I need help," she said.

"With getting in to see Bruce? I don't think so, *sweetheart.*" The word was not an endearment. "What you *need* is to go back home."

Elissa took another breath, mind racing. Telling Mr. Play-by-the-rules the truth was out of the question. He never even broke curfew, for goodness' sake. He might deliberately crash an auto-operated flyer in a flash of adrenaline-driven determination to keep his perfect flight score, but he wasn't going to even *consider* breaking the law the way she'd found herself forced to do.

"You don't know what's been going on," she said, the last bit of truth she was going to give him. "I'm not trying to see Bruce. I didn't even know he was in quarantine. I came to ask him to help me out with something."

"Well, like I said, he's not here."

Elissa thought fast. "Look, my friend Lin—Lynette—she came over from—from Agera, to stay with her boyfriend while he was off school next week. And she just found out he's been cheating on her, so she's walked out of his family's house and she has to get back home—"

"Hang on a minute." Cadan put up a hand. "I realize this is a complete crisis and everything, and I probably should be *totally* upset for her . . ."

Oh. My. God. Once more, heat fizzled over Elissa's skin. He was mimicking the way she talked. He was *making fun* of her.

She forgot about her careful cover story. She raised her chin and stared at him. "My friend needs a ride back to her own planet," she said. "I said I'd go with her, and we can pay you to take us there."

Cadan's eyes widened, but when he spoke, his voice stayed level, as if he weren't suddenly a hundred percent more interested. "And since when do I work in public transport?"

"You take *charter passengers*, don't you? And you're booked to pilot a goods transport flight to Mandolin?"

"Tonight. Twenty-two-hundred." He shook his head as if to refocus. "But—no, look, Elissa, I can probably take your friend as a passenger, but I'm not taking *you* off-planet, not while Bruce is in quarantine. Your mother's going to be frantic. You need to stay here, give her some emotional support."

Emotional support? Elissa's temper flared. "Don't tell me what I need to do!"

"Don't walk in here like it's my job to be useful to you!" For the first time real anger, not just irritation, sparked in his face. "You might be used to getting everything handed to you on a plate, but that doesn't fly here, sweetheart. This is where you *work* to get what you want, you don't just—" He broke off, and his eyes flicked away from her as if she weren't worth wasting energy looking at.

Out of nowhere a trickle of memory came. *It's not a chip on his shoulder, you know?* Bruce had said. *Not really. But there are guys there who you know only squeaked in 'cause Daddy paid to get them there, and when you're Cay, full-scholarship guy, and you're going to be in debt to SFI until you're in your thirties . . .*

Not a chip on his shoulder? Yeah, right. Well, she had more to worry about than his feelings, or his pride.

She folded her arms. "I'm not asking you to help me out of the goodness of your heart," she said. "I'm offering you a chance to earn some money. If you're not interested, I'll go elsewhere."

He didn't look at her. For a moment, silence hung in the room. *Oh, come on. Give in.* If that split second of memory had reminded her of anything, it was that Cadan, who'd had SFI pay for every bit of his education since he was eleven years old, who even after he graduated would be in debt to them for as long again, couldn't afford to turn down any legitimate way of making money.

Bluffing, willing him to look at her, to take the bait, she moved toward the door.

He didn't move out of the way. "How much?"

She caught the breath of relief before it could escape to betray her, and named a price.

His eyes snapped wide, incredulous. "What did you say?"

Elissa shrugged. "My friend really wants to get home."

Irritation flashed across his face again. "She's here for no more than a week, and she can't wait a bit longer for her scheduled flight?"

Arrogant ass. You don't have a freaking clue. She tilted her chin, not caring if he thought she was nothing but a spoiled rich girl with a princess complex. "She *could* wait. Why should she have to?"

His eyes met hers, flat and angry, and her stomach clenched a little. He'd tell her to go to hell if he could. *Well, if I didn't need his stupid ship, I'd never have asked him for help. So we're even. He despises me, and I don't care what he thinks.*

"What about your parents?" Cadan said. "They're okay with you just taking off like that?"

Doubt colored his voice. Elissa tried not to let the tension gathering within her show in her face, in the way she stood. If he decided to be all responsible, to override what she was saying and call her parents, she was screwed. But she'd offered him a whole lot of money, more than he'd make taking most charter passengers, and she knew he needed it.

A tendril of guilt wound itself into her thoughts. He needed the money she was offering, and he didn't know it wasn't real money at all. When she and Lin hopped ship at Mandolin and changed the IDs on the morph-cards, the money would disappear as if it had never existed.

She ground down on the guilt tendril, crushed it out of her thoughts. What choice did she have? Anyway, if he'd been halfway a gentleman, he'd have *offered* to help, and she wouldn't have needed to lie to him.

She met his eyes unflinchingly. "Sure. School let out this afternoon. I'm on vacation now too. I can do what I like for a week."

"So it'll be okay to call them and let them know you're here, yes?"

Elissa's heart jumped straight back into her throat. *"No."*

"Right." He raised his eyebrows, superior and infuriating, like he was the grown-up and she was some little kid. "Why do I feel I'm missing something?"

"You're not *missing something*. I—"

"Isn't your operation scheduled soon? The one for your headaches?"

She stared at him. Of course Bruce would have told him—last night, probably—but she hadn't expected him to mention it. "Yeah," she said, trying to be vague about the details. "Fairly soon."

"Bruce said it was scheduled for this Monday."

"I . . ." *Oh, hell.* "Yes, but . . ."

"Hey." He put a hand up. "It's not my business. I guess you'll reschedule, right?"

"Yes." She tried to make her voice firm.

He flicked her another glance. "It's short notice. I'd be a bit freaked. If it was me."

"I . . . okay." She bit her lip, wondering what he was getting at. Then— *Oh.* That was what he meant. He thought she was using her friend's so-called problem as an excuse to postpone the op. And he didn't blame her. He wouldn't call her parents the moment she got out of here. He thought he knew what she was doing, and he was—of all things—being sympathetic.

The guilt twined around her stomach, so hard that she felt sick. She couldn't look at him. "Thanks. I—um, takeoff is at ten, right?"

"Yeah. Flightpad eighteen. Be there at nine, okay? You've got your IDs, both of you?"

She assured him they had and she left, heading down the stairs and out into the waning daylight, pushing the guilt back, focusing instead on the happy circumstance that taking a flight off-planet wouldn't occur under high security. The morph-cards would be all they'd need. Coming back through the maze of immigration control would be a whole other matter.

But I'm not coming back.

The thought hit her out of nowhere, knocking her breathless. She stopped walking, automatically putting out a hand to brace herself against the side of the building. She'd known that already, she'd *known* it. But somehow, talking to Cadan, making up her safe little story that she was just helping a friend get home and then she'd be back—for a few minutes she'd convinced herself it was true. It wasn't true. She was leaving her home planet, her parents, brother, ex-best friends, every school she'd ever gone to, everything that had been familiar her whole life—and she wasn't coming back.

For a moment she wanted to push everything away, cram the last two days into a box and drop it off the edge of a cliff. Wanted to take a taxi straight to Dr. Brien's clinic and tell him to burn the link away, burn out her memory, too, delete every-thing to do with finding out about Lin, about Spares, about electrokinesis that was strong enough to kill, about her mother telling lies and locking her in her room, about her father not doing *anything* except telling her to run, about having to ask Cadan for help and cheating him out of money he needed . . .

It was no good. Even if she did forget everything, it would all still be there, all the horrible ugly truth, like a disease wait-ing to break out. And right now . . . She took a breath that shuddered through her teeth. Right now Lin was waiting for her to come back, waiting for Elissa to tell her they were saved.

Flightpad number eighteen was at the end of a row, a long way from the busy, brightly lit central area where the big commercial flights took off, carrying tourists and business-people across the star system.

Terrified of something going wrong, of missing takeoff, Elissa had made sure she and Lin had set off with plenty of time to spare, with the result that they'd arrived more than half an hour before the time Cadan had said, and had to wait in the enclosed shelter for waiting passengers, reading the flickering, endlessly repeating safety notices on the walls.

Nearby on the flightpad the sleek squid-shape of the spaceship gleamed, first in the setting sun, then, as the rusty golden light drained out of the sky, in the glare of the color-less spaceport lights. It was already tilted into launch posi-tion, the dark figures of the maintenance crew darting in and out around it.

Lin sat, knees up to her chest, on one of the benches in the waiting area. She was biting the edge of her thumbnail.

Elissa had tried to sit, but she couldn't. She stood by the window, trying not to bite any of her own nails. The window was reinforced, as one of the safety notices kept informing her, to withstand mega-high temperatures, explosion shock waves, and flying metal shards. The air that filled the shelter came through pollution filters that removed all but the most infinitesimal percentage of airborne pollutants.

It's a shame I'm not worried about any of those things.

She peered through the patchwork of bright lights and gathering dusk to try to make out the figures of the main-tenance crew. She'd known goods transports didn't use the little two-man ships Bruce and Cadan had done most of their training in, but all the same she hadn't expected this one to be so big, or to require so many crew members. She'd somehow—vaguely, stupidly—thought that she and Lin would have to deal with meeting Cadan and a copilot, and maybe one or two more crew. Not seven, eight . . . ten and more strangers who might want to know about them, might be curious, might pay enough attention to notice that, despite the hair and makeup, they were far too identical to be just friends.

Another figure detached itself from the shadows around the spaceship, came across the no-man's-land between the flightpad and the shelter.

Elissa jerked upright. "Lin—"

"I know." Lin unknotted herself and bent to pick up the bag Elissa had bought for her earlier. The edge of her thumb showed red and sore.

As Elissa glanced down to pick up her bag, she noticed her own fingernails. Every one of them was bitten down to the quick.

The door whooshed open and Cadan stepped in. He looked freshly showered, his face shaved smooth, and he was wearing the familiar dark blue SFI jacket, but with the silver gleam of a pilot's bar pinned to the shoulder.

"We're boarding passengers now. If you'd like to step across for security checks?" His voice held none of the sympathy that had made her feel so guilty that afternoon. It was crisp, authoritative, what she'd always thought of as Cadan's "watch the world spin around me" voice.

They followed him out into no-man's-land, past the sign warning of the penalties if you passed it unaccompanied by authorized personnel. A hot, dusty wind blew Elissa's hair across her face, filled her nostrils with the scent of rocket fuel. Away across the plateau, beyond the perimeter of the spaceport, there was the drainage ditch where she'd found Lin. An instant of disorientation hit her, a feeling that this couldn't really be happening, it *couldn't*, not to *her*, Elissa Ivory. Then the sensation vanished, leaving behind a loneliness so intense, it was like a cold blanket dropping over her.

They came into the shadow cast by the looming spaceship, which was held in position by landing arms that created its squidlike appearance. Elissa pulled her hoodie closer around her, an attempt at comfort. She'd been on a ship twice before, on a family vacation and on a school trip, but those times she'd departed straight from the central spaceport area, surrounded by soothing indoor lights, the cheerful busyness of embarking tourists.

Beside her Lin reached out and put a hand on Elissa's arm. Elissa glanced at her, anxious, wondering if Lin was finding this as intimidating as she was. Lin's face was tight with the same tension Elissa was trying to hide, but when her eyes met Elissa's, she smiled. Elissa's hoodie hadn't provided any sort of comfort. Lin's smile, weirdly, suddenly did.

Then they came under the huge silver curve of the spaceship itself, its entrance gaping directly in front of them. Lin's eyes left Elissa's, and her head tilted back. "The *Phoenix*," she read. "That's its name?"

Cadan glanced at her. "Her name. Ships are feminine."

Lin's gaze went back to him, a fascinated smile growing on her face. "Really?"

"Yes." His eyebrows rose a little, but Elissa couldn't tell if it was in impatience or just amusement. She prickled, waiting for him to say something—how many times had he and Bruce taken pains to point out when she'd gotten their terminology wrong?—but all he did was gesture to the entrance. "This way."

It took them straight into the cargo hold, a cold echoing

space with steps running up all the sides and metal walkways cutting back and forth overhead. Cadan led the way up a long flight of stairs and along a walkway that followed the inner contour of the ship's wall, then into a corridor lit with bluish strip lights at its edges, curving away in front of them. The position of the ship meant that the floor sloped gently downward, then, as the corridor took them around the far side of the ship and up onto the next level, more steeply upward. Doors dilated to let them through, then snapped shut behind them, isolating each section of the ship—one of the many safety functions that Bruce and Cadan had found so very impressive when they'd first learned about them.

"The passenger areas are lit with amber lights," Cadan said over his shoulder. "For your own safety I'm going to ask you to make sure you stay within those areas."

Around them, a hum began, a vibration that went through the walls and the floor, raising the hairs on Elissa's skin.

"What's that?" said Lin.

"We're running a test on the engines. You'll feel it less in the passenger area."

Lin ran a hand along the wall as she passed. Her face was intent, fascinated.

They climbed a short flight of stairs, and the strip lights turned amber. Cadan gave a quick sideways nod. "That's the way to the dining area. There are nutri-machines in your cabin, but they're prepacks only—there's no link to fresh supplies. The crew will be eating meals in the dining area. If you'd like to join us, please let the chef know in advance so he can prepare." He pointed along the next side turning. "There's an exercise room down there. The crew has priority use, but you're welcome to use it if it's not booked."

His voice didn't sound as if they really were welcome. Irritation prickled along Elissa's spine as she looked at the uncreased back of his jacket, at his tidily cropped hair.

As he swung up the next flight of stairs, she caught a glimpse of his face. He looked the way he had in the cadet accommodation, as if he owned everywhere he walked, everything he touched.

You're not even the real captain. You're only in charge of this flight for a few days, then you're back to being a cadet.

The irritation sparked into words. "What's wrong with the real captain?" she said.

He glanced back at her. "The real captain?"

"Well, you're only pilot for the duration. This ship—it's not yours, is it?"

Cadan paused, his hand halfway up to a door panel. His voice was a little stiff as he answered. "This is an SFI-owned ship. She has no captain permanently attached. The captain is whoever is in charge for any particular flight. So right now, I *am* the real captain." He hesitated. "Bruce and I must have explained that kind of thing to you years ago?"

She shrugged. "You told me an *awful lot* of things, Cadan." Without quite meaning it to, her voice hovered on the edge of outright rudeness.

Cadan's eyes met hers with an icy little jolt. Then he looked away and touched the door panel to open the door. "This is your cabin. I'll take security details and payment here." His eyes flicked briefly to Elissa's. "As part of my *captain's* role."

He couldn't just win a point; he had to win it *again*, driving home that he was—*always*—the expert, that she was nothing but some stupid little schoolgirl with no specialist knowledge of anything ever.

She looked away and around the cabin. It wasn't quite as tiny as the pod-motel, but, barring a window, it had all the same kind of facilities. Bunk beds, toilet, shower cubicle, nutri-machine with a newsscreen above it. Except of course it wasn't a newsscreen—it was for ship information and announcements only.

Cadan touched the screen to wake it and tapped in a code. "Elissa, I'll take your details first."

She handed him the morph-card, the now-familiar tension twisting through her. She'd had a horrible moment earlier when she'd realized she could no longer use a fake name on the card, not if she was showing it to Cadan. But if she used her real name, would it spark a security alert, like the known aliases of terrorists and interplanetary criminals did?

She'd come up with a solution she was pretty sure would work, but she'd had no way of pretesting it. As she watched him slide the morph-card through the scanner below the screen, all her muscles tightened as if they were trying to tie themselves into knots.

Her name flashed up on the screen. *Ellissa Layne Ivory*. A difference of just two letters from her real name: enough to slip under the system's detection, but not enough to catch Cadan's attention as a name that wasn't hers. She hoped.

If it does catch his attention, if he starts asking me questions like he did in his room, if he does it in front of Lin . . . Her muscles tightened further, in a painful jerk that made her stomach cramp. She was back on the shaking staircase, watching that awful smile spread on Lin's face. *If something goes wrong now and she feels trapped* . . .

Cadan tapped the screen, then drew the card out and gave it back to her. Elissa took it in a suddenly clammy hand, not daring to meet his eyes, in case he saw the relief in hers. *It worked. I did it.*

"Ms.—?" He was holding out his hand for Lin's card now.

"Lynette May." They'd gone over Lin's new name a million times before they'd left the motel, and now her voice sounded natural, convincing.

Cadan slotted her card into the machine, waited for her name to appear, then tapped the screen to bring up a menu. "And you're paying the full amount?"

The full amount blinked onto the screen. Phantom money, dead leaves disguised as gold. Elissa swallowed, refusing to think about it.

"Yes." Lin's voice was calm and cheerful. They'd rehearsed this, too. What they hadn't rehearsed was how it would feel to do it for real, to look at those numbers on the screen and know they should read nothing but zero. Elissa looked away, folding her arms across herself. *I can't help it. I don't have a choice.*

"Thank you, Ms. May."

Lin took the card, her smile wide and bright.

It doesn't make any difference to her. Practicing cheating someone, doing it for real . . . it's all the same to her.

"Okay." Cadan stepped back into the doorway. "We'll be taking off within the hour. The passenger lounge has a viewing window if you're interested. You'll find it on the plan. Please take some time to read through the full safety procedures first. Breakfast will be served at oh-eight-hundred. Shall I tell the chef you'll be joining the crew for that meal?"

Elissa stopped herself from throwing Lin an anxious glance. They were on the ship for just two days. It wouldn't do them any harm to stay in their cabin, get their meals from the nutri-machine. *Keep Lin out of the way of as many people as possible.* "No, thanks," she said. "We'll just eat here."

"That's your choice, certainly." Elissa looked up at Cadan, and his eyebrows were raised again, as if he were mocking her. "But I can assure you, you'll find much better food if you join the crew."

As if she didn't know that. "No, thank you." Again her voice came out too abrupt to be courteous. It wasn't really deliberate this time, instead born out of fatigue and over-frayed patience, but it was too late to fix it.

Cadan's eyebrows went up farther, and his eyes were suddenly cold. "Suit yourself, Elissa. Ms. May, it was a pleasure to meet you." The door snapped shut behind him.

Elissa sank onto the edge of the bottom bunk. Her knees were kind of shaky. With tiredness, of course. It wasn't like she cared if she'd offended Cadan. He was transport, that was all. She didn't even need to see him again till she and Lin left the ship.

"Okay," she said. "Let's unpack. Then do you want to go watch liftoff from the lounge?"

Lin didn't answer the question. Instead she asked one of her own. "He's your brother's friend?"

"Yes." Elissa reached for her bag and dragged it over to her feet.

"I've seen him before, in bits, in your memories. I can't tell . . . Is he around much? Do you know him well?"

Elissa gave a short laugh. "Not really. He and Bruce left for SFI training four years ago. They've been far too busy to know anyone not in flight school."

She pulled out the wash bag she'd bought at the motel and unzipped it, resisting Lin's gaze. The faint persistent hum of the engines shuddered into silence. The crew must have finished running their tests, then. Liftoff couldn't be far away.

"That made you . . . angry?"

Elissa jabbed her hand into the bag, searching for the handle of her toothbrush. "*Angry?* Please, what did I have to be angry about? He was Bruce's friend, not mine. And he's way older than me. We have nothing in common."

Lin said nothing. After a moment, unwillingly drawn to do so, Elissa looked up and caught her gaze. Lin was biting her lip, her eyes narrowed in confusion and worry.

Oh, hell, it's not fair to confuse her about—of all things—human emotions. She might have started her life out seminormally, but since then, since what they did to her . . .

Eissa let the bag fall onto the bed. "Okay. I *was* kind of angry. He was always nice to me—nicer than Bruce a lot of the time. He only has an older sister and a bunch of older cousins, not any younger ones, and I was so *much* younger than him, I guess he thought I was sweet."

She could see now, at seventeen, what she hadn't understood at seven, when Bruce had first brought him home to visit, or even at eleven, twelve, thirteen, when they'd left for the full SFI training program. Back then she'd known he was Bruce's friend, but she'd thought he was *her* friend too, had mistaken his amused kindness to his friend's little sister for genuine friendship.

"When they went off for training," she said, "I knew they wouldn't have time to visit much, or even call or e-mail. But I was so excited when they were coming home. I thought it would be like it used to be." The old embarrassment washed over her, burning. The second day Bruce was home, he'd arranged to go over to Cadan's house for lunch, then bring

Cadan back for dinner. Elissa had spent half her month's allowance on just the right white strappy top to wear with her favorite skirt; she'd washed her hair at lunchtime to make sure it was as clean and bouncy as possible; she'd got a stack of things that had happened at school that she thought Cadan would find funny. Unable to wait, she'd already told them all to Bruce, and he'd laughed, so she was sure Cadan, who she thought had a *much* better sense of humor, would find them even funnier. She'd saved up a whole lot of questions, too, about flight training and what safety gear they had to wear, and how soon they'd be allowed up into space.

"And it wasn't like it used to be?"

When Elissa answered, she couldn't help the anger that sparked through her voice. "No. They'd only been away a couple of months. I had no idea it would make any difference. But for them it was like they'd been away for years, like they'd turned from children into grown-ups." She paused, rolled her eyes, and corrected herself. "No, not grown-ups. Into *men*. They were so *pleased* with themselves. They talked about themselves all the time—about what they'd done, what they'd learned, about their latest grades—about the latest grades of everyone in their whole class. When I asked them questions, they answered with all this flight jargon. I didn't even know what they *meant*. Then I tried to tell Cadan something funny from school, and Bruce just cut me off, said Cadan wouldn't be interested."

Elissa, he'd said, in the new grown-up drawl he and Cadan had both adopted, *please don't inflict all fifteen of the eighth-grade classroom tales on us. Not quite so soon after the last time.*

But I haven't told Cadan any of them, Elissa remembered replying. She'd been taken aback but not wounded—not yet.

Not until Bruce had laughed and said, *Trust me, little sister, once was more than enough.*

She picked up the wash bag again, shook it to arrange the contents. "And that was it. From then on, they both made it clear they were on one side of this big adult divide, and I was on the other, still just a kid. Bruce was annoying, but I'd grown up with him, I knew what to expect. But Cadan—he was getting the highest scores on nearly every test; he was the first to be chosen for fast-track pilot training, and the better he got, the more pleased with himself he was. He started giving me *advice*—about working hard at school, about it never being too early to specialize. I mean, *jeez.*"

She gave the bag another shake, shaking the memory off too. "I got over it. At least"—she couldn't help laughing at herself a little—"pretty much, anyway. I started high school and I had my own stuff, my own specialties. But then the symptoms started, and I wasn't just a little girl not bright enough to get into SFI training. I was this freak who kept fainting and screaming and throwing up and who started failing the sort of classes that Cadan and Bruce had just sailed through—"

She caught herself, hot with shame, shocked at her own thoughtlessness. "Oh, jeez, I'm *sorry.* I know *anything* I went through—it's nowhere near what was happening for you. I—" It sounded so stupid to say it, but it was the truth, and the only excuse she had. "I forgot. I know that's dumb, and I don't blame you if you don't believe me—"

"I believe you. It's okay."

"It's *not* okay. As if I can even *compare*—"

"It is okay." Lin's voice was firm and certain. "The bits of your life I used to see through the link . . . like I said, they were just flashes. As if, every time I reached out to you, dragged you into what was going on in my life, I pulled in some of your memories, too. I knew the link was wrecking things for you, but I thought if the link hadn't been there, everything else would have been okay. I guess I didn't put the pieces together right—I thought the rest of your life was all smooth and easy."

Shame still burned in Elissa's face. "It *was* smooth and easy. Compared to what they did to you."

"Yeah, I know. But just because no one strapped you down and plugged a machine into your head, it doesn't mean you don't have scars too."

Elissa had her mouth open to say something else, but at that she shut it. She hadn't expected Lin to say that. Hadn't expected her to even be able to relate to pain so minor, so trivial. Hadn't expected her to understand.

She remembered now that when she was very small, she used to wish for a sister. She'd always known she couldn't have one, of course. She was the second child, and her parents had been sterilized according to Sekoia's legal requirements. She'd made girl friends instead, and she and Carlie and Marissa had gone through a stage of calling themselves sisters, and it had been fine. It had been enough.

Except now she knew it hadn't.

She had to clear her throat before she could speak again. "Come on. Let's leave the unpacking and go wait for lift-off. I've only seen it twice before, and the last time was on a school trip to Seraphon, when I was only eleven. I bet I didn't fully appreciate it."

They reached the passenger lounge by following the plan Elissa pulled up on-screen, traveling along two corridors joined by a flight of stairs, then through a final set of doors.

It wasn't a large room, but the viewing panel made up one entire wall, curving to follow the line of the ship, running up into the ceiling and down into the floor, forming a slight lip so travelers could stand with their toes over emptiness. At the moment, with the bright lights that had jumped to life when they'd entered the room, the glass reflected the girls, distorted in its slight concave surface, back to themselves.

"I can't work out which way we're facing." Elissa looked around for an override switch. "There must be a way of dimming the lights so we can see. Lin, can you—"

She stopped. The first rumble of the engines vibrated through the floor, the walls, the insides of her ears. A steel shutter slid smoothly across the glass of the viewing panel.

Lin's face fell. "I thought we'd be able to see liftoff. Isn't that what he said? He— *Oh*."

Elissa's stomach dropped. Her ears crackled. There was antithrust cushioning built into all the ships, but it would take more than that to stop their bodies from registering that all at once they were climbing at hundreds of miles an hour, picking up speed enough to blast them out of the planet's orbit. "It's okay. It's just an auto-safety precaution. They'll raise it in a moment."

Elissa's stomach lurched a little more, and she looked over at Lin. During Elissa's first spaceflight she'd been scared, and Lin hadn't even traveled in an airplane or high-speed train before. But Lin's eyes were shining, her lips parted in a smile. She crossed to the shuttered window and put a hand on the gently thrumming metal, not for support but as if to feel the ship blasting up into space.

"You can *feel* it," she said. "I didn't know. I . . . Wow."

Elissa felt her own face break into a smile. For the first time since she'd met her, Lin looked utterly, completely happy.

Around them the vibration lessened. The distant roar of the thruster rockets died. They were out of orbit, completely off-world, in territory owned by no planet and no government.

"Did you feel that?" Lin's voice was a whisper. "We're—"

Elissa knew perfectly well that the gravity drive of the ship exactly replicated the conditions of Sekoia, but all the same, when she took a breath, it felt as if her lungs were working more easily than they had planet side, as if she'd been laboring under gravity turned up a little too high. "We're outside planetary jurisdiction. We made it, we did make it."

The steel shutter slid away from under Lin's hand. Around them the lights dimmed. Their reflections melted into blackness. Far away against that blackness, green and blue and white-misted, Sekoia hung. And beyond it were points upon points of white fire, endless and unobscured, stars beyond imagining.

In the dimness Lin's face showed lit by starlight, pale and spellbound, her eyes huge. "In space," she said, finishing the sentence Elissa had interrupted—and completed wrongly. "We're in space."

NINE

AN HOUR LATER, dizzy with tiredness, Elissa managed to drag Lin away from the window with the promise they'd come back the next day. She found their way back to their cabin, stripped down to T-shirt and underwear—she hadn't managed to get them nightclothes, but at least the ship would have a laundry facility, and it was only for two days, after all—scrubbed her face in the tiny sink, and crawled into the soft coolness of the top bunk.

She woke three times in the night, thick-headed with sleep, heart banging so hard, she felt sick. Once it was the dreamed sound of sirens that woke her. The second time it was her father calling her name, his phantom voice echoing in her ears even after she woke up. The third time she woke with a jerk to a real sound—a choked whimper from the bunk below.

She touched one of the side lights. It came on with a glow so soft, it scarcely lightened the darkness. Elissa peered down over the edge of the bunk.

Lin's eyes were tightly shut, and although the whimpering noise came from her, she was making it in her sleep. Elissa watched her for a moment, chewing her lip, wondering if she should do anything, but she was still so tired that she found herself drooping, her forehead knocking on the edge of the bunk, and so she gave up, pulled the covers over her ears, and fell miles down into sleep.

In the morning—by Sekoian time and Elissa's body clock, at least—the room lights woke them, creeping around the edges of the ceiling like a gently rising sun.

Lin looked pale under her fake tan, but calm and clear-eyed, not at all as if she'd been crying during the night. They dialed breakfast from the nutri-machine. Coffee, cereal with reconstituted milk, and dried-fruit bars. Cadan had been right, they would have gotten a better breakfast by eating with the crew, but the lack of quality food was a small price to pay for not having to keep remembering the portfolio of lies Elissa had built up.

She made sure Lin's disguise was as flawless as possible—checked that the fake tan wasn't fading, got her to wash her hair and reapply the straightening serum, stuck her false eyelashes back on—and then they returned to the lounge and viewing panel.

Sekoia was tiny in the distance now, the stars still endless all around it. Looking out, Elissa felt as if she were on the only ship in the whole of the universe, and on a ship that wasn't really moving, that was only floating in space, stars and moons and planets hanging motionless all about her.

"It's something, huh?"

Elissa looked around. A young man stood in the doorway.

He wore a uniform similar to Cadan's and had brown hair cropped close the way all the pilots had it. His friendly face was spattered with freckles.

He put out a hand. "Copilot Stewart James."

"Elissa Ivory. And my friend, Lynette May." She half turned to include Lin and saw she hadn't looked away from the window. Elissa laughed. "I'm sorry. She's a big fan of space travel." The half-truth came easily to her lips.

Copilot James grinned. "Well, I can understand that. Cadan says you're Bruce Ivory's sister?"

Somehow she hadn't thought he'd tell anyone. Hadn't wanted him to. Which was stupid. There was no reason for him not to mention that one of the *Phoenix*'s paying passengers was his friend's sister.

"That's me." She smiled, going for charming, something she'd once been able to do without effort. "I'm just keeping Lynette company to Mandolin. She's on her way home to Agera."

"How is Bruce? Such bad luck, to get himself put in quarantine before he had the chance to take this flight."

Elissa squashed guilt. If she didn't know how her brother was, it wasn't her fault. "He's . . . well, disappointed, I guess." She smiled again, deliberately bright. "By the time I get back, he'll be out—and if he's not, he'll be demanding to be allowed out!"

The copilot laughed. "You're probably right. We'd all feel the same—miss a few days, and you get so far behind—" He broke off. "I'm sure Bruce will be fine, though. He'll catch up."

Elissa bit back a smile at the belated attempt at tact. She was still trying to remember if she knew anything about this guy. Stewart James, hadn't he said his name was?

He was about to say something else, when Lin interrupted him. She'd finally turned from the window and was looking at him, a frown between her eyebrows. "Shouldn't you be flying the ship?"

"Lin!" *Oh, goodness, please act as if you've been on a ship before. You must know something about them.*

"Not right now," Mr. James said politely. "I stood by during liftoff, but we're well outside orbit now, Cadan's on the flight deck, and the autopilot's engaged. Our route has been set in advance, but I assure you that the moment either of us needs to be hands-on at the controls, we will be."

"Oh," said Lin. Then she hesitated, seeming to notice, for the first time, Elissa's expression. "I don't mean to be rude."

"That's quite all right, Ms. May." He paused a moment, then turned back to Elissa, his smile going from polite to warm. "Ms. Ivory, would you like a visit to the flight deck? I don't know how much you've flown, but it's usually pretty interesting if you haven't been on one before."

"Oh—" Elissa spoke quickly to cover her instant negative reaction. "I don't want to disturb Cadan."

Mr. James grinned. "The ship'll be more or less flying herself now. He'll just be running diagnostics. Trust me, he won't mind a little bit of a distraction."

Oh, I think he might. She was trying to think of a better excuse, when she caught sight of Lin's expression, all saucer-eyed excitement. If Elissa refused this invitation, they might not get another, and Lin might not get to see any flight decks. "Thank you. We'd love to come."

"Great!" His smile flashed out again. "If you'd like to follow me, I'll show you the way."

He led them through the center of the ship, up the

staircase that spiraled around the core that housed, among other things, the air-filtration system, the gravity drive, and the fuel tanks. Then up through one of the safety doors—this one set directly above their heads, the stairs leading through it—into a circular room that opened onto endless, star-strewn space.

For a moment it felt like being at the top of a miles-high tower, surrounded by a nighttime sky dazzling with darkness and brilliant with stars. Elissa went momentarily dizzy, the universe spinning around her, her feet feeling as if they might float off the ground. Beside her Lin gave an awed gasp.

Then Elissa's eyes adjusted, the room came into focus, and she realized they'd reached the flight deck in the nose of the spaceship, and that the bridge stood on a shoulder-high platform in front of her.

"A little safety protocol," said Mr. James, at the foot of the short flight of steps leading up to the bridge. He cleared his throat, then rattled out the next words. "I have to warn you that, as untrained persons, SFI laws strictly prohibit you from touching any of the control panels, touch-screen displays, or instruments unless given direct permission to do so from authorized SFI personnel, namely the pilot or copilot."

He took a breath. "In addition you are strictly prohibited, under any and all circumstances, including a directive from ship personnel, no matter how senior, from attempting to gain entry to the hyperdrive chamber"—he gestured briskly to the base of the platform, to the outline of a sealed door Elissa hadn't noticed—"and you are warned that this law is enforced by SFI and by the elected planetary government of Sekoia, and that contravening it carries the penalty of imprisonment." He mimicked running out of breath, grinned, and gestured up the steps. "If you'll follow me?"

The bridge was surrounded by what looked like no more than a waist-high wall, until Elissa reached it and realized that was just the lower part of the barrier. The wall, made of treated glass, almost as invisible as a force field, extended up as far as the curve of the ceiling, enclosing the whole of the platform. Mr. James pressed his thumb to a control panel at the top of the steps, and a section of the barrier slid out of the way to let them through.

Cadan, his back to them, sat on the other side of a railing and in front of a bank of screens, his hands flickering over a console as wide as the span of Elissa's arms.

"Stew—" he said as the door opened, then checked himself. He turned slowly to look at them. Where his gaze touched her, Elissa's skin prickled. She shouldn't have given in to Lin's obvious excitement about seeing the flight deck. Cadan didn't want her there—didn't want either of them there—and he'd insulted her enough yesterday. She really didn't need to give him *more* opportunities.

Oblivious to Cadan's cold gaze, to Elissa's sudden discomfort, Mr. James—Stewart—was explaining that he'd invited them for a tour of the bridge. Cadan listened, not speaking, eyes back on the screens in front of him. On the largest, code scrolled endlessly upward. It was gibberish to Elissa and moving too fast for her to read. She remembered Bruce saying they'd all been put through an intensive course in speed-reading in order to deal with just this type of thing.

Stewart finished his cheerful explanation and turned back to Elissa and Lin. "Like I said, Cadan has engaged the auto-pilot, and the ship's following her programmed route. He's just running a diagnostic program now—to tell us if there are any problems thinking about germinating, either in some part of the ship or on the projected flight path."

"What sort of problems?" Lin's eyes were still like saucers. She was standing very still in the center of the flight deck, hands tightly clasping each other.

"Oh, a glitch in one of the engines, or metal fatigue causing flaws in the outer shell. It's smart-metal—it mends itself to some extent, but you have to be aware of what's happening, whether a sheet might need replacing."

"And that code?"

"That's what tells us if something's wrong. Those colors—" He turned to point something out, then tensed. "Cadan."

Cadan had reacted at the same moment. His hand flew up the screen, froze the scrolling code. "I see it."

"What is it?" said Lin, her voice unalarmed, fascinated.

Cadan reached over to another of the screens and opened up a window. "The forward-scanner's picked up a cluster of debris on our flight path."

"It can't do us any damage." Stewart glanced toward Elissa and then back to Lin, his smile reassuring. "It's not big enough. But getting through it's likely to cause turbulence, which is an inconvenience we can do without."

Cadan had pulled both hands back to the keyboard and was tapping out new combinations, watching the seemingly infinitesimal changes they made to the patterns on yet another screen. His voice was distracted. "At least Ivan might finally appreciate that he's *not* cooking over naked flames."

Stewart laughed. "Ivan's the chef we've got for this trip. He swears the only way food tastes good is if it's cooked the old-fashioned way, with direct heat, but of course all the ships' kitchens are full of nothing but safety burners."

Fascinated, her attention fixed on the screens, Lin walked across the bridge to stand near Cadan. He shifted a little, his shoulders tensing. Behind him Lin unclasped her hands.

Déjà vu hit Elissa like something grabbing hold of her. Lin, controlling currents, interfering with electric circuits to make doors leap open and fires start, with that intent look on her face, her hands opening in concentration. Lin, who didn't react like normal people—neither in the way she treated others, nor in thoughts for her own safety.

Elissa was across the bridge in three quick steps, her hand tight on Lin's arm, fingers digging in, trying to send a silent message. *Lin, don't do anything. Don't use your electrokinesis. Don't interfere.*

"Can you not do that, Elissa? Stewart *told* you to stay clear of the control panels."

"I *am* staying clear," she said, taken aback. "I'm not doing anything."

Cadan flapped an irritated hand at her. "You're . . . jigging around behind me. Can you—" He broke the words off, then paused, making an obvious effort to drag his voice back to civility. "Would you please stand a little farther back?"

"*Completely* no problem." Elissa backed to the center of the platform, stiff with resentment, half-dragging Lin with her.

Stewart cleared his throat. "You're working out alternative routes, Cadan? You don't want to just hop past it?"

Cadan gave his head a quick sideways jerk. "Using hyper-speed this early in the flight, knowing the chief's going to be asking for a full explanation for every particle of energy I've used when we get home? I'd rather find the slow way around this time." His shoulders relaxed. "That's it. *Okay.* We're done."

He hit the enter key, unfroze the diagnostic code, and set it scrolling again, then twisted his chair around to face them. His face held some of the same stiffness Elissa knew was showing in her expression, as if maybe he felt bad about snapping at her. Well, he should. Like she *needed* to be told not to touch the controls?

"Look," he said. "I'm sorry, but I was working the flight path out, and I really didn't need to have someone jog my elbow or—"

The injustice stung. "I wasn't *going* to jog your elbow. I was nowhere *near* you."

Unexpectedly, his mouth quirked in a tiny smile. "Come on, now. You were *somewhere* near me."

"Oh, *whatever*." Fury broke over her. "I was *behind* you—you couldn't even *see* how close I was."

His eyebrows went up, making her feel like a badly behaved little girl. "Elissa, come on, this is the bridge. Do admit I have some right to not have people hopping around behind me when I'm in the middle of flying the ship."

"Yeah, well, don't worry. We're going anyway." She turned, pulling Lin around with her, and took a step toward the exit.

And a blast rocked the ship from end to end.

It knocked Elissa off her feet. She hit the floor with a bump that jolted through her hip and all the way up her spine. Lin lunged for the railing, swung one-handed, and banged against it, only just managing to stay on her feet.

At the controls Cadan reacted instantly, swinging his chair around to grab the throttle and drag the ship's speed down. The *Phoenix* gave a shudder as the stability drive kicked in.

Stewart, at the screens so fast that Elissa didn't see him cross the platform, pulled up full-perimeter visuals. "Pirates."

Elissa's stomach turned upside down. The screens showed four spacecraft surrounding the *Phoenix*. They'd come out of nowhere, jumping from God knew what distance away—small, sleek, built for speed, their sides bristling with guns that could tear a ship's sides open. All SFI ships had shields—shields that were second to none, if Cadan and Bruce could be believed—but even the best shields, if hit hard and often enough, would degrade, leave the ship herself open to attack.

Above Cadan's head the communication unit gave a sudden beep, lights flashing along its lower edge. Cadan, one hand on the throttle, didn't even look up.

At the controls, flipping switches—*please let them be to arm the ship's weapons*—Stewart said, "Captain . . ." He sounded breathless. Was this his first sole-charge flight too? Had he, like Bruce and Cadan, only been in simulated combat before? And now, on their first flight, just hours out of Sekoia's protection . . . *How can there be pirates now? So soon after we left orbit?*

Cadan didn't answer.

"Cay, they want to talk."

"No." Cadan's voice was cold and calm.

"Cay, if it just gives us time to fully arm the ship—"

"I said no." Cadan didn't take his eyes off the viewscreens. He moved the hand that was not on the throttle to another lever. His fingers whitened, closing their grip, easing the lever upward, and the ship gave another tiny shudder. "You know the protocol as well as I do. No negotiation with pirates."

Something cold lodged in Elissa's chest. Without volition she found her gaze moving up to where Lin clung to the rail. Their eyes met. *They want to talk,* Stewart had said. To talk? Or to demand that Cadan hand over his two passengers? Were they pirates, or were they something else entirely?

I thought we'd gotten away. I thought once we were off-planet, we'd be safe.

Another blast. Fire flared in the viewscreens as the missiles hit the *Phoenix*'s shields, but this time, stability drive fully engaged, the superbly built SFI-engineered ship scarcely shivered.

Thank God. As long as the gravity drive kept working, it didn't matter which way the ship was "up"—in space all directions were the same. But in a battle, Elissa knew they couldn't afford to be tipped out of position. *Is this a battle now? If they're after us and if Cadan won't negotiate, what will the pirates do? They don't want us killed, surely, but if they keep firing and firing and Cadan has to give in . . .*

"Weapons ready, Captain."

Cadan gave a jerk of a nod. "I've got her steady. Fire in three, two, *one*."

Flames shot out, obscuring the vicious little spaceships behind momentary, instantly disappearing fireballs. Two direct hits against their shields, one miss as a little craft dropped abruptly out of sight, and a glancing blow that sent the remaining ship spinning out of control.

"Three, two, *one*." Cadan's voice was so steady, he might have been doing nothing more than directing Stewart to get him a coffee.

Stewart fired again. Another fireball disintegrated the shield around one of the ships and exploded against its side. Flames bloomed over the punctured hull, and the ship flipped, tumbling over and over.

"Three, two, *one*."

But this time, as Stewart fired and the rockets shot out

across the viewscreens, all four pirate crafts winked out, leaving nothing but the split second of their afterimage floating in front of Elissa's eyes. She blinked, and the afterimage was gone. On the communicator unit the lights died.

"Good God," said Stewart. He put up a hand and wiped his sleeve across his forehead.

"Keep her armed," Cadan snapped. "It could be a diversionary tactic. Let me scan for hidden craft." He moved his throttle hand to the keyboard. His voice remained steady, and his hands, too, but his fingers had left prints on the throttle that showed dull for a moment, damp patches on the smooth metal.

Long seconds passed. The viewscreens stayed empty. Elissa became aware that she could hear her heart beating, and next to her Lin's breathing, fast and shallow. She pushed herself up to her knees and reached for Lin's hand. The fingers that wrapped around hers were ice cold.

"All clear." Cadan eased the other lever—some sort of manual steadying control?—back into place and moved the throttle forward. On one of the screens a line flickered, showing the *Phoenix*'s speed as it picked up.

The view from the transparent sides of the ship didn't change, nor did the images on the viewscreens, but as the speed line climbed on the control panel, Elissa knew they were moving fast away from the scene of the attack, leaving it behind them, and her stomach began to unknot.

"Sorry," said Stewart. His voice was flat, almost a mutter. Elissa flicked a glance at him. He was looking at Cadan, his face flushed. "I shouldn't have suggested that you open to communication with them. I know the protocol. No negotiation with pirates. Ever. I *know* it. I just—"

"I know," said Cadan. "But that's exactly why we have the protocol. Heat of the moment—no one thinks straight by themselves."

"You did."

Elissa's attention sharpened at the change—a very slight change—in Stewart's tone, and Cadan threw him a quick look, as if searching for what might be behind it. Then, after a moment, he grinned. "Yes, this time. There'll be something that hits me like that one day, though, Stew, and then it'll be the protocol that saves *my* skin." He glanced around at where Elissa knelt, clutching Lin's hand. "Elissa? Ms. May? Are you all right?"

Elissa nodded, fighting with herself not to start shaking, or crying, or something. The danger was over. It hadn't ever been much of a threat—not against an SFI ship—and she knew about pirates, they weren't that unusual. She didn't have to start thinking it was anything other than a random attack. *But if it wasn't . . .*

Lin's hand gave a convulsive twitch in hers, and Elissa's chest tightened. *Either I'm picking up her fear or she's picking up mine. But either way, one of us is so freaked out, she's going to start having hysterics any minute.*

Elissa got to her feet, her hip aching. She'd really gone down hard—she'd have a bruise there later for sure. "We're okay," she said. "We'll just go back to our cabin for a bit."

"Of course." Cadan looked at her a moment, then stood up. "Stew, take the controls for a moment, would you?" He came over to them. "I'm sorry. That's a hell of a thing to happen on your first day out—and to see it firsthand from the flight deck too. It wasn't as risky as it felt, though, I promise. They didn't even breach our shields. I think they just wanted to intimidate us into opening communications."

"Why?" Lin's eyes, wide and dark, came up to his.

"Because once we're talking to them, they can threaten us even further, try to trick or frighten us into letting them on board, paying them protection money . . . any number of things."

"So if anyone else attacks, you'll just refuse to talk to them? You'll never find out what they want?"

Cadan laughed. "I *really* don't anticipate any more attacks, I assure you."

"But *if*—"

"Okay, *if*, then yes. We don't communicate, we don't negotiate. Those are the rules we agreed to when we joined SFI. We live by them, and we all stay safe." He gave Lin a brief smile, and after a moment she nodded, her hand relaxing a little within Elissa's. But Elissa didn't relax. She was abruptly as cold as Lin had been, a prickling cold that went all over her body.

"Elissa?" said Cadan. He was looking down at her, his smile gone, his brows drawing together in a frown—not of disapproval but of concern. "What is it? What's wrong?"

For an instant he didn't look like the high-flying SFI cadet, the arrogant young man who'd left her behind a long time ago. He looked like the teenage boy the thirteen-year-old Elissa had adored, the boy she'd have trusted with nearly anything, whom she'd trusted more than she trusted her brother, more than her best friends.

She swallowed, making herself look away. He hadn't been that boy for a very long time. And she wasn't the thirteen-year-old to whom everything had come easily, who thought everyone she loved would automatically love her back.

Those are the rules we signed up for. Not only was he not that boy anymore, but now he worked for the SFI, owned by the

Sekoian government. They might be outside planetary juris-diction here, but if an SFI ship came with a message that he had fugitives on board, he wouldn't hesitate a microsecond before handing them over.

They haven't done it yet, at least. Which means those ships—maybe they were just pirates. Maybe we are still safe. But, oh God— her stomach lurched—*if they do track us, if they do send a message out to him—*

"I'm fine," she said, and tugged at Lin's hand, backing toward the doorway.

He was still frowning. "All right. Look, you don't want to be sitting all alone in your cabin all day, not after that. Come and eat with the crew later, okay? Thirteen—one p.m, in the dining area. You can follow the signs on the walls, yes?"

"Okay." She nodded, not caring what she was agreeing to, just needing to get away. "We'll come." She reached the door, managed to find the button to open it, and pulled Lin down the steps.

At the bottom, drawn by an instinct she didn't recognize, wasn't expecting, she glanced back. Cadan was standing where she'd left him, his brows still drawn together, watching her leave.

"Was it pirates?" asked Lin. They were outside the flight deck, still hand in hand, descending the staircase that would take them back to their cabin. Lin's lips were pale, and when she spoke, they moved as if she couldn't quite feel them.

"It could have been. They do exist—you hear about them all the time. SFI flies orbital patrols specially to protect the planet from them—and lots of other planets do too. They completely could have been."

"But if they weren't—"

Elissa's hand twitched tightly around Lin's. "*Not here.* Wait till we get back to the cabin." She didn't think the ship corridors had security cameras or hidden mics, but among all this echoing metal their voices would carry. And they kept passing doors—shut, locked doors, but how did she know which crew members might be behind them, able to catch what she and Lin were saying?

In their cabin, with the door clamped shut, Elissa caught sight of herself in the tiny mirror in the shower cubicle, and for a ridiculous instant nothing but self-conscious vanity took over. Her face looked as if all the blood had drained out of it, leaving her skin a muddy shade of pale, her freckles and the fading bruises standing out like dirt. Cadan had seen her looking worse—well, probably everyone she knew had seen her looking worse. But all the same . . . No wonder he'd had that expression on his face, as if he thought she might throw up in front of him.

"They won't communicate with anyone? That's what he said?" Lin's voice jerked Elissa back to urgent—*real*—preoccupations. The fake tan meant that Lin didn't look quite as awful as Elissa, but her lips still moved stiffly, and one hand, now released from Elissa's hold, twined tightly around the other.

Elissa pulled herself together, hit the buttons on the nutrimachine for two hot chocolates with extra sugar, and handed one steaming cup to her twin. "That's right. It's SFI rules, and like he said, he won't defy them."

"So they . . . if it wasn't pirates, if it was people from Sekoia, they can't get through to the ship? They can't make him give us back?"

Lin's fingers curled around her cup, and her lip showed bloodless where she was biting it. For a moment the impulse to lie, to offer comfort whether it was true or not, rose within Elissa. It would be so easy to say *no* and to see Lin's face relax, to see her hands lose that careful jerkiness that showed she was trying not to let them tremble.

She couldn't do it. Not to Lin.

"Kind of," she said. "If it's law enforcement pretending to be pirates—or if it's pirates sent by law enforcement—then Cadan won't talk to them unless they manage to force him to. But"—she swallowed, hating to say it—"if they turn up as themselves, with SFI authorization codes, telling him he's got to hand us over . . ."

Lin's whole body seemed to shrink, as if she were pulling herself tighter. "Yes. I see."

Elissa made herself take a sip of chocolate. "It's why I wanted Bruce to help us. You're *his* sister too—if I'd gotten him to accept that, I think I could've gotten him to agree just to take us somewhere else and dump us and forget it had ever happened. But Cadan, he's practically the SFI poster boy. Ugh, *hell*." She had to stop her fingers from clenching on the flimsy cup. "I was stupid to get us on his ship. If I'd waited for Bruce to come out of quarantine . . . But if I'd done that, we might have ended up without a ship at all. Bruce could have missed his chance by then. And anyway, we couldn't afford to wait—"

She halted. Something had flickered across Lin's face. "What?" said Elissa.

"You really think your brother would have helped?"

"Well, I think so." She stopped. "You don't think he would?"

Lin was no longer chewing her lip, although she still stood as if bracing herself against something. "He's SFI too, isn't he?"

"Yeah, but it's different." She hesitated, thinking how to explain. "See, Cadan's family—they're not well off; they'd never have been able to afford to put him through flight school if SFI hadn't spotted him and paid for his education. Since he was, like, eleven, he's been in debt to them." It ambushed her suddenly, the thought of what she'd done to him. Let him think he was earning money to pay off that debt. Tricked him into helping a fugitive from their own government's law enforcement agents.

She pushed the thought away, focusing on the skeptical look on Lin's face. "You don't think Bruce would be any different?" Elissa asked.

Lin lifted a shoulder in a tiny shrug. "Well, you know, your parents . . ."

"I know," Elissa said, too fast. That was another thought lurking in the undercurrents of her mind, another thought she couldn't look at yet, not until it had stopped hurting so much. She took a gulp of chocolate. "And you could be right. I mean, I knew going to Bruce was a risk too, but we were *so* out of options." She sighed, combing the fingers of her free hand through her hair, as if by doing so she could comb the thoughts out of her head.

"I just mean," said Lin, "that you weren't stupid. Your brother might not have been any safer than Cadan."

Elissa blinked. Once again, just like last night, Lin had offered comfort and understanding that Elissa hadn't been expecting. She certainly hadn't expected it from Lin, but as well as that—it had been a long time since she'd expected it from anyone.

"Thanks," she said finally. She drained the last, gritty mouthful of chocolate. The shock and fear of the attack had receded a little; she was thinking more calmly again. The attackers *could* have been nothing but pirates. And the flight would be over in less than forty hours. Once she and Lin got to Mandolin, they could get new IDs, get on a standard passenger flight with people who didn't know them at all, and lose themselves somewhere in the whole of the rest of the star system.

We've gotten this far, and I never would have thought we'd manage it. Our luck only needs to last a little while longer. Just two more days and we'll be done, we'll be safe.

Something familiar about the cadence of her thoughts caught at her, sparked memory. She'd been thinking something very like that about two days ago, forty-eight hours in the other direction, as she'd stood in phys ed, waiting to be picked last, telling herself that all she had to do was wait a little longer and her whole life would be okay.

Four days, and everything will be better.

No, that wasn't what she'd thought. It came back to her now. With the sudden unexpected clarity of total recall, she smelled the sweat-and-rubber scent of the gym, felt the prickle of hostile or mocking stares on the back of her neck. She hadn't been thinking, *Four days, and everything will be better*, but, *Four days, and they'll make everything better.*

She hadn't known then what that meant, or how definitely she was going to defy the way they—the doctors, her parents—had intended to make things "better." But there'd been so much comfort in the thought that someone else was going to sort out her problems, that all she had to do was obey, submit, go along with what they told her. No questions, no second-guessing.

That comfort had gone. No one was going to take over her

responsibilities, the decisions she had to keep making. It was just her now, her and Lin, and if they didn't fix things for themselves, no one else would do it for them.

Elissa had agreed that they would eat lunch with the crew of the *Phoenix*, and at the time it had seemed like the easiest answer to give. But now that she and Lin were following the wall-markers to the crew's dining area, she wished she'd thought of an excuse. Their cover story had been enough to get them onto the ship, but was it enough to hold up through half an hour or more of talking with the whole crew?

Heart beating so hard that she felt the blood pounding inside her head, felt it vibrating under her skin, she touched the door panel.

The door opened on a blast of conversation and the scent of spices and rice. The crew—fifteen people—was gathered around a long table, slightly curved to follow the curve of the spaceship wall.

Stewart James stood up the moment they came in, his smile flashing out at them. "Our newest passengers! Ms. Ivory, Ms. May, come find a seat." The look of shock he'd worn after the pirate attack was gone, and he was once again the cheerful young man who'd invited them to the flight deck, assuring them Cadan would welcome the visit.

Which he completely didn't.

Elissa pushed away the thought, plus any others threatening to distract her, and smiled back, as bright and bland as if her head had nothing important in it at all.

Cadan wasn't there, and Stewart made the introductions— a jumble of names and positions she couldn't keep track of and wouldn't remember. The only person who stood out was the chef, Ivan, a long-armed gorilla of a man, untidy even in his white chef's uniform. He wasn't just the chef, obviously. Everyone on an SFI crew had to be multifunctional. *Does he wear a different uniform the rest of the time?* Elissa wondered, a random, fleeting thought.

After spending the first few minutes vibrating with nerves, Elissa realized that although the crew was polite and relatively friendly, they weren't interested enough in either her or Lin to be the risk she'd feared. They were all a good ten years older than Bruce, so although either Cadan or Stewart had told them she was Bruce's sister, and several of them were courteous enough to say they hoped he'd be out of quarantine soon, they were not his fellow cadets in the way Cadan and Stewart were, and they had no personal interest in Elissa as his sister.

Cadan came in just as Ivan uncovered the long metal dishes in the middle of the table. Cadan looked as relaxed as if the earlier attack had never happened, but he was wearing not only the obligatory wrist unit that connected him to the bridge, but also the nonessential earpiece, a small black clip that fitted over the top of his ear. He threw a quick greeting around the room, then took a seat at the head of the table, a couple of places away from where Elissa and Lin sat.

Elissa looked down, twitching her napkin into her lap. Earlier, on the flight deck, the thought of telling him everything had flashed, tempting and treacherous, into her head. It had been wiped out almost instantly, but all the same, seeing him in his official garb, uniform jacket buttoned up to his neck, earpiece snug against his ear, taking without hesitation the highest-ranked place at the head of the table, her stomach dropped with the horrified realization that she could have betrayed herself and Lin to him.

It was another danger she hadn't thought about: the danger of the weakness within herself that had driven her to ask help of her parents, of her brother, that could drive her into asking help of even SFI officials if they looked at her with kindness, if she let herself think they could be trusted.

The crew's conversation flowed over and around them, letting them sit undisturbed, a huge relief after what Elissa had feared. And the food was delicious—*real* food, after the snack bars and machine nutri-packs they'd been eating for what seemed like days. Fragrant fish curry and long-grain rice, pale yellow, spiked with cumin seeds and cardamom pods. But Elissa only enjoyed it until she glanced sideways and saw Lin, both elbows on the table, napkin lying ignored, scooping up forkfuls of fish and sauce far too fast to be polite.

Embarrassment flashed over Elissa even quicker than fear. She'd seen Lin eat before, but it had always been in hurried, informal circumstances—she hadn't noticed, hadn't thought to anticipate, that Lin's table manners wouldn't be the same as those of the upper sections of Sekoian society.

Of course they aren't. Of course*—I was stupid not to think about it. And I should be ashamed to be embarrassed of her. It's not her fault.*

Elissa gritted her teeth against the instinctive cringing as Lin put down her fork and picked up her water glass without first wiping her fingers, leaving a smudge on the smooth surface of the glass. She shouldn't be embarrassed, but she was right to be afraid. Anything that showed Lin as different, anything that drew suspicion onto them . . . they couldn't afford that. Not on this Sekoian ship.

At Elissa's right, Stewart stood up and stepped over the bench to go refill his water glass at the wall dispenser. As Lin picked her fork back up and speared a piece of fish, Elissa seized the opportunity and slid her left hand over to touch Lin's elbow. Lin glanced at her questioningly.

Elissa flicked a look down at Lin's fork, then at where her own right hand was poised just above the table, her elbow tucked neatly down at her side, her napkin laid across her lap.

Lin's eyes followed her gaze, then came back up, a look of bewilderment in them. Elissa leaned over so her mouth was next to Lin's ear. "Table manners," she murmured as softly as she could.

For an instant, understanding showed in Lin's face; then color swept over it, a wave of visible humiliation. All at once Elissa remembered how Lin had looked when Elissa had discovered the hole in the back of her head. Ashamed, as if it were her fault. As if somehow she were responsible for every horrific thing that had been done to her.

Lin moved her elbows off the table, then pulled her napkin into her lap, her fingers tight on it, crumpling the thin paper. When she next picked up her fork, her movements betrayed an almost painful caution, and her cheeks still burned.

I had to warn you. I had to. We can't afford to make anyone suspicious. Now that it was too late, Elissa thought of a host of other ways she could have warned Lin without humiliating her. Tense with remorse, with the knowledge that she'd hurt her sister and couldn't take it back, she stole a quick look up to see if anyone was watching—and met Cadan's eyes.

His gaze jolted her, turning her skin cold. *Oh God, of all people—it has to be Cadan watching. He'll have noticed. The lies I told him—they won't hold up if he decides to investigate.*

But after a second she realized it wasn't suspicion in his eyes. It was something close to distaste.

He reached for his napkin, then leaned forward, speaking past Elissa. "Ms. May, can I pass you anything?"

Lin looked up, already shaking her head, and as she did, Cadan planted both elbows on the table, fork still held in the fingers of one hand. With the other he crumpled his napkin, then dropped it to lie, creased and messy, next to his plate. He smiled at Lin, the warm smile Elissa remembered from a long time ago. "Ivan tells me he has something else delicious prepared for tonight's meal—I hope you'll join us again?"

"I . . ." Lin shot an indecisive look at Elissa. "I'm not sure."

"I don't think so." Elissa spoke quickly, trying to sound polite. "It's very kind of you, but we'll be fine in our cabin."

Cadan didn't even glance at her. He spoke again to Lin, his words very clear, elbows still firmly on the table. "That's a shame, Ms. May. We'd be very happy to have you join us, if you'd like to. There's entirely no need to feel you should stay in your cabin." Then his eyes did flick to Elissa, and the emphasis in his last sentence was beyond clear.

He'd seen her gesture to Lin. He'd seen Lin's embarrassment, seen her careful changing of the way she ate. But of course he couldn't know that Elissa was trying to keep them both blended in, unremarkable, unmemorable. He thought— *Oh, for God's sake!* Heat rushed into her face, until she knew it must be glowing as hot as Lin's had a minute earlier. *He thinks I'm criticizing Lin's table manners, humiliating her, for no other reason than that I want her to fit in. He thinks I'd do that to someone—someone who's supposed to be my friend.*

For a flaming instant she wanted to set him straight, wanted to tell him she didn't *care* about table manners, that he had *no idea* what was going on in her head. And that even if that had been what was going on, it was none of his business—it wasn't his duty to defend Lin against her. She bit back the impulse, looked away, and, despite her appetite having disappeared, took another mouthful of curry.

"That's both of you, of course, isn't it, Captain?" Stewart stepped back across the bench into his place. Elissa looked up and found him smiling down at her. "He should have insisted you join us for breakfast, too. The nutri-machines will keep you alive, sure, but it's not like we're a warship—there's no reason you should stay in your quarters."

"I did extend an invitation," Cadan said, his voice cool and detached.

Stewart laughed. "Yes, but did you *insist*?" He sat down and smiled again at Elissa, as if inviting her to join him in his lighthearted mockery of Cadan. "He sometimes overlooks these little niceties, Ms. Ivory—you'll have to excuse him."

Out of politeness Elissa responded to his smile, but she was rigid with discomfort. Surely Cadan's copilot must be able to pick up the stiffness in Cadan's voice, the flush still burning in her cheeks? Was he a particular friend of Bruce's, that he felt he had to make his sister welcome on board the ship? But if so, surely she'd have heard about him before?

At that point someone at the other side of the captain's place spoke to Cadan, and his attention was drawn away for a moment.

Stewart leaned a little closer. "Hey. Honestly, Ms. Ivory, we'd be happy to have you both join us. You don't need to be shy. And you don't need to wait for an invitation from the captain, either!" He smiled at her again, and suddenly Elissa saw in his smile what she should have seen before.

What maybe she would have seen if she hadn't been out—
way out—of the dating scene for so long.

He wasn't being kind to a friend's little sister. He wasn't
looking at her like she was anyone's little sister at all.

It threw her into instant confusion—partly flattered surprise, but shot through with pure alarm. She didn't know
how to do this anymore. And she couldn't afford to have
him interested in her—not like that, not like *any* way.

She felt the blush climbing back into her face and fought
to suppress it. The last thing she needed was for him to think
she was interested in him. If she left the ship and he wanted to
keep in touch, she'd have to lie to him, lead him to think he'd
be able to do so, that Elissa Ivory wasn't going to change her
hair and name and disappear. She couldn't do that, couldn't
be so ruthless.

*But if I do, if I do lead him on to think I'm interested, at least it
will take his attention away from Lin.* The thought came as if
from somewhere outside her own head—or from a part of her
she hadn't known about or acknowledged, a cold, calm streak
slicing through the confusion.

She didn't need to think about it anymore. She let the
blush come, glowing into her cheeks. She dropped her eyelids for a single, confused-looking second, then raised them
again so that for a moment her eyes met Stewart's. *Flirting—
turns out you don't forget how. Just like riding a skycycle.*

She leaned back in her chair, twirling some hair around her
finger, not letting herself despise what she was doing. "That's
superkind of you. If you're sure that's okay . . ."

His smile widened, and she'd been right, that was interest—attraction—in his eyes. "Oh, absolutely, Ms. Ivory."

She laughed. It came out a little breathy with nerves, but

given the impression she was trying to convey, that was probably okay. "Please, that just sounds like my mother. Everyone calls me Lissa. I mean, all my friends. And you know my brother and everything, don't you? You're, like, almost family or something."

His eyebrows went up quizzically. "*Or something*, I hope. 'Family' sounds a little bit too close, you know?"

This time she managed a giggle. "Okay. How about a distant cousin?"

"How distant?"

"Oh, *really* distant."

He grinned at her. "Yeah, I can live with that."

Elissa let the twisted lock of hair go and ran a finger up to tuck the strands behind her ear. "Bruce completely hasn't told me enough about you. You're in the same year, right?"

"Right." He said something else, kept on talking, but suddenly Elissa wasn't listening. Cadan had looked back toward them, and his eyes were such a cold blue that when they met hers, every cell in her body seemed to stop still.

She held his gaze with an effort, defiance standing in for courage. *What?*

He raised his eyebrows. *Nothing.*

Fine, then. She began to slide her gaze away, determined not to let her face show anything other than indifference, when all at once the ship seemed to shiver.

Around the table people froze in place, hands stopping dead midmovement, voices as instantly silent as if a soundproof barrier had fallen.

Elissa's heart seemed to stop dead too. That shiver—it hadn't been like the blast of the pirate attack, but it hadn't been normal, either. Her hand went automatically out, meeting Lin's as it moved toward hers. Their fingers clasped like magnets locking together. *Not pirates. Surely it's not pirates.*

"Cadan?" said Stewart.

Cadan was already on his feet, his wrist unit open. His voice was clipped and tight. "I don't know. There's nothing. We're picking up nothing." He stepped backward over the bench. "I'm getting to the bridge."

Then the speaker up in the corner between wall and ceiling whined into life, and a voice spoke.

"Attention, *Phoenix*. That was your first warning. We have jammed your shields, we have you surrounded, and we are prepared to fire. We demand communication with the captain."

TEN

LIN'S HAND tightened so hard around Elissa's that Elissa felt every fingernail. She couldn't breathe, her body frozen, her eyes fixed on Cadan.

There was a white shade around Cadan's mouth. His eyes were like ice. He clicked a button on his earpiece and spoke, his voice coldly furious. "Get the hell off my public speakers. You've hacked this far into the system, switch to private band."

Not-quite silence stretched out for a moment that lasted forever, then the speaker went dead.

Cadan swung around, took two strides to the wall, and jabbed a code into a little keypad Elissa hadn't noticed. Metal slid to the sides to reveal a control panel and screen, dark and blank. Cadan pressed his thumb to it, and the screen woke faster than Elissa had known was possible.

As Cadan swiped open windows and summoned Stewart over with a jerk of his head, as the rest of the crew moved to standing, some of them drawing weapons from holsters she hadn't even realized they carried, Elissa's heart slammed back into motion, banging so hard against her chest, she had to fight for breath. Alone at the table Lin sat as if turned to stone, staring up at the speaker as if it would tell her what was going on.

"It's them," she said. "They've come back—"

"It's all right." Elissa spoke across her without even thinking if it was the truth or not.

Lin shook her head, a tiny quiver. "They've jammed the shields. They're going to fire."

"Lin." Elissa tried to say her name calmly. "This is an SFI ship. This is what they're built for. Cadan will get the shields back up. He won't let them hurt you."

"I might," said Cadan. Elissa jerked around to look at him in disbelief. "If you don't stop talking for a minute so I can . . . Okay. Markus, I need you here. Stew and I have to get to the bridge."

"Yes sir." Markus, a man about thirty years old, tall and deeply tanned, seemed to be there before Elissa caught up with who Cadan was talking to. Cadan stepped back to make way for him at the control panel. "I've locked them out, but they're jumping—you need to keep changing the band so they can't hack in again. As long as you're keeping them out, I can get the shields back up. Stew, bridge."

He strode past Elissa to the door.

She had to stop herself from clutching for his sleeve. But she couldn't stop herself from speaking, taking the attention she knew he couldn't afford to give her. "Cadan—they're not still talking to you?"

He swept her with a glance as he went past. "They can't.

They're locked out. Go to your cabin. If you hear the seat belt alarm—"

"I know."

As he left the room, he cast a split-second grin back at her. "You *did* pay attention, then." And then he was gone, Stewart moving quickly after him.

Elissa forced herself to take a deep breath. *Cadan's in control. He knows what he's doing; he won't let anything happen.* She turned to tell Lin that, and was just in time to see her scramble to her feet and over the bench, and then run out the door.

Elissa hurried after her. If Lin was too panicked to find the cabin, and the seat belt alarm sounded when she wasn't near any safety harnesses—

But Lin was making no effort to follow the signs to their cabin. She was running along the corridor where Cadan and Stewart had disappeared, the one leading up to the flight deck.

"Lin! That's the wrong way."

Lin neither answered nor looked back. Elissa picked up her own pace to catch up. "Lin! We have to get to our cabin. You heard what Cadan said."

"I have to hear. They'll talk to him. They'll tell him—"

"*Lin*, they won't. He's locked them out. You *heard* him."

But Lin didn't respond. She was beyond panic, no longer able to think halfway reasonably, not even able to hear what Elissa was trying to tell her. The memory of what had happened last time Lin was this frightened swept over Elissa. She tried again—"Lin, we *have* to get to our cabin in case we need seat belts"—but it was no use.

Cadan had told them to go to their cabin, and Elissa still could. But she couldn't let Lin go to the bridge alone, not like this. *Last time, in the mall—if she'd been running away by herself, if I hadn't been there to stop her, how far would she have gone?*

Elissa dragged in a lungful of processed air and concentrated on keeping up with her twin, following her up and around the central staircase to the door that opened, as it had that morning, above their heads.

They erupted, out of breath, onto the flight deck. Lin made straight for the steps, stopping only when she reached the half-visible barrier. She stopped, hands spread against the glass like a toddler at a window, chest heaving for breath.

Across the bridge, at the controls, Cadan threw a glance over his shoulder. "What the hell? Lissa, what are you—"

Elissa had come up the steps behind her twin. She spread her hands. "I'm sorry, she panicked. I couldn't—"

Cadan's eyes swept over Lin. "Okay. I see." He frowned for a second, his eyes distant, then refocused on her. He punched a button, and the barrier slid back to let them in. "Just keep her quiet, all right? And for God's sake, Lissa, get yourselves belted in."

"Okay." There were safety harnesses all along the rail that ran behind him. Elissa fumbled with one, trying to work out the straps. "Lin, here, this is how they work." But when she looked up, Lin was already clicking the buckles into place, the smart-straps drawing close around her body to hold her against the rail. Her eyes were still huge and panicked. Elissa wouldn't have thought she could work out a normal safety belt in her state, let alone the intricacies of the SFI-installed five-point harnesses.

She got her own harness fastened and felt it tighten, pulling against her shoulders, waist, and crotch, clamping her against the cushioned edge of the safety rail.

Cadan hadn't glanced back at them. His hands flickered over the controls, so fast he seemed to hardly touch them. It was as if the displays on the screens—the shields racing their way back up to a hundred percent, the little sinister flashes on the enhanced scan Stewart was running that were the only sign of the cloaked ships' presence—were responding to his will, not his touch.

They're not just pirates. She'd known it before, really, but now she knew it all the way through her, a feeling as if her spine, all her bones, had turned to melting ice. *Ordinary pirates don't work in groups that big. Ordinary pirates don't have technology that keeps them hidden from SFI ships.*

Cadan moved one hand off the keyboard and reached for a lever among a bank of them. The manual control for the stability drive, the one he'd used before? No, a different one, marked with a thin blue stripe, that he had to unlock with his thumbprint before he could ease it out of its starting position and move it up.

Elissa found herself watching him as if just the act of doing so could help him keep control of the ship—or as if it could keep her thoughts from exploding into unthinking panic.

Not just pirates. They're bounty hunters. Powerful, tech-rich mercenary ships, available to anyone who could afford them, open to any assignment that would pay enough to make it worthwhile. Piracy was the least of it. Abduction, murder, terraforming sabotage . . .

Our own government hired them. Our own government sent them after us.

But if they were prepared to do that—*and how much do they want Lin back, to pay bounty hunters to come after her?*—why not send their own ships? Why not do what she and Lin had feared and send SFI officials to demand access to the *Phoenix*, arrest her and Lin then and there, save time and money and all the risks involved in attacking their own ship?

As Cadan slid his hand back onto the control panel, the answer came to her. *They're still trying to keep it quiet. Arresting us openly, revealing the existence of Spares, of what they're doing to them . . . they don't want to do it. Not yet, at least. They hired bounty hunters because they don't need to tell hired mercenaries why. All they need to tell them is how much they'll pay.*

Half-beneath her notice, like the beginnings of a headache, a faint whine had been building in the air. Now it intensi-fied, the headache blooming into migraine, shaking Elissa's mind from her thoughts. The noise seemed to come from everywhere, seemed to travel through every metal surface, a vibration she felt in her bones, in her teeth, shivering at the corners of her eyes. She hadn't felt it before, but back in the days of hanging on Bruce's and Cadan's words, she'd heard plenty about it. She knew what it was.

The hyperdrive. Cadan was engaging the hyperdrive, SFI's ultimate technological triumph, the machine that would take the ship to a speed so much faster than light, it would be as if they'd teleported instantly from one coor-dinate to another.

It was the only thing to do. The only way to escape. But Elissa's gaze went, as if drawn by magnets, to the screen where the shields now showed at a hundred percent. The one flaw of the hyperdrive: At the point when the ship kicked from normal into hyperspeed, the shields would drop. They couldn't stay up during hyperspeed—which, once you were actually in hyperspeed, or once you'd hopped to your destination, didn't matter. But for that tiny fraction of time while you were still under potential fire . . .

Her mouth went dry. She was clamped against the rail, but all the same her hands came up as if of their own accord to curl around it, so tightly that her fingers went numb.

"Cay," said Stewart, "they're moving into attack formation. We have to move—"

"Okay. Nearly there."

"*Cay—*"

Stewart's voice was drowned out. The whine became a shriek Elissa felt all through her body. The ship gave one shudder, all the screens went dark, and the stars outside blinked into blackness. Then, with a jerk that felt as if the whole universe had shifted, they were elsewhere.

The control screens all flicked back on in blurs of scrolling code. Then, a split second later, the viewscreens came on too. The flashes of cloaked ships were gone, but Elissa held her breath while Stewart's fingers raced over the controls, scanning and rescanning.

An endless two minutes later, he said, "We're clear."

Cadan had his hand up to his earpiece. "Markus? . . . Yes. We're good. Great job. Seal it up for me again, would you? Then— Yes, right away, please. Come to the bridge to debrief. Thanks. . . . Yes. Seriously, great job."

He clicked a switch on the earpiece, then pulled it off and slid it into his breast pocket. He moved the hyperdrive lever back into its locked position. Then, for a moment so brief that Elissa would have missed it entirely if she hadn't had her eyes fixed on him, he tilted his head back slightly, drew in a breath, and let it out through his teeth.

Then he unclicked his seat and swung it around to face

Elissa and Lin. His eyes went first to the safety straps hugging them to the rail, and he nodded. "Good girls. It's okay, you can unbuckle now. We've hopped right off-route, they won't be able to work out where we've gone."

The straps slipped under Elissa's fingers. She had to pause and rub her hands hard on her top before she could finish undoing them. Lin slid out of them a little more easily, then looked at Cadan. "Doing that—"

"Using the hyperdrive?"

"Yes. Does that mean *no one* knows where we are now?" Urgency jumped through Lin's voice, making the words sound jerky.

"No one we don't want to." Cadan gave Lin a brief smile. "I think those ships must have been working with those in the earlier attack. Maybe the earlier attack was mostly to soften us up. Anyway, don't be alarmed. I'm quite sure that'll be it for this flight!"

Except it won't. Elissa wrapped her arms around herself, her stomach giving a cold lurch. He'd said it himself: *No one we don't want to.* Which meant the bounty hunters by themselves might not be able to keep on tracking them, but SFI still could.

She met Lin's eyes and didn't need telepathy to see her own fear reflected back at her. They still had more than twenty-four hours left of the flight, and these two attacks had come within hours of each other. Her stomach lurched again, a feeling like a cold pancake flipping inside her. There was nothing they could do. Nowhere else to run. The ship had seemed as if it offered so much freedom, but all that coming on board had done was trap them in the exact thing that could be most easily tracked.

She clasped her arms tighter, trying to hold herself together, trying to think. There must be something else that would help them. If she and Lin could just go back to where they could talk properly . . .

"Lin, let's go back to our cabin."

But Lin shook her head.

Elissa stared at her for a second. "*Lin*. We shouldn't even *be* here—we should have been in our cabin to start with."

Lin flashed her a look. "Then we wouldn't know what's happening. I want to stay here."

Something close to panic tightened all the way up through Elissa's body. She *couldn't*. She couldn't stay here, trapped in this room, under Cadan's and Stewart's eyes, having to pretend she didn't know danger was coming closer and closer. "*Lin*. Come *on*."

"*No*. They're going to attack again, and I—"

"Oh my God, will you *shut up*?"

Elissa's voice was overlaid by Stewart's. "Ms. May, honestly, there's no danger of that now—"

And then, raised over them both, Cadan's. "That's *enough*."

The snap of authority in his voice brought Elissa automatically around to face him. He had one hand back on the control panel, and his eyes were bright with irritation. "Ms. May, Elissa is quite right. You should be in your cabin. We are highly unlikely to be attacked again"—Lin opened her mouth, but Elissa shot her a furious look and she snapped it shut once more—"but if we *were* to be attacked, the safest place on the whole ship is the passenger section." His gaze shifted briefly as a footstep sounded on the steps leading to the bridge. "Markus, thank you. Come on up."

He looked back at where Lin still stood, her hands clenched

on the rail. "Ms. May. I'm afraid that if you don't retire to your cabin immediately, I do have authority to order that you be taken there."

Lin went white. Elissa began to reach out to her, before she realized her twin hadn't gone pale from fear but from rage. Lin's hands came up off the rail, a movement that, if you didn't know, if you hadn't seen it before, would have looked like one of capitulation. "No one," said Lin, and her voice was like a hiss, "*no one* is touching me."

Cadan stood, his face all at once devoid of expression. "Mr. James, would you take over. Mr. Baer, your assistance, please."

As Elissa watched, caught and horrified, Cadan came around the end of the rail toward Lin. The other man—Markus, whom he'd left to guard the downstairs control panel—came forward from behind Elissa.

"Ms. May," said Cadan, his voice flat, "I'm going to ask you again."

And as Lin's gaze whipped toward him, Elissa felt it. The building *something* in her palms, as if all the rage in her body were focused in just those places. Lin, fueled by panic and fury, drawing on her electrokinetic power. *I can control electrical currents*, she'd said. And here, on the bridge of the spaceship, they were surrounded by enough power to . . . What could she do? Set the ship on fire? Electrocute someone?

No. Oh, no no no.

"Lin."

Lin's eyes met hers, blank and glittering. And the sensation, the heat, still built and built in her hands, ready to fly out, to strike . . . who? Markus, who was just doing his job? *Cadan?*

Elissa acted before she could find out. Before Markus and Cadan could reach to take hold of Lin's arms, she took two quick steps forward and seized Lin's shoulders. "Don't you *dare*," she said. "Don't you dare even *think* about it."

The heat stayed, pins and needles prickling up into her wrists. Lin's eyes glared into hers. Her teeth were clenched, her face set.

For an instant, fury rose up through Elissa, a wave that blocked out everything, and a jumble of fragmented thoughts. *Never going to be touched again. Kill them before I let them—*

She struggled, gasping, getting her head above the thoughts and feelings that weren't hers, and clenched her hands onto Lin's shoulders, digging her fingers in as hard as she could. "*Stop* it. *Lin.*" A blink of memory, and suddenly she had the right words. "Lin, listen to me. I don't want to have to hate you."

The heat died. The heat and the fury and everything, as suddenly as if they'd been flash-frozen. Lin's face went still.

Elissa let go of her shoulders and turned, linking her arm instead. "She gets panic attacks," she said to Cadan and Markus, part of her mind noticing the embarrassment on Markus's face, the narrow-eyed look on Cadan's that indicated he might not be buying the quick and easy lie. "I'll take her to our cabin now." She hesitated half a second longer. Lin was right, there *would* be another attack, and he wasn't expecting it. *If it's even worse than this one . . . and oh, it's his first sole-charge flight . . .*

It was no good. She couldn't warn him, and she didn't dare let Lin stay. She let her gaze slide away from his and led Lin off the bridge and away from the flight deck.

"Do you hate me?" said Lin when they were back in their cabin.

Elissa leaned back against the tiny section of wall between the nutri-machine and the shower cubicle and let her knees collapse slowly under her so she slid down toward the floor. She shut her eyes. "Not yet."

She said the words without thinking, and only realized their impact when she heard the tiny sound Lin made. She opened her eyes to see her twin's face rigid with hurt. "I'm sorry. I didn't mean to say it that way. I just mean, you didn't do anything to make me hate you."

Lin's face tightened, the pain morphing into anger. "Yeah, well, I was going to."

"What?" said Elissa, her voice jumping. "What were you going to do?"

"*Hurt them.*" Lin's teeth snapped together on the words. "Lissa, you *heard* him. He said they were going to take hold of me, make me—"

"It's *his ship.*" The spark of anger in Elissa's voice surprised her. "He *gets to do* that. They were only going to bring you here."

"I didn't want them to!" Lin's face went suddenly stony. "And I don't know why you even care. You said—you don't like him—"

Elissa pushed herself to her feet. "That's got nothing to do with it. You can't just hurt people, whether you like them or not."

"But—"

"*No.* Lin, you have to listen to me. If we're trying to escape, like back on Sekoia, or if we're, like, I don't know—*fighting*—then using your electrokinesis to help us get away—it's kind of justified. But just now, just because you didn't want to leave the flight deck, that's not okay. You can't *do* that." She looked at Lin, sudden despair sweeping through her. Was she getting through at all? Did Lin even grasp the distinction Elissa was trying to make?

She didn't get the chance to try again. The whole room gave a violent jolt, sending Lin crashing backward against the cabin door, banging Elissa into the side of the shower cubicle.

Even Elissa's brain seemed to freeze. She'd known this was coming—they'd both expected it—and yet, for one long instant between the first and the second blasts, somehow there was time to think, *Maybe it's not, maybe it's not, maybe it's not—*

The second blast came, knocking her off her feet, knocking her back into reality. The bounty hunters. Using whatever information or tracker technology SFI had given them, they'd used their own ships' versions of hyperdrives and come after the *Phoenix* again.

She got hold of the rail at the edge of the lower bunk bed, braced herself against the next blast. "Lin—"

Lin looked at her, her eyes unfocused. She'd banged the back of her head on the door.

"Lin," Elissa repeated, "we're supposed to get onto the bunks, strap ourselves in. You use the lower bunk, okay?"

Lin nodded, lips pressed together so hard that they'd almost disappeared.

Another blast came as Lin pulled herself up to the bunk, drew the straps across her body. The blast flung Elissa sideways again, banged her elbow on the side of the nutri-machine. Tears of pain jumped to her eyes. *We just did this. They're not supposed to be able to come after us like this, over and over, with no chance of us getting away.*

She reached for the rail that would steady her as she swung

up into the upper bunk, just as an alarm split the air.

Elissa jerked around. Lights flashed red—one over the door, one along the top edge of the screen. Then came the unnaturally calm mechanical voice of the warning system. "Air lock B activated. Security breached at Section B-twelve."

Elissa stopped breathing.

Bright white text blinked suddenly on the screen, but she couldn't focus enough to see if it was simply reiterating the message. *Security breached,* she thought. *They're on board. They got on board.*

The warning began to repeat then from the screen's speakers, and Cadan's voice came clearly over it.

"Attention, armed personnel. We have a security breach. Section B-twelve, pirates. Assume armed. Shoot to kill."

A pause, half a breath long, then his voice came again. "Attention, all passengers. Please remain in your rooms. Repeat, please remain in your rooms."

Lin's feet thumped down onto the floor next to where Elissa knelt. "We have to hide." She grabbed at Elissa's arm. "Quick. We have to hide."

"No. We have to stay here. You heard him—"

"Lissa!" Lin shook her. "They're on the ship. They're coming for us. We have to hide!"

"There's nowhere *to* hide! Lin, no, we have to stay—"

"But this is where they'll come! I can open one of those locked rooms. We can—"

The alarm sounded again. For a moment Elissa thought it was no more than a repetition, but then the spoken warning came. "Air lock J activated. Security breached at Section J-seven."

More? Oh God.

"Lissa," Lin said, dragging at her.

Elissa let herself be pulled, unresisting, to standing. But she was shaking her head even as she did so. "It's no good. I don't know where either of those sections *are*. If we leave the cabin, for all I know, we'll end up running straight toward them."

Lin's hands were shaking on Elissa's arm. "We can't just *wait*. Lissa, we can't—"

But it was too late. Outside the cabin the corridor echoed and clanged with the sound of booted running feet.

Lin's hand flashed out to hit lock on the door panel, then back to clutch at Elissa's arm. Elissa's heart was pounding so hard, she couldn't hear properly. Above her head the alarm kept on shrieking, the lights reflecting red flashes off Lin's face.

Something crashed into the door. The door shook, and the little red LOCKED light flickered but held. *Maybe they won't be able to get in. Maybe—*

Sparks jumped from the crack between door and wall. The LOCKED light winked out. Black-gloved fingers closed around the edge of the door and slammed it all the way open.

Somehow Elissa had thought that if the bounty hunters caught up with them, they'd still have time. Time to protest innocence, to use one of their cover stories, to insist the bounty hunters had gotten their facts wrong. Time to delay while they worked out how to escape.

There was no time. The moment the door was open, the cabin was full of men in black spacesuits, helmets folded back. Two of them seized Elissa, and before she knew it, she was being bundled down the corridor between the back of one man and the front of another, the one behind her racing her along so fast, she was half off her feet, feeling any moment she was going to fall.

She screamed, twisting around, trying to see what they'd done with Lin, and one of the men closed his hand across her face, cutting off most of her air supply so that within seconds she was struggling to breathe. *Lin!* Were the men bringing her, too? Or was she being taken somewhere else? There was security on the *Phoenix*—there was *always* security on SFI ships—but where was it?

The bounty hunters came to an abrupt stop before a door clamped so tightly shut that only the faintest swirl of hairline marks across the steel surface showed that it was a door at all. The hand across her mouth and nose shifted a little, and she gasped in a huge gulp of air, watching through blurry, oxygen-deprived vision as the man in front put his blast-gun to the central point of the door.

Sparks sprayed around him as he fired. The door shook a little in its frame but didn't move. As he drew out another instrument, Elissa tried to twist her head to see if Lin had been brought with her, to see if she was all right. To see—*oh, please, God*—if anyone, anywhere, was coming to save them. But the moment she moved, the man holding her tightened his grip, jerking her head back to face front so hard that pain jabbed through the top of her spine.

Lin! There must be something you can do. All that electrokinesis—there must be something.

But either there was nothing or Lin was frozen, too terrified to think of it, because nothing happened.

The door sprang open. Almost before it finished dilating, something cracked through the air and snatched the blast-gun from the hand of the man in front of Elissa. The weapon flew up, clanked against the wall, then hit the floor and skidded away down the corridor.

Figures leapt through the doorway. One crashed into the first man, throwing them both against the side of the corridor. A knife blade flashed.

Then Elissa was being dragged backward by an arm across her throat, being held tightly against her captor's chest. *Like a shield.* The realization flashed into her head. *He's using me like a shield.*

He brought his blast-gun up, and a bolt of heat sizzled over Elissa's head. A direct hit on the chest of the second man who'd come through the doorway—Elissa saw the fabric of his jacket smoke and singe. But he came on—*he must be wearing a blastproof vest*—knife in one hand, and in the other the whip—*oh, that's what it is*—cracking out faster than she could see.

Her captor gave a grunt of pain. The gun spun out of his hand. The whip flew out again, streaking along the arm across Elissa's throat. The arm jerked, and then Elissa found herself staggering forward as the man let her go, shoved her toward the man with the whip.

She managed to stumble to the side, knowing she had to get out of the way of the man who'd saved her, but she couldn't keep her footing. She went down on one knee and both hands, and, as the man with the whip leapt past her, her brain caught up with itself and she realized it was Cadan.

Back along the corridor the men holding Lin had turned to race the other way, only to meet more crew members: Markus, another man, and two women she recognized from earlier, their reinforced jackets deflecting knives and blast-guns.

You couldn't fire bullets or high-powered lasers on spaceships, not unless you wanted to risk puncturing the hull and killing everyone on board. All combat had to be close-range, the only weapons knives, shock-guns, or short-range blasters. And Cadan's whip. She remembered now: A couple of years into the SFI training, the cadets had been offered the chance to learn the use of an alternative weapon. Bruce and Cadan had both gone for the whip—*Coolest weapon ever*, Bruce had said at the time. She didn't know if Bruce had continued past the initial year of basic training. Cadan obviously had.

He was fighting Elissa's captor now, too close to use the whip again. The bounty hunter was big, his movements brutally fast, and Elissa found herself flinching, expecting every moment to see his knife slice into Cadan's unprotected throat or face.

The knife came up in a thrust that looked as if it couldn't help but drive home. Somehow Cadan's own knife flashed out to block it, slammed the blade up across its owner's nose. Bone cracked. Blood spurted. The man slid to the floor, unconscious.

Cadan spun back into combat. The whip snapped out again and again, faster than Elissa's eyes could follow, snatching weapons from hands before they came near him, leaving the pirates with nothing but bleeding fingers, then curling back to snatch their legs from under them and send them slamming to the floor.

And then, all at once, it was over.

The bounty hunters—six of them—sprawled, unconscious. There was blood smeared up the wall, and more blood in spatters along the floor. And blood on the blades of the knives some of the crew members were holding.

Elissa became aware that there was a buzzing in her ears, and her heart was beating far too hard, up at the top of her chest so she couldn't draw a full breath. That man—the one who'd opened the door—was slumped against the wall, his head sunk far forward on his chest, his neck—

Sweaty, hot nausea swirled up over her. *That's wrong. His head shouldn't be at that angle. No one's head should be at that angle.*

She moved her own head, stiffly, taking in the other men lying along the floor of the corridor, and once again her brain seemed to suddenly leap forward, catching up with what she should have seen before.

They weren't unconscious. None of them were unconscious. They were dead.

The buzzing in her ears seeped away, but no other sounds replaced it. Instead all the other sounds she knew there must be—people's voices, a boot scraping on the floor as Markus stepped over a bounty hunter's body to help Lin to her feet— seemed to go with the buzzing, flowing away, leaving nothing but a thick silence like cotton wool in her ears. She didn't want to look at the dead men, but she couldn't make her gaze move away from the one slumped against the wall, from the other one, who'd held her, the one Cadan had . . . *oh God, killed. Cadan killed him . . .*

"Elissa. Put your head down."

Cadan's voice. Cadan's hands on her arms, pulling her to a kneeling position, gently but firmly pushing her forward so that the floor came up toward her and her hair swung all around her face.

Sound returned in a crash of voices, boots, and the ever-present background noises of the ship: the whisper of the air-filtration system, the faint hum of the gravity drive. Elissa put her hands up to push her hair off her face, grateful that her right hand blocked out the sight of the blood, of the bodies—and she met Cadan's eyes.

"Are you all right?" he asked

She nodded.

"Okay. Just hang on, all right. Stew?" That confused her for a moment until she realized he was speaking into his wrist unit. "We're done. Status? . . . Good. Yeah—they're not going to fire when they think their men are on board. . . . No, don't wait. Make the hop now. I'm coming back to the bridge."

The hop. Hyperspeed again. *But it won't help. They tracked us so fast. They'll do it again. And again. Until they catch us.*

"Let's get you out of here. And Ms. May, too." As she got to her feet, he moved his hand to under her elbow, support-ing her, and glanced over her head up the corridor. "Ariel, leave cleanup for now, okay? All of you, stand by for further breaches. Markus, give Ms. May a hand."

She heard the voice of one of the women. "Yes, sir."

Then Lin's, far calmer than Elissa knew her own voice would be, should she attempt to speak. "I'm okay."

Elissa couldn't look up the corridor toward her, to see if the calmness was just the false calm of shock. She couldn't look again at the dead bodies, at the— *Oh God.* She wouldn't faint. She *wouldn't.*

As the bone-deep whine of the hyperdrive built around them, Cadan, his hand steady on her elbow, steered Elissa through the door the bounty hunter had opened, into another stretch of corridor and along a little way to where a side door stood. He thumbprinted it open, and, followed by Lin, they went through into a second corridor that ran parallel to the one they'd just been in, like its narrower cousin. In this smaller space the noise of the hyperdrive was magnified, a strong enough vibration to make Elissa's teeth chatter.

Cadan said something, but she couldn't hear. The vibration went through everything, raising every hair on her body, prickling over her scalp. Then there was that universe-shaking jerk, and they'd made the hop to . . . no, not to safety. Not this time. Not anymore.

"Listen," said Cadan. "I have to get back to the bridge, and I need the crew standing by." He paused. "Lissa?"

She looked up at him.

"Are you with me?"

She nodded.

"Okay. Look. You and Ms. May, you can go back to your cabin. Or you can come to the flight deck. You don't have to be alone. You've never seen hand-to-hand combat before, and that was—" He broke off suddenly, shutting his mouth hard on the words, his whole face rigid.

"Neither have you." She didn't realize she'd spoken out loud until she heard the words echo. She shouldn't have said it. He'd think it was a jab at him, the same kind of jab she'd made before. "I mean—"

"You're right." His eyes met hers and he swallowed. "We've done a hundred training exercises, though. At least I've been prepared for this." He swiped his hand across his forehead, and she realized his hair was sticking up, dark blond and damp with sweat. He'd killed someone. All she'd had to do was watch it happen, but he—he'd had to do it. And now he had the memory, a physical memory, lodged in his hand and arm muscles, of what it had been like to break bone, to smash a man's nose hard enough to drive it back into his brain. How could you prepare for something like that?

He brought his hand down, and she saw him pull himself together, straighten his shoulders, ready to deal with the next crisis. "Lis, I'm sorry. I have to get to the bridge."

"We'll come too." She said it without thinking any further, without checking with Lin to see if she agreed.

Once they were both hurrying after Cadan as he strode up the corridor, Elissa glanced at her sister. Lin's face was pale and tight, a bruise darkening on her cheek.

"You got hurt? Your cheek."

Lin blinked. "I don't know. I—oh, the men pushed me out of the way when that guy—Markus—came up from behind. I hit my face, I think."

"You don't want to go back to the cabin?"

"*No.*" Lin spoke vehemently. "I want to know what's happening."

Elissa dropped her voice, although Cadan, striding fast, was much farther ahead now. "I think we need to. Those men . . ."

Lin dropped her voice too, as low as a whisper. "They weren't just pirates, were they." The tone of her voice made the words not a question.

"Bounty hunters, I think—no, I mean, I'm sure."

Lin's eyes met hers. *They've sent them after us?* hovered, unspoken, in the air.

Elissa nodded, then put her hand out to grasp Lin's. Lin's fingers were ice cold. They hurried after Cadan, unspeaking, hands tightly clasped.

On the bridge Stewart sat at the controls. He didn't take his eyes off the screens—or his hands from the keyboard and control panel—as they entered.

Cadan was across the platform in three strides. "Status, Stew."

"No tail so far. External damage at three percent, auto-repair taking place. I'm running the enviro-scan."

Cadan slid into his seat, tapped a screen to bring up a display. "These are the coordinates?"

"Yes. I did a basic-distance hop—"

"Do you think that's enough?"

"I . . ." Stewart hesitated.

"No, don't think about it. Just answer."

"No, then." Elissa caught a glimpse of Stewart's face, set in anxious lines, as he turned a little toward Cadan. "They shouldn't have caught up with us so quickly, Cay. It doesn't make sense."

"Just my thought. Keep the scan open. I'm taking her into a longer hop."

"*Now?*"

"Before they catch up with us again? Yes, now." He eased the hyperdrive lever back, his other hand flickering over the controls; once again the noise of the hyperdrive built and built, shivering under Elissa's fingernails, tickling the insides of her ears. She found her gaze clinging to the quick, deft movements of Cadan's hands, and with the gathering buzz of the hyperdrive came a sensation of relief, of safety. He'd been super well trained, was top in his class. *He knows what he's doing. He'll keep us out of danger long enough for us to escape.*

A flicker of a thought came: *I always thought he was so arrogant, so pleased with himself. Maybe it's not exactly arrogance— maybe it's just that he's really good at what he's doing.*

Cadan's hand moved on the controls. Elissa's thoughts

fled. She braced herself, one hand gripping Lin's, the other tight on the rail.

At the very last moment, a fraction of a second before the screens would go dark, before the massive jerk that would take them into hyperspeed, something jumped on one of Stewart's screens. There was a sound like a dull thud.

"They're here! They—"

But at that point the shriek of hyperspeed rose around them, the screens blinked out, and they'd made the hop.

Coming out of hyperspeed was different from before. The ship jerked as she reached her destination, then jerked again, as if something had damaged her balance. The screens flashed first blankly white, then dark, then began to scroll information that looked as if it were moving even faster than before, surely too fast for even Cadan and Stewart to read.

"Cadan, they got us. They hit us." Stewart's voice was panicky. "Damage up to seven percent. And the shields—I can't get them back up. The shields aren't coming fast enough."

"Don't waste the energy. We're taking another hop." He turned his head a tiny bit, not enough to see the twins, just enough so that Elissa glimpsed his profile. "Lissa, are you two strapped in?"

Elissa grabbed for the straps. "We are now."

"Okay. Keep the scan open, Stew. Forget about the shields."

He took the ship into another hop—and into another bad, jerky exit, the screens flickering from dark to light to dark.

Stewart glanced up at the screen and swore between his teeth. "The coordinates are off."

"I know. She's falling short."

"Because of the damage?"

"I don't know," Cadan said curtly, one hand on the

controls, one hand pulling information down across yet another screen.

"Damage is still at seven percent. Going into hyperspeed again so soon—the auto-repair hasn't had a chance. Can we risk another hop?"

"We have to. We have to get farther away. If they catch up with us now, with the ship damaged and our shields down—" Cadan bit the words off and forced the ship back into hyperspeed.

This time they came out of hyperspeed not just clumsily, but with a clash, a shriek of tearing metal. For an instant every warning light around the whole flight deck went to red.

"Something's wrong," said Lin. Elissa shot a look at her. Lin's eyes were glazed, distant, as if she were not seeing the flight deck but instead focusing on something somewhere else. *The electrical system inside the ship? She can control electricity—can she see it too?* Elissa looked back at where Cadan sat, her mouth twisting wryly. *Not that it takes freaking electrokinesis to tell that something's wrong.*

Cadan eased the hyperdrive control back into place, reached up to clear a screen of the frantically scrolling information, and pulled up what looked like a view of some part of the outside of the ship. Elissa heard his breath go in a short gasp.

What is it? What's he looking at?

Then the picture resolved itself and she realized what it was.

In that first moment of going into hyperdrive, when the *Phoenix*'s shields had been down, the ship had taken a hit. A hole gaped in her side, the metal peeled back in ragged shreds like paper.

Without speaking, Cadan threw open another screen—an inside view of the damage. Elissa could see that the automatic repair Stewart had mentioned was in process. The adjacent chambers were already sealed off, and spider-bots were swarming out onto the *Phoenix*'s hull to drag the edges of the smart-metal back together so it could begin the process of repairing itself.

But all the same, looking at it, Elissa felt sick. With damage like that, no wonder the *Phoenix* hadn't handled hyperspeed well. Her balance would be affected, her fuel efficiency impaired. A hole like that—even with the next-door chambers sealing themselves, she'd have hemorrhaged gallons of precious oxygen out into space. And if they were attacked again before the auto-repair was complete, Cadan wouldn't dare take her back into hyperspeed. That sort of weakness, under the stresses of hyperspeed—it could tear the whole ship open.

There are sixteen crew members on this ship. They could all die. Cadan, Markus, the others—they could have already been killed, fighting the bounty hunters. All the air seemed to leave her lungs, and she bowed over the rail, trying to steady her breathing. *Because of us. Because I lied to Cadan and took advantage of him and got us onto his ship.*

The familiar defense rose to clamor within her. *What else was I supposed to do? Lin has no one—no one but me to help her.* But it didn't carry the same force as before. She was bound to help Lin, bound by guilt and the beginning of a bond she hadn't expected and didn't yet understand. But was even Lin worth the lives of sixteen other people?

"What in God's name is going on?" The new tone in Cadan's voice snapped her head guiltily up. But he wasn't talking to her. He'd spoken without looking up, his attention focused on the controls, working on getting the shields back up to full strength, while Stewart was again running the environment scan to check for hostile craft.

"Tracking us like that—they should never have been able to do that."

"The hop I made?" said Stewart. "If it was too short . . ."

"No. Yes, it turned out to be too short, but it shouldn't have been. You made a standard defensive hop—it took us plenty far away to be out of range of tracking beams. But they caught up so fast, they must have locked onto our signal within minutes. *Nothing* can do that, not once the ship's gone into hyperspeed."

"They couldn't have hacked into SFI?"

Cadan laughed, a short, unhappy sound. "I'm about ready to believe even that—or I would be, if we hadn't had it drilled into us it was all but impossible." He rubbed the back of his arm down over his face. "But nothing else makes sense either. They got through our defenses to jam our shields, they tracked us through hyperspeed—*twice*—they knew where the passenger—" He stopped dead. Even his hands, for just a second, froze on the controls. "Lissa?"

Her stomach turned over. "Yes."

"You felt the impact when they blasted our air lock?"

"Yes."

"How soon after that were they at your cabin?"

She didn't need to think back to remember those frantic moments between the sound of the alarm and the men bursting through the door. "Really quickly."

"Five minutes?"

"Less."

"Yes." He was speaking to Stewart once more. "They were after the passengers, that's obvious. But they knew exactly where to go to reach them—and more importantly, they knew exactly where to hit the ship, close enough to gain access as fast as possible, but not close enough to risk hitting the girls themselves." He scrubbed his sleeve across his face again. "I can only think of one explanation." His voice was heavy, as if he had to drag the words out, force himself to say them. "They're being fed information about the ship. Stew, we're going to have to start asking questions of the crew."

"No." Stewart's voice jumped, suddenly loud. "Cay, they're handpicked, a hundred percent loyal. You can't—"

Cadan was done with the controls. He turned fully to face Stewart now, his mouth set grimly. "What else can I think? God knows, if I could think of another answer . . ."

"Cadan, this is *SFI crew* you're talking about!"

"I *know*." For the first time Elissa could hear the strain in Cadan's words. "Stew, you're going to have to help me think this through."

"In front of *them*?"

Elissa jumped. Sudden, real anger had sprung into Stewart's voice.

"Where the hell is your loyalty?" he said. "You want us to—"

"My loyalty's not in question!" Cadan's voice was raised now as well. "I have everyone's safety to think about. I can't afford to be sentimental."

"*Sentimental?* That's what you're calling it? Fine, if loyalty isn't enough, you might remember your damn protocol. You seriously want to talk about which of your crew is in league with bounty hunters in front of *civilian passengers*?"

Cadan, his expression exasperated, on the edge of anger, had been opening his mouth to say something else, but at that he broke off and shut it with a snap. "Okay," he said after a moment. "You're right. I apologize. Lis"—he turned in his seat—"I'm sorry, you'll have to excuse us. I . . ." He looked as if he were going to try to sum everything up for her, but in the end he just gave a hopeless, all-encompassing gesture.

His eyes had bags under them, she noticed suddenly, and there was a bruise darkening on his wrist and around the base of his thumb. A long, ragged scrape running up over his jawline and across his cheek showed where a knife had caught him—way too close to his throat and left eye for her to be able to look at it without her whole body clenching against the thought of what could have happened. *Because of us. Because of me.*

It was worse than the physical marks on him, though. For the first time she could remember, he looked out of his depth, as if his well-trained world had turned on him, growing teeth, snatching him by the scruff of his neck, shaking him while he dangled, helpless and afraid.

There was nothing she could do to help. Nothing except keep out of his way and let him do his job.

She unsnapped the safety harness. "It's okay," she said. "We'll go."

"Not to your cabin. The captain's quarters are just below here. If I give you the override code, can you remember it?" He rattled it off, too long for Elissa to keep track of, but Lin, stepping out of her safety harness, nodded.

"I can remember it."

Cadan gave Lin a brief smile. "Thanks. Lissa—"

"Yes?"

"I can't give you any reassurances of safety this time. All I can say is that we'll do everything possible to keep you and Ms. May out of danger. You have my word on that."

His eyes were too intent on hers. A sudden unease prickled through her. Part guilt, part embarrassment, part something else—something like the hero worship she'd once felt for him, that she was way too old to feel now. "The captain's word?" she said, her voice coming out even more flippant than she'd meant it.

Cadan's face didn't change. He might as well not have recognized the note of not-quite-intended mockery in her voice.

"No," he said. "Just mine."

ELEVEN

ELEVEN

THE CAPTAIN'S quarters turned out to be a suite of three rooms opening off a narrow slip of an entrance lobby. The bedroom and shower room were only a little bigger than the twins' cabin, but the suite included a tiny sitting room with a drinks machine, armchairs that unfolded from the wall, and a table that could sink into the floor.

Lin climbed into a chair, bringing her legs close up to her chest and wrapping her arms around them. She looked beaten and exhausted, the bruise horribly vivid on her cheek.

Elissa dialed them hot chocolate from the machine. Her stomach was churning, her hands clumsy as she bent to set the cups on the table. She seemed to have made a decision— or rather, in that moment when Cadan's eyes had met hers, a decision had made itself. And now she knew what she had to say, but the words kept sticking on her tongue.

Lin interrupted the tumble of Elissa's thoughts. "I think something's wrong with their hyperdrive."

"Wrong with it? How can you tell?"

Lin shrugged. "When they did those last two hops, I could feel something wrong with the electrical currents. Like they weren't connecting properly . . . like they kept cutting out. Lissa, we can't stay on this ship. We have to get them to take us somewhere else. If their hyperdrive dies and those men—bounty hunters—catch up . . ."

Elissa straightened. She couldn't put it off any longer. "Lin."

"What?" Lin had picked up her cup. She looked at Elissa over the rim.

"We have to tell him what's going on."

"*What?*" The same word, but everything else—Lin's expression, the sudden tension in her body, the tone of her voice—had changed.

Elissa folded her arms across her body, holding herself steady. "We have to tell Cadan what's happening. We have to tell him who's after us, that they've probably got SFI's help. We have to tell him who you are."

Lin put the cup down on the table. When she straightened and looked back at Elissa, her eyes were blazing. Elissa couldn't help flinching. She'd known Lin wouldn't like it, had known she'd argue, but she hadn't been quite prepared for a look of such black rage.

"I'm sorry," she said. "He has to know. All these things are happening and he's promising to protect us, and it's not fair—he doesn't even know why. If we tell him the truth, ask him for help—"

Lin interrupted her. "You *never learn*." She spat the words out.

"What? What do you mean?"

"You never *learn*. You're doing it *again*. You make all that fuss about what I have to do to get us out of places, and then you just go and get us back into them!"

Elissa stared at her, bewildered. "What do you mean, I get us back into them?"

Lin's voice rose. "Calling your father! Telling your parents! I *told* you not to, I *said* they wouldn't help. And you did it *anyway*."

"Okay. I understand. But, Lin, listen. It's not like that this time. I was wrong—completely wrong, I know, and I'm really sorry. But this time—honestly, I've thought about it. Cadan's not like my parents. My mother's always just wanted me to fit in, and my dad, he never interferes—"

"And Cadan's the *SFI poster boy*." For a moment Elissa frowned at the phrase, recognizing it, then she realized Lin was echoing something she'd said, even mimicking the tone she'd said it in. "You think telling him it's *SFI* who's after us is going to keep us safe? He'll hand us over, you said so!"

"I don't think he will. He's—I think he's changed from how he used to be. You can see—he's having to think through stuff. He's facing really hard decisions—"

"No, he's *not*!" Lin's voice went up to a shriek. "He's not making any decisions! He's doing everything by protocol. He *said* so. You *heard* him."

"I *know* that. But he's not doing it blindly. God, *Lin*, you're not listening to me—"

"I listened last time! I let you call your father, and we ended up nearly getting caught! And then you blamed me—you blamed me for doing what I had to do and getting us out of there. You said you'd hate me if I did it again."

"That's *not* what I said. Lin, that's not fair."

But Lin was beyond listening. She was trembling, her fists

clenched, a hot flush around her eyes and on her cheekbones. "No, what *you* keep doing isn't fair. You don't know what it's like to grow up knowing you're meant to be subhuman, a spare copy of the person who's real. *You* just jump into trusting everybody, you think it's okay to ask them to help you. It's not. It's *not*. You can only do it because everyone knows you're human—legally, officially human—and you know you're safe. I can't do that. I don't count. You have *no idea—*"

Heat swept through Elissa. *No idea? I have no idea about not being able to trust people?* She opened her mouth to snap back—and stopped. In front of Lin on the low table, steam was rising in clouds from the two cups of hot chocolate—more steam than had risen from them when they were fresh out of the machine. As Elissa stared, bewildered, the dark liquid began to bubble, jumping furiously as if it had been placed on direct heat. As if the electrics that folded and unfolded the table had turned into a heating pad, as if someone— *Oh*. Elissa was suddenly aware that the heat in her veins, in the palms of her hands, was not just anger, hers *or* Lin's. It was the building power she'd felt before—the power that belonged not to her but to Lin.

She found that she, like Lin, was shaking. Her teeth chattered in a sudden spasm, and in order to talk she had to bite them together, speak through them. "What are you doing?"

Lin's eyes, dark and blank with fury, met hers. "Making you pay attention. You're not to tell him. *You're not to*, do you hear me?"

The chocolate bubbled more violently. Scalding liquid leapt over the sides of the cups to splash onto the table. Elissa curled her fingers up into her palms, feeling the bite of her nails. "What if I say I'm going to anyway?"

A spark cracked from the metal corner of the table. "Don't

think I won't do it, Lissa. Don't think I won't use my power to make you listen."

Their eyes held. Elissa stopped shaking. Something went through her, stiffening her spine, lifting her head upright—something that after a second she recognized as unyielding, ice-cold rage.

"Fine," she said. "Go ahead."

Lin's hands clenched tighter. "I will! I'll—"

"Electrocute me? Burn me? Like I said, *go ahead*."

A new kind of panic shone in Lin's eyes. "Lissa, you have to listen—"

"Listen to someone who's threatening me? I don't think so!"

"Lissa . . ." The furious bubbling of the boiling hot chocolate started to diminish. The steam thinned, moving in languid curls away into the air. "I wasn't really going to do it. I just— I . . ." Lin's flush of anger drained away, but her eyes were still shiny with panic.

And Elissa was still frost-cold, furious in a way she would have thought would make her incoherent but that instead made her words come out with an ice-hard emphasis. "You *never* threaten me," she said, her gaze holding Lin's. "Never again, do you hear?"

"I'm sorry. I—you're not listening, and I'm scared you're—"

"*It doesn't matter*. You *don't do* that. It's not how relationships work—you don't threaten people to get them to do what you want."

For an instant, anger snapped through the fear and anxiety in Lin's eyes. "You mean *real humans* don't do it."

Elissa made a noise of contempt. "Please. 'Real humans' do it all the time. Terrorists. Dictators. Pirates and bullies and criminals. But *we* don't. I don't, and you don't either."

Lin bit her lip. "Okay. All right. I'm sorry. But, Lissa, you have to listen—"

"No. *You* have to listen to *me*. All that time we were linked, did you not pay any attention to what was going on in my life?"

"I said, it was only flashes. You never pulled me right in like I did with you."

"So you really think I jump into trusting everyone?"

"I don't mean it's because you're stupid or anything," Lin said anxiously. "It's because you're legally human—you know you can—"

"No, I *don't*." Within her the icy anger shivered and broke apart, splintering all through her in a shower of tiny points of pain. "I don't trust *anyone*. Not since the symptoms started. I haven't trusted anyone apart from my parents for years."

"You did trust them, though—"

"And now I don't! I don't trust anyone! The symptoms showed me I couldn't trust my friends, and finding you showed me I couldn't trust my parents or the doctors or the police of *my own planet*. I don't trust *anybody*, Lin!" She stopped, finding that her hands were trembling again. In her anger she wanted to leave it at that, throwing the words at Lin as if they were weapons, letting her know that because of her, Elissa had lost everything and gained nothing in return. But it wouldn't be true, and it wasn't fair to give Lin less than the truth.

She took a breath. "Except you," she said. "I trust you."

Lin's head came up, and her face was furious all over again. "You don't. You think I didn't see how you looked at me when I caught up with you in that playground? You think I've never been looked at as if people don't know whether to be scared or disgusted—you think I can't recognize it when you do the same?"

Shame swept across Elissa. Shame and guilt. *I hoped she didn't know. I hoped she couldn't tell what I was thinking back then.*

Well, I wanted honesty, didn't I?

"Okay," she said. "Yes, back then, in that playground, and in the pod-motel, and before, when I came to find you—*yes*, I was scared. I didn't know what you wanted, I didn't know what you were like, and I was scared of you. Now I'm not."

"But you don't *trust* me," Lin said mulishly. "You don't. You keep thinking I'm going to hurt someone."

"Well, for goodness' sake, you keep *acting* like you're going to hurt someone!" Lin opened her mouth to reply, but Elissa kept talking, bulldozing over her, determined to make her understand. "You don't trust *yourself* not to hurt someone. You said so, back on Sekoia, so don't go blaming me for thinking the same thing."

"Then what do you even mean? You keep saying how you don't trust me, and then you say you do, and it doesn't make any sense, Lissa! If you hate me and you just want to get rid of me, then just say so! Just say so and I—"

"Oh my God!" All Elissa's patience slipped, and she heard her voice go loud, out of control. "Will you listen to what I'm trying to say? It's not that I trust you not to hurt *anyone*. I trust you not to hurt *me*!"

Lin stopped dead. They stared at each other across the table, across the no-longer-steaming cups.

Elissa took another breath, forcing her hands to stop shaking. "I knew you weren't going to use your electrokinesis on me," she said. "I knew it was just a threat. And that's why you can't do it. Well, you can't do it to anyone, but you especially can't do it to me. Because you *don't threaten the people who trust you.*"

Silence stretched out between them. Silence filled with faint background noises—the quiet hum of machinery, the distant vibration that might be the continuing auto-repair of the damaged ship.

"I—" Lin started, then broke off. "Okay."

Her face seemed naked, as vulnerable as a child's. Elissa had to fight the impulse to cross her arms and break eye contact. She wasn't used to this. For years she'd had to expose so much about herself—all the weird physical and mental symptoms—to doctors, to her parents. But her *feelings*—she'd kept them locked away, private beyond private. She'd said that she'd trusted her parents, and it was true. But she'd never shared her feelings with them. *Maybe it's not just Lin who doesn't have practice in how relationships work.*

Elissa cleared her throat. "I won't hate you," she said. "Whatever you do, I won't end up hating you."

Lin's eyes snapped wider. "If I— You said if I killed someone—"

"Even then." The words hung in the air, and suddenly they were too scary not to qualify. "I mean, it's not *okay* if you kill someone. And you *can't*—and if you do I'll be really, really upset—and you really *can't*." She couldn't think of words that expressed the gravity of what she was trying to say. She stopped, frustrated and a little freaked out by what she'd kind of given Lin permission to do, and Lin giggled.

"It's okay. I understand." Lin hesitated. "Thank you."

"Oh—" Elissa waved her hands, dismissing the issue. "It's not a thank-you thing. I mean, it's not some *decision*. I just—I realized—" She checked herself, determined to ignore her out-of-practice-with-all-this-stuff discomfort, determined to say it clearly. "Whatever you do, it doesn't make any difference."

The silence stretched out again. Elissa took a breath. There was something else she had to say, something else she had to stick to.

"I have to tell Cadan," she said. "He's trying to help us, and his whole crew is in danger, and he's having to think that there might be a traitor among them. It's not fair. I have to tell him."

"I don't want you to." Lin's voice shook.

"I know." Elissa forced herself to hold her sister's gaze. "I'm scared too. But, Lin, there's sixteen other people on this ship. I can put *myself* in danger for you. But I can't do it to sixteen other people. At least—God, I've *already* put them in danger, but I have to at least let them know what they're dealing with."

"And you think he'll still help us?"

"Yes."

"Even though he'll be acting against the government?"

Elissa bit her thumbnail. That was the fear, wasn't it? That was the risk. That she'd tell him, and then she'd have to watch while his expression turned to shock and distaste. *You broke the law, Elissa? You're on the run from our own planet's police? You're using property that's been confiscated from criminals?* And the money—*oh God*, the fake money she'd given him.

But at the same time she remembered the argument he'd had with Stewart. Stewart couldn't believe they had a traitor on board—*they're handpicked*, he'd said, as if SFI's judgment were all the guarantee needed. But Cadan—Cadan might want things to be black and white, but he knew they couldn't always be that way. He knew that SFI crew could be in league with pirates. He knew SFI wasn't infallible.

And he promised to keep us safe.

She looked steadily at Lin. "Yes," she said. "He does stick to the rules, because it's worth it, and because he agrees with them. Like the rule not to communicate with pirates? You could see, he was sticking to the protocol because it works, because it makes sense. But if there's a rule he doesn't agree with—if he thinks it's wrong—I don't think he'll feel bound to keep to that, too."

"You don't think."

"I can't know. Not until I do it. But yes."

A long pause, then Lin drew herself up, straightened her shoulders. "Okay," she said. "You think he'll break rules he thinks are wrong. Then let's convince him this one's wrong."

The door slid open, the quiet sound making them both jump. Cadan came in.

His eyes went straight to Elissa. "I need a word."

Her heart thumped. "We were coming to see you. We—"

"No." His voice was polite but definite. "Just you, Elissa. I need a word with just you."

Her heart thumped again, knocking some of the breath from her lungs. Now it came to it, admitting to the lies she'd told him, trying to explain who—*what*—Lin really was . . . *Oh, I don't want to.*

Cadan had his hand on the door, preventing it from closing. "Elissa."

"I'm coming." She cast one look at Lin, then went out of the tiny sitting room into the even tinier entrance lobby.

Cadan followed her. As the door clamped shut behind

him, he spoke immediately, with no preamble. "I have to ask, Elissa. Before I destroy my crew's morale by asking them. Is it Lynette?"

For a moment she just stared at him, blank. Then what he was asking registered. "*No*. No, Cadan. Lin's not in league with the pirates. No, I swear."

"You're sure, right? Her story—her boyfriend breaking up with her, needing to go home right away—it's not just something she's told you? You know for a fact that it's true?"

Oh God. Elissa's hands were shaking. She shoved them into her pockets. "Cadan, listen. I have to tell you something."

"Lis, I'm sorry, I don't have time. Whatever it is, it'll have to wait. Please, just tell me if Lynette's a danger to my ship."

In her pockets Elissa's hands clenched. She gulped in one last too-shallow breath and forced herself to meet his eyes. "We both are," she said. "The pirates—I'm pretty sure they're bounty hunters. They're coming after us."

She stopped there automatically, expecting him to say *What?* or *Why?* But he didn't. He neither moved nor spoke, waiting expressionless for her to give him the rest of the information.

She dragged in another breath and told him. Told him what Lin was, told him how she'd found her, about how they'd both become fugitives. About the news alert, the chase in the mall, about how her father had told her to run.

Cadan's expression didn't change. He watched her as she told him everything that had happened over the last three days, listening to her voice as it stumbled over the details— the wound at the back of Lin's head, Elissa's own conviction that if she was caught, the doctors meant to burn the link out from her brain.

She reached the end of her account and paused, but he didn't say anything, and after a nervously silent moment she found herself talking again, repeating things she'd already told him, backtracking over justifications for what she'd done, using the words to fill the space and the silence, because anything was better than just waiting for him to speak, waiting for him to hate her—

"Okay," he said, cutting her off, and she stopped, feeling sick, unable to look at him, cringing from the expression she didn't want to see on his face. "You're saying, back home, it was law enforcement agents chasing you?"

She nodded. "My—my mother called them, and I saw the symbol on their flyer."

"And at the mall as well?"

"Yes."

"You're sure? You saw the symbol there, too?"

"Yes—" She broke off. She hadn't questioned that they were Sekoian law enforcement, but now as she looked back at that twenty minutes' blur of flight and terror, she couldn't remember if she'd even seen the flyers clearly enough to see their symbols. "I—they must have been. That's who was after us—after Lin. It's some kind of secret government facility—"

"Elissa." His voice was very calm, and it was that calmness that made her throat close up. He didn't believe her. He was going to insist she'd gotten it wrong, that the right thing to do was give Lin up. *I was wrong. Oh God, I told Lin we could trust him and I was wrong again. I've thrown her into danger again, and all for nothing.*

She looked at him, cold with despair.

"Elissa, it can't really be government agents, you know that. The Sekoian government would never be involved in something like this. And as for thinking SFI is helping bounty hunters track the *Phoenix*, come on, now!"

"Then who *else* would it be? The place she was in—the facility—it's huge, it's completely equipped."

"It's something pretty big," said Cadan. "You've got that right, I'm sure. Equipment, money—"

"Cadan, the *doctor* was involved!"

"Elissa, this is *illegal*. This has *nothing* to do with any legitimate government." He looked steadily at her, full of experience and expertise and the complete, unshakable assurance that he was right. The look he'd been giving her for years. The look that had made her hate him.

She didn't have the energy to hate him now. She let herself slump back against the lobby wall, miserable and defeated. "Please," she said. "Don't hand us over. Don't take us back. If there's just another planet you can drop us on—any kind, it doesn't matter, even if it's completely third-grade—"

His eyebrows went up. "Drop you on a third-grade planet? What do you take me for?"

Okay, maybe she did have enough energy to hate him. "If you're going to hand us over to those butchers who carved a hole in her skull, you don't want to know what I freaking take you for! God, Cadan, for *once* can't you just accept I might know what I'm talking about?"

"And for once can't you listen to me instead of reacting to what you think I'm saying?" Cadan snapped. "For God's sake, Elissa, I'm not going to 'hand you over' to anyone. Just because I don't agree with your interpretation of who's doing it doesn't mean I'm going to refuse to help you!"

For a moment she stared into angry blue eyes, then her own gaze dropped. As easy as that? Shame swept over her, scalding hot. *If I'd asked him for help back on Sekoia, the way I was going to ask Bruce . . . would he have helped us then? Lying to him, cheating him—did I even need to do it?*

"So," said Cadan. His voice was still clipped, impatient. "You and Lynette—Lin—are both fugitives from some very powerful organization. One that, given that they are tracking us somehow, obviously has access to some very high-quality tech."

"It's the government, honestly. I just *know* it is."

"I can't accept that, Elissa." She wasn't looking at him, but she sensed him flick a glance at her, and his voice took on the heavy tone of enforced patience. "I'm sorry, it simply makes no sense. But whoever they are, I can well believe they've accessed technology that has no place outside official government use. Even with that, though, we took a long enough hop that they'll have hard work catching up with us. Whatever their hyperdrives are like, they won't be up to the speed of ours. We're going to land on the nearest planet available and make some repairs so we can safely start using it again."

But if they're from SFI . . . It was no use. Even if she kept arguing, she wasn't going to convince him, and as long as he was going to help her and Lin anyway, there was no point freaking out about it now.

"Lissa."

She looked up.

"I don't think you've got all the facts right," Cadan said, "but you've dealt with a hell of a lot in an incredibly short space of time." He smiled at her, a tiny lift of the corner of his mouth. "Color me impressed."

She wasn't thirteen anymore. It didn't matter that she'd

impressed him, that he was smiling at her with more approval in his face than she'd seen in years. It didn't *matter*. But all the same she found herself responding to him, her own mouth relaxing into a smile.

The look of helplessness, of the fear of being out of control, had gone from his face. He was dealing with a situation that, while it might be unexpected, unwelcome—and just as dangerous as it had been before—didn't make him feel out of his depth. It was a crisis, but, after all, he was trained to deal with crises.

He turned briskly to the door. "I have to get back to the bridge and explain this to Stew. Get Lynette—Lin—and come up too. I'd like to get a fuller picture of the story." He half-raised his hand to open the door, then stopped. "Lissa?"

"Yes?"

"Do I have all the details I need for now? I realize there will be all kinds of minor things you haven't been able to tell me yet, but what you have told me, is that basically it? There's nothing else I should know?"

There were. Two things. Two things she hadn't been able to bring herself to say during the account she'd given him. One of which he definitely needed to know. One of which . . . *he doesn't. He doesn't have to know it, not now, not yet, not while he's got all this to deal with. He's probably worked it out for himself already anyway. And if he hasn't, and I tell him, and I have to watch his face change . . .*

"There's one thing," she said.

"Okay." He took his hand down from the door panel and stood, watching her, waiting.

It was hard to say. It felt like a betrayal of Lin, unfairly exposing her to someone who couldn't understand the way she'd grown up, didn't understand the fear she was living with still.

"It's Lin," Elissa said. "I'm afraid they've . . . damaged her, kind of. The electrokinesis—it's not like she *can't* control it, but she panics sometimes, and then she doesn't see why she *should* control it if it will help her—or me—escape."

"That's what you were afraid of, on the bridge."

"Yes."

"Okay." He nodded, frowning, assimilating the new information. *Crisis-management mode,* Elissa thought. It would take an awful lot to shake him right now. *I should tell him. I should tell him and then it'll be done and he'll deal with it and then—*

"Cadan."

He looked at her.

"There's another thing."

"Okay." This time something in her expression must have caught at him. His eyes flickered with something like apprehension. "Go on."

"When we came on board ship, the money we paid you . . ."

His face froze as her meaning hit him. "It was stolen."

She shook her head, shutting her eyes so she didn't have to look at him while she said it. "It was fake. The cards—they're not real. We can wipe our IDs off them, and as soon as we do—"

"The money will disappear." His voice was as heavy as lead.

She nodded, eyes screwed shut.

"And you knew that when you did it?"

"Yes." Her voice came out as a whisper.

"You didn't think to—" His voice jumped, anger sparking through it. "For God's sake, Elissa, have the decency to look at me! It didn't cross your mind to just *ask* me for help?"

She'd opened her eyes, but she couldn't meet his gaze. She

focused instead on the shiny silver bar on his uniform jacket. It winked in the lobby's overhead light, blurring a little at the edges. "That's why I was looking for Bruce."

"But once you found his full-scholarship buddy instead? Oh, don't bother. Money talks, right? And who am I to act like it's an insult? I took it, didn't I?"

She had nothing to say. He *had* taken it, the way she'd gambled on him doing. She'd known he needed money in a way that Bruce didn't . . . in a way that most of the cadets on the training course didn't. She'd known his weakness, and she'd used it.

His voice had hardened. "Did it even take an effort to lie to me? Or was that a foregone conclusion? It's not worth wasting the truth on someone like me, is it? Not when you can just throw some money at them and tell them to jump?"

Elissa bit her lip. She'd never heard him so angry—not with her, not with anyone. Like she'd told Lin, she'd known his family didn't have the money hers did, but she'd never realized he felt like this. And it wasn't fair, what he was saying to her. He *hadn't* offered to help her, he *had* done it for the money, so acting as if she'd deliberately insulted him was just unreasonable.

But even as she thought that, realization came to her. She'd dumped a major crisis on his shoulders, she'd put his ship and his crew and everything at risk, and he was dealing with it way better than she could ever have expected. But on top of all of that, he'd just found out she'd lied to and manipulated him, and he wasn't even any closer to paying off his debt to SFI.

There was anger in his voice, lending every word an edge

sharp enough to cut. But there was also a whole mess of disappointment and hurt. And whether it was fair or not for him to blame her, she had created it.

She bit her lip harder, then forced herself to meet his eyes. They met hers with a shock like a blow that she felt in the pit of her stomach. "It did take an effort," she said. "I hated lying to you, and I felt really bad about the money. I was desperate, that's all. I was only going to tell Bruce the truth 'cause Lin's his sister too. But with everyone else—anyone else I might have found to help me—all I had was the money. And"—she swallowed—"and I'm sorry."

He looked away. For a moment she thought he was going to ignore her apology, but then he lifted one shoulder in a shrug that was a sort-of acknowledgment. "Okay."

"Cadan—" A couple of days ago she'd have been able to tell herself she didn't care if he hated her. She couldn't do that anymore.

He hit the door panel to open the door. "It's okay. Just . . . give me a few minutes to process it, all right? Bring Lin up to the bridge—she can help me explain this to Stew." He paused a minute, head down. "I can't even imagine what he's going to say."

TWELVE

TO BEGIN WITH, Stewart said nothing. He sat silently while Cadan repeated what Elissa had told him, his gaze moving between both sisters, although it remained longer on Lin. Taking in, Elissa assumed, the similarities they'd done their best to hide. His face didn't stay as blank as Cadan's had, but although she saw his lips tighten, saw a muscle jump in his jaw, she didn't know him well enough to be able to read his expression. *He's been really nice to us—mostly me, but Lin, too. And it was Cadan I lied to, and he doesn't hate me—I don't think—so there's no reason for Stewart to . . .*

But as he continued to sit there, unspeaking, listening to what Cadan was saying, tension wound itself tightly inside her. *If he wants to turn us in, if he won't even believe as much of the story as Cadan did . . .*

"That's the situation as far as I have it," Cadan finished. "Elissa is convinced it's actually the Sekoian government involved in this, but I strongly disagree. However, it's more than obvious that *whoever's* behind it has got some high-up contacts and some pretty sophisticated tracking technology. It's also more than obvious that Lissa and Lin need our help. I'm thinking our best bet, once we've patched up the *Phoenix*, is to get them to the Interplanetary League's headquarters on Sanctuary so they can claim refugee status under the Humane Treatment Act. It's going to take some major evasive action, if what's been happening so far is anything to go by, and we'll have to use the hyperdrive more than I like, to ensure we're not in one place long enough for anyone to get a lock on us—"

Which was when Stewart spoke. He'd been staring at Elissa and Lin—mostly Lin—for the last minute, but at this his head snapped back toward Cadan. And now Elissa could read his expression. It was anger—sheer, incredulous anger.

"What the hell is wrong with you?" he said. "Have you gone freaking insane?"

"I have not." Cadan's voice was suddenly coldly polite. "If there's a flaw in my plan, then I suggest you let me know in a more reasoned manner."

"A *flaw* in your plan?" Stewart gave a bark of laughter. "By her own admission the girl's on the run with stolen government property, she's lied her way onto our ship, and you're planning on *helping* her? I would say that's a pretty big freaking flaw!"

"Hang on a moment there," said Cadan. "Did you listen to what I was telling you?"

"I listened." Stewart pushed himself out of his seat so that he and Cadan were standing face-to-face across the safety rail. "I just couldn't believe you were really saying it. Sure, she's a pretty girl, but do you not get what she's asking of you?"

All at once there was a nasty twist to his voice, and Elissa flinched. Cadan didn't seem to have noticed, though. He was frowning, intent on what Stewart was saying, not the tone he was saying it in.

"You're saying—you seriously think she's right, it *is* government authorized?" Cadan asked.

Stewart made an impatient gesture. "I'm saying it could be. And if it is—God, Cadan, think about what you'd be doing if you helped her! Theft—*grand* theft, if the property's so valuable they're sending spaceships to get it back. You know how much clones cost, and they've only ever managed partial clones. And now we've got *this*." He jerked a nod at Lin. "As close as you can get to a full-body clone, God knows, *and* it's telepathic and electrokinetic. It could be a secret government weapon! We'll end up on treason and terrorism charges before we know it!"

"But"—Cadan gave his head a quick shake as if to clear it—"you can't think our government would be involved in something like that."

At the same time Lin said furiously, "I'm not a clone. I'm *me*."

Stewart flicked a glance at Lin, a glance that seemed to skate over her and move straight back to Cadan. She might as well not have spoken.

"I don't *know*, Cadan! What I'm saying is, if it is the government, you can't afford to go on the run with their property. Fine, we'll make for the Interplanetary League HQ, but for God's sake, going off-route without SFI's permission? At least send them a message that that's what you're doing."

"*No.*"

"No!"

Elissa and Lin spoke at once, their voices blending so that

for a moment Elissa didn't realize she was hearing her sister as well as herself.

"Please," she said. "Cadan, don't. You don't have to believe me, but please, please, just in case I *am* right—"

Stewart cut across anything Cadan might have been about to say. "Yeah, if you are right, then you're a thief, aren't you? Stop trying to make him feel guilty—stop trying to use him. This is his career here. And mine. And I'm not risking them for you and the freak double you stole."

Elissa stared at him, speechless for a moment. If she hadn't known this was the same pleasant young man who'd invited her to the flight deck, who'd flirted with her over the lunch table just a few hours ago, she'd have thought he'd been replaced by his own double. He wasn't even trying to understand what this was like for her and Lin—and the way he was talking about Lin, calling her "property," calling her "it," what was wrong with him? Why couldn't he see?

She tried to speak calmly. "You're not understanding. Lin's not a clone. She's my sister. My twin."

"Oh, for God's sake. Your *twin*? It's not even a real word."

"It *is* a real word. It means double—"

"Double. Yeah, like a—guess what?—*a clone.*"

"*Not* like a clone!" Her voice went shrill, and she forced it back into calmness. It was no good arguing with him. He just wasn't listening—it was too much for him to handle and he couldn't grasp it. *I couldn't grasp it at first, and I'd shared her thoughts.*

She tried another tactic. "Look," she said. "Like Cadan said, Lin and I are linked. For three years I felt what they were doing to her. I only got it secondhand, and it was the worst pain ever. That's what you'd be handing her over to. Please.

What does it *matter* if it's the government or someone else?"

"It matters because *we work for them*! Do you know how long we've trained just to get a chance at flying this ship for a pathetic four-day round-trip? Do you know what would happen to us if we helped you evade them?"

"Oh my God!" Elissa's calmness splintered into a million shards. "This is all about your *job*? This is Lin's *life*. Do you know what will happen to *her* if you make her go back? Why can't you grasp what we're telling you?"

A wave of color rose behind Stewart's freckles. He opened his mouth to say something, but Elissa overrode him. "You want to see what they did, your precious government you want to report us to?" She flung her hand out toward Lin. "Come show him. Come show him what they want you for."

Too late, as she saw the blankness hit Lin's face and freeze it still, Elissa realized what she was asking. She stared at her twin, a mute apology. *You have to show him. He has to know.*

For a moment Lin just looked back at her, frozen, not moving. Then she came forward to stand next to Cadan at the rail and turned, putting her hands up to lift the dyed-blond hair from the back of her neck.

"*What*? What am I supposed to be looking—" Stewart stopped. And Cadan took one step back, as if the floor had lurched under him.

The hole, neat and clean-edged, stood out against the pale skin at the back of Lin's neck. Elissa saw it more clearly this time, saw the details she hadn't seen before. Saw that although the flesh had healed around and inside it, it was shiny with scar tissue, the sort of scar tissue that came from burns, repeated over and over again.

"This is what they do to me," Lin said, her voice thin and

remote. "Twice a week since I was fourteen. This is what they keep me for. This is why they want me back."

After a long moment Cadan said, "What—what is it for?" His voice cracked as he spoke, and Stewart threw him an irritated look.

Lin made a little noise that would have sounded like a laugh if there'd been any real mirth in it. "They didn't tell us *that*."

"And it—" Cadan swallowed, then continued. "Lissa said it hurts?"

"Hurts?" Lin let her hair slide back over her neck, raised her head to look at him. "Yes, it hurts." Once again there was a sound like laughter in her voice, but with a note to it that made Elissa go cold.

"That's it," said Cadan. "I don't care if it is our own government behind it. I'm not letting them get hold of her, *whoever* they are."

"Then what?" Stewart's voice seemed to explode into the room. "You're going to go on the run, on the spaceship they own? Cadan, for God's sake think about this."

"*Think* about it? Take a look at her, Stewart! Look what they've done to her!"

"I saw, thanks." Stewart's voice dismissed the horrific wound, put it aside as something merely distasteful that didn't need to be mentioned. And that was when it fully hit Elissa.

Arguing with Stewart, trying to persuade him—even trying to get his pity for Lin—none of it was going to work. The moment he'd learned she was a Spare, something like a shutter had closed across his mind, cutting him off from the necessity of feeling anything toward her that he would feel for a legal human.

I didn't really think people would be able to do that. Everyone knows about partial clones—it makes sense for someone to see Lin and me together and think she could be a full-body clone. Human-based but not human. Not a person. But I thought that once people met her, once people knew that she was born the same as me—I didn't think anyone would be able to continue thinking of her like that.

She told me people would want her sent back, and I didn't believe her.

"And that's not the point," Stewart was saying to Cadan. "Aren't you forgetting something? You've got a crew of fifteen here. You're going to force us all on the run with you?" He came around the end of the rail. "You're the captain. You have duties to hold to. The crew didn't sign up for this."

"I know." Cadan's face was grim. "I've thought of that."

"Then what? What are you going to do? Force them to turn their careers to shit with you? Make them traitors too?"

"That's enough!" Color ran up into Cadan's face, a flush under his eyes, on his cheekbones. "I'm going to give them the choice, of course. They can stay with me, help me get the ship to Sanctuary—"

"Or what? What if they don't want that choice?"

Cadan's face drew itself into grimmer lines. "Then *Shuttlebug One* takes twenty."

"That's it? You're going to tip us out into the lifeboat and keep the *Phoenix* for your pet thief and her freak nonhuman clone?" The venom in his voice was clear now, and Elissa physically flinched, putting an automatically protective arm around Lin.

"I said that's enough," said Cadan, his voice like steel.

"Really? Enough? That's it, is it? Just like that? Four years, thrown away?"

Cadan opened his mouth to say something, then shut it.

He looked at Stewart for a long moment. Then, "If you want to look at it that way. Four years. Thrown away."

They stared at each other for a moment, then Stewart turned on his heel and walked off the bridge. His boots thumped briefly on the stairs, then he was gone.

Elissa didn't dare speak. She hardly dared look at Cadan. *Everything Stewart said—losing his career, committing treason . . . if it's too much, if Cadan decides it's not worth it . . .*

Cadan's hand was clenched, white on the rail. For a long moment he said nothing, just stared at where the barrier had slid shut behind Stewart. Then he looked away, visibly gathering himself.

"He'll come back," he said. "This has knocked him, and I told him the wrong way, but he's a good man. He'll see reason. He'll come back."

Elissa didn't reply. Cadan knew Stewart better than she did. For all she knew, he was right. But that venom in Stewart's voice, the way he'd instantly dismissed Lin as a clone, a *thing*, something that belonged to other people rather than herself . . . She thought Stewart *was* seeing reason, but it was his own reason, not Cadan's.

Cadan took a deep breath. "Okay. Now I have to speak to the crew. I won't ask you to leave—this is your concern now, after all. If you would sit over there?" He gestured to a couple of pull-down seats on the wall around the bridge.

As Elissa and Lin took the seats, Cadan threw open a com-channel and issued a crew-wide instruction to come to the flight deck. Then he paused for a minute, head down, hand braced on the console next to the com-channel switch.

Elissa watched him, wrung by helpless pity. *His career, that he's worked for since he was eleven. And he's not even hesitating.*

He's just doing one unpleasant task after another. The Cadan I used to know, the one so hung up on his career that he forgot how to be polite, he would never have done this.

Or would he? Was he always like this, and I just never noticed?

The door slid open. Cadan straightened, ready to face his crew.

He made it brief. Partly, Elissa guessed, because they didn't have time to waste, if they were to repair the ship and get back into another hyperspeed hop. Partly, maybe, for the sake of the crew themselves? But also—*oh, this must be awful for Cadan, right after Stewart's reaction, Stewart's accusations, having to explain himself all over again.*

"I have to do this," Cadan said at the end of the explanation, his voice flat. "I don't expect anyone to agree with me. I don't expect anyone to stay on board. *Shuttlebug One* is ready for evacuation, and the nearest planet with a Sekoian embassy is less than a twelve-hour flight. The shuttlebug will be leaving in the next half hour." He paused there, and Elissa saw him swallow before he continued. "Beyond that I can only offer my apologies. It has been my honor to serve as—" He stumbled. "To work with you all. If, one day, I can make reparation—" He got stuck again, and this time didn't recover.

They were watching him. Some of the faces did mirror Stewart's. Shock, disgust, anger. Some of them showed only discomfort—a desire to get out as quickly as they could, before their careers got dragged down with Cadan's. *It's not just a job—it's a life choice* was one of the SFI recruitment slogans, Elissa remembered. She hadn't really bought it—of *course* it was just a job—but now, watching Cadan's crew preparing to leave him, it looked as if it were, after all, literally true.

Cadan didn't speak again. He gestured instead, one of the universal, easy-to-read signs Elissa knew they used for signaling across distances outside the ship. *Proceed without me.*

Elissa looked away as the crew left. Trepidation prickled down her spine. *How will Cadan run this whole ship without his copilot and his crew?* But overriding that unease was a wrenching pity she knew she shouldn't show. *What must this be like for him, seeing his crew leave him? Knowing they—like Stewart—think of him as a traitor to his own government?*

She listened to the last pair of feet go down the steps, but she, Lin, and Cadan were not alone. Elissa looked up.

Three of the crew hadn't yet gone. Ivan the chef. Markus, who'd come earlier to the flight deck. A tall fair-haired woman, one of those who'd helped defeat the pirates.

Cadan cleared his throat. "You're free to go, all of you. I believe Mr. James will be coming with you, and he'll take charge of the shuttlebug. It'll be set for Charonial, of course, but if it needs piloting—"

Ivan gave the other crew members a glance. "Looks like we're staying, sir. To offer our services on the *Phoenix*."

"The *Phoenix*'s not going to need your services." Cadan's voice was flat, all expression ironed out of it. "I'm going to be right off-grid. I don't even have full plans yet—"

"We can see that." Ivan interrupted him. "I'm telling you, if there was anyone who looked as if he had *less* plans I wouldn't want to let him have charge of a ship at all, let alone two runaways."

The woman rolled her eyes. "Way to help his confidence." For the first time Elissa noticed her properly. She had very angular features and skin so pale it was almost translucent, both marking her out as not a native-born Sekoian.

"Wait," said Cadan. "What are you talking about? What are you doing?"

"We're staying." The woman gave him a brief smile. "We're staying to help."

Cadan's shoulders slumped. "You can't, Felicia. All of you. I explained. I'm making myself a fugitive, as well as Lissa and Lin. I don't even know how I'm going to do it—I'm going to be on the run from the bounty hunters. Possibly, if Lissa's right, even SFI themselves. The ship's damaged and we can't yet use the hyperdrive—"

"We know," Felicia said. "That's what we're helping with."

Cadan's eyes moved from her to the others, then back to her. He looked completely thrown, a million times more than he had been by Stewart's reaction. He'd braced himself to do this, to dismiss his crew and watch them leave, and now here were these crew members, determined to stay with him. Out of nowhere a thought crossed Elissa's mind. *Sometimes finding you can trust someone is as devastating as finding you can't.*

"But why?" he said. "I—look, I know you're supposed to treat me no different from a captain you've served with for years, but this is . . . You hardly know me. I haven't done anything to deserve your loyalty."

Ivan folded his gorilla arms across his chest, his expression deadpan. "You think you need to have gone through pilot school to have ethics of your own, Captain?"

"*No*. God, no. I just—"

Felicia laughed. "He's messing with you, Captain. Ivan, be nice."

The hint of a smile narrowed Ivan's eyes. "Nice? Who'd recognize me if I was nice?"

Markus had been standing near the entrance of the bridge,

arms folded. He'd been looking weirdly calm, and Elissa had wondered if he was as shocked as Stewart had been, if any minute he was going to explode with the same disgust the copilot had showed.

He moved now, a tiny jerk of a movement, and Elissa saw what she hadn't grasped before, that his fingers showed white and bloodless against the dark blue of his jacket, that his face was so tense, the skin seemed stretched taut over the bones beneath. Then he spoke, and she realized he wasn't calm. He was violently angry.

"*Why*, Captain?" he said, so much suppressed anger in his voice that it felt as if it would shatter something. "I would have thought the real question was *why not*?" He cast a glance around the bridge. "A crew of sixteen, and only four of us willing to stand against something like this? God, I *knew* it. I *said,* you start with the sliding moral scales, and you'll find you can justify every freaking obscene thing some insane scientist comes up with."

Felicia put a hand out. "Markus, this isn't the time—"

"Yeah, I *know.*" His jaw clenched, then he looked across at Cadan. "I've been protesting the cloning laws since I was sixteen," he said. "I'm in one of the groups that forced the interplanetary ban on continued research into full-body cloning. We've been asking for tighter laws on existing cloning for years. And some—some freaking megalomaniac sadists— they've chosen this way of getting around the ban?" He took a breath, looking as if he were going to continue, then shut his mouth hard, waiting for a second before speaking again. "All right. I'm done. I'm done."

"About time," said Ivan drily, and laughed when Markus threw him a knife-edged look. "Captain, you want more grandstanding, or you want us to get on with something?"

Cadan gave his head a shake as if to clear it. Then he straightened, his shoulders going back, snapping back into role. He sent Felicia and Ivan to oversee the evacuation, and Markus to run an extra safety check on *Shuttlebug Two*. Elissa knew it was against all sorts of safety protocol to deliberately leave a manned ship with only one lifeboat—the least Cadan could do was make doubly sure the one they had left was ready for emergency use.

She watched the crew as they left. Markus's jaw was still rigid, and Felicia had her lips pressed tightly together. And on each of their faces—Ivan's, too—was a look of set determination.

They weren't leaving. She didn't know if Ivan and Felicia were driven by the same feelings as Markus, or whether they had their own, different reasons for staying with a captain who was rebelling against SFI. But they'd heard the full story. They'd heard what Lin was, what Elissa had done, and they were staying. They weren't leaving. They were going to help.

Twenty minutes later Elissa watched in the viewscreen while the shuttlebug detached itself from the dock low on the *Phoenix*'s flank and dropped slowly away from the main ship. Its booster rockets flared. Cadan cleared the viewscreen, and the shuttlebug became no more than a steadily blinking dot on the enviro-scan.

He didn't speak, just moved his hand to the controls, taking the ship back up to speed. Lin leaned on the rail behind him, watching the numbers climb. Her face held none of the strain that Elissa knew showed in her own expression. It was as if knowing that they were, for the moment, safe had wiped the terror of the previous hours out of her head.

Elissa sat carefully out of the way, watching Cadan's hands on the controls, watching the side of his face that she could see. His face was as calm as Lin's, but calm as if, in his case, the strain had been not wiped away but deliberately pushed down until he had leisure to deal with it.

She'd learned to do something similar over the last three years, pushing away hurt she wasn't yet ready to look at. But she'd only managed it by shutting off completely, like the button-snails on the cliffs near her house that could draw themselves up smaller and smaller until they fit into the smooth flat shells that looked like buttons stuck to the cliff face. She'd never managed to withdraw and still remain as calmly competent, as focused, as Cadan was now.

If his last few years—all his time training—had come as smoothly, as easily as I'd thought they had, how did he learn to do that?

He'd set their course for the closest habitable body—not a planet but a moon, Syris II. The planet it orbited was not eligible to be terraformed, nor was its larger moon, but Syris II was in the second stage of the process, meaning that it would be bleak and inhospitable, but with breathable air and no immediate danger to human life.

They had to get somewhere they could repair the ship as quickly as possible, Elissa knew that. But going to the very closest place, the place Stewart must know they'd be making for . . .

"Cadan?"

"Yes?"

"Stewart—he'll know where we're going."

"I know," Cadan said shortly.

"Won't he . . . tell someone?"

Cadan's jaw clenched, and his fingers moved, suddenly jerky, on the controls. "I'm sure he will."

Elissa swallowed. "Then shouldn't we go to a different place?"

Cadan swung around on her. "For God's sake, Lissa, will you stop talking and let me do my job?"

"I'm just saying—"

"There *is* no other place! The ship's running at over five percent damage. I've got a whole sector shut down. If I don't get her patched up so we can use the hyperdrive, we're no better than floating wreckage waiting to be picked up. Whoever it is who's after you can track the ship. Our only chance is in not staying still long enough for them to catch up with us." He shut his teeth hard on the last word, took a deep breath. "Now, please, either stay quiet or go away."

They touched down on the surface of the moon two hours later. Cadan told Elissa and Lin to strap themselves in even before he brought the *Phoenix* into orbit, and entering the atmosphere was a stomach-dropping ride, with Cadan fighting to keep the ship stable. They landed with a last sideways lurch that kicked Elissa's heart up into her throat.

She'd known the *Phoenix* was damaged, but after that landing she couldn't help but wonder if the ship would even make it back into space.

If the repairs didn't take too long—if they could be made at all—the ship could stay ahead of their pursuers. If not . . . *We're no better than floating wreckage waiting to be picked up.*

Cadan stood, clipping his earpiece over his ear, checking the reading on his wrist unit. "There are padded jackets in that cupboard," he said, pointing. "The atmosphere is thin enough to be pretty cold, but you might as well save the ship's oxygen by breathing what's outside." His voice was curt, and his gaze skated over Elissa. He had the right to be angry, she knew that, but all the same, resentment crept up inside her. She'd apologized for what *she'd* done, and it wasn't her fault Stewart had turned out to be such an ass.

They came down the ramp of the cargo hold onto gray sand so fine, it was like ash. It puffed up around their feet as they stepped onto it. A thin breeze licked an icy damp tongue over Elissa's face, and she pulled the jacket hood around her head and shoved her hands into the deep pockets.

Cadan strode away from the ship, then turned so he could get a clear view of the damage. His face tightened.

When Elissa caught up with him and looked, even she could see that it was bad. A mangled scar ran across the *Phoenix*'s smooth silver hull.

Markus had followed Cadan and the twins. He was no longer taut with anger; his face showed nothing but focused attention on the problem at hand. "At least the auto-repair worked."

Cadan rubbed a hand across his face. "All too well. It's going to be a hell of a job pulling the metal back out."

"What's wrong?" Lin asked Elissa, her voice low. "I thought the auto-repair was a good thing?"

"It is. But it's, like, just an emergency fix. The metal clamps tight, seals it all off, but then, if you want to get it back to how it was, you have to peel the metal back up and fix it back in its original place so it can cope with hyperspeed. They have these massive machines that do it at home."

"We have the equipment to do it here," said Markus, overhearing. "Or a good enough job, anyway. It's getting the equipment up there that's the problem."

"Can't you reach it from inside?" said Lin, her face interested and curious.

"We can," said Cadan. "But it'd mean breaching the work of the auto-repair, and if we can't get *that* back, we'll be stuck not being able to fly at all, let alone making hyperspeed." He rubbed his face again and squinted up at the ship's side. "If I can maneuver *Shuttlebug Two* close enough . . ."

Markus nodded. "We can rig up a platform for Felicia and me to work from."

"That's a lot riskier than I like to ask of you, Markus. I'd do it myself—"

"But we need you to keep the shuttlebug steady while we work. It's okay, Captain."

It didn't sound okay. It sounded completely dangerous. But Elissa couldn't say anything. She couldn't do anything to help, she didn't have any advice, and Cadan had already made it pretty clear he didn't appreciate her interfering.

"What do you need to do?" said Lin.

Cadan gave her a distracted, irritated look. "Not now, please. We're trying to work out how to fix it. I don't have time to explain the process."

Elissa felt Lin bristle next to her. When she spoke again, her voice was determined. "Yes you do. It'll take you about half a minute."

The next look Cadan gave her was no longer distracted—but it was a lot more irritated. "Do I look as if I want to spend even half a minute being your teacher? We're working hard to keep you safe here—"

Lin glared at him. "And *I'm offering to help*."

"*Help?* How?"

Lin didn't answer immediately. Instead she just dropped

her gaze to the front of Cadan's jacket. He looked disconcerted, following her eyes down to where they'd focused on the little silver pilot's bar. "What are you—"

The bar twitched. Cadan's head jerked back, surprised bewilderment flashing across his face. "What the hell?"

Lin frowned. One of her fingers moved. The bar gave another twitch, then slid sideways, its pin coming free from Cadan's jacket, and fell onto the ground. A tiny cloud of dust billowed up around it.

Markus took a big step back. "Whoa."

Lin grinned at him, then at Cadan. "Come on. I *know* Lissa told you I'm electrokinetic."

"Yes. She did." He blinked. "I just . . . forgot." He bent to pick up the bar. "The clasp's undone. You . . . can actually do that?"

Lin's grin spread until it was almost smug. "Among other things."

Cadan cleared his throat. "But that's just a clasp. What we need for the ship is a hell of a lot more challenging."

Lin rolled her eyes, just a little. "So *tell* me."

For the first time since before the last pirate attack, a glint of amusement crept into Cadan's eyes. "All right, then. We need each of those sheets of metal pulled away from the ship. We need them beaten out flat, and we need them reattached so their curvature matches the curvature of the ship's side. It doesn't look like too much from here, but the metal is extremely heavy. It'll take all Markus's and Felicia's strength to do it, and only then with the help of lifting equipment. Do you really think you can do it?"

"Yes. Well . . ." She made a face. "I've never done anything quite like it before. But"—she flexed her fingers, and once more Elissa felt that prickle of electricity in the palms of her own hands—"I can try."

Cadan frowned. "Is it dangerous? If you expend too much energy?"

"How would I know?"

"Ah, look . . . I don't like it. Letting you do something that could be dangerous—"

Lin shrugged. "I can stop if it's getting too hard, can't I? Anyway"—she grinned again—"it's nowhere near as dangerous as having Markus and Felicia balancing on a platform built on a shuttlebug."

She looked back at the ship, eyes narrowing in concentration, and the prickle began to build again in Elissa's hands. But for a moment she hardly noticed. She'd thought Lin was offering to help with the ship just because they—she and Lin—needed it. But with Lin's last words, a new thought dawned in her mind. Maybe Lin *was* offering to help solely for her own and Elissa's benefit. It made sense: If she could get the job done faster, she could leave Markus and Felicia free to do whatever other tasks needed seeing to. But on the other hand, was she actually doing it for *their* benefit? For Markus's and Felicia's sakes, to save them from undertaking a dangerous procedure?

And if so, if Lin, for the first time, was thinking about people other than herself and Elissa, people who were full, declared-legal humans, people whom she'd once described as meaning nothing to her . . . what was going on in her head? What had changed? Was it because they—Cadan and Markus and the others—were helping protect them?

Then the prickle climbed up into Elissa's wrists, a feeling like pins and needles making her fingers twitch, and the thought dissolved under more immediate preoccupations.

Lin stood still, face tilted up toward the damaged area, eyes crinkled in concentration, hands in front of her. It wasn't possible that she'd be able to do anything—the piece she was supposed to fix was so far up, the metal pressed in on itself in tight inflexible folds, as if it had been pinched by giant fingers. And before, back on Sekoia—okay, she'd controlled the mechanism in a moving staircase, but that had been in an extremity of fear and fury. And wouldn't just shaking something be easier than uncrumpling a bunch of massive sheets of metal?

Now, if she tried and tried and couldn't, would it damage her? *Is she going to get hurt?*

Elissa bit the edge of her thumbnail. Lin looked so normal, so *small*, standing there, hair scraped back, face set in concentration. The task was way too big for her, she'd never be able to—

Above them metal screeched.

Elissa shot a look upward. A section of the damaged area was bellying slowly outward, as if it were being blown from the inside, pulling away from the other metal with a grating, slithering sound that set her teeth on edge. Markus drew in a sharp breath.

Lin shifted her feet a little, but other than that she didn't move. The metal sheet swelled farther, lining itself up with the curve of the undamaged section next to it, then froze in place with a definite *clang*.

"Will that do?" she asked.

Cadan nodded. "That will absolutely do."

Lin grinned a tiny bit, clearly registering the approval in his voice, and something seemed to stab through Elissa, unexpected and so fast she didn't quite recognize it.

Lin screwed her eyes up again, curled one hand into a fist. Her other hand made an infinitesimal twitching movement, and another piece of metal began to unroll itself from the ship.

The whole process seemed to take forever. The metal uncrumpled so smoothly, without all the normal paraphernalia of machinery and power tools, that once Elissa had gotten over her first incredulity, it seemed as though Lin were unrolling nothing but foil, paper thin. At points, when she hesitated, when a corner of metal hung just outside the right position, Elissa's own fingers itched to reach out and press it lightly into place. A couple of times she had to stop herself from offering Lin advice—*just a bit to the right; if you stretch it out farther it'll be easier to fit in place*... It looked so easy, something that anyone, if they could reach, could do as easily with their hands as Lin was doing with her mind.

But after half an hour Elissa noticed Lin's fingers. They'd been moving in tiny twitches as if she were touching the metal, as if it were real, physical work. And now they were trembling, and the skin of her forehead, half-hidden by her hair, looked clammy. She was approaching what seemed—even from Elissa's position of ignorance—like the hardest part of all.

The spider robots had not salvaged all the metal. Some had been blown to dust in the blast, and some had been torn into shreds and thrown far from the *Phoenix* to float in emptiness. Cadan and Markus had brought a new sheet out and it now lay on the ground, gathering dust in a gray film on its shining surface.

Lin's job was to lift it—way up, three stories above their heads—and slide it into position over the remaining space, then rivet it with the lightweight rivet gun Cadan held ready to pass to her. The new sheet, like the rest of the *Phoenix*'s outer shell, was smart-metal. The moment the ship hit the outer atmosphere of the moon, the smart-metal would bond to the other sheets as if they'd never been anything other than whole.

Lin relaxed her hands for a moment and rolled her shoulders back, stretching. Elissa opened her mouth to suggest she take a break—she couldn't possibly do this, Cadan was crazy to let her—but it was too late. The muscles along Lin's jaw tightened as she clenched her teeth, and in front of them the sheet of metal shivered, making a noise that would have been almost musical had it not been so harsh. Then the sheet rose into the air.

This time it was Lin who gasped, a quick indrawn breath that sounded as if she were in pain.

"Lin," said Elissa. "It's too hard, you'll hurt yourself—"

But she wasn't being listened to. Lin gritted her teeth—actually gritted them, Elissa heard them grate together—and the sheet rose higher, wavering, making wobbly, metallic noises, and then it clanged against the side of the ship.

Then slowly scraping along, metal on metal, with a squeaky sound that set Elissa's teeth on edge, the sheet inched up the bulk of the ship.

Elissa looked at Lin. It didn't seem easy anymore. Her sister was sweating, moisture forming under her hairline, running down the sides of her face. Red pinpricks appeared beneath her eyebrows, tiny bursting blood vessels.

"Lin. You need to take a break."

Lin gave the smallest sideways jerk of her head, not speaking, keeping her mouth tightly shut. Above them the metal quivered, hesitated, and continued to slide up toward the damaged area.

"Lin." This time Cadan spoke. "You don't have to finish it now. Lissa's right. Take a break."

She didn't even make a gesture of reply this time. Her face was set and stubborn, and suddenly Elissa knew that she wouldn't stop, wouldn't give up till it was done.

But what's it going to do to her? It must be using up so much energy. What if it's too much? What if she hurts—really hurts—herself?

She didn't dare try to force Lin's attention away from the sheet—if she let it fall now, it would crash down on both of them—but she slid her hand over her sister's, feeling the quiver that seemed to come right through Lin's bones. Elissa reached out, trying to silently let Lin know that it was fine to give up, that she could continue later, that she wouldn't let anyone down by taking a break.

Pain rushed up Elissa's arms. Her shoulders suddenly ached and trembled with fatigue so intense, it hurt. She was looking through Lin's eyes, thinking Lin's thoughts. *They need to leave me alone. Stop distracting me, and I can do it. I can do it.*

Her fingers, so cramped and sore, flexed suddenly. She felt as if she'd slammed both hands onto the metal sheet, pushed hard and felt it slide. Above her the reluctant scraping became a sudden metallic rush of noise.

The sheet slid exactly into place.

She dragged in a breath, mentally leaning against the sheet to keep it steady—so much easier than pushing it farther and farther up the side of the ship—and held out her hand for the rivet gun.

After the metal sheet, the gun seemed almost ridiculously easy to maneuver. She sent it floating up around the edges of the sheet, punching in the rivets.

As the last rivet went in, disorientation swooped through

Elissa, then she found herself looking again through her own eyes, her fingers going slack on Lin's hand. Next to her, Lin staggered. The rivet gun, floating halfway down the side of the ship, turned over and fell. It thudded onto the ground, sending up a puff of gray dust.

For a moment Elissa thought the dust had gotten into her eyes: Everything went dim, blurry. She dropped Lin's hand and wiped her eyes, and after a moment the blur cleared.

Lin was staring at her. "I felt you." She put a hand up to her head. "You . . . linked to me."

"I didn't mean to, it just . . . happened. I was scared you were going to hurt yourself."

"I *was* hurting myself. But you . . . You've never done that before. It was always me. I didn't know you even could." She glanced up at the mended ship. "And you just helped me. You helped me move it. But you don't have electrokinesis— at all. Do you?"

"No." If she had, wouldn't she have discovered it earlier, like Lin had? Wouldn't it have been yet another freaky-weird thing about her for the doctors to try to get rid of?

Lin was watching her, and now Cadan and Markus were too. Elissa found herself hunching her shoulders, an auto- matically defensive move. *If I did have a power anything like Lin's . . . God, I wouldn't want everyone analyzing it.* She shook her head vehemently. "I don't. I don't have anything like that. I've only ever felt it when I'm linked to Lin. It's not *me*."

Lin shrugged. "Whatever it is, we did it." She turned to look at Cadan and Markus, triumph in every line of her body. "How about that, Mr. Captain?"

Cadan's face lit in a smile. "Amazing. Thank you, Lin." A hairsbreadth of a pause. "And, Elissa, for whatever you did."

She couldn't look at him. She'd hardly done anything. She was just a burden on his ship, with no specialist skills and no superpowers. Abruptly his words from a few days ago came back to her. *We wouldn't want you slipping up and, you know, excelling . . .*

Suddenly she knew that if she opened her mouth to say anything, she'd start to cry. And that, after everything, would be more humiliation than she'd be able to bear.

"Markus," Cadan said, "would you take Lin to get something to eat from the nearest nutri-machine?" A little amusement lightened his voice. "About the only thing I know about any type of electrokinesis is that it expends a good deal of energy."

"Sure thing," Markus said. "Lin, do you want to come grab something?"

Lin hesitated. "Lissa? Don't you want . . . ?"

Elissa managed to shake her head and give her sister a little smile, keeping her teeth shut tightly against the threatening tears.

"We'll bring her back a chocograin bar," Markus said to Lin.

"Chocograin?"

"You haven't had a chocograin bar? That's it, the first thing on your menu . . ." Their voices disappeared up into the cargo bay.

Not that it helped. It was *Cadan* she didn't want to freaking cry in front of. Elissa bit the inside of her cheek. If she could just keep the tears back a bit longer, the urge to cry would pass. God knew, she'd done it enough times at school.

"Lissa."

She looked up, keeping her face as stony as she could possibly manage.

"I'm not blaming you," said Cadan. He wasn't smiling anymore, and the look of strain in his eyes gave his face a grim expression. "You were saving your sister. You—" He hesitated, broke off. "That's all, really. You had to do it. I understand."

She swallowed, forcing the tears down. "Giving you that fake money—it wasn't meant as—I wasn't thinking of you as for *sale*."

"It's okay. I know. You already said." He hesitated, then reached out and brushed her upper arm. All unexpectedly her stomach flipped. "Look," he said, "I'm *extremely* irritable right now. Don't take it personally, okay?"

Something—the release of tension, that out-of-nowhere stomach flip—made a laugh burst out of her. "Please. As if I hadn't learned by now to ignore the mean things you say to me."

"'Mean things'?" He was laughing too, but with a question in his eyes.

"*Extremely* mean things." In the interests of fairness she added, "Well, sometimes they're more just superpatronizing."

"They are?"

She raised her eyebrows, taking a little bit of revenge. "Completely."

Cadan was frowning, looking as if he were searching his memory for the last mean—or patronizing—thing he'd said to her. She saw the moment the results came up, because a sudden flush swept over his face. "Oh," he said. "Yeah, all right. I'll give you patronizing." He hesitated again. "I guess . . . This stuff with Lin, it's been going on over the last three years, right?"

"Yes."

"So, there are quite a lot of things I might have the wrong idea about?"

"There really could be." Although it hadn't been funny at the time and *still* kind of wasn't, she found her lips quirking into a smile.

His eyes met hers. He didn't return her smile, but something in his face changed.

"I meant it, you know," he said as they turned to walk back up the ramp. "What I said before, about how you've handled all this. I'm impressed, honestly."

And when Elissa flickered a look at his face, he was smiling at her.

THIRTEEN

CADAN TOOK another hour and a half to run maintenance on the *Phoenix*, aided by the three remaining members of his crew. Halfway through, Elissa and Lin raided the nutri-machine in their cabin and took the crew a collection of the most dinnerlike items they could find. Curly grain featured heavily, and something called "savory protein wafers" that did not at all taste of the ham they were supposed to. The crew ate hungrily, though, standing around the cargo bay, watching the sun rise swiftly over the horizon. Elissa knew very well that Syris II didn't match Sekoian time, and she kept checking her watch, which agreed with her body clock that it was late nighttime, not morning at all. But all the same she found the sunrise utterly disorienting, as if she were trapped in a day that was never going to end.

Felicia was standing near her, by the cargo bay exit, and when Elissa looked at her watch for what must have been about the tenth time, Felicia glanced at her, smiling. "You get used to it."

Elissa looked up. "If you're on a planet for, like, a few days, does your body clock reset itself?"

"Some people's, yes." Felicia laughed. "I've found out that mine, though, is pretty intransigent. I've been on Sekoia more than twenty years, and part of me's still set on Freyan time."

For a moment Elissa thought she must have misheard. "I'm sorry—which planet is that? I didn't catch—"

"No, you heard me right. My home planet is—well, *was*—Freya." She sent a half smile Elissa's way. "Did you know, there was an Old Earth goddess named Freya? Goddess of fertility, apparently. Which, I have to say, seems particularly ironic."

Well, yeah. The planet Freya was the universe's worst example of what they called post-completion terraforming failure. It had been settled a thousand years ago, reclaimed from the receding edge of an ice age and turned into something very like Old Earth itself, with busy oceans and temperate landmasses. It had evolved its own cultures, even different strains of language. And then Freya—a planet with an established, entirely stable global ecosystem—had moved into a stage of orbit the scientists had calculated incorrectly, and despite all efforts to reverse the process, the planet had entered its next ice age.

It had taken most of the next fifty years for them to bring themselves to do it, but eventually every Freyan citizen had been forced to abandon their dying world. Probably forever.

"I'm sorry," Elissa said, knowing the words were beyond inadequate but needing to say them all the same.

Felicia smiled at her again. "I was a good bit older than

you and your sister before I had to leave, though. So maybe I didn't know how lucky I was, hm?"

Except now, because of us, you might not ever get back to your adopted home planet. God, was there never an end to all the people whose lives she was managing to wreck?

"Stop that," said Felicia.

Elissa blinked.

"That. Hunching your shoulders. Looking as if you want to start chewing on your nails. I'm forty-two. I made my own decision to stay with the ship. Just like we all did."

"I know. I just . . ."

"You feel guilty. Well, yes, I imagine you do. But you shouldn't." She paused, catching Elissa's gaze, the angular lines of Felicia's face settling into an oddly gentle expression. "Did you not wonder why I—as well as Markus—stayed to help?"

"Yes. But I— Maybe it's not my business . . ."

"You know all Freyan citizens were given interplanetary citizenship?"

"Yes."

Everyone knew that. It had been one of the Interplanetary League's landmark rulings. Freyan citizens had been declared to be refugees first, but then, after protracted arguments and petitions and appeals, had been given the newly created status of interplanetary citizens, with the legal right to settle on any planet they wished and be treated no differently from full native citizens.

"We—my family—came to Sekoia. There were other planets, of course, but after what we saw on Freya, there was something about settling on a planet that was sure of its own safety, sure that its terraforming had worked, that what had happened to us was one of those one-in-a-million aberrations that could never happen to them . . . Well, my mother said the complacency made her skin itch. Sekoia was only just dragging itself out of its own environmental crisis—if there was one thing it wasn't going to be, it was complacent. So we settled there. Interplanetary citizens, right? Welcome anywhere?"

Elissa nodded.

"Except not," Felicia said.

"You got . . . discriminated against? But that's illegal. Sekoia has *stringent* human-rights laws."

Felicia's mouth twitched, and Elissa, suddenly aware that all she was doing was quoting a phrase she'd heard a million times and hadn't ever thought to challenge, stopped.

Felicia lifted a dismissive shoulder. "It's a nice little legal fiction, that's all. I'm trained to use every currently licensed type of firearm—and a good few that aren't licensed at all. I'm a black belt in three different types of martial arts, and my IQ is two points off genius level. But by the time I left college, I knew my only employment opportunities were cleaning jobs."

"But it's— I don't understand how people could get away with—"

Felicia gave her that oddly gentle look again. "People can get away with most things if they're determined to." A smile flickered across her face. "And people can overcome most things if they're determined to, as well. I joined SFI as a cleaner, and I worked my way up. Once you're in SFI, under the eyes of the people who really count, all they care about is how good you are, not whether you've got that pesky special citizenship they'd never have voted for if it had been up to them." The twist to Felicia's voice indicated that this time it was she who was doing the quoting.

"Anyway." She shrugged. "It's not a sob story I'm telling you. It's an explanation. I don't trust government bodies. I don't trust them when what they say sounds like a good thing, and I don't trust them when what they say sounds like a clever bit of twisted logic. 'Nonhuman human-sourced entities,' for God's sake." Her lip curled. "One guess which category *that* falls into."

Elissa swallowed, aware that at some point in the last few minutes Lin had wandered over and was silently listening, that Cadan, Markus, and Ivan had stopped talking and were watching them. "But . . . Cadan doesn't think I can know it, but I *do*. It's not just some random organization doing this. It's the government. You—SFI gave you a job—"

"And you think if it comes down to it, my loyalty might ultimately be to them? No. I *earned* my position with SFI. They gave it to me because I was that good, not because they wanted to. I don't owe them anything." Her face hardened. "And if it was the government who authorized what happened to both of you, I'll find myself another damn job."

"We all will," said Ivan, crumpling his coffee cup in his big hand.

Lin looked across at him. "Why did you stay?" she asked. "Markus gets all angry about clones, and Felicia doesn't trust the government, and Cadan always does the right thing—"

Cadan choked on his coffee. "Hardly—"

"That's what Lissa says." Lin's voice was matter-of-fact, and she didn't even bother glancing his way. It was as if she were making a statement that everyone already knew. Elissa felt a flush climbing all through her face. She couldn't look at Cadan. It was one thing for *her* to know she trusted him; it was quite another for him to know exactly how much.

Lin was still watching Ivan, her face full of calm interest. "Why? Why did you stay?"

Ivan tossed the crushed coffee cup into the disposal chute, watching as it hit the rim and bounced down out of sight. "It's not politics, I can tell you that much. I'm just a working man—I don't have time for any of that activist stuff."

Lin waited, her gaze on him.

Ivan looked up at her. "I have daughters," he said. "They're not on Sekoia, and they lived with their mother even before they left home. But you and your sister—you remind me of them when they were teenagers."

Lin waited.

"That's all," said Ivan. "I told you, it's not politics, and it's not complicated. That's it." He glanced at Cadan. "I'm going to start those safety checks, Captain, okay?"

He climbed up one of the staircases and disappeared into the body of the ship.

They took off in a sudden rainstorm that came up as they were leaving, up through raindrops that spattered against the glass all around the flight deck, then through banks of cloud followed by a momentary blaze of sunlight like fire. Then the sound of the engines changed, Elissa's stomach dropped in the fraction of a second before the gravity drive kicked in, and they were in space once again.

The crew were already at their posts around the ship, doing, Elissa imagined, the most vital tasks of all those intended to be undertaken by a full crew. She and Lin were strapped like good passengers into two of the seats at the edge of the bridge.

"So," said Cadan, half his attention on the enviro-scan, "this is what we're doing." He glanced across at them, then gestured toward two of the seats at the controls. "Here, come and sit where we can talk."

He waited for them to change seats, frowning at one of the side screens.

"Is that the hyperdrive?" asked Lin.

"The hyperdrive status display, yes. It's . . . it's not *show-ing* anything wrong, but the last time I used it, it didn't feel . . . But it's built to be good for at least five years, and, anyway, no one on the ship even begins to be qualified to investigate it." He gave his head a shake, filing the problem away—Elissa could tell he was doing it—to consider later.

"We're making for Sanctuary," he said. "I can't plot a course from here, though—I don't dare do anything that makes us easier to track. And even using the hyperdrive, I can't take us straight there, for the same reason. We're going to do it in a series of short random hops to keep anyone from getting a full lock on our signal. Doing it that way, we should reach Sanctuary in the next twelve hours. And once we're at IPL HQ, you—Lin at least, and probably Lissa as well—can claim refugee status under the Humane Treatment Act."

"Does that work—the Act, I mean—even if Lin's not legally human?"

Cadan gave her a half smile. "Will I sound patronizing if I say that the Act has nothing to do with being human?"

Elissa flushed a little, but his eyes were kind. "I can cope. I guess I should already know about it, yes?"

"I guess," Cadan said, echoing her, "that you've been

otherwise occupied. Basically, the Act deals with cruelty, and it applies to all life-forms. It didn't just get mammal-hunting abolished, it's what led to the banning of foods like foie gras and ikuzukuri and dead-and-alive fish. So, and thank God for it, the fact that Lin isn't declared human on her home planet is irrelevant."

Relief seeped through Elissa's bones. She looked at Lin, wanting to share it, but Lin, with one of her out-of-place reactions, had found her attention caught by something else entirely. "I could be a *fish*," she said, amusement all over her face.

Cadan shrugged. "Pretty much. Look"—he glanced at Elissa—"it's very late by Sekoian time, and you both look tired. Why don't you get some sleep? If you go down to my cabin, you can use my bunk and the couch in the lounge area."

If we can sleep, after everything that's happened—everything that's still happening. "When will you sleep?"

He gave her another little smile, and she had to suppress an impulse to reach out and touch his hand. "When we get to Sanctuary? It's okay, Lis, we've practiced plenty of ultralong shifts. If you could dial me a coffee before you go, I'll be fine."

He didn't look fine. He was pale, with bags under his eyes. For a moment, as he turned to frown at a screen, rubbing his forehead with three fingers, he looked like the skinny, too-tall boy he'd been years ago. Markus and Felicia and Ivan were making sacrifices and taking risks, but at least they were completely grown up. Cadan wasn't even supposed to have graduated yet, and right now he looked horribly young, coping with problems far too big for him.

Well, Lin and I are doing that too. But all the same her chest tightened in pity so strong, it felt like grief.

Elissa did manage to sleep for a while, although she woke each time Cadan took the ship into hyperdrive, and she spent a good part of the rest of the time jerking awake, hearing phantom explosions or running footsteps. After a couple of hours she couldn't cope with it anymore. She slid off Cadan's couch, washed her face and brushed her teeth with items from the toiletries machine in his shower room, and went quietly out, leaving Lin in the bedroom.

The whine and shriek of the hyperdrive vibrated all around her as she climbed through the doorway up to the flight deck, and the jerk as they took another hop made her grab for the rail at the bottom of the steps to the bridge.

Cadan was standing by the nutri-machine when she tapped on the security door. He turned, coffee cup in hand, to let her in. "You couldn't sleep longer?"

"I'll have to sleep when we get there too."

"Good plan. Coffee?"

She nodded, and he dialed for her. "I'm having it with extra caffeine. You want that?"

She couldn't suppress a little shudder. "No, thanks. Regular's plenty strong enough. I only started drinking it, like, three days ago, when Lin and I first ran away from my house. Before that, when I was getting all the symptoms of what Lin was going through, one of the doctors I saw said going caffeine-free would help."

"Sadistic freaking bastard."

Elissa blinked. That was a reaction she hadn't expected.

Cadan turned from the machine, the coffee he'd just dialed in his free hand, his face set in lines of anger and distaste. "For God's sake, they knew all along what was doing it, and they recommended things like going caffeine-free? For disconnecting a telepathic link?"

"Oh, no." He wasn't handing her the coffee, so she took it from him. "I don't think they all knew. I mean, some of them definitely did, and I'm sure my parents knew all along too. But that doctor—he was kind of early on, and I think the others—the ones who did know—I think even they were maybe hoping it was nothing but nerves and hormones and stuff. Right at the beginning I was just getting the pain, before the bruises started appearing. So to start with, they sent me to ordinary doctors as well—doctors who didn't have all the information, I mean."

Cadan's face had gone, if anything, even grimmer. "And that's how it started? With the pain coming from what they were doing to her?"

Elissa sipped sweet hot coffee and nodded.

"How often did it happen?"

"Two or three times a week, usually."

Cadan muttered a swear word that Elissa thought it would be polite to pretend not to hear. "And what they were doing— plugging stuff into the back of her skull—that's what you felt? All along, that's what it was?"

"Yes." She frowned at him. "But you know that. I told you earlier today—yesterday." She shook her head. "Whenever. I already told you. And back then, you must have known? Not what was doing it, but that I was sick and stuff. I mean, *everyone* knew."

"Bruce said you got headaches," said Cadan.

"Well, it was difficult to know what to call them. I guess they were sort of headaches—" Then his tone, the look on his face, hit her. "Wait, what? You mean—Bruce said I got *just* headaches?"

Cadan's eyes met hers. There was still anger in them, but now there was shame as well. "Pretty much. A few times he said they were migraines, but he— I never got the impression they were any worse than that. And *definitely* not even as often as once a week."

"Bruce said . . ." She couldn't take it in. Bruce had *known* how bad the symptoms were. He'd seen the bruises, had seen her when she was so sick with pain that she couldn't sit up or stand. And he'd told Cadan they were *headaches*?

"Yeah." Cadan was watching her. "I should have known there was more to it than that. Bruce . . . he doesn't like things he can't define, give reasons for. I guess saying your symptoms were just headaches, it didn't embarrass him like having to admit—"

"What did *he* have to be embarrassed about? It was me it was happening to!"

"I'm not defending him. I just—that's the way he is."

Elissa let out a long breath, trying to let her shock and anger ebb. "I guess so. My mother's pretty much the same. She kept insisting it was just hormones or something until it was so way beyond obvious that it wasn't. Which is crazy, because I *know* she knew—I guess she just kept refusing to believe it."

She sipped coffee, trying to calm down, trying to put it behind her. What did it matter, how her mother and Bruce had tried to deal with what had been happening to her? What did the opinion of anyone back on Sekoia mean anymore?

Then a thought struck her, and she had to force her fingers not to clench on the cup and make coffee spill. "You believed him."

Cadan flushed. "I didn't think not to. If I'd thought about it more . . . but we were in the middle of training, and I just—"

She put the coffee down on the shelf next to the nutri-machine. "So was *that* why? All that freaking advice you kept giving me, about making the most of my opportunities at school? The jabs about me not excelling in class? You thought all I had was headaches? You thought I was lazy?"

"Not lazy."

"Then what?"

"Look, I just thought you were in the position of not having to work for what you wanted. I thought you took it all for granted. Bruce kept mentioning that you were having time off school, that you'd dropped your swimming club and weren't taking driving lessons. And . . ." He sighed. "Okay. I thought you were using the headaches as an excuse. And I thought you were doing a bit of attention seeking."

Attention seeking? Anger swept through her, so strong she felt her face heat. She could only stare at him, hands clenched.

Cadan looked alarmed. "It's not that bad, Lissa. Look, you're a teenage girl—that's the sort of thing they do—"

"Oh my *God*. Tell me you did *not* just say that."

Cadan's flush deepened. "Okay, look—"

"You don't get to make big huge statements about teenage girls and assume they apply to me! You don't *do* that!"

"I know. I'm sorry. I'm sorry." He put his hands up, a gesture of capitulation and defense. "I said it the wrong way. God knows I did my own attention seeking when I was in my teens."

"*Please*. You're twenty-one. Like you're *so* far out of your teens now."

"Point taken. And"—he grinned a little, ruefully—"it's not like I'm immune to seeking some attention now, either. I had the wrong information, and I drew the wrong conclusions. I'm sorry. Really."

"I *cared* what you thought," she said before she could catch the words back. "I *wanted* you to approve. I thought you were awesome when I was little."

Cadan's mouth twisted into a wry look. "You hid it pretty well when you were a bit older, though."

"Of *course* I did! You with your career advice and your 'Oh, Lissa's not up on current affairs,' despising me and making fun of me. Of course I wasn't going to show you I—" She stumbled, suddenly scared of what she might end up saying if she kept talking.

Cadan's eyes were intent on hers. "I didn't despise you," he said. "I *never* despised you."

"Well, then, you *hid it pretty well*," she shot back at him.

"I guess I must have."

The words hung between them, seeming to gather meaning like static electricity. Elissa's heart was suddenly beating up in her throat. *He always thought of me as a little girl. Bruce's baby sister. That's all I was to him. Wasn't it?*

Cadan opened his mouth, then shut it again. Then folded his arms. "Look. I was pretty pleased with myself when I was a little younger, when I was training. I know I must have been all kinds of irritating. And I made some pretty harsh judgments of you. But I did *not* despise you."

"Okay." She wouldn't ask him what he had thought about her. She'd put herself out there enough already—she couldn't do it anymore.

She shifted her position instead, took a gulp of coffee. "I

didn't have to work for what I wanted," she said suddenly. "Before the symptoms started. You were right about that. So if you thought I was kind of spoiled, well, I guess you weren't totally wrong."

"Yeah, I did, a bit," said Cadan carefully. "But only kind of."

Elissa lifted a shoulder. "I guess that's fair."

Cadan had been glancing at the screens at intervals while they talked. Now he moved back to take his seat at the controls again. "You've changed, though," he said, eyes intent on the screens. "Since you've been on the ship. Seeing everything you've had to do—everything you've given up for Lin . . ."

Elissa sat down two seats away from him. She wasn't going to ask. It was enough to know that he hadn't despised her; it was enough that he knew she hadn't been faking the symptoms.

"So I'm not so spoiled now?"

Cadan glanced at her. "Not at all spoiled." Their eyes met, and held, and once again the words hung in the air, gathering electricity that hummed and sparked between them. Cadan took one hand off the controls. "Lissa . . ."

Behind them someone tapped on the glass. Elissa jumped and turned around, and Cadan hit the button to open the door.

Lin came in, yawning, hair sticking up all over the place, and walked straight to the nutri-machine to dial a hot chocolate and chocograin bar. "How far are we now?"

"No more than eight hours away now," Cadan said. He glanced back at the screens, and Elissa noticed his color seemed a little higher than it had before. What had he been about to say, before Lin came in? *And will he get another chance to say it?*

He didn't look as if that were on his mind now, though. "Lin," he said as she came over to take a seat next to Elissa, "when you were in the facility, did you have any idea what purpose it was for? Why they were doing it?"

Lin had turned toward him as he'd said her name, but at his words her eyes went blank, as if she were looking not at but through him. "No," she said, and the word was like a barrier clamping down.

Cadan paused a moment, looking at her. "No idea at all? After three years?"

"No."

As Cadan opened his mouth again, Elissa put a hand out to stop him, an automatic impulse. Couldn't he see that Lin didn't want to answer? That he was pushing some button that needed to be left alone?

But either he didn't see her gesture or he chose to ignore it. "Lin, I'm not asking for fun. I'm asking because it might be useful information."

"It's not useful information. I don't know."

"Okay," said Cadan, in a voice of deliberate patience. "Then I'll tell you what I've been thinking instead." He moved a hand over the controls, opened up another window to check something, then glanced back at Lin. "Lissa said it had to do with your greater telepathic ability. And probably your electrokinetic ability too. Like I said, about the only thing I know about that is that it takes up a lot of energy. But I've seen what you eat, and, in terms of calories, I don't think you're taking in anything like the amount of energy you can give out."

"So?" said Lin.

"*So* I'm thinking what they were doing was using you like

some kind of energy amplifier. Drawing energy through you—"

Every part of Lin's body seemed to flinch. For a moment she looked as if she'd actually shrunk. Elissa flung out a hand toward Cadan. "*Stop*. Stop it. Can't you see she can't handle you talking about it?"

Cadan's eyebrows twitched together. "Look, I know it's not pleasant, but—"

"Not *pleasant*?" All the former understanding she thought they'd reached exploded into dust. "What's wrong with you? You know what happened to her!"

"Yes, I *do* know," Cadan snapped. "And I'm trying to find ammunition to ensure it doesn't happen again! The more information I have, the more of a case I can present to the IPL."

"You said we'd get refugee status anyway." Elissa couldn't help the accusing tone that came into her voice.

"You will. But do you want to live as nothing more than refugees forever? With Lin never being recognized as a legal human? Right now all we can get these people on is contravention of the Humane Treatment Act. If we can find out they've broken other laws, if we can get you compensation, if we can get Lin legal human status, it'll make things a hell of a lot better for you both. So please, both of you, stop treating me like the enemy!"

His eyes held Elissa's, and after a second she looked away.

"I know one thing," said Lin abruptly. "People—Spares—once the procedures started, they didn't last long."

Elissa's stomach clenched. Once again she heard what Lin had said that first day: *Some of the other Spares . . . they burned out.* Elissa had tried not to think about it. It was over for Lin, and she, Elissa, couldn't do anything about the Spares still left there. But sometimes the words came back, and so did images, of Lin burning out, used up, gone.

Lin was watching her. "Lissa, no, that's not what I'm talking about. Some of us"—she glanced at Cadan—"couldn't cope with the procedure. It burned out something in their brains. But some of us got taken away." She hesitated. "At least, that's what I guessed. I mean, there weren't any corpses. They could have died and been removed without us knowing. But we all thought . . . The rumors were that they were taken away alive." She swallowed. "And it was always people a bit older than me. A year, two at the most."

"People reaching the end of puberty," said Cadan. "At the height of their powers, maybe?"

Lin shrugged, her face shutting down again, as if, having given the information she could, she was once again blocking it out of her brain.

"Okay." Cadan reached to unlock the hyperdrive, ready to take yet another hop. "Thank you."

He was still frowning, thinking, while he engaged the hyperdrive.

The familiar whine filled Elissa's ears.

As they made the hop, the ship lurched in a way that was also becoming familiar. Warning lights lit up, and when the display screen for the hyperdrive came back on, it was flashing red text. Elissa's eyes went straight to it, and the message on-screen made her go ice cold. *Error. Error. Error.*

"No," said Cadan. "Damn it, not *now.*" He flicked open a panel below the screen, tapped in a code, and waited. The error message flickered, blinked slowly, and then was replaced by a page of gibberish code. The warning lights went off.

"It's going wrong, isn't it?" said Lin.

"No, it can't be!" Elissa's voice jumped with nerves. "Cadan, it's working again now, isn't it? It could have been just a glitch? A display problem? You said the hyperdrive lasts *five years*."

Cadan clicked the panel back into place, his fingers moving slowly, carefully. "I wish I thought it was just a glitch. I think . . ." He scrubbed a hand over his face. "I think it's malfunctioning." A pause. *"Damn!"* He flung his hand down, thumped the edge of the control panel. "We can't afford this now! Our only chance of getting there without detection—" He broke off, hand clenched, visibly getting himself back under control, then opened up the communications channel. "Markus, can you come to the bridge? Thanks."

He looked at Elissa and Lin. "We're going to have to fly straight for a while. I'm setting up the widest enviro-scan I can manage running. We'll see if anyone's coming." His face tightened, a grim look. "That is, if they're using normal flight. If they track us precisely enough to hop here . . ."

He opened the door for Markus and turned briefly in his seat to summon him to the control panel, then gestured to the hyperdrive screen. "Markus, can you make sense of this? I don't even recognize what it's saying. God, I always *thought* they should give us training in maintaining the damn thing. I have to use it again, I *have* to, but if I just knew what it might do, what strain it'll put the ship under if the whole thing breaks down halfway—"

But Markus was shaking his head. "I'm sorry. I don't know any more than you. It's not meant to break down at all. The only thing they ever told us was that *if* it malfunctioned—and they were very firm that it wouldn't—we were authorized to call for the emergency maintenance crew." He and Cadan shared a look of frustration.

"If we're attacked now, and I have to deal with that when I don't know if I can safely use the hyperdrive . . ." Cadan's hand was still clenched. For a moment he rested his forehead on his fist, staring at the screens. Then he straightened. "Okay. Markus, we have to get into the hyperdrive chamber. If there's any chance at all we can find out what's happening with it, we have to do it."

"It means breaking government seals."

"Does it look like my big concern is not breaking government seals?"

Despite everything, Markus laughed, a sudden bark of laughter. "Mine neither. They're tricky, that's all."

"Can you do it?"

Markus shrugged. "I can certainly try."

Cadan engaged the autopilot and stood. "Try."

The two of them went down the steps to the sealed door Stewart had shown Elissa and Lin when he'd first brought them to the flight deck. Elissa remembered his cheerful, humorous voice rattling out the penalties for attempting to gain entrance to the hyperdrive chamber.

After a couple of seconds' hesitation, she and Lin followed Markus and Cadan off the bridge and stood a distance behind them while they bent to inspect the door.

"It's fingerprint-locked," Markus said. "Laserproof, of course. And I can't unscrew the hinges. The heads of the screws—look, they're unique. We don't have any tools that'd fit them." He ran his finger down the edge. "I'd suggest crowbars, but look at this thing. It's sealed so damn tight—I'm not going to be able to get anything in to pry the edges apart."

"How about pushing the door in?"

"If we can do it without damaging the hyperdrive," said Markus. "I don't know where it is in relation to the door. I'd consider a controlled explosion if I knew what the risk was, but as it is . . ."

"Okay," said Cadan. "If we can push it in just enough to open up a space at the edge, we can get a crowbar in." He straightened, scrubbing his face with both hands. "What have we got that'll do that?"

"I can do it," said Lin behind him.

He snapped a look at her. "You can?"

"Yes."

Relief swept over his face. "Okay, then." He stepped back to make room for her. Markus grinned, looking at her with approval and respect.

Lin went forward. She'd just bent to touch the door when the attack came.

From the first second it was as if the other attacks had been nothing but rehearsals. There was no warning at all. Just, all at once, other ships exploded out of hyperspace around them, blasts hitting on every side. Flames shot over the glass nose of the ship, licking fast across the glass walls before they winked out of existence.

The impact rocked the *Phoenix* sideways—almost ninety degrees, too powerful for her stability drive to withstand and too fast for the internal auto-cushioning to keep up. Elissa was thrown right off her feet and halfway across the flight deck. She landed hard, pain cracking from her shoulder down her arm.

Lin fell forward, hitting her head against the door of the hyperdrive chamber so hard, it made a hollow clang. She went boneless, a rag doll on the floor.

"Lin! *Lin!*"

Cadan had been knocked off his feet too. Now he shoved himself upright again, grabbing for the stair rail and leaping up the steps to get to the control panel.

Another blast came as he jumped onto the bridge. Elissa went sprawling again. Lin, still limp, slid across the floor to end up against the glass wall of the flight deck. For a heart-stopping moment Elissa's brain played a trick on her, made her think the glass wasn't there, that Lin was going to slide right over the edge to fall and fall and fall . . .

"*Lin.*" Elissa managed to crawl across to where her sister lay. Pain shrieked through her shoulder.

Markus was behind her. "Get her up to the bridge. Get her into a harness."

They managed to do it, one on each side of Lin, who slumped, almost unconscious in their hands as they brought her across the shuddering floor, up the steps. She started to come to as they reached the bridge, and Elissa strapped Lin and herself into the side seats with fingers that shook on the buckles, her brain blanking out as if it couldn't hold the knowledge of how to fasten them.

We were so close. We were nearly there. And now, with the hyper-drive going wrong . . .

Warning lights flashed, and the beep, beep, beep of an alarm. "Shields at seventy-five percent," came an uninflected, mechanical voice.

Cadan swore, arms braced against the console as he fought to get control of the ship. "Markus, check that for me. They can't be taking our shields down that fast. What the hell kind of tech have they got—"

He broke off as suddenly as if someone had struck him

across the throat. One of the ships had just swooped up into the view on a screen, and the logo on the side was plain to read. SPACE FLIGHT INITIATIVE. They were SFI ships.

Elissa's stomach dropped so fast, it was as if she were falling. Falling out of control, losing hold of everything she'd fought for, seeing it slip out of her hands and spiral away like dust.

"No freaking way," said Markus from Cadan's far side, his voice so shocked, it sounded flat.

Cadan's face had gone bone white. "Elissa, I apologize," he said.

Another blast. "Shields at seventy percent . . . Shields at sixty-eight percent . . ."

Cadan's hands flashed over the controls. Elissa knew he couldn't return fire, not while the *Phoenix* was wallowing as the power of the blast fought with her stability drives, and not while the shields were dropping so fast. But he was busy taking power from every nonessential function on the ship, shutting everything down he could, throwing everything he had into getting them shielded again.

He moved his hand to unlock the hyperdrive. He wouldn't dare use that yet, not with the *Phoenix* as heavily under fire as she was, but the minute he could, the minute he could fire back, distract them for long enough . . . He could get them out of this. He could save them the way he had before—

Even as she had the thought, the ship rocked with another blast. Were the SFI ships actually planning on destroying the *Phoenix* and all her crew? Had they decided she and Lin were too much of a risk to allow them to live?

Or were they just trying to intimidate them? Were they planning on pounding the ship half to pieces, sure that, before Cadan and his crew were anywhere near in danger, he'd have to give in?

And he will have to. He can't sacrifice everyone just to save us.

Oh God. She'd never thought it would come to this.

Cadan swore again, viciously, and put his hand up to the com-channel. Elissa's throat closed. He was opening dialogue with them. But to do what? *He won't give us up. I know he won't. Not Cadan.*

"*Phoenix,*" Cadan said, his voice coming out like a snarl. "What the hell do you think you're doing to one of your own damn ships?"

Silence. A long silence that crawled out forever. Elissa kept expecting a voice to come through, an official-sounding voice demanding that Cadan release her and Lin. But after an endless minute, punctuated only by the sound of the blasts against the ship's sides, by the automatic warning voice—"shields at sixty-five percent . . . sixty-three percent . . . sixty"—she realized that no response was coming.

The SFI ships didn't want to communicate. They didn't want to bargain. They were beyond stealth now, beyond discreet damage control. They just wanted to wipe them out.

She saw the realization hit Cadan, saw his face go stiff. He switched off the com-channel. "Okay," he said through his teeth, throwing open all the viewscreens he could. "Hang tight. The second I get a chance, we're going into hyperdrive."

A million *but*s exploded across Elissa's thoughts. *But we'll get hit. But it's faulty. But it could tear the ship apart.* She knew, though, that none of those things mattered. If the *Phoenix* didn't get out of here, within minutes her shields would be down at zero, and it would all be over.

Next to her Lin gave a sound like a bitten-down sob. Elissa reached out and took hold of her twin's cold hand. "I don't regret it," she said, even though she wasn't sure it was true, even though terror broke through her like a wave. "I don't regret it. I don't care."

Lin said nothing. Her hand was shaking, and her nails dug into Elissa's skin.

The hyperdrive whine began, powering up to maximum, Cadan's hand on the controls, his head whipping back and forth to check every screen he had open. *"Now,"* he said, as if he had to command himself to do it, the way he'd have snapped out a command to his copilot or his crew, and threw the ship into hyperspeed.

The whine became a shriek, the power kicked up to full, and the ship made the hop—

Except it didn't.

The shriek of the hyperdrive cut out so suddenly, it was like going deaf. The ship gave a horrible shudder as if she would shake herself apart. And the lights on the hyperdrive display went dead.

No. Oh no, not now.

The hyperdrive, the thing that was going to hop them out of range of the attacking ships, that was going to take them to safety, that was irreplaceable unless you could get to SFI headquarters . . . it wasn't just faulty. It had stopped working.

Another explosion rocked the ship.

"We have to get into the hyperdrive," said Cadan. "Lin, tell me you're up to opening the door."

Lin raised her head. There was a nasty purpling lump on the side of her forehead, and her eyes were huge and black in her white face. "I'm up."

"Okay, then. I'm going to reroute everything to get our shields and stability up to full. I can buy us some time. If we can get the hyperdrive working for another hop . . ."

It still won't be enough. One hop won't do it. They'll come straight after us. There was no point in saying it. It was a feeble hope, but it was their only one.

Cadan snapped a warning through the internal com-system, received confirmation from Ivan and Felicia that they'd moved into the core sections of the ship, then began to shut sectors down. Elissa watched on one of the screens as, on the plan of the ship, section after section showed outlined in amber, then red, then went dark. Cadan was pulling everything—oxygen, heating, electricity—from those sectors, concentrating energy on the essential core of the ship. On the plan, dotted lines became solid as door after door clamped shut, sealing themselves so tightly, it was as if they were forming a ship within a ship.

The shields began to climb. Sixty-six percent, seventy, seventy-two . . . The stability drive climbed too, and although Elissa could still hear the blasts hitting the ship, the floor didn't heave with each impact.

"Shields at ninety-five percent," came the computer's bland announcement.

"It's as good as it's going to get," said Cadan. He snapped to his feet, adjusting his earpiece. "Markus, you stay here. Okay, Lin."

Having seen what Lin had done with the ship's repairs, Elissa hadn't expected her to have any difficulty easing a door open. But within minutes Lin was shaking all over, her teeth clamped into her lower lip, her breath coming so heavily, it sounded as if it must hurt her chest. And the door hadn't so much as trembled.

"It's not just locked," she said on a gasp. "It's sealed all around. And there's a force field."

She went heavily down on one knee, then on both. Then she reached out a hand. "Lissa, I'm sorry, I can't do it by myself."

Oh, of course. Feeling stupid that she hadn't thought of it herself, Elissa gripped her sister's hand. And once again there was a moment of blindness, of disorientation, before she was looking at the door through Lin's eyes, though a blur of fatigue, fury, and determination. And the door . . . it felt like trying to push over a skyscraper, like trying to get your fingernails under the massive buttresses at the end of a bridge.

She—*they*—gritted her teeth, focused everything on the part of herself that was trying to push the door open. It hurt. It was too hard. They couldn't—

The door gave. Just a tiny bit, a millimeter of a crack appearing at one edge.

"That'll do," said Cadan. "You can stop—"

But at that point something else gave, something that snapped like a rubber band. *The force field.* And as Elissa jerked back into her own consciousness, gasping for breath, Cadan stepped past her and Lin, took hold of the edge of the door with both hands, and, muscles straining, dragged it free of the remains of the seal that held it, and away from the doorway.

From within the chamber came a faint, pulsing glow. Hope leapt inside Elissa, flaring through her exhaustion. If the energy cell that powered the hyperdrive wasn't entirely dead, then there must be a chance of getting the drive functioning again.

Cadan strode forward into the shadowy chamber, Elissa and Lin close behind him.

The energy cell was the first thing Elissa noticed. It lay, a pale, glowing cylinder the length of her arm, strapped into a padded hollow in the floor.

Wires ran through it, ghostly blue, giving it the look of a jellyfish squished into a glass container. At each end the wires collected into a single cable, glossy silver, no thicker than her wrist. One cable extended just a little way outside the cylinder, making an S-shape across the floor and connecting to a slim black box.

"Is that . . . ?"

"The hyperdrive," said Cadan. "Yes. I know that much." He bent, picked it up in one hand, and turned it over. A tiny unlit bulb caught an edge of pale light from the glow of the energy cell and glinted suddenly as if his touch had turned it back on. "Okay, the power's dead. But I can't see any sign the drive is broken." He gave a breath of laughter. "If it's as simple as a loose connection . . ."

Elissa had stopped listening. While Cadan inspected the hyperdrive itself, Lin had gone forward, past the energy cell, following the other cable. It snaked away into the shadows at the far end of the chamber. As Elissa's eyes became accustomed to the dim light, she realized Lin had come to an abrupt halt, looking down at where the cable had led her.

"Lin?"

Lin didn't answer. And suddenly something stabbed through Elissa, a shock of emotion so intense, so sharp-edged that it came like a physical pain. Sweat broke out over every inch of her skin.

"Lin?"

"Lissa?" said Cadan sharply. "What is it? What's wrong?"

But now Elissa couldn't answer either. Horror had overtaken her, a creeping horror that raised every hair on her body, prickled all the way up the back of her scalp. Lin stood by a second, much larger cylinder, sunk so low in the floor she could only see its uppermost curve. It reflected the scant light in the room, making it opaque, impossible to see what was inside.

Elissa didn't want to see inside. She didn't want to know what else was in the room that should only contain the hyperdrive and the energy cell it ran from. The room that had been locked and sealed by SFI themselves. The room they hadn't been supposed to enter.

She had to make herself walk forward, only peripherally aware that Cadan followed her. She got to Lin's side and looked down.

This cylinder was dark. Almost too dark to see what it contained.

But not quite. There were wires, distorted by the curve of the glass and the colorless fluid within, and a fine network of tubes—a self-contained life-support unit. And what the cylinder held was—

Behind her Cadan made a choked, horrified sound.

The cylinder held a person. A young man, maybe a couple of years older than Elissa and Lin. He floated in the colorless liquid: naked, motionless, pale. The wires and tubes ran in and out of his body, an obscene network.

And he was dead.

"What the—" Cadan's breath went in a harsh gasp. "What the hell is that?"

The cable from the energy cell entered the cylinder by the young man's head, ran a short length through the liquid inside, then attached to the corpse in a neat plug that exactly fitted the socket at the base of his skull.

This was where the hyperdrive's power came from. It wasn't from an energy cell. It was from a Spare. The hyperdrive's power, the SFI's top secret superfuel they'd been using for the past thirty years—it came from Spares.

FOURTEEN

ELISSA BECAME aware that she had both hands held out in front of her, as if to push the sight away, as if to make it not real, not true, not *there*. She'd known they were doing something awful to Lin, to the others, but she'd never imagined something like this. Never imagined they were shutting them away in the dark, trapped and drowning, every moment waiting for the pain that would tear through them when the ship went into hyperspeed.

A memory pierced her. "You said others—other Spares— were taken away. It was this. It was for this."

Lin's face turned to her, as pale as that of the dead Spare. In the dim room, her eyes were black hollows. Her jaw was slack with shock.

"*No,*" said Cadan. "No. It can't be. This can't be what they—" He broke off. "Oh, God in heaven, hyperdrives last five to seven years."

For a moment Elissa didn't pick up on what he meant.

Then it hit her, a huge fist clenching in her stomach. "*Seven years?* That's how long he's been there?"

"No. Not this one. The *Phoenix* is only two years old. This one—something's been malfunctioning all along. He must—" Cadan choked again. "Ah, God, what have I been doing to him?"

"Two years." Elissa found her head turning back toward where the Spare floated, limp and helpless. Out there, in all the other spaceships, other Spares were floating in the same way, kept alive by tubes, kept— Oh God, were they conscious the whole time?

As she looked, unable to turn away, other details revealed themselves, details she didn't want, things she didn't want to know could happen anywhere, *ever*.

Blood floated in the fluid near the dead Spare's lips, transparent ribbons of pale scarlet, and the lower lip showed dark bruises, vivid against the bluish color of death. He'd bitten himself.

The Spare's hair was longish, trailing like seaweed around his head. Except at the back, around the . . . the hole, the socket. There his hair was frizzled, shriveled as if it had been burned.

Unbidden, Elissa's gaze dragged itself up to the cable itself, to the inner wall of the cylinder. The cable showed signs of corrosion, uneven blackened marks on the smooth surface. The cylinder seemed almost untouched, except at its very edge, where the cable ran through it. There the glass showed the tiny hair-fine crazing that came from excessive heat.

What had happened? Had the connections been overheating? Had the Spare's brain waves been too much for the cables? Or had the settings been wrong? Had they tried to drag too much energy from the Spare, set off some kind of feedback that meant that whenever the ship shifted into hyperdrive—*It was us, we did it; we kept using the hyperdrive to get away*—the Spare, trapped, bound, helpless, had been subjected to the sort of pain Elissa had only felt secondhand but that she could hardly bear to remember?

"I don't know why the hell we're still standing here," said Cadan suddenly, violently. Lin jerked as if she'd been slapped, and for the first time her eyes left the sight of the Spare lying in the glass prison that had become his gruesome tomb.

Elissa dragged her last shreds of self-control together, put her arm around her twin. "Let's get out of here. Cadan's right, there's no point staying."

Lin still didn't speak. Her hand came up, ice cold, closing around Elissa's. Elissa wasn't sure if the next words in her mind were Lin's or her own. *I knew it would come. It has. It's over.*

It can't be over! That was definitely her own thought, frantic, on the edge of panic. "Not like this. There must be a way through!"

She didn't realize she'd said it aloud till Cadan answered her, turning to look at her as they stepped out of the chamber with its hideous, faintly pulsing light.

"Lissa, I'm sorry." His face was bleak. "We're done. We're not going to make it to IPL."

"Cadan . . ." Her voice came out like a desperate accusation. There had to be *something*. After everything they'd gone through, every narrow escape, it couldn't all be ending here.

"I'm sorry," he repeated. His eyes met hers, and they were bleak too. "If there was anything I could think of, any bargain I could make . . ."

They climbed the steps to the bridge. Markus snapped around as Cadan opened the barrier. "The shields are going down again. Did you—?" His eyes took in Cadan's expression and he stopped. "It's no good?"

Cadan crossed to the controls. "No good." He gave the shortest explanation possible, the strain of describing what they'd seen—what still lay under the floor they stood on—drawing lines in his face.

Elissa looked away and realized for the first time that Ivan and Felicia had come up to the bridge as well. The thought came, cold and detached: *So we can all die together.*

Lin's hand stayed icy in Elissa's. As icy as if she, like the pitiful burned-out corpse below them, were already dead.

Cadan turned to the display screens. "The rate the shields are deteriorating, we're not going to last longer than an hour."

An hour. After all they'd gone through, in the end that's what it came down to? One more hour. Despite everything, despite what had happened to innumerable Spares only a little older than her, it seemed impossible that she, Elissa, was going to die before she'd ever really lived.

Fear had left her. She felt . . . kind of lost, dizzy, as if she stood on the very edge of a cliff, the escape route she'd been supposed to take nothing but a tangle of snapped rope and broken harness before her. It had been for nothing. All that fear, all that effort. Getting away, and getting away *again*, and putting Cadan and his crew in so much danger, and it was all worthless.

She found herself speaking without meaning to, out of that weird, chilly detachment. "If you offer to hand us over . . ."

"No."

For a moment she assumed it was Cadan who'd answered,

but then, as she took it in, she realized Felicia and Ivan had spoken at once, and Markus was shaking his head.

"Hand you over to those butchers?" said Ivan. "Now that we know exactly what they want you for? I don't think so."

Somehow she couldn't stop herself from answering him. "If you don't, they're going to kill all of us."

Beside her Lin raised her head. "You could save yourselves. All of you. Lissa, too."

Her voice was curiously flat. Elissa shot a glance at her but couldn't catch what she was either thinking or feeling. And before Elissa could form words, Lin spoke again.

"None of you need to die. If you handed just me over, kept Lissa here."

"Maybe," said Ivan. "Maybe not. It's pretty damn likely they'd kill us off as witnesses even if we did hand you over."

"But maybe they wouldn't."

"Even so." Cadan's face was as hard as steel. Elissa looked at him, at the crew, and something flickered to life within her, sudden heat in the midst of the cold.

Lin formed her next sentence slowly, as if she were puzzling something out. "You're willing to die . . . when you don't need to. When you could get a chance at surviving." Her eyes moved across them all. "And you're not doing it just for Lissa. You're doing it for me."

The crew was staring at her now. Ivan shrugged. "Why not?"

Lin's eyes met his. "But I . . . I'm not even really human."

"Oh, of course you damn well are," said Ivan. "All that— it's so much fake legal crap. Anyone can see you're human."

"But I . . . my brain's not . . ."

"Your brain's as normal as your sister's," Ivan said. "And

even if it wasn't, since when did a bit of difference make someone not human?"

"Just look at Ivan," interjected Felicia.

Lin blinked at her.

"Well," said Felicia, "you think arms that length are normal?"

Ivan gave a sudden snort of laughter, and after a second of incomprehension Lin's face broke into a smile—a smile that was not because of Felicia's joke but because she finally understood what the crew was trying to tell her.

Inside Elissa the little flicker of heat licked higher. Like Lin, she hadn't expected this, not of the crew, not at this last extremity of danger. It was one thing for her to die with Lin, and another thing for Cadan, who'd promised her that he'd help them—

Her thoughts broke off. She hadn't expected it of the crew. But she *had* expected it of Cadan. Not because she thought it was fair that he should die for her and Lin, but because she'd known he'd be willing to. Somehow, in the last horrible few hours, she'd gone from hoping she could trust him to knowing, without question, that she could.

"And," said Markus, "we can at least go down fighting."

The flicker became a fire. Elissa's head came up; her spine straightened. Beside her Lin's face flushed suddenly bright. No longer dead, but twice as alive as before. "We can fight?"

Cadan's back had straightened too. When he swung around from the controls, his face was blazing, his eyes like bits of blue glass. "We damn well can. The ship's stabilized now, and we've got no reason to conserve our firepower." A shut-teeth grin flashed across his face. "Lin, you want to come shoot at the bastards?"

Lin was sliding into the seat next to him before he finished speaking. "These switches, right? That's how you arm the weapons?"

"Yes. That's right. Now, these are the controls—"

But Lin's hand was already skimming over them, a practiced, familiar movement. The display screen changed.

"What the hell?" said Cadan. "How are you—how did you ever learn to do that?"

Lin moved her hand again, and a different set of code blinked on the screen. "I can read things. Mechanisms, systems, computers . . . This one's complicated. It took me a while of watching you before I could work it out."

Everyone was staring at her now. Even Elissa. The electrokinesis was one thing, the odd ability to use machines and fasten harnesses before anyone had shown her how to. But understanding the controls of a spaceship?

Even if the process itself were as simple as flying a beetle-car, the control panel was deliberately set up to be incomprehensible to anyone untrained. It was a mass of obscure symbols, all the switches at the sides unlabeled and uncoded. She knew it had taken Bruce two months to even remember what they all meant, let alone learn to use them correctly, and here was Lin saying it had taken her "a while" of watching—just *watching*.

"It's armed," said Cadan, his voice fascinated.

Lin nodded. Elissa had crossed to where she could see her sister, and she noticed Lin's eyes had slid a tiny bit out of focus. It was as if whatever she was doing were shortcutting her conscious mind, instinct leaping straight to where her fingers touched the controls.

Cadan was frowning. Then he shrugged—a "what have we got to lose" gesture. "Fire at will."

Lin fired. Rockets shot across the viewscreens, splintered fire against the shields of the attacking ships. Within seconds came answering blasts like a silent echo, hitting the *Phoenix*'s shields, sending them inching down.

Lin laughed, a glinting, savage sound, and fired again. She was flushed, her eyes fever bright. After the years of being trapped and controlled, here she was, fighting for her own freedom, being given the chance to hit back against the organization who'd imprisoned her, even though she had to know she had no real hope of taking any of the attacking ships down with her.

At least I gave her that much. A few days of it. Terror, and grief, and horror, but freedom, too.

That was worth it, at least. *For Lin, I did it right. I did the right thing.*

But . . .

Elissa's gaze slid over to Cadan. He was watching the screens, his profile showing in a hard, set line. He'd been around for half her life, but it seemed like it had only been in the last two days she'd come to know him at all. There were things she should say to him—things she *wanted* to say, if she could gather enough courage—but it was too late. After years of thinking of him as a big brother, then a friend, then an antagonist; after years of hero worship and hurt and irritation; now, in the shadow of death, she knew exactly what he was to her. And it was too late. She'd run out of time.

Cadan turned his head, first to glance at Lin, then farther. His eyes met Elissa's. She felt the look—a blazing look the bright blue of a summer sky—all the way through her, tingling under her skin. She couldn't look away. It was *too late*. There was no time to find out whether he still saw her just as his friend's little sister, or whether he, like she, had found things changing in the last couple of days, like puzzle pieces breaking, shaking down into a new pattern. No time even to tell him . . . tell him *anything*.

Cadan spoke briefly to Markus, who had come to stand at his shoulder. Then Cadan got up and came around the end of the safety rail and over to where Elissa stood.

She looked up at him.

He said nothing, just tipped his head toward the door.

Elissa took a last look at Lin, bright and alive, surrounded by people who'd told her she was human, who'd told her she was worth as much as any of them, who were prepared to die with her. *I did that. I gave her that. And it's okay that she's not even noticing me, not thinking about what I had to lose to do it. I didn't do it for what I could get. But if I can just have a few minutes—here at the end of everything—just a few minutes to get something for myself . . .*

She followed Cadan down the steps from the bridge.

As she stepped onto the lower area of the flight deck, the ship shook, the shields dropping another increment. Once through the trapdoor that led into the corridor, Cadan turned, taking hold of one of the grab handles set into the wall. Elissa climbed down after him and curled her fingers around the grab handle nearest her. Above them the door clamped shut.

"Elissa."

He'd never said her name that way before. She felt it the way she'd felt him look at her, as if he'd reached out and touched her skin. Her heartbeat picked up.

"I didn't want you on the ship," he said.

Oh. She took half a step back, feeling slapped.

His face changed. "No. Wait. I need you to listen. I've gone through a hundred ways of saying this, and none of them come out right. But if I don't—if I don't say it now—" His eyes were intent on her face, his hand white on the grab handle. "I've run out of time. I have to say it now, whether it comes out right or not."

Another blast hit the deteriorating shields. Elissa felt it go through her, a vibration through every nerve and bone and muscle.

"I didn't want you here," Cadan said. "For ages I've thought you were—okay, I thought you were spoiled, and self-centered. And way too pretty for your own good. And I"—he flushed—"I wanted you to be impressed by me. When I'd been at flight school for a while, there was this time, I remember I came back and you—you weren't a little girl anymore. And like I said, *far* too pretty. But anything I did that you should have been impressed by, you *never* were. You always just gave me this *look*, and it was like whatever I did, however high I climbed, I'd always be the kid who was lucky to be there, who'd never really belonged. It's when I started calling you princess—do you remember?"

"I remember. But, Cadan, I *never*—"

"No. No. You have to let me say it. You've changed. You're brave, and tough. I mean, it's not like I can see you fighting pirates—or firing against other ships like your sister's doing. But you're . . . well, I wouldn't like to have to work against you, I can tell you that. And thinking you were self-centered— I don't think you even remember *how* to put yourself first anymore." He hesitated. "Maybe that was always there, and I just never noticed it. Maybe it's me who's changed. Or maybe it's just this last couple of days, with everything that's happened . . ." He paused again, swallowed, and she saw that the corners of his lips, as well as his hand, were white.

"I love you," said Cadan. "I know it's the worst possible time to say it, and it won't mean anything because it can't, because it's too late, and I'm an idiot to even want to tell you—" He swallowed again. "I just wanted to tell you. That's it. I love you."

She felt that go through her too. She stared at him, her body locked into motionlessness, the words vibrating through every nerve and bone and muscle.

"I wrecked your career," she said.

"Yes."

"I'm in the middle of getting you killed."

Cadan gave a tiny, rueful smile. "And again, yes." There was a breath of a pause, then he shifted, made a little dismissive gesture with the hand holding the grab handle. "Like I said, I'm an idiot. I wouldn't even be telling you if we weren't in the middle of getting killed. So, please, feel free to finish it off by telling me that you wouldn't be interested even if I were the last person on the last ship in the whole of the known universe—"

"I can't."

He'd begun to look away, but now his gaze jerked back to her. "You can't?"

"I can't. I can't tell you that. I . . . it's crazy, and it's—oh my God—so the wrong time, but I—" Their eyes met, and suddenly she was shivering. "I was in love with you when I was *thirteen*," she said. "Then you got all grown-up, and were such a *pain*, and I told myself I didn't care, and I didn't even like you. Then, on the ship . . ." It was difficult to keep looking at him. She dropped her gaze, talking to the floor, heat rising in her cheeks. "Like I said, I thought you were amazing when I was a kid. And now, seeing you doing your job, everything you've done to help me and Lin . . . how I used to feel about you—it all came back."

"'It all'? You mean . . . the stuff you felt when you were thirteen?"

Her face was flaming now. She still hadn't raised her head, but she heard all the layers of questions in his voice and forced herself to look up. "An awful lot more than I felt when I was thirteen."

Cadan stepped across the space between them, taking hold of the grab handle above where she held it. Their hands brushed. Her mind short-circuited at the jolt of his skin against hers.

"It *is* crazy," he said. "And the wrong time. And there's probably no point to any of it, because, like you said, you're in the middle of getting me killed." Pain flashed in his eyes, but amusement, too, and she couldn't help laughing a little, dizzy with the feel of him standing so close to her.

"I'm sorry," she said, for the sake of saying something.

"Oh, well," Cadan said. "I'm not looking to change anything." He leaned down, his hand sliding to cover hers, his other hand braced against the wall next to her waist, and he kissed her.

Another blast rocked the ship, tipping them sideways, Cadan's arm close around Elissa and his body between her and the wall.

The ship wouldn't hold out against the attacks forever. She hadn't told him yet that she loved him. She must, she must say the words before it was too late. As soon as she had breath to speak, she needed to tell him . . .

Above them the door to the flight deck sprang open. They both jumped, heads jerking up to look.

Lin's face was pale, her eyes wide. "You have to get back to the bridge. Quick!"

Cadan leapt up the steps, pushing past where Lin stood. Elissa hurried after him to grasp her sister's arm. "What is it? What's wrong?"

"You have to get up there too."

"But why? What's happened?"

Lin yanked her arm away. "Don't ask questions. Just go, Lissa, please!"

Elissa ran up the steps to the bridge, confused, heart pounding. What could have gone wrong that needed both Cadan and her to fix it? What was the crew doing? And why was Lin not following—?

She got onto the bridge. "What is it? Cadan?"

He whirled to face her. "Lissa! Don't let the door shut!"

But it was too late. Behind her the barrier thumped closed. Cadan raced toward her, slammed his hand on the panel that should have reopened it. There was no swish of it obeying him, but Elissa's attention was on the sight in front of her.

On the floor Ivan and Felicia lay sprawled, as if they'd fallen where they'd been standing. Markus was slumped in his seat, held up only by the safety harness.

It was so not what she'd expected, so inexplicable, that Elissa just stared for a moment, unable to take it in.

"Lin!" shouted Cadan, and Elissa spun to see him bang his hand against the barrier. Above the thumbprint panel a little red *X* shone out. The door was locked. "Lin, open this door!"

"What are you doing?" Elissa asked. "How can she have locked the door? Against *you*?"

Cadan didn't answer. He banged on the glass again. *"Lin!"* No answer.

Elissa pushed in next to him, panic icing her blood as she saw the flight deck stretching empty beyond the suddenly impenetrable door. What was going on? Where had Lin gone? And what had happened to the crew?

Lin came out of the hyperdrive chamber. The ship lurched beneath another blast as she did, and she grabbed, one-handed, for a hold. With her other arm she cradled a slim black box. The hyperdrive.

The hyperdrive? Elissa banged on the door. "Lin! What are you doing? Why have you locked us in?"

Lin bent, laid the hyperdrive carefully on the floor. Her hair swung over her face, and she didn't answer.

"Lin!"

Lin went back out of sight. Elissa looked up at Cadan. "She's in the hyperdrive chamber again. What is she doing? Can you open the door?"

His face was overcast with confusion and anger, his hand still pressed hard against the glass. "She's overridden it some-how. It's not responding to my thumbprint. She— I had no idea she could do that, operate machines so precisely. And I don't know what she's doing. She—"

He broke off. Lin had come back, on hands and knees this time, presumably because it was safer to roll rather than carry the thing she was bringing back with her. The energy cell.

She rolled it across the floor, then reattached one of its cables to the hyperdrive. The other lay slack beside her. Its two-pronged plug was clearly visible from where they stood, and a little shiver ran over Elissa's skin. Lin must have pulled it out of the place where the dead Spare was, must have—*ugh, how could she?*—broken the glass cylinder and pulled it out of his skull. Elissa had hardly been able to bear seeing it. What was Lin doing, salvaging the disgusting thing?

"Lin!" said Cadan again, and this time his voice was sharp not with irritation but with fright. "Talk to us. You've locked us in, you've incapacitated my crew—you can't be worried we'll interfere."

Interfere? With what? What was Lin doing that she wouldn't want them to interfere with? And why did Cadan sound suddenly afraid? In the back of Elissa's mind, like the slow drip of a faucet, a little voice began to repeat a single word. *No. No. No. No.* If Lin could lock the barrier without touching it, overriding even Cadan's thumbprint, she could operate the spaceship controls from outside the bridge. The spaceship controls, including the hyperdrive.

Lin stood up, pushed her hair back, and looked at them. There were tears running down her face. In Elissa's head the drips got faster, louder, all joined together. *Nonononononono.*

"I don't see why everyone should die," Lin said clearly, through the glass.

"I don't know what you're talking about!" Elissa's voice came out shrill. "What are you doing? What are you doing with that thing?"

"It didn't break," said Lin. Despite the tears her voice was so calm, it sounded flat. "The only thing it needs is an energy source."

"No!" It came out as a shriek. "Lin, don't even think about it!"

Lin shook her head. "Ssh. It's just stupid, us all dying when we don't need to. And no one else can do anything."

Elissa fought to make her voice come out quietly, trying to get through to her sister. "Lin, you can't. You know how it hurt you before, you know what that thing does. And that one doesn't even work properly—"

"It worked properly for years before it went wrong."

Elissa felt another shriek pressing against the sides of her throat. Lin just kept talking so *calmly*, as if she actually thought she was talking about something reasonable, something that made sense.

"It didn't just *go wrong*. It killed that boy! It doesn't work. It'll kill you, too."

Just a shiver of emotion ran over Lin's face before it tightened again. "Probably not right away, though."

"Lin." Oh God, it was no good trying to control her voice. She was crying too now, much more messily than the slow slide of tears down Lin's face. She had to force the words out through sobs. "Lin, the pain, it's too much. It killed him. It'll kill you."

"Maybe not." Her eyes met Elissa's. "And if it does, it still makes more sense than all of us dying."

"How does that make sense? It doesn't make sense! It *doesn't.*"

Behind Elissa, Ivan spoke. "What . . . ? Cadan, what's going on?"

Elissa snatched a look back. He and Felicia were sitting up, and Markus was straightening in his seat, hand to his head. Whatever Lin had done to them, it had been precisely timed. She hadn't intended to make them unconscious for any longer than it took her to get Cadan and Elissa here, to shut them up so they couldn't stop this awful, insane plan. *How did she even do it? If I'd known she could do that . . . But oh God, all this worrying about what she might do to other people—I never thought to worry about what she might do to herself.*

Frantic, Elissa turned to Cadan. "*You* talk to her! Make her listen!"

"No," said Lin, speaking to Cadan as well. "You listen to me instead. You need to give Elissa something—a sedative or a painkiller or something. When I use the hyperdrive, it's going to hurt her if she's not drugged."

How long had she been thinking about this? It had to have been since they'd discovered the Spare. If Elissa had never left her, if Elissa had stayed, Lin wouldn't have gotten the chance to knock out the crew. And oh, to think she'd *wanted* Lin to develop empathy, to care about other people. *If I'd known, I'd never have made her feel bad about what she'd done, I'd never have tried to get her to be different. Oh God, Lin . . .*

With a shock Elissa suddenly realized Cadan was no longer looking at Lin, but down at her. She didn't need a telepathic link to know what he was thinking.

"Don't you *dare*," she said. "Don't you dare even *think* about drugging me. You have to get the door open. You have to find a way to stop her!"

Cadan was white, his mouth set as hard as she'd ever seen it. "Lin," he said through the door, "you're making a mistake. You do this, and the shock could kill Lissa as well as you."

Lin's face settled into stubbornness. "Not if you give her a sedative like I just told you."

"You're telling me to drug her without her consent? Lin, I told you, this is a mistake. Unlock the door. We'll work out something else."

For a moment Elissa thought they'd won, because Lin's face changed and her hand made a quick movement. Then she straightened, her body set in lines as stubborn as the expression on her face.

"No. There is nothing else. There's no time. Cadan"—her eyes locked on his—"I know you'll drug her. I know you won't let it hurt her, too." She turned her back on them.

Elissa opened her mouth to scream at her, and couldn't. Her breath seemed to have stopped, her heart, all the blood in her veins. Her sister, her twin . . .

If she dies, I'll never be whole again. Like a lightning flash, agonizingly clear, she knew it. Knew, too, what would have happened to her if she'd let the doctors burn the link out of her brain back on Sekoia. She'd have been a half-person, always, not knowing what she'd lost, just knowing *something* had gone, something she'd never been meant to live without.

For an instant, weird and out of time, the lightning flash showed her father's face, gray and tired and detached the way it had been her whole life. *Oh my God. My dad—did he—*

Then her mind snapped back to the present. Beyond the glass, Lin had knelt next to the energy cell and gathered up the hideous two-pronged plug.

She turned a little as she settled herself, looking up toward the bridge. Her face was wavering now, tears slipping down it, her mouth trembling around where she'd set her teeth into her lower lip. The light of the energy cell pulsed weakly.

"Lissa." It was Cadan's voice.

Elissa looked up at him. He looked beaten, hopeless, and she knew what he was asking.

"No."

"She's doing it anyway. Look at her. I can't stop it. Do I have to watch what it could do to you as well?"

Fear flared into fury. "You're giving up just like that? You have to be able to stop her! You have to be able to do *something.*"

"You don't think I would if I could? Lissa, you know I can't drug you without your consent, but look at her, she's set on this, she's trying to save the rest of us. If she does, and you die too—"

"No. *No. Lin!*" Panic swept back up through her, blanking out thought. She beat on the glass. "Lin! Lin, don't, don't!"

Cadan took hold of her arm. "Lissa, come away."

"To be drugged? No. No, *no*."

"Not to be drugged!" Panic and anger leapt into his voice, tightened his hand so it bit into her arm. "Just come away. If you're standing here when she does it, if you're this close and she does die, you could die too."

Elissa wrenched away. "She's not *going* to do it. Not if she knows it could hurt me."

"She's relying on me to get you away. Lissa, damn it—"

Lin put a hand under her hair and swept it up off the nape of her neck. She didn't look up, didn't even give Elissa one last glance. She took the plug, positioned it above her neck, and with one swift, steady movement, punched it home.

Inside the cell, the fluid glowed, brightness seeping through it. The thin, building whine of the hyperdrive reached Elissa's ears.

"Lissa." Cadan dragged at her, both his hands biting into her flesh now, trying to make her go, trying to make her leave her sister. She fought him, clawing at his hands, pushing away. She no longer had breath with which to scream, but she couldn't give up, not yet, not yet. She reached out with the only thing she had left, the link, tenuous and incalculable, that she'd never really known how to use, that only Lin had mastered. If Elissa could just reach her sister now, reach her for long enough to distract her—

The energy cell flared bright white, bleaching the color out of Lin's face, silvering the loose ends of her hair . . .

. . . shining straight into Elissa's eyes. The energy cell lay in front of her, the hyperdrive beside it. She was here. She'd made the link. She was looking through Lin's eyes, feeling Lin's tears on her face, feeling . . .

. . . the whine turned into a shriek, filling the air around her . . .

. . . feeling nothing.

For a minute Elissa didn't even know where she was. Her vision had gone black. She was numb, couldn't tell whether she sat or stood or lay. Couldn't tell whether she was still in Lin's head or back in her own.

I'm not dead, at least.

With the thought came consciousness, just a single thread of it creeping through the black, like a shutter opening on daylight. She opened her eyes and found herself slumped at the bottom of the bridge's barrier, Cadan's arm around her, his hand against where her pulse beat in the side of her neck.

"Lissa. Lissa. *God.*" He put his head down to hers. "I thought—"

"Lin?" She scrambled up on unsteady legs.

Down on the flight deck Lin raised her head. She dragged the plug out from under her hair. "Lissa?"

The locked symbol flicked off and the door to the bridge slid open. Elissa was down the steps and across the flight deck in four strides, shaky legs or not. She slammed her hands down onto Lin's shoulders, her face inches from her sister's. "Never do that again! Never, do you hear me? You don't get to make that kind of choice for me, do you understand?"

"Lissa—"

"Shut up!" She was shaking so hard, she could hardly speak. "You don't *do* that! You think I did all this stuff for fun? You think it doesn't matter to me if you get yourself killed?"

"Elissa."

"What?"

"We did it. Look." Lin waved a hand around them, at the glass sides of the flight deck, and after a blank moment of staring, Elissa understood. The other spaceships were gone. Nothing showed but the far-off stars.

"We made the hop," said Lin. "We made hyperspace."

"But . . ." Elissa put her hands up to her head. "I hardly felt it. And that—the boy who was powering it before, it hurt him terribly. It killed him."

"You linked." Cadan had come up behind her. "Just before, you linked with your sister, didn't you, Lissa? I was holding you, I felt you go."

"Yes." Elissa took her hands down and glared at Lin. "That was the first time I ever had to do it because you were trying to kill yourself, though. Don't *ever*—"

"Wait a minute." Lin wasn't paying attention. She looked up at Cadan. "Is that what did it? Both of us, together? Is that how we made it work, without it hurting, without what happened to that boy?"

"It *can't* be that simple," said Cadan. "They'd have figured it out before."

Elissa stared from one face to another, seeing the same light dawning that rose now inside her head, flooding everything, making everything make sense. "But they couldn't figure it out. They never got further than taking the strongest twin. The way they had it set up, they never got a chance to try their disgusting experiments on both twins. Once they said one of us was human, they couldn't do anything."

"And it worked well enough already." Lin shrugged. "They got the power they wanted. And it wasn't like *they* cared about it hurting." She jerked her head up to look at Elissa. "Maybe they only think they're taking the strongest twin. Maybe they're really taking the least *controlled* one, the one who's all . . . splashing around. Maybe that's why so many of us burn out. Maybe that's why"—her eyes widened—"maybe that's why I kept reaching out to you, when they harvested the power from me, when it started to hurt. But it didn't really work because you didn't know I was real, you didn't reach back."

"But this time I reached out to you . . ."

"And it worked." Lin's face lit up, blazing with her seeing-the-stars smile. "You saved us. We escaped."

"And it *didn't hurt*." Elissa still couldn't believe it. She was so used to the idea that the link brought pain, stuff she couldn't control. *But that was because it was always Lin doing it. I didn't think to try controlling it; I just tried to make it stop. All I did was freak out and react. If I'd known . . .*

Cadan stood and started back up to the bridge. Lin scrambled to her feet to follow him. "Where are we? Are the coordinates right?"

He glanced back, a sudden frown creasing his brow. "How the hell did you even know where to take us?"

Lin laughed. "I'm not *that* clever. You set the coordinates already."

"Oh. Of course." He flushed a little, rubbing a hand up over his face, and tenderness caught at Elissa. They'd thrown so much at him, she and Lin, and he'd dealt with it all. *And fell in love with me at the same time.* But that was a miracle she didn't have time to dwell on now, something warm and glowing to take out and marvel over later, when they'd reached safety.

Safety. That seemed like a miracle too—but a miracle she'd had to make happen.

Cadan slid into the pilot's seat. Next to him Markus gave Lin a steady look, and she flushed. "I *had* to."

"Yeah, okay," said Ivan. "Just understand you're forgiven only because you probably saved our lives."

"We can reach Sanctuary in one more hop," Cadan interrupted them. He swung around in his seat. "Lissa, Lin, this link, it's not something I understand . . ."

Lin caught Elissa's eye, grinning. "You want to know if we can do it again."

"Well, yes. If we can get there now, before they catch up again—"

Elissa jerked a look at the screens. "Will they? This quickly?"

Cadan gave an exasperated head shake. "Your guess is as good as mine. God alone knows how they did it before. I'd rather not wait around to find out. But if that was a fluke, if doing it again will hurt you, or if it's left you weak . . ."

Elissa glanced back toward her twin and found herself smiling too, filled with a sudden confidence that fizzed inside her head like rising bubbles. "Can we do it again?" she asked. "*Oh,* yes."

Back next to the hyperdrive, taking her sister's hand, ready to make the link again, Elissa watched the smile lighting up Lin's whole face. She concentrated on that, ignored the still-hideous cable that once again trailed out from under her sister's hair. *If we ever do this again, it needs to be without using that freaking disgusting thing.*

Then she shut her eyes and thought of nothing but Lin, of making the link between their brains that had once been the source of everything wrong in her life, the link that had changed her whole world . . .

The shriek of the hyperdrive went through her. The energy cell flared bright light against her shut eyelids, dyeing them red. Her nails dug into her hand, and this time the small pain anchored her, kept her from dissolving into the blackness, held her steady until the whine died, the light disappeared, and she heard Cadan speak, triumph in every syllable.

"We made it. We're there."

FIFTEEN

AT ITS INCEPTION the Interplanetary League had been granted land on Sanctuary, one of the first terraformed planets in the whole star system. Over the decades of IPL's existence, the buildings of its headquarters had spread and been extended, until it formed a kind of sprawling village all over the southern slope of the hill where it had first been built.

The window of the room Elissa and Lin had been allocated, in a building halfway up the hill, looked out over a view that could not have existed on any of the more recently colonized planets: a forest of trees that were thousands of years old, with leaf shapes Elissa didn't recognize and names she had not yet learned.

Now, on an evening a week after Cadan had landed the *Phoenix* in the spaceport fifty miles away, she leaned on the railing of the tiny balcony outside their room, watching dust-like seeds and specks of insects drifting in and out of the golden sunlight and long shadows of early evening.

Behind Elissa, in the bedroom, Lin lay on her bed, feet waving in the air, skimming through college brochures on a handheld screen. She was humming to herself, a tuneless, wordless sound of contentment. Lin was a legal human now. The whole "nonhuman human-sourced entity" thing had been judged universally unlawful two days after they'd landed on Sanctuary, by an emergency summit of IPL officials. Both Lin and Elissa were due to receive compensation. The notification of exactly how much that compensation was going to be had come earlier that day, and Elissa was still kind of reeling from how much they were going to get.

Lin's was more than hers—the information that had accompanied the notifications had included the formula the authorities used for working it out: *Loss of freedom plus trauma (physical) plus trauma (emotional) multiplied by years affected (directly and indirectly), etc., etc., etc.*

Nothing would ever be enough to make up for what the Sekoian government had done to Lin, but this amount . . .

For a moment Elissa's fingers relaxed where they'd been gripping the balcony railing. Okay, this amount—it was *nearly* enough.

But the moment of calm was gone almost as soon as she'd felt it, washed away by a prickling wave of returning tension. Her hands tightened again.

She was standing here, in this golden sunset light, waiting for an interplanetary call to come through. From Sekoia. From her parents.

Sekoia had been all over the news for the last week, scrolling across every newsscreen, being narrated by every newscaster, beginning just hours after the *Phoenix* had landed on Sanctuary.

Interplanetary League takeover of Sekoian government . . . Space Flight Initiative disbanded . . . Thirty secret facilities uncovered . . . Warning, this broadcast contains material some viewers may find disturbing . . .

Then the images. Rooms and machines like the ones Elissa had seen in her long-ago visions. Children and teenagers being ushered out of huge buildings, some alert, some blank-faced, sleepwalking out into daylight, the bruises showing starkly on their faces and necks. Worse bruises—and burn marks—on the pale skin of corpses being rapidly zipped into body-bag stretchers.

Entire Sekoian government deposed and under arrest for contravention of interplanetary law under the Humane Treatment Act . . .

A takeover. There hadn't been a whole-planet takeover in her lifetime, but she remembered covering them in history at school. A planet's economy could survive them, but it was never easy, and it took generations to recover. And unlike most first-grade planets, Sekoia's economy had only been stable for the last twenty years.

In the last week there'd already been reports of rapidly rising crime, of growing social disorder—both of which the newscasters were attributing to the catastrophic double loss of both Sekoia's autonomy and its spaceflight industry. There'd been riots, too, and, as panic buying took hold, projected food shortages.

This was Elissa's family's home. These were the conditions she'd left her family living in.

Even though she'd been jittering, on edge, for the last hour, expecting the call, when the electronic voice sounded from the com-screen in the room behind her, every cell in Elissa's body seemed to jump.

She hurried into the room as Lin sat up on the bed; heart

pounding, hands suddenly damp, she touched the screen to accept the call.

Even with the most modern tech available, interplanetary calls were neither easy nor reliable. It took several seconds for the operator to get them connected, and when the connection was finally achieved, the screen filled with white static, raining sideways from edge to edge. The speakers hissed and spat, as if the static were real rain, falling across the space between the planets.

Then the static cleared, all but a few unsteady lines of interference, and there they were in front of her.

"Lissa?" Her mother's voice shook, rising over Edward Ivory's quieter greeting, and even behind the interference lines her face seemed to waver. "Lissa, is that really you? My God, are you safe?"

Elissa's throat tightened. Back on Sekoia, once she'd known they weren't going to help her, she'd had to push away all thoughts of her parents, deliberately put them into her past, focus on nothing more than herself, on Lin, on the future they were going to have to build for themselves. But now, seeing her mother's face looking, for the first time, almost old, marked with lines of anxiety . . .

"I'm fine," she said, and her voice shook too.

"Lissa, my God, this has been such a nightmare. You *ran away*, we had no idea where you were. We thought you were in the most dreadful danger. And then it turned out you were with *Cadan!*"

Elissa bit her lip hard. Her voice would be distorted enough without letting herself cry. *I've been through a million things in the last two weeks—it's crazy to hear my mother's voice and want to burst into tears.*

And her dad. Had he always looked this . . . gray, not just tired but drained, or had she done that to him too?

"I didn't want to run away like that," she said to both of them. "I just had to save Lin—I mean, my twin—"

Static buzzed briefly, and she wasn't sure they'd heard, because her mother spoke across her.

"It doesn't matter anymore. We all made mistakes. The pressure from the government, law enforcement at the house . . . People can't be held accountable for what they do under that sort of stress. We had people questioning us, your father and I, can you believe it? But of course we can't be blamed—it was our own government. And oh, everything that's happening here . . ." She put a hand to her head. "You know your brother's career is over."

"I—I guessed, when they said SFI had been dissolved. I . . ." Guilt enveloped her, but she couldn't say sorry. She *couldn't*. Surely—surely?—they didn't expect her to?

"God knows what he's going to do now. It's so unfair. This will be the ruin of Sekoia. The planet's never going to recover. It was the *government* who acted illegally. All the decent people just doing their jobs, they're innocent victims of this, they shouldn't be made to suffer for it. And Bruce—he's worked so hard, and he was so close to graduating . . ."

Hang on a minute. Elissa snapped out of the cloud of confused guilt, out of the compulsion to apologize. *Innocent victims?* Her mother had watched the news, seen the uncovering of the secret facilities where Spares had been imprisoned, heard where they'd gone after that, known it had been happening to her own *daughter*—and she was talking about *Bruce* as an innocent victim?

Her mother was still talking. "Lissa, we spoke to IPL officials. They said you'll be receiving your compensation money soon, and you're free to settle where you like?"

Elissa nodded, not sure where this was going, still distracted by what her mother had been saying, by her whole manner. Elissa had been expecting anger, blame—had been expecting to have to explain and explain and justify herself—and it hadn't come. But all the same, this whole conversation . . . Her mother wasn't saying any of the angry things she'd expected, but she wasn't saying anything Elissa wanted to hear either.

"We're being offered relocation. As one of the affected families. We're being offered a place on Philomel." Her mouth tightened. "It won't be anything like we're used to, but we can't stay here. The situation . . . it's just getting more and more unstable. You can fly straight to Philomel from Sanctuary, Lissa. We can put all this behind us."

Put all this behind us? For a moment Elissa could only stare at her parents' faces on the screen. *She can't mean that. She can't think—*

Static flickered again, blurring their expressions, making her mother's lips look as if they'd dragged down at the corners. "Lissa? Did you hear me? This connection is terrible."

"I heard you. I—" She hesitated, but then it burst out. "What about my twin?"

This time it wasn't the static. Her mother's lips did tighten briefly before she spoke again. "Lissa, we understand you did what you believed you had to do. You helped uncover an illegal operation. You've done what you felt was your duty. Now you can come home, forget the whole thing."

Elissa's gaze had moved to her father's face, looking for his answer, but at those words she snapped back to look at her mother. "Forget the whole thing? How can I? I've found my twin. I— Look." She took Lin by the arm, drew her over so both their faces would appear on-screen. "This is Lin. She's your other daughter."

Even in the tiny screen, through the static, she saw her mother's whole face stiffen, saw her upper lip lift slightly as if in disgust. "What are you suggesting, Elissa?"

"Suggesting? I'm not— Mother, look. This is *your other daughter*."

"It's my other *nothing*." That was disgust in her mother's face. And a sudden white blaze of anger. "It's a Spare. Nothing but a Spare. I donated it years ago, it's not even *human*."

Beside Elissa, Lin didn't make any sound, any movement, but Elissa flinched as if her mother had hit her. "Don't *say* that about her."

"There is no *her*. My God, Elissa, isn't this enough? You ran away from home to liberate your Spare. And enough people are saying it was a noble act that I—well, I suppose I have to concede. I acknowledge that you were brave, and selfless, and I'm"—she hesitated almost imperceptibly on the words—"of course we're proud of you, Elissa. But that's enough. You've done what you set out to do. You're done. You can come home."

"No. I can't come home. I don't want to. Not without my sister."

"She's *not*—"

"She *is*. She's my sister. She's my *twin*."

Elissa met her mother's eyes and knew it was no use. She was never going to make her mother understand. Not because Mrs. Ivory lacked the imagination but because . . . In a flash of insight Elissa realized the truth. In Laine Ivory's world she was always right. She might make small mistakes, but *only* small mistakes, ones she could take back, ones she could say she hadn't meant, that she could smooth over and fix. She would never admit to making an unfixable mistake. She would never admit to the mistake she'd made with Lin.

"*Elissa.*"

"No." Elissa held her mother's eyes, knowing it could be for the last time. "I'm sorry. I'm not leaving Lin. If she's not your daughter, neither am I."

Sheer fury flashed into her mother's face, obliterating the pain and grief that had—very briefly—flickered in her eyes. "Very well!" she said, and her hand went up to—presumably—cut the connection.

But Elissa's father's hand came up too, just as quickly, catching his wife's fingers before they could get there. "Just a minute," he said.

"*What?*"

"Just a minute. We've got a little longer. I'd like to talk to my daughter."

Elissa's mother snatched her hand down. "Very well. Go ahead. Good luck getting through to her!"

Her face vanished from the screen.

Elissa's eyes filled with sudden tears. She blinked them back angrily, determined not to cry.

"Lissa."

"What?" She snapped the word, afraid of breaking down, furious all over again that he hadn't interfered, that he'd let her mother say all those things, *awful* things, and in front of *Lin.*

"Lissa, would you introduce me to my other daughter?"

Elissa's head came up. Beside her a quiver ran through Lin's body.

"I— Dad?"

His face was still tired, as tired as it had been for as long as she could remember, but there was a slight smile on his lips. "My other daughter, Lissa." His eyes went to Lin. "Your name's Lin?"

Lin nodded, a tiny jerk of her head, and her voice came out as a whisper. "That's the name we chose—Lissa and me."

"I'm very glad to meet you, Lin." Edward Ivory smiled again. The static shivered across his eyes, making them blur. "And I'm glad—gladder than you can imagine—that you've found each other." For a moment his smile disappeared, and at the look on his face Elissa's stomach lurched as if she'd stepped out over emptiness. In her head, pieces began to click together.

"You helped us," she said. "As much as you dared to."

"Yes."

"Why? Why, when you knew, as well as she did—"

She stopped. Her eyes came slowly back to her father's face. The face that for as long as she could remember had been gray with fatigue rather than gray with age, distant . . . lacking.

"It happened to you, didn't it?" she said. "You had the operation they wanted to do to me."

"Yes."

It felt like an invasion to ask, but she had to. "Did you know? Did you know what it was doing to you?"

Her father gave a slight shrug, not one of indifference but one of helpless loss. "I thought it was hallucinations. I didn't find out until later."

"Dad . . ."

Her father shrugged again. "It's all right, Lissa. It had to happen. They tried a lot of other things first. Not everything they tried with you, but then those methods weren't all available. They exhausted all the options they had at the time. And the surgery—it stopped the pain. Enabled me to live a normal life. Work, get married."

But you never had a normal life. They took away your twin, and you've been living nothing but a half-life ever since. She couldn't say it. Either he knew it himself or he'd managed to deny it the way her mother had managed to deny she'd ever done anything wrong. Either way, saying it to him would do no good.

Was that what he'd thought he was giving her? A normal life, without the pain of the link with her twin? Had he really thought that would be better for her? Or had it just been fear? Fear of their government, fear of what her mother would say if he interfered with the normal life she had planned out for their daughter?

But whatever it had been, she couldn't resent him for it anymore. He'd lost his twin, allowed them to burn out the link that Elissa could no longer imagine living without. He'd been surviving as half a person ever since.

"You found out?" she said. "About your twin? You found out afterward?"

"Yes. I . . ." He gave another hopeless movement. "When your mother was pregnant with you, she had too much information for them to just take the Sp—the baby. They had to tell her—us—and get her official consent." His mouth twisted a little. "They said it was for humane medical research, and we were well compensated. But . . . yes, that was when I found out."

And you had to mourn something—someone—you hadn't known you'd lost. By yourself, with no one even acknowledging he'd been a person at all.

Her father's eyes had come back up to hers. There was shame in them, and in that moment she knew he was aware of how he'd failed her.

"You helped us," she said. "You helped us escape."

He sent her his familiar faint smile. "I did do that," he said. "Tell me, Lissa, Lin, was it the right thing to do?"

"Yes." They spoke at once, their voices blending into one, and their father smiled at them both, across miles of space, across a distance they might never bridge again.

"Then I'm glad," he said. "Take care of each other."

The static quivered across the screen, blurring his eyes again, sending a shimmer into them that, at the last minute, Elissa thought might not have to do with the static at all.

Then there was nothing but static, filling the screen with white rain, filling her ears with the sound of it, and Edward Ivory was gone.

Later that evening Cadan came to find Elissa. She was sitting in the little courtyard outside the rooms they'd been given, her back against the trunk of an impossibly ancient tree whose branches stretched over half the courtyard. She'd brought a handheld out with her—she, like Lin, needed to look at college courses—but she'd left it lying on her knee so long that the screen had switched itself off.

"Lissa?"

She looked up. He stood, a dark silhouette against the lights mounted around the walls of the courtyard, holding out a cup that steamed slightly in the cool air.

"Lin said you'd be out here. I brought you a hot chocolate."

She came back to the here and now as if surfacing from immersion in deep, cold water, and smiled at him. "Thank you. How were the interviews?"

He laughed, sitting next to her. "We were always told SFI was renowned all over the known universe. Turns out the government might have been a set of freaking vicious criminals, but they told us the truth. I need to train for another year—IPL craft aren't set up the same as SFI ships—but after that there'll be a place for me in the IPL spacefleet, if I want it."

Relief swamped her, as warm as sunlight. "I didn't get you killed *or* wreck your career?"

He stopped her from lifting the cup to her lips so he could lean in and kiss her, a spark of amusement in his eyes. "That's right. You didn't."

"And Markus—the crew?"

"Markus is in the same kind of position as me. Felicia and Ivan—their skills are entirely transferable, and they've got years of experience. They'll have no problem finding work. So you didn't wreck their careers either." There was laughter in his voice, but this time she couldn't respond. The momentary warmth had gone. She was suddenly back looking at her mother's face, hearing her voice. *You know your brother's career is over.*

"That's good," she said, because the silence had gone on a breath too long and she had to say something. "Lin and I—we're still looking at what colleges we can go to. I never thought of going off Sekoia, and there are so many . . ."

"Lissa, Lin told me about your parents."

Elissa didn't say anything. If she said anything, she was scared she'd start to cry.

Cadan put his arm around her. He was warm, and his jacket smelled of coffee, and the bark of the tree they were leaning against, and him. "You know," he said conversationally, "I don't much like your mother."

Elissa gave a splutter of laughter that was almost a sob. "Oh, what she *said* about Lin. And that *SFI employees* are the innocent victims! After what she *knows* was happening."

Cadan's arm tightened around her.

Elissa gave another almost-sob. "I want to just say screw it, forget about it all. I *had* to leave. It's not my fault. But my dad, knowing what they did to him . . . And Bruce, losing his career . . . And I can't *do* anything, I can't help. And—oh God, did you see the news this evening?"

"I did." His voice was grim.

As the IPL military police had clamped down, as the fear of food shortages rose, as different political factions formed, the first terrorist act had taken place.

A bomb. A real bomb, small and primitive, nothing like the sophisticated nonlethal devices the ecoterrorists had been using for years. Twenty people had been killed immediately, with more fatally injured. The newscasters had been repeating the figures during every update, on every channel.

Sekoia was falling into chaos.

"I didn't think I cared," Elissa said. "I thought as long as I could get Lin to safety, nothing else mattered. But seeing what's happening, seeing our planet—our safe, *civilized* planet—going insane . . ."

"It's your world," said Cadan. "Of course you care."

She took a long breath, determined not to be a brat. "I know it's worse for you. At least my family's being relocated."

"Yes."

Something in his voice caught at her. "Cadan? What is it?"

"I . . . nothing, really. I haven't heard anything since I spoke to them yesterday. But with what's happening . . . I'm afraid of reprisals. Against them—against anyone associated with SFI." His breath ruffled her hair. "Like you, if I could do anything . . . But even if there were any public flights to or from Sekoia, even if they hadn't shut down transport, even if I could get there, what would I do that'd be any use?"

Elissa spoke quietly, not looking at him. "If you could go, though . . ."

"Yeah. I would." He hesitated. "God knows I don't want to leave you, but knowing my family's stuck there . . ."

"No, I know. I . . ." She was edging closer to the elephant in the room, the thing they both knew they weren't talking about. She didn't want to—if you couldn't do anything about it, wasn't it better to go on pretending it wasn't there? But somehow, with every sentence, she got closer and closer to the time when there'd be nothing left for her to do but point it out.

"I'd go with you," she said in a rush.

His arm stiffened where it touched her. "You've thought about it?"

"I *keep* thinking about it. My compensation money—I could refuel the *Phoenix*. Even with the hyperdrive not working, it'd get us back to Sekoia eventually. Airspace isn't closed off yet. We could get your family out at least. I mean, the *Phoenix* is still technically yours, right—you're still the captain?"

"Technically, yes. SFI isn't in any state to try reclaiming it, and IPL's not going to stop me from taking a ship that doesn't even belong to them. Lissa, I didn't realize you'd thought about it that much." But his voice didn't lift in relief. He knew as well as she did why it might have been better not to talk about this at all.

She looked up at him, aware that her helplessness showed in her expression. "If it were just me."

But it's not just me. It's Lin. I can't leave Lin. And I can never even suggest the possibility of going back to Sekoia, not to her, not ever. It felt like a betrayal to say it out loud, but in Cadan's eyes she read understanding. As she would never ask it of Lin, he would never ask it of her.

But as she lay, sleepless, later that night, the thought—unwanted, unasked for—returned. It wasn't just about rescuing Cadan's family. Once again she saw the pale, shocked faces of all those Spares, coming out of imprisonment into a world they didn't understand. Lin had said the telepathic link between one twin and another usually died out when they were still young. Would it have survived for any of them, or would they be totally adrift, without the anchor, the safety net that Elissa knew she'd been to Lin? Would the Spares ever adjust to the outside world? And if they didn't, would they be as dangerous as Lin had been—still could be? Lin's wasn't the only brain that had the power to fuel a hyperdrive—it couldn't be just Lin who had some kind of electrokinesis.

Elissa thumped over in bed, tugging the covers with her. She and Lin, linked, could move a spaceship. Without hurting themselves, without putting themselves in danger. If the links between other Spares and their twins hadn't died out completely, could the pairs be as powerful as she and Lin?

Sekoia needs its spaceflight industry. It needs hyperdrives. But the only way it can power them—

Oh God, though. It's not okay to even think it, after what's been done to them.

She flumped back onto her other side.

She and Lin, going back, voluntarily, to show how Sekoia's spaceflight industry could be restored, to let other Spares see that their power could be used without pain or danger, that might be the one thing that could rebuild a shattered society. She and Lin might be able to turn the tide of anger and desperation, stem the inexorable march of events dragging Sekoia down into the poverty from which it had so recently struggled free.

If we went back, we could get Cadan's family to safety, and help other Spares recover, and even . . .

"Lissa?" said Lin's voice in the dark.

Elissa's heart skipped a guilty beat. "Yes?"

"I don't want to go to college."

Irritation jabbed fingernails into Elissa. She had to think about Lin's education *now*?

"What do you want to do?" she said patiently.

"I want to go back to Sekoia."

"*What?*" Elissa snapped upright in bed and clicked the light on. Across the room Lin blinked at her. "What are you talking about?"

Lin's chin set in a stubborn look that was becoming familiar. "Cadan will take us if you ask him."

"Yes, I know he—" Elissa shook her head. "Wait, what are you *talking* about? What do you want to do on Sekoia?"

Lin gave her a sidelong look. "I just . . . I don't like seeing the news. Your family's being moved off-planet, and Ivan and Markus don't have family there, but Cadan and Felicia do. I keep thinking, if it was *you* stuck down there, and I was here and couldn't do anything . . ." She wriggled to a sitting position, wrapping her arms around herself. "When I got out of the facility, I knew where I was going. I knew I was going to you. Some of those Spares—their link will have died off like it's supposed to. They won't have anyone—if they meet their twins, it'll be just like meeting some stranger. And their twins, they might not be like you. They might be like your mother, or Stewart." Her eyes came up to Elissa's. "If you'd hated me . . . if I'd gotten out and come to find you and you'd looked at me like Stewart looked at me when he found out what I was . . ."

Her arms tightened around herself, a movement like a shudder. Her eyes were dark, distant. "I don't like it, that's all. And I keep thinking, we could help them. The Spares. And their twins. And Cadan's and Felicia's families—even if it's just getting them off the planet. But . . ." She met Elissa's gaze again. "We're *millions* of times stronger now, Lissa. It wouldn't have to stop with just that. If the planet got safer again, no one would have to leave it. If we went back, together, we could . . ." She trailed off, biting her lip, her expression suddenly full of uncertainty.

Elissa looked at her. Into the face so like hers, the face she'd seen bleak with terror, lit with happiness, bone white with the determination that had saved them both.

Lin's face was anxious now, anxious and hopeful, waiting for Elissa to speak.

"If we went back . . . ," Elissa repeated, and Lin's eyes lit up as she recognized what Elissa was going to say an instant before she said it. "We could help Cadan's family, and the Spares, and save our world."

Through the viewscreen the stars were a distant mist of lights. Paths and signposts all over the galaxy, pointing the way back across the star system to Sekoia. To the planet Elissa would once have called home.

"Take the speed up a notch," said Cadan.

Elissa slid her finger over the control panel, watching the line on the display climb, feeling the *Phoenix* respond to her command.

"It *has* to be my turn now," said Lin, leaning over the railing for the third time.

"Oh, good God," said Cadan, exasperated. "You learn every damn thing twenty times faster than your sister—can you just give her a bit longer?"

Lin sighed, breathing down Elissa's neck. "I could be your *copilot* by the time we get there, if you just let me practice some more."

"That's assuming I want you as my copilot," said Cadan crisply. "Right now I'm about ready to drop you off on the nearest deserted moon."

"Oh, please." Lin pushed away from the rail and wandered over to get herself a chocograin bar. "I saved your life, *and* paid to refuel your ship. You owe me *forever*."

Cadan slanted a look at Elissa. "To think I ever thought *you* were a brat."

"Tell me what you think I am now." A smile pulled at her lips, and Cadan grinned at her.

"Maybe later." He reset the controls to where they'd been. "Okay, you want to try that sequence again?"

Elissa went through the routine, ticking procedures off in her head. She was probably years away from ever learning to really fly a ship, and she'd never keep up with Lin, but it felt good to be learning a few of the basics. They were no longer being pursued by SFI, of course, but there were other dangers out here between the planets. If the *Phoenix* were attacked again, she wanted to be able to do more than buckle up and wait for Cadan to save her.

She'd reached saturation point now, though. When Lin next came to lean hopefully over the rail, Elissa got up and let her sister take the controls. She moved to the seat at Cadan's other side, watching him as he explained another complicated maneuver to Lin.

Ivan, Markus, and Felicia had joined them for this return to a planet in chaos. She hadn't expected them to want to, had thought they'd already risked more than enough for her and Lin. But they had wanted to come—people with whom she would once have had nothing in common, who were fast turning from friends into something like family.

And the *Phoenix*, the ship she'd once seen as nothing but an escape route, a means to an end, was becoming home.

Elissa edged her hand over so it just touched Cadan's. He didn't turn from the screen, from the code he was translating for Lin, but his fingers closed around hers, warm and firm.

All her life she'd just wanted to be normal, ordinary. She was a long way from either now.

She'd wanted safety, too, something else she was a long way from. Sekoia was a different place now, a dangerous place. There'd be people there who'd see her, Lin, Cadan, and the crew as the people who'd caused the planet's disintegration, as bad as terrorists themselves.

But going into danger yourself, of your own will—it was so very much better than having your will taken away, than having other people's decisions imposed on you. And there were things more important than a guarantee of safety—or of being normal.

And, anyway . . . Elissa looked past Cadan to what she could see of Lin, whose eyes were intent on the screen, fingers flickering over the controls. Her twin, her double—stubborn, freakily talented, frighteningly powerful—linked to Elissa by a bond neither of them fully understood.

Anyway, she wasn't normal. She never had been normal. And it didn't matter anymore.

ACKNOWLEDGMENTS

Flowers, chocolate, and Twitter shout-outs
are due to the following people:

My agent, Mandy Hubbard, who saw the potential in this book
when it didn't really have much *beyond* potential, and whose
insight changed it into something immeasurably better.

Everyone involved in its production at Simon & Schuster,
especially my editor, Navah Wolfe, whose editing made it
immeasurably better all over again, Lizzy Bromley, who designed
the drop-dead-awesome cover, production editor Katrina Groover,
and production manager Angela Zurlo, as well as copyeditor
Christina Bryza, and proofreader Bara MacNeill, who saved me
from a great deal of continuity-related embarrassment.

The Lucky 13s, who kept me company in the months
leading up to publication in the way only other debut
young adult authors can.

Michelle and Dayna, who have supported me since we were all unpublished authors, and who kept me from biting my fingernails off during the days this book was out on submission.

Jossy, who was the first audience for my stories, and who has been an *excellent* sister ever since.

Finally, thank you to Philippa and Elinor, most awesome, entertaining, and beautiful daughters ever, for putting up with being manuscript orphans and for *still* being excited when I sell another book;

And to Phil, for everything.

Don't miss the thrilling sequel to LINKED

UNRAVEL

Coming **Summer 2014**

Quercus

www.quercusbooks.co.uk